Acknowledgments

Thanks, once again, to the members of my writers' workshop: Matthew Claxton, John Hart, Barry Link, Fran Skene, Peter Tupper, and David Willis. Your critiquing and suggestions were invaluable, as always!

It was for food, at first, a hunger profound and demanding. Living creatures, scrambling and scrabbling, a ball of thousands rolling and biting and kicking. No alliances, no sharing, a million individual spiderlings feasting upon their siblings, crunching on carapaces and sucking on sweet life juices.

Those that survived the first minutes of freedom from the egg sack found their physical hunger satiated, found their eight-legged bodies bloated. And for a moment, there was rest.

But physical hunger proved no more than the catalyst, and these beasts, offspring of the Lady of Chaos, were elevated from physical need to the demands of the ego, from simple hunger to the first taste of power, and the war raged once more. They bit and they ate. They attacked and they fed, nourished as much by the exquisite pain of their rivals as by the smell of flowing ichor.

The shriek of a victim's agony.

The fear in eight tiny eyes as one gained advantage and another realized its doom.

The joy of spilled lifeblood.

This marked the second level, beyond the physical, for those who survived the first wave of feeding. This marked the satiation of ego, the sense of supremacy, the sweet taste of victory. And the thousands rested.

But they were not done.

For beyond the hunger and the power came the need for thrill, the true mark of Lady Lolth, the ultimate and paradoxical craving to walk on the very edge of disaster.

And so it began anew. The thousands attacked, consumed and were consumed, and to those who survived the first few moments of the renewed trial came the sense of self, for these were beings of Lolth, beings of chaos, and in that swirl of battle, where oblivion loomed on every side, the offspring lived, truly lived, basking in the realization that each moment could be the last moment.

This was the beauty of chaos.

This was the beauty of Lolth.

This was the doom for all, but one.

Pharaun lay on the forest floor, staring up into the angry eyes of five hissing serpents. Their fangs bared and dripping with poison, their mouths open wide, the red-and-black-banded vipers strained against the whip handle from which they grew.

The woman holding the whip stared down at Pharaun with tightly contained rage. Taller and stronger than the Master of Sorcere, she was an imposing figure. Pharaun could not see her face—the bright light streaming down from the sky above flooded his vision, turning her into a dark silhouette with bone-white hair—but her tone was as venomous as her serpents' hisses.

"You stepped on that spider on purpose," Quenthel said.

"I did not," he spat back, wincing at the slush that was soaking through his elegant shirt, chilling his back. He was glad the other members of their group had scattered in different directions to search—that they weren't there to observe him in such an undignified pose. "I can't see a gods-cursed thing in this wretched light. Would I have let my trousers get into such a state if I could see well enough to step around the brambles that tore them? If there was a spider on the path, I didn't know it was there."

He glanced to his left, at the spot Quenthel had indicated a moment before. As she looked in that direction, he slid his right hand out from behind his back.

One of the whip-serpents hissed a warning to its mistress, but too late. The moment Pharaun's hand was clear, he spoke the word that awoke the magic in his ring. Instantly, the steel band around his finger unfurled, elongating and expanding into a sword. Quick as thought, it spun in mid-air, slashing at the serpents.

The vipers recoiled, narrowly escaping the scything blade. Quenthel leaped back, her mail tunic clinking. Pharaun scrambled to his feet and pressed her with the sword.

"Jeggred!" Quenthel screamed, her *piwafwi* whirling out behind her as she dodged the dancing sword. "Defend me!"

Pharaun whipped a hand into a pocket of his own *piwafwi* and pulled out a pinch of powdered diamond. Flicking the sparkling powder into the air, he shouted the words of a spell, at the same time whirling in a tight circle to scatter the powder. A dome of force sprang up all around him, shimmering like an inverted bowl.

And not a heartbeat too soon. An instant after the magical dome had materialized, a vaguely drow-shaped form hurtled out of the forest. The draegloth leaped onto the dome, the claws on his oversized fighting hands screeching like the shrieks of the damned as they scrabbled for a hold on the diamond-hard surface. The half-demon jumped again and again onto the dome, sliding off.

At last giving up, the draegloth crouched just outside the magical barrier, his smaller set of hands balled into fists on the ground while his larger hands flexed claws in frustration. He glared with blood-red eyes at Pharaun, then jerked his chin in defiance, sending a ripple through the coarse mane of yellow-white hair that cloaked his shoulders.

Pharaun winced at the stench of the draegloth's breath, wishing the magical barrier was capable of blocking odors.

Behind Jeggred, Quenthel kept a wary eye on the sword that hovered just over her head, shielding herself from it with the buckler strapped to her arm. The serpents of her whip hissed at it, one of them straining upward in a futile effort to snap at the weapon. Quenthel started to reach for the tube at her hip that held her scrolls, then paused. She seemed reluctant to waste the little magic she had left on such a petty quarrel.

"Call off your nephew, and let's talk," Pharaun suggested. Squinting, he glanced up at the harsh blue sky. "And let's get out of the sun, before it turns that pretty adamantine buckler you're wearing to dust."

Quenthel's eyes narrowed in fury at Pharaun's insubordination. No doubt she was thinking that though a Master of Sorcere he might be, as a male he should remember his place. Quenthel certainly lusted to use the spells once granted her by Lolth to pin Pharaun in a web and subject him to a thousand slow torments, but the Queen of Spiders had fallen silent. Save for her scrolls, Quenthel had no more spells to cast.

"Jeggred," she snapped. "Withdraw."

Reluctantly, Jeggred backed away from the barrier.

"That's more like it," Pharaun said.

He lifted his right hand, fingers extended, and spoke a command word. His sword shrank, then streaked through the air toward his hand and coiled into a ring once more. He started the gesture that would lower the barrier, then paused as he saw Jeggred tense.

"I should remind you, Quenthel, that I could kill this demon spawn with a single word," Pharaun cautioned.

"Jeggred knows that," Quenthel said, indifference turning her beautiful face into an expressionless mask. "He makes his own choices."

Jeggred growled—whether at Quenthel or Pharaun, it wasn't clear—and spat against the magical dome. Rising to his feet, he stalked back into the forest.

Pharaun let the barrier fall.

"Now then," he said, straightening his elegant but travel-worn clothes and smoothing back an errant lock of white hair from his high forehead. "I apologize for stepping on one of Lolth's children, but I assure you it was entirely an accident. The sooner we leave the Lands of Light, the better. Not only did we just stir up all of Minauthkeep by killing the high priest of House Jaelre—"

"Your decision, not mine," Quenthel spat. Then, after a moment, she smiled. "Though Tzirik did deserve to die."

The serpents in her whip hissed their assent.

Pharaun nodded, glad that she was in agreement that the death had been necessary. Tzirik's magic had allowed their group to travel through the Astral Plane to the Demonweb Pits, domain of the goddess Quenthel served—a goddess who had fallen alarmingly silent, of late. There, they had discovered why Lolth's priestesses could no longer draw upon her magic: the goddess had disappeared. Her temple appeared to have been abandoned, its door sealed with an enormous black stone carved in the likeness of her face.

There had been no time, however, to learn whether that was a situation of Lolth's own choosing. As Pharaun had expected,

Tzirik betrayed them, using his magic to gate in the god he served. Vhaeraun had attacked the stone face and nearly succeeded in breaching it when Lolth's champion—the god Selvetarm— appeared to defend it.

Realizing that Tzirik had no intention of letting them return, Pharaun had ordered Jeggred to kill Tzirik—telling the draegloth the order came from Quenthel. The priest's death had ejected Quenthel's group out of the Demonweb Pits, leaving only the gods behind. For all Pharaun knew, Selvetarm and Vhaeraun were battling there still.

If Vhaeraun won and succeeded in destroying Lolth, it would be the beginning of a new era for the drow. The Masked Lord favored males opposed to the matriarchy; his victory would no doubt spur the disenchanted males of Menzoberranzan to an even greater insurrection than the one that city had recently seen. But if Selvetarm succeeded in defending the Spider Queen, Lolth might one day return and restore her web of magic, lending power to her priestesses' spells once more. Whatever happened, Pharaun wanted to be on the winning side—or appear to be serving its interests, anyway.

"As I was saying," Pharaun continued, "not only is House Jaelre seeking us, but this forest is infested with wood elves. The sooner we get below ground, the better."

He paused to glance at the forest, squinting against the sunlight that bounced harshly off the white, slushy snow that covered trees and ground alike. The wizard regretted his decision to teleport the group there. His spell had allowed them to escape House Jaelre's keep, but the portal he'd hoped to use to put even more distance between them only functioned in one direction. They were trapped on the surface at the mouth of a shallow, dead-end cave.

"I wonder if any of the others have found a way down yet," Pharaun muttered.

As if in answer, Valas Hune appeared from out of the forest, emerging from a tangled clump of underbrush with a silence that was only in part due to the enchanted chain mail the scout wore. A pair of magical, curved kukri daggers hung at his hip, and to his vest was pinned a miscellany of enchanted talismans fashioned by more than one Underdark race. The mercenary, his amber eyes watering slightly as he squinted against the sunlight, had a squared-off jaw that seemed permanently clenched. He habitually held himself tensed and ready, as if he expected to take a punch. His ebony skin was crisscrossed with dozens of faint gray lines, fading legacies of two centuries' worth of battles.

Valas jerked his head in the direction from which he'd just come and said, "There's a ruined temple a short distance away. It's built around a cave."

Quenthel's eyes glittered, and the serpents in her whip froze in rapt attention.

"Does it lead to the Realms Below?" she asked.

"It does, Mistress," Valas said, offering a slight bow.

Pharaun strode forward and clapped an arm around the scout's shoulders.

"Well done, Valas," he said in a hearty voice. "I always said you could smell a tunnel a mile away. Lead on! We'll be back in Menzoberranzan in no time, quenching our well-earned thirst with the finest wines that—"

"I think not." Quenthel stood with hands on her hips, the serpents in her whip matching her venomous stare. "The goddess is missing, possibly under attack. We must find her." Her eyes narrowed. "You are not suggesting, are you, Pharaun, that we turn our backs on Lolth? If so, I'm sure the matron mother will see to it you receive proper punishment."

Valas glanced between Pharaun and Quenthel, then took

a slight step to the side, dislodging Pharaun's arm from his shoulder.

"Turn my back on Lolth?" Pharaun asked, chuckling to hide his nervousness. "Not at all. I'm merely suggesting we follow the matron mother's orders. She bade us find out what's happened to Lolth, and we have. We may not have all of the answers yet, but we have some pretty important pieces of the puzzle. The matron mother will no doubt want us to report what we've found out so far. Since the archmage is no longer answering my sendings, we can't be certain he's receiving our reports. I assumed we would report in person."

"Only one of us need go," Quenthel said. "But it won't be you. There are other, more important things for you to be doing." She paused for a moment, thinking. "You have the ability to summon demons, do you not?"

Pharaun raised an eyebrow.

"I have summoning spells, yes," he said. "But what does that have to do w—"

"We will return to the Demonweb Pits—in the flesh, this time," answered Quenthel. "And with a more trustworthy guide than Tzirik."

Valas shuddered and asked, "A demon?" The normally taciturn scout saw Quenthel's glare, seemed suddenly to realize he'd spoken aloud, and bowed. "As you command, Mistress."

Pharaun was more blunt.

"Assuming I do summon a demon, how can we possibly hope to prevent it from tearing us limb from limb, let alone coerce it into becoming a tour guide for some little jaunt to the Abyss? Even Archmage Gromph wouldn't think of whistling up a demon without a golden pentacle to bind it. We're in the wilderness—in the Realms of Sunlight, in case you hadn't noticed. Where am I supposed to get the spell components to—"

LISA SMEDMAN

"Jeggred."

Pharaun blinked, wondering if he'd heard Quenthel correctly.

"Jeggred," she repeated. "We'll use his blood. You can draw the summoning diagram with that."

"Ah . . ." Pharaun cursed silently as he realized that Quenthel was, unfortunately, right. The blood of a draegloth could indeed bind a demon, but only one: the demon who had sired Matron Mother Baenre's half-demon son. The demon that was Jeggred's father.

Pharaun had no desire to meet him, in the flesh or otherwise, but he could see he had little choice in the matter. Not if he wanted to maintain his delicate balancing act of apparent loyalty to Lolth—necessary if he was to keep his position as Master of Sorcere. Just as Valas had done, Pharaun bowed.

"As you command, Mistress," he said—with just enough of a sarcastic twist on the final word to remind her that her title was a hollow one. Mistress of Arach-Tinilith she might be, back in Menzoberranzan, but he was hardly one of her quivering initiates. He swept a hand in the direction Valas had indicated earlier. "Let's do the spellcasting below ground, shall we? I'd like to get out of this wretched sunshine."

As Valas and Quenthel set off, Pharaun pretended to follow them. He paused, picked up a twig, and used it to collect a bit of spiderweb from the trail. Lolth might be silent, but the sticky nets woven by her children were still useful; spiderweb was a component in more than one of his spells. Tucking the web-coated twig into a pocket, he hurried after the others.

TWO

Halisstra stood on top of the bluff, staring out across the forest. Snow-blanketed trees stretched as far as the eye could see in every direction, here and there dimpled by a lake of an impossibly bright blue or divided by a road as neat and straight as a part through hair. For the first time, Halisstra understood what the word "horizon" meant. It was that distant line where the dark green of the forest met the eye-hurting, white-streaked blue of the sky.

Beside her, Ryld shivered.

"I don't like it up here," he said, holding a hand to his eyes to shade them. "It makes me feel . . . exposed."

Halisstra glanced at the sweat trickling down Ryld's ebony temple and shivered herself as the chill winter wind blew against her face. The climb had been a long, hot one, despite the age-worn stairs they'd found carved into the rock at one side of the bluff. She couldn't explain what had compelled her to lead Ryld up there, nor could she explain why she felt none of the apprehensions the weapons master did. Yet despite his anxiety, Ryld—who stood fully as tall as Halisstra herself, even though he was a male—was in every respect a warrior. He wore a greatsword strapped across his back; a cuirass with a breastplate wrought of dwarven bronze; and vambraces, articulated at the elbows, that sheathed his lean, muscled arms in heavy steel. A short sword for fighting at close quarters hung in a scabbard at his hip. His hair was cut close to his scalp so that enemies could not grab it during combat. Only a fine stubble remained: hair as white as Halisstra's own shoulder-length locks.

"There was a surface dweller—a human mage—who dwelt for a short time in Ched Nasad," Halisstra said. The vastness of the sky above them made her speak softly; it felt as if the gods were lurking up there just behind the clouds, watching. "He spoke of how our city made him feel like he was living in a room with too low a ceiling—that he was always aware of the roof of the cavern over his head. I laughed at him; how could anyone feel enclosed in a city that was so loosely woven—a city balanced on the thin lines of a calcified web? But now I think I understand what he meant." She gestured up at the sky. "This all feels so . . . open."

Ryld grunted and asked, "Have you seen enough? We're not going to find an entrance to the Underdark up here. Let's climb back down and get out of the wind."

Halisstra nodded. The wind found its way inside the armor she wore, even through the thickly padded chain mail tunic that covered her from neck to knees, and from shoulders to elbows. A silver plate attached to the tunic's chest was embossed with the symbol of a sword, standing point-up across a full moon surrounded by a nimbus of silvery filaments. It was the holy symbol of Eilistraee, goddess of the surface-dwelling drow. The padding of the chain mail still smelled of blood—that of the priestess Halisstra had dispatched. The smell haunted the armor like a lingering ghost, even though the blood was several days old.

Halisstra had not only claimed the armor from Seyll after her own armor was stolen, but also Seyll's shield and weapons—including a slender long sword with a hollow hilt that had holes running the length of it—a hilt that could be raised to the lips and played like a flute. A beautiful weapon, but it hadn't helped Seyll any—she'd died before getting a chance to draw it. Lulled by Halisstra's feigned interest in her goddess, Seyll had been utterly surprised by Halisstra's sudden attack. And despite Halisstra's treachery, Seyll had told her, "I have hope for you still." She'd said it with such certainty, as if, even in her final, dying moments, she expected Halisstra to save her.

She'd been a fool. Yet Halisstra could no more get the priestess's dying words out of her mind than she could get the smell of blood out of the armor she'd claimed.

Was this what guilt felt like: a lingering stench that wouldn't go away?

Angered by her own weakness, Halisstra shook the thought out of her head. Seyll had deserved to die. The priestess was stupid to have trusted a person who was not of her faith—even more foolish to trust a fellow drow.

Still, Halisstra thought, as she paused to let Ryld descend the stairs first, Seyll had been right about one thing. It would be nice not to *always* have to watch your back.

❦ ❦ ❦

Ryld descended the stairs in silence, listening to the faint clink of Halisstra's chain mail and trying in vain to pull his mind away from the shapely legs he would see if he would just turn around.

Where was his concentration? As a Master of Melee-Magthere, he ought to have more control, but Halisstra had ensnared him in a web of desire stronger than any Lolth's magic could spin.

At the bottom of the stairs, away from the chilling wind of the open bluff, Halisstra paused to finger a crescent shape that had been carved into the rock.

"This was a holy place, once," she said, looking over the scatter of broken columns that lay among the snow-shrouded trees.

Ryld scowled. In the World Above, vegetation covered everything like an enormous mold. He missed the clean rock walls of the caverns, empty of the smells of wet loam and leaf that choked his nose. He scuffed at the snow with his boot, uncovering a cracked marble floor.

"How can you tell?" he asked.

"The crescent moon—it's the symbol of Corellon Larethian. The elves who once lived in these woods must have worshiped here. Their priests probably climbed these stairs to work their magic under the moon."

Ryld squinted up at the ball of fire that hung in the sky.

"The moon's not as bright as the sun," he said, "at least."

"It casts a softer light," Halisstra replied. "I've heard that this is because the gods who claim it as their symbol are kinder to those who worship them—but I don't know if that's true."

Ryld stared for a while at the ruined masonry then said, "The gods of the surface elves can't be very strong. Corellon let this temple fall into disrepair, and Seyll's goddess was powerless to save her from you."

Halisstra nodded and replied, "That's true. Yet when Lolth tried to overthrow Corellon and establish a new coronal in his place all those millennia ago, she was defeated and forced to flee to the Abyss."

"The Academy teaches that the goddess left Arvandor

willingly," Ryld said. Then he shrugged. "More of a strategic retreat."

"Perhaps," Halisstra mused. "Still, I can't help but think that what we saw in the Demonweb Pits—that black stone in the frozen image of Lolth's face—was a lock, a seal that made Lolth's own temple a prison. A prison fashioned by some other god's hand. Will Lolth eventually emerge from behind it—or will she remain trapped for eternity, her magic forever stilled?"

"That's what Quenthel means to discover," Ryld said.

"As do I," Halisstra answered. "But for different reasons. If Lolth is dead, or trapped in eternal Reverie, what point is there in following Quenthel's orders?"

"What point?" Ryld exclaimed. He was beginning to see the dangerous fork in the road down which Halisstra's musings had taken her. "Only this: spells or no spells, Quenthel Baenre is both Mistress of Arach-Tinilith and First Sister to the Matron Mother of House Baenre. Were I to defy Quenthel, I'd lose my position as Master of Melee-Magthere. The moment Menzoberranzan learned of my treachery, everyone in the Academy would have their daggers out and be thirsting for my blood."

Halisstra sighed and said, "That's true. But perhaps in another city—"

"I have no desire to beg for scraps at someone else's table," Ryld said bluntly. "And the only city in which I might have made a home for myself—with the sponsorship of your House—has been destroyed. With Ched Nasad gone, you have no home to return to. All the more reason to get in Quenthel's good favor, so that when we return to the Underdark you can find a new home in Menzoberranzan."

After a long moment of silence, Halisstra said, "What if I don't?"

"What?" Ryld said.

"What if I don't return to the Underdark?"

Ryld glanced at the forest that hemmed them in on every side. Unlike the solid, silent tunnels he was used to, the wall of trees and underbrush was porous, filled with rustling and creaking, and the quick, tiny movements of animals flitting from branch to branch. Ryld couldn't decide which was worse: the shrinking feeling he'd experienced under the empty expanse of the sky; or the feeling he had then—as though the woods were watching them.

"You're mad," he told Halisstra. "You'd never survive out here alone. Especially without spells to—"

As anger blazed in Halisstra's eyes, Ryld suddenly regretted his rash words. With all Halisstra's talk of surface gods, he'd forgotten, for a moment, that she was also a priestess of Lolth and a female of a noble House. He started to bow deeply and beg her pardon, but she surprised him by laying a hand on his arm.

Then she said something, in a low murmur he had to strain to hear: "Together we'd survive."

He stared at her, wondering if his ears were playing tricks on him. All the while, he was overwhelmingly aware of her hand upon his arm. The touch of her fingers was light, but it seemed to burn his skin, flushing him with warmth.

"We *might* survive up here," he admitted, then wished he hadn't spoken when he saw the gleam in Halisstra's eyes.

The alliance he'd just unintentionally committed to would probably be no more solid than his friendship with Pharaun. Halisstra would maintain it as long as it furthered her goals, then would drop it the instant it became inconvenient. Just as Pharaun had abandoned Ryld, leaving him to face impossible odds, when the pair of them were trying to escape from Syrzan's stalactite fortress.

Ryld's meditative skills had saved his life then and allowed him to fight his way free. Later, when he'd met up with Pharaun again, the mage had clapped him on the back and pretended that he'd fully anticipated, all along, that Ryld would survive. Why else would he have abandoned his "dearest friend?"

Halisstra gave Ryld a smile that made her look both cunning and beautiful in one. "Here's what we'll do . . ." she began.

Inwardly, Ryld winced at the word "we," but he kept his face neutral as he listened.

※ ※ ※

Danifae watched from behind a tree as Halisstra and Ryld stood in the ruined temple, talking. It was clear they were plotting something. Their voices were pitched too low for Danifae to hear, and they leaned in toward one another like conspirators. It was also clear, from the quick kiss Ryld gave Halisstra as the conversation ended, that they had become, or would soon become, lovers.

Watching them, Danifae felt a cold, still anger. Not jealousy— she cared nothing for either Ryld or Halisstra—but frustration born of the fact that she had not seduced Ryld first.

Danifae was more beautiful than her former mistress by far. Where Halisstra was lean, with small breasts and slim hips, Danifae was sensuously curvaceous. Halisstra's hair was merely white, whereas Danifae's had lustrous silver tones.

As for Halisstra's face, well, it was pretty enough, with its slightly snubbed nose and common, coal-red eyes, but Danifae had the advantage of skin softer than the blackest velvet, lips that curled in a perpetual pout, and eyebrows that formed a perfect white arch over each of her strikingly colored, pale gray eyes. An advantage she should have used earlier, judging by the display of mawkish sentimentality Danifae had stumbled upon.

Quenthel was already in play, though the older, more experienced priestess was not wholly unaware of Danifae's immediate desires. It didn't take a genius to see why Danifae had seduced the Mistress of Arach-Tinilith. It was almost to be expected.

Danifae anticipated a more complicated time of it when she'd have to take on Pharaun and Valas. The Master of Sorcere was wily. He would surely be difficult to fool once things began to turn, but his open dislike of Quenthel gave her something to use. Valas was bought and paid for by House Baenre, and that kind of gold was something Danifae wouldn't likely happen upon anytime soon. That would be delicate. And Jeggred, well. . . .

But Ryld, with this strange infatuation with her soon-to-be former mistress, would be a tougher nut to crack.

What good was playing *sava*, she thought, if you don't control all of the game pieces?

Valas strode into the ruins, followed by Pharaun and Quenthel, and, a moment later, by the loping Jeggred. The false smile Halisstra gave Quenthel and the way Ryld deliberately met Pharaun's eyes, confirmed Danifae's suspicions. Halisstra was preparing to betray her fellow priestess and Ryld his former friend.

Danifae smiled. She didn't know what they were up to—yet—but whatever it was, she was certain it could be turned to her advantage. She walked out into the clearing, joining them.

With a quick snap of her whip, Quenthel motioned for the others to gather around her.

"Valas has found an entrance to the Underdark," she announced. "Once we're safely below, Pharaun will cast a spell. We're going back to the Demonweb Pits. But not all of us. One of you will carry a message back to Menzoberranzan, to the matron mother."

As Quenthel's eyes ranged over the group, Danifae noted the indecision they held. Quenthel was obviously uncertain whom she could spare—or trust. Seizing her chance, Danifae prostrated herself before the high priestess.

"Let me do your bidding, Mistress," she said. "I will serve you as faithfully as I have served Lolth."

As she spoke, she cast a baleful eye on Halisstra, hoping Quenthel would take her point. Halisstra had acted blasphemously during their recent journey to the Demonweb Pits and was not to be trusted.

Of course, neither was Danifae. She had no intention of going to Menzoberranzan if she was chosen. Not when there was a wizard in Sschindylryn who might be able to help her to free herself, once and for all, from the odious Binding that tied her to Halisstra.

Danifae felt Quenthel touch her hair, and she looked up expectantly.

"No, Danifae," Quenthel said, the touch turning into a gentle stroke. "You will stay with me."

Danifae ground her teeth. Apparently, she'd done too good a job of seducing Quenthel.

Halisstra stepped forward—and, to Danifae's astonishment, also fell to her knees in front of Quenthel.

"Mistress," Halisstra said. "Let me carry the message for you. I know that I failed you earlier, in the shadow of the goddess's own temple. I beg of you now. Please let me . . . redeem myself."

"No!" Danifae spat. "She's up to something. She has no intention of going to Menzoberranzan. She—"

Halisstra laughed.

"And just where *would* I go, Danifae?" she asked. "Ched Nasad lies in ruins. I no longer have a House to return to. I need to make a new home for myself—in Menzoberranzan. And what better way to start than by braving the dangers of the World Above to carry a vital message to the First House?"

Danifae's eyes narrowed. She could sense that Halisstra was up to something.

"You'd travel to Menzoberranzan on the *surface*?" she asked, spitting out the word. "Alone? Through woods crawling with House Jaelre? You'd be captured again before night fell."

Danifae was pleased to see Quenthel nodding—she was obviously about to reject Halisstra's foolish notion and send Danifae, instead. Then Halisstra's lips quirked into a smile—and Danifae realized that, somehow, unwittingly, she'd just played right into Halisstra's hands.

"This will see me through," said Halisstra, patting the leather case that held her lyre. "I know a *bae'qeshel* song that will allow me to walk on wind. Using it, I could reach Menzoberranzan in a tenday, at most."

Danifae's eyes narrowed and she said, "I've never seen you use a spell like that."

"What use would it have been in the Underdark?" Halisstra said with a shrug. "There's no wind—and if there were, I'd only walk straight into a cavern wall. Regardless, I have not been, nor am I now, in the habit of justifying myself to a battle-captive. Our situation has changed some, Danifae, but not entirely."

Not yet, Danifae thought, then she grasped Quenthel's knee and pleaded, "Don't send her. Send me. If Halisstra dies, I—"

"You'd be very, very sorry, wouldn't you?" Quenthel said with a smirk. She was well aware of the particulars of the Binding. "Halisstra will go. With you here, we will be able to trace her, and at least know that she still lives. And the two of you Houseless wretches are the most expendable."

Danifae lowered her eyes in acquiescence, even though inwardly she burned with impotent anger. Halisstra, on her own in the World Above, would almost certainly be killed. It would only be a matter of time.

And when she died, the magic of the Binding would see to it that Danifae died, too.

Valas felt the knot of tension between his shoulders relax—just a little—as familiar darkness enveloped him. The harsh sunlight had been left behind after the third bend in the tunnel. He could still smell the earthy tang of wet leaves that told him the Surface Realms were just above their heads, but the air around him already felt cleaner. As they descended the twisting fissure that led ever downward through the stone, he felt his eyes adjusting to the darkness. Gone was the itching glare of sunlight, allowing him to fully open his eyes and use his darkvision for the first time in too many days.

Behind Valas, Quenthel and the others followed in a line. They'd fallen quiet instinctively as soon as they'd left the sunlight behind. Even the upper Underdark could be a dangerous place for the unwary, and that particular tunnel was unknown territory. Yet compared to Valas, they hardly moved in silence. He could hear the scrape of armor against stone as someone behind him squeezed through a spot where the tunnel had narrowed, forcing them to turn sideways to slip through. A moment later he heard the scuff of a boot and a faint intake of breath as one of the females missed her footing. He turned and angrily started to sign *Move more quietly* to her, but dropped his hands when he realized it was Quenthel and not Danifae who had slipped. Danifae had once again positioned herself near the back of the group, just ahead of Ryld—not because of the potential dangers ahead, Valas was sure, but, with Halisstra gone, to keep a wary eye on her companions.

What have you stopped for? Quenthel signed from behind Pharaun. *Keep moving.*

One of the vipers in the whip tucked into her belt gave a slight hiss.

Nodding his head, Valas led the way through the tunnel once more. As before, Pharaun was close behind him, continually peering over Valas's shoulder as if he was searching for something. Ryld, on the other hand, was constantly looking back the way they had come. Whenever Valas caught his eye, the weapons master would signal that he thought someone was following them. Valas had never seen him so jumpy before.

The first two times Ryld had done that, Valas had doubled back to check for himself, but there had been nothing: no sounds, no signs of pursuit. Thereafter he ignored Ryld's anxious glances behind them.

Since Halisstra had been sent back to Menzoberranzan there were only six of them left. Personally, Valas thought that was a foolish decision on Quenthel's part. He doubted that Halisstra would make it without Lolth's magic to protect her. But no doubt Quenthel thought the same. She probably hoped to eliminate a rival priestess who might claim credit for discovering what had happened to Lolth—assuming that a return to the Demonweb Pits was even possible.

For the hundredth time since Quenthel had announced her plan to have Pharaun summon a demon, Valas wondered how that was going to help. In all likelihood, the demon would turn on them and swallow them whole without guiding them a single step of the way.

He reminded himself that the lot of a mercenary was not to question how, but to do—and bow. And so he led them on. As he moved cautiously ahead into the unknown darkness, Pharaun still crowding close behind him, Valas fingered one of the magical amulets pinned to his shirt—his lucky, double-headed coin—and hoped it would give him the edge he'd need when the demon eventually turned on them, as he was certain it would.

❁   ❁   ❁

Halisstra stood on the bluff that overlooked the ruined temple, staring out at the horizon. The others had descended into the Under-dark some time before, and the sun was slowly sinking below the horizon, painting the clouds shades of pink and gold. Though it made her eyes water to look at the sunset, Halisstra stared in fascination, watching the colors shift into ever darker shades of orange, then red, then purple, gazing as new patterns formed each time the sun's slanting rays struck the clouds at a different angle. She was beginning to understand why the surface dwellers spoke in such rapturous tones about sunsets.

As the forest below darkened, her sight began to shift toward darkvision. She could see birds flitting through the branches below and could hear the thrumming of numerous wings as a flock of birds moved through the trees toward the bluff. She'd heard that surface-dwelling creatures followed the cycles of day and night, and it struck her that Ched Nasad's magic-controlled lighting and Menzoberranzan's famous pillar Narbondel—used for marking the passage of "day" and "night"—must have been holdovers from a distant time when drow still dwelt upon the surface. Had House Jaelre simply been following a call that other drow had not yet heard when they returned to the surface, forsaking the worship of Lolth?

The flock of birds had come closer, filling the treetops just below the bluff with strange whistling cries. One of them rose above the treetops, its wings beating so quickly they were a blur. Only when it was within a few paces of her did Halisstra recognize the "bird" for what it truly was. The furry body, the eight legs, the long, needle-shaped proboscis—all added up to a creature she hadn't realized was also a danger on the surface. Especially when there was not just one of the creatures flying toward her at the speed of an arrow, but dozens: an entire flock.

"Lolth help me," Halisstra whispered. "Stirges."

They were too close for a crossbow shot. Whipping out Seyll's long sword, Halisstra braced herself to meet the threat. Grimly, she realized her chain mail wouldn't be any help; the stirges' needle-thin noses would slip between its links.

As the first stirge dived in to attack, Halisstra swung the long sword. It was still awkward in her grip, heavier than the blade she'd been used to. Even so, her blow connected, slicing the stirge cleanly in two.

Then half a dozen of the creatures were on her.

For several frantic moments, Halisstra fended them off, killing two more with the sword and crumpling the proboscis of a third with a blow from the small steel shield she wore on her left arm.

She felt a piercing pain in her right shoulder as a stirge struck. A moment later, another plunged its proboscis into the back of her left leg, just behind the knee. The force of it caused her to stagger. Only by ducking frantically was she able to avoid the stirge lancing in at her neck. Whirling, she struck it with the sword as it flew past.

As still more of the creatures dived at her—nearly two dozen of them—Halisstra reached down with her shield hand and grabbed the stirge that had plunged into the back of her knee. She squeezed—and heard a satisfying pop as the creature's bloated midriff burst. Yanking it from her, she threw its body away, dimly noticing the spray of blood that had soaked her gloved hand. Meanwhile, the stirge in her shoulder continued draining her of blood.

The flock dived en masse, and four more stirges plunged into her flesh. One bit deeply into her left arm, two into her right leg, and the fourth into her shoulder, beside the one that was already greedily sucking away. Halisstra killed two more with the sword—which, with the air rushing through the holes in its hilt, was making constant, discordant noises like a badly played flute. Halisstra, rapidly losing strength as the stirges drained her of blood, suddenly shivered as she realized she might very well die there. Lolth was no longer watching over her, blessing her with the magic she needed to drive the foul creatures away. The only darksong spell that would affect so many creatures at once required a musical instrument as its arcane focus—and she could hardly pluck out a tune on her lyre and fight at the same time.

Then she realized something. Perhaps there was another instrument she could use, closer to hand. . . .

Abandoning her attempts to strike the stirges—there were too many of them—Halisstra reversed Seyll's sword and brought its hilt to her lips. Closing her eyes, she blew into the hilt, fingering the holes so the rush of air escaped through a single hole. Even though she sagged to her knees as blood loss weakened her, she felt magic flow from her lips into the hilt of the sword and out through the hole in a piercing blast. Her own ears rang, then went numb as a single note—sweet, high, and impossibly strong—shattered the air. All around her, stirges tumbled from the air as a magic blast hit them. Those on her body wilted, hung for a moment, then slowly slipped free of her flesh, hitting the ground around her with soft thuds.

In the silence that followed, Halisstra could hear only the sound of her own breathing. Opening her eyes, she saw dozens of stirges lying on the ground, some of them still twitching. She picked up the closest one and squeezed it. Its blood—her blood— soaked her gloves as its body burst. Dropping it, she continued from one stirge to the next, killing them one by one. Then she pulled off her blood-soaked gloves and cast them aside.

Perhaps the surface was not a place of beauty, after all.

Then she realized that something had disturbed the stirges— something that was moving through the forest toward the bluff where she stood. Hunkering down, she crept back toward the stairs, looking for a place to hide.

Valas signaled for the party to stop when the tunnel, which had been twisting its way ever deeper toward the Underdark, opened into a jumble of broken stone that led down to a medium-sized cavern whose floor was hidden by a deep pool of water. Pharaun gave a low chuckle, breaking the silence.

"Perfect," he breathed.

Keep quiet, Valas chastised, but Pharaun only laughed.

"It's going to be loud enough in here in just a moment," the mage said with a wink. Then he called back to the others, who were higher in the tunnel, up beyond where Valas could see. "Mistress, I've found a spot that will do nicely. Get Jeggred ready."

Valas heard Quenthel ordering the draegloth to kneel and the sound of a drawn dagger. Pharaun, meanwhile, laid a hand on Valas's shoulder.

"Excuse me," he said. "I need to get by."

Valas still wasn't certain what the mage was doing, but he flattened obediently against the cold stone, allowing Pharaun to squeeze past him into the cavern. Pharaun reached into a pocket of his *piwafwi* and pulled out a tiny cone of glass. Rolling up his sleeve, he pointed the cone at the water at his feet.

"Chalthinsil!" he cried, his shout filling the cavern.

In that same instant, a cone of bitterly cold air erupted from the glass cone, filling the air with swirling frost. The magical cold struck the pool, instantly turning it to solid ice. Frost continued to roil in the air for a few moments more, coating the walls and ceiling of the cavern with sparkling white ice crystals. Then it vanished, leaving a chill in the air that made Valas shiver.

Pharaun tucked the cone of glass back into his *piwafwi*.

"Perfect," he said again, staring down at the expanse of ice. "Nice and smooth. Just the thing to draw on." Then he shouted back over his shoulder, "Quenthel. I'm ready."

Behind him, in the tunnel, Valas heard a hiss of anticipation from one of the vipers in Quenthel's whip. A moment later he smelled the tang of freshly spilled blood. Quenthel appeared at the entrance to the cavern, and passed a cup to Pharaun. The mage clambered down the slope, holding the cup so its contents wouldn't spill,

Quenthel and Danifae crowded in behind Valas to peer past him at the cavern. Quenthel snapped her fingers, and Jeggred stalked down the tunnel as well, panting clouds of foul-smelling breath into the ice-cold air. One of his massive fighting hands was clamped around a spot on the wrist of his smaller arm. Blood welled out between the clamped fingers and dripped onto the stone at his feet. A moment later, Ryld joined them, having at last given up his cautious watch over the tunnel behind them.

Pharaun was already out on the ice, moving across it in a skating slide. As the others watched, he pulled out a dagger and traced an enormous hexagonal star onto the surface, carving its lines deep, like troughs. When he was done, he stood a minute, looking for imperfections.

Quenthel frowned down at the mage. "Six sides?" she asked. "Why not a standard pentagram?"

Pharaun shrugged and said, "Anyone can summon a demon with a pentagram. I like to do things with a bit more panache." He moved around the diagram, dribbling the blood from the cup into one of the lines he'd cut in the ice. After a few moments, he raised a hand and beckoned. "Jeggred, come here."

After a quick glance at Quenthel—who nodded her permission—the draegloth loped down toward the pool, dislodging rocks that tumbled down the slope to skitter across the ice. He crossed the frozen surface to the mage and obediently opened his hand, releasing his bloody arm when Pharaun gestured for him to do so. Taking that arm, Pharaun held the cup under the slashed wrist. When it was once again full, he motioned for Jeggred to re-clamp the wound, then continued limning the diagram in blood.

The mage had to repeat the process twice more before the pattern was complete. Despite the loss of blood, the draegloth remained impassive throughout the procedure. When Pharaun at last dismissed him, Jeggred loped up the slope to join the others.

"Now," Pharaun said, cracking his fingers as he stretched, "for the difficult part."

From a pocket, he pulled a candle. He cut it into six pieces, trimming each back to expose the wick. He walked around the star, boring a hole at each of the points and pushing one of the candles into it. Then he stood back and snapped his fingers. Six flames sprang to life as the candles began to burn. Their meager heat magically spread through the blood that had frozen inside the troughs in the ice. The blood melted and began to circulate, pumping through the veins of the hexagram.

Valas squinted as the flickering yellow light disrupted his darkvision. The frosted walls of the cavern picked up the illumination and sparkled like a million tiny diamonds. The candles flickered, their flames guttering slightly to one side. Seeing that, Valas nodded. The cavern wasn't completely a dead end. There must have been some tiny fissure, hidden from view, through which air was circulating.

Standing with his hands extended over the hexagram, Pharaun began to chant. As his words echoed back and forth across the confined space, the candles burned at a terrific rate, melting down to puddles of wax against the ice. Yet still the wicks burned, and as soon as they touched the ice, the color of the flames turned a brilliant blue. The flame pulsed out along the lines of the symbol and, mixing with Jeggred's blood, turned a ghastly, glowing purple.

As Pharaun's chant rose to a crescendo the mage clapped his hands together over his head. The boom of thunder that resulted all but obliterated Valas's gasp and Jeggred's harsh grunt. For an instant, the frigid air in the cavern seemed to wrench itself in two. Through the split, Valas could see the roiling red-black clouds and furnace-hot flames of the Abyss. Then came a roar of utter rage and indignation as an enormous, humanoid figure hurtled through the portal between the planes, staggering as though it had been pushed by an invisible hand. Pharaun, facing it, backed up a step or two on the ice, then recovered his composure.

"He's done it," Quenthel said.

"So he has," Danifae agreed, and she sounded impressed.

Valas realized that he was gripping his lucky coin amulet and quickly moved his hand to the hilt of his dagger, instead.

The demon—a glabrezu—was nearly three times as tall as a drow and powerfully muscled. It had four arms—two with hands, and two with enormous, snapping pincers—and a dog-like head. Its body emitted a stench that smelled like putrid corpses roasting over a sulfur fire. Its skin was so utterly black it was difficult to see its features clearly, save for a truncated snout filled with gnashing yellow fangs and eyes that glowed with penetrating intensity, as if all the fury of the Abyss swirled within their violet depths.

"You dare summon me?" it roared in a voice that filled the cavern, shaking loose small stones that tumbled down the slope onto the ice. "You dare!"

In what seemed a mockery of the gesture Pharaun had used to summon it, the demon flung its hands above its head. Intensely bright flame erupted between the outspread fingers, filling the cavern with a blinding light. Leering, the demon thrust its hands at Pharaun, sending the flame at him in a horizontal wave.

Instead of washing over Pharaun, the flame was contained by the lines of the hexagram. It licked along the veins of blood, roaring from point to point of the star in a dizzying blur, then gradually began to slow. Rather than melting the ice, the flame seemed to freeze in place. Then it shattered with a tinkling sound, like breaking crystal.

A corner of Pharaun's mouth twitched up into a half-smile.

"Are you quite finished, Belshazu?" he asked dryly.

The demon's eyes narrowed.

"You know my name," it said, its voice dropping to a deep rumble.

"We do," Quenthel said from behind Valas. "And unless you

wish to be trapped inside that hexagram for all eternity, you will tell us where we can find a gate that leads from this realm to the Abyss. Tell us that, and the mage will dismiss you."

Belshazu grunted, then dropped to its knees and sniffed at the symbol that bound it. When the demon looked up, its eyes fastened on Jeggred.

"Draegloth blood," it growled. "So that was why the drow bitch mated with me. What was her name? Tral? Tull? No . . . *Triel*." The demon spat a gob of foul-smelling phlegm onto the ice, then added, in a disdainful rumble, "That whore."

It stared past Pharaun at the group of drow above, its violet eyes burning with a terrible challenge that caused Valas to draw his kukris in readiness.

Jeggred returned the demon's growl. Tensing, he hunched into a crouch. Quenthel's hand darted to his back and clenched the draegloth's tangled mane. She jerked Jeggred back just as he was about to spring.

"Stay beside me," she commanded.

Jeggred complied.

Valas heaved a sigh of relief, glad the draegloth hadn't sprung forward to attack his father. Had Jeggred taken a single step across the symbol that had been wrought with his blood, the lines of magical force that bound the demon would have stretched—and snapped. Which was what the demon had obviously intended, all along.

Pharaun cleared his throat, and the demon returned its attention to him.

"Now then," the mage said. "We need to get to the Demonweb Pits. Where's the nearest gate to the Abyss?"

Belshazu bared yellowed fangs in a smile and stared down at Pharaun as if contemplating which of the wizard's limbs to tear from his body first.

"Right here, in this cavern," it rumbled. "Just beneath my feet. Let me show you."

Summoning its magical fire again, the demon directed the flame from its hands downward, onto the ice at its feet. Because the magic was not trying to cross the hexagram itself, the flame took effect. Enormous clouds of steam rose from the melting ice, obscuring the spot where the demon stood. A crater appeared beneath the demon's feet, and as melt water rushed to fill it, Belshazu plunged flaming hands into the water and set it aboil.

Pharaun was leaning forward, intensely curious to see the gate the demon had promised. He reached into a pocket of his *piwafwi* at the same time. Jeggred was still flexing his claws in barely suppressed anger at the insult to his mother. Danifae and Ryld stood closer to the tunnel entrance, and were talking in rapid sign. Their backs were turned to Valas, making it impossible for him to see what they were saying.

Beside him, Quenthel suddenly tensed.

"Pharaun, stop Belshazu!" she shouted. "He's trying to—"

Her order was lost in a furious hiss of steam and the loud bubbling of boiling water. Valas himself could only hear Quenthel because she stood right beside him. Then he saw what Quenthel was pointing to: the edge of the crater of knee-deep water Belshazu was standing in was crumbling back toward the line of the hexagram. At last awakening to the danger, Pharaun saw it too—but too late.

With a hissing roar, the line of flowing blood tumbled into the boiling water and was gone.

The hexagram was broken.

"Wizard—you are mine!"

Roaring his triumph, Belshazu waded through the boiling water toward Pharaun, eyes blazing violet fury at the mage who had so foolishly dared to attempt to bind him.

Chapter

F O U R

Ryld pulled the bag of sand out of the pocket of his *piwafwi* and placed it on a ridge in the rock wall at the point where the tunnel forked, then carefully balanced a large stone on top of it. He pulled from his quiver one of the crossbow bolts Halisstra had taken from the surface elves and checked its barbed head for traces of poison. Seeing none, he used it to cut his palm. He smeared blood on the tunnel wall, then snapped the point off the bolt. As he placed the broken bolt on the tunnel floor, he glanced nervously back down the fork that led to the cavern, worried that someone might have heard the sound.

Silence. The noise had been slight, and no one was coming to investigate.

He balled his hand around a rag to staunch the flow of blood, then dropped it to the floor beside the broken crossbow bolt. Then he pulled his portable hole out of a pocket and flipped the folded piece of phase-spider silk open, laying it on the ground just below the sand-filled bag. Carefully, he loosened the bag's drawstrings until just a trickle of sand began to fall from it into the portable hole. Then he hurried back down the steeply sloping corridor to the cavern where the others were.

He'd been worried that Jeggred would smell the fresh blood on his palm, but the draegloth seemed to have been doing a little bloodletting of his own. It was Danifae who stared at him as he returned.

Ryld paid little attention as Pharaun summoned the demon, his mind instead focused on the silent count he'd begun after leaving the bag. He did glance down in alarm, however, when the demon told Pharaun there was a gate to the Abyss directly under the frozen pond. It was obviously a ploy of some kind, but Pharaun didn't question it. Instead, when the demon's hands flared with fire for the second time, Pharaun merely stood and watched, as if curious to see what the demon would do.

Ryld concentrated on his count: fifteen, fourteen, thirteen . . . almost time.

"Listen," he said, touching Danifae's arm. "Do you hear that?"

Danifae gave him a suspicious look. Then, from farther up the tunnel, came the sound of a dislodged stone hitting the tunnel floor and rolling toward them. Danifae's eyes widened slightly.

"Someone *is*—"

Her words were cut off by a violent hiss of steam from the cavern below. Glancing down, Ryld saw that the demon was melting the ice. He opened his mouth to shout a warning—

—then he pursed his lips shut. The demon was Pharaun's problem.

Ryld shifted to sign language, in order to speak over the hissing roar of boiling water.

Whoever it is, I'm going to make them sorry they followed us. Tell Quenthel where I've gone.

You're running off after Halisstra, Danifae accused.

Ryld, startled, was surprised by her bluntness—and by the approval he saw in her eyes. Was she glad that her mistress would have someone to protect her, after all?

No, he told her, determined to keep up his bluff. *I'll be back. As proof, you can keep this.*

He pulled the lesser of his two magical rings from his finger and passed it to Danifae, intentionally dropping it. The ring bounced off a rock and began to roll down the slope toward where the others stood. Danifae scrambled after it, trying to grab the ring before Quenthel or one of the others claimed it.

Ryld turned to hurry back the way they had come. He saw Valas shoot him a quick, questioning glance. Then Quenthel shouted a warning to Pharaun. An instant later a roar of triumph filled the cavern. The demon was free.

Ryld was already several paces away, climbing swiftly up the narrow tunnel that had led them to the cavern. Behind him he could hear more roaring, violent splashing, and terrified shouts. An explosive rush of cold air whooshed past him—the blast of a spell. There was no way to tell whether it was one of Pharaun's—or one cast by the demon. Then a male voice screamed in mortal agony. Pharaun's?

For a heartbeat or two, he actually considered turning around. Then he decided against it. Pharaun deserved to know what it felt like not to be able to count on a friend.

He climbed upward, ignoring the sounds of battle behind him until he reached the flattened bag, which he plucked from its ledge. He dropped it into the portable hole, then folded the hole shut. He'd shake it out later when he reached the surface. If the others survived the demon attack and came looking for

LISA SMEDMAN

him, there would be no clues to alert them to the trick he'd played.

Ryld pressed on, retracing the route they'd taken from the surface. He'd taken careful mental notes as they descended, pausing several times to turn around to view landmarks from the opposite direction.

He passed the place where they'd been forced to crawl over a jumble of rock because the ceiling had partially collapsed, then the long, narrow cavern where a trickle of water had encouraged a faintly glowing patch of lichen to grow. Next came the natural chimney that rose more than a hundred paces above and below to dead ends, with several narrow tunnels opening onto it.

Reaching it, Ryld looked up the chimney and counted. The third tunnel above and slightly to the right was the one they'd come through. Touching the magical brooch pinned to his shirt, Ryld stepped out into the chimney and levitated toward it.

As he drew closer to the tunnel mouth, he heard a faint clink from somewhere inside it. Instantly recognizing the sound of chain mail links clinking against each other, he whipped up the hood of his *piwafwi* and drew his feet up under its hem. The magic of his cloak enfolded him, throwing his body into shadow. He drifted past the mouth of the tunnel he'd been heading for—to one side of it, so the person he'd just heard wouldn't spot the movement of shadowed gray against shadowed gray—then he halted the equivalent of a dozen paces above the opening. He hung there, carefully controlling his breathing so that not even a whisper of sound escaped his lips. He waited.

A moment later, a dark face appeared in the tunnel mouth. The strange drow's ebony skin blended with the darkness of the tunnel behind it, as did the black mask that hid his lower face—the symbol of a cleric of Vhaeraun—but his white hair and faintly glowing red eyes stood out in sharp relief. He peered up

34

at where Ryld floated. A chimney was a natural place to expect an ambush.

Slowly, Ryld slid his finger into the trigger of the crossbow that was strapped to his wrist, but the cleric didn't appear to have spotted him.

After a quick scan of the chimney above, the cleric turned his attention downward. Pulling a forked bit of bone out of a pocket of his *piwafwi*, he grasped it with the thumb and forefinger of each hand and held it over the chimney, then spoke the words of a spell. The bone glowed with a soft purple light. A moment later, the light coalesced at the point of the V-shaped bone, then erupted into a sizzling purple spark. The spark began to drift up, then hesitated and drifted slowly and steadily downward. It came to a halt in front of the tunnel Ryld had just climbed out of before it winked out.

The priest turned and signed to someone in the tunnel behind him, *They went this way.*

That seen, Ryld's suspicions were confirmed. The cleric was from House Jaelre and was seeking vengeance for the death of his high priest.

Ryld watched in silence as the cleric and two well-armed males descended toward the tunnel. The cleric and one of the warriors simply stepped out of the tunnel and drifted magically downward, but the second warrior was forced to climb down the narrow corner of the chimney, his back braced against one wall, hands and feet against the other. Tactically, that was the moment for Ryld to strike—or to flee, since the grunts and scuffing noises the climbing male was making would cover the sound of him entering the tunnel they'd just left.

Ryld didn't care about Quenthel Baenre. He had accompanied her because he'd been ordered to. Valas could take care of himself in a fight, and Danifae was from another city, and no concern of

Ryld's. But Pharaun, even though he was a powerful mage, had just been in a fight with a demon. He would be easy pickings for those three. . . .

Flipping back his *piwafwi*, Ryld shot his crossbow at the cleric. The tiny bolt struck the drow's cheek, plowing a furrow of red across it. As the powerful poison on the barb entered his bloodstream, the cleric sagged in mid-air and was forced to grab at the mouth of one of the tunnels as his levitation magic failed him. Crawling into it, he lay trembling on its stone floor, his lips moving in whispered prayer.

Ryld touched his brooch and dropped like a stone. He twisted as he fell, simultaneously drawing his short sword and lashing out with a foot as he passed the climbing drow. Braced against the rock as he was, the man could do nothing but close his eyes against the kick Ryld aimed at his face. The blow rocked his head back, smashing it into the wall with a loud crack. An instant later, his unconscious body tumbled after Ryld.

Pushing off from a wall, Ryld activated the magic of his brooch a second time, checking his fall. The unconscious drow tumbled past, landing with a bone-snapping thud against the floor far below. In the meantime, the levitating warrior had drawn his weapon: a spiked mace.

Ryld floated down toward him, short sword at the ready. His opponent shouted something—a command word—and the head of his mace burst into bright, magical light. Blinded by the sudden brilliance, Ryld instinctively twisted aside—and heard the mace strike a shattering blow against the wall beside his head. His foot lashed out a second time but missed its target. The warrior was used to fighting in sunlight and had easily avoided the kick.

Cursing, Ryld summoned a magical darkness that filled the chimney. Neither of them could see, so both had to listen carefully over the sound of the cleric's prayers for the faint shifts of fabric and armor in order to locate his opponent.

A rush of air warned Ryld of a second mace blow. He twisted violently back, inadvertently falling a little as his levitation magic was interrupted. His sword arm brushed the chimney wall—and an instant later the mace smashed into his elbow, numbing his arm to the fingertips. He tried to swing, but the sword slipped from his fingers.

The mace smashed in a second time, catching him in the stomach. Ryld's breastplate stopped the spikes from penetrating, but even so, the force of the blow made him grunt. His opponent was better than Ryld had expected.

Ryld heard his short sword clatter against the bottom of the chimney, far below. Meanwhile, the cleric's prayer had increased in volume from a whisper to a chant. The cleric must have been using his magic to neutralize the poison, which meant that Ryld would soon have two threats to face. In the narrow chimney, the greatsword strapped to his back was useless. He wouldn't be able to bring Splitter to bear. That meant close fighting. Very close.

Kicking off from a wall, Ryld launched himself horizontally at the sound of his opponent's breathing. His fingers brushed against a mail tunic, but then he heard the rush of a mace. He twisted, but the weapon connected with his shoulder. He was saved from injury by the dragon-shaped ring on his finger—the ring that marked Ryld as a Master of Melee-Magthere—for its magic made his skin and flesh as tough as that of a dragon. The spikes of the mace bent as they struck, and the weapon glanced off.

Meanwhile, Ryld clawed his way up his opponent's body, stabbing fingers into pressure points. The man grunted, gasped—then made a loud, choking gurgle as Ryld found his throat and crushed his windpipe. His body went limp, and he too tumbled away.

They must have been losing elevation during the fight. Ryld emerged from the magical darkness and could see again. And the cleric could see Ryld.

Shouting an invocation to his god, he tore the mask from his face and hurled it at Ryld. The weapons master twisted and dropped, but the mask followed him with the speed of a swooping bat. It slapped against his face and adhered tightly against his nose and mouth with a wet sucking sound.

Ryld tried to tear the mask from his face, but it clung to his skin like fungus to a rock. Unable to breathe—a single indrawn breath would draw the contagion the mask carried deep into his lungs—Ryld did the only thing he could. He touched his brooch and dropped. Somehow, he was able to avoid drawing a breath as he caught the ledge where the cleric stood. He held his breath still as he wrenched his head up to the level of the ledge, then swung his legs up in a graceful leap. The mental discipline taught to him by the masters of Melee-Magthere sustained him as he sprang toward the startled cleric, hands poised to strike. Dark sparkles danced before his eyes as he reached the limits of what his body could do without air to sustain it—and he passed those limits, still rushing forward.

The cleric, red eyes wide with fear, danced backward, avoiding Ryld's charge. Then, nerve broken, he turned and fled, screaming the words of a prayer. A circle of darkness appeared in the air just ahead of him, and he hurled himself into it. Then he was gone.

An instant later, the mask vanished from Ryld's face. Able to breathe again, Ryld drew a shuddering breath and steadied himself against one wall. For the moment, all was well. The cleric was gone, his magic having spirited him away, and the two warriors of House Jaelre who had accompanied him were dead. Even if the cleric did find Pharaun and the others, Ryld had greatly improved the odds. In the meantime, the two dead bodies would give his excuse about going back to see who was following them the ring of truth. If the others came that way they would find the dead warriors, would be able to tell from the tracks that there had been a third man, and would assume, when Ryld failed to return, that he had been captured and dragged back to Minauthkeep. Perfect.

Stepping out into the chimney once more, Ryld levitated down to retrieve the sword he'd dropped. The bodies of the two warriors he'd killed lay in a tangled heap, wedged into the bottom of the chimney.

Ryld's sword was sandwiched between them.

Flipping the top corpse over, he reached for his sword—then gasped when he spotted a pair of leather gloves that had spilled out of one of the warrior's torn pockets. He recognized them in an instant by the insignia of House Melarn embossed onto their wide cuffs.

They were Halisstra's gloves—and the soft leather was stiff with dried blood.

Fear washed through Ryld like an icy river. Did that mean Halisstra had been killed? If so, the logical thing for Ryld to do would be to return to the others—assuming they weren't demon meat by then—and give up the insane notion of remaining on the surface. It had all been Halisstra's idea, anyway. If she was dead, there was no point in him continuing alone.

But if she wasn't dead. . . .

Ryld shook his head, angry at himself. He didn't owe Halisstra anything, he told himself. Going after her was simply insane.

His fist tightened on the bloody gloves. Stuffing them into a pocket of his *piwafwi*, he touched his brooch and levitated up the chimney.

Chapter

FIVE

Pharaun smirked as Belshazu surged across the boiling pool of water toward him.

"Demons are *so* predictable," he said, *tsk tsking*.

He raised the cone of glass he'd palmed earlier and spoke a command word. A blast of freezing air burst from the cone, smashing against the demon. Sweat crystallized to sparkling ice on Belshazu's broad chest but cracked and melted away under the heat and motion of the demon's charge. When the cone of cold struck the knee-deep water that surrounded Belshazu the pool instantly froze solid again.

The demon, finding himself trapped in knee-deep ice, directed the flames that surrounded his hands downward, but the ice did not melt.

Pharaun's smirk grew as he saw that his plan had worked.

"Thanks for stirring up the pool," he told the demon. "You

mixed Jeggred's blood into it quite nicely. Oh, and here's a bit of trivia for you. Did you know that ice crystals always have six sides? So do crystals of blood, since blood is mostly water. They always form perfect little hexagrams. Millions of them."

It took a moment for the demon to realize what Pharaun was talking about. When it did, it roared even louder than before, smashing its pincers down on the ice that bound it. While the blows were hard enough to fill the cavern with booming crashes, the ice neither cracked nor splintered. The effort seemed to tax the demon. After just a few blows, it was panting in great, wheezing gasps.

"Now then," Pharaun continued. "You were going to tell us where the nearest gate to the Abyss can be fou—"

With a lurch that sent bile rushing into his throat, Pharaun fell upward as gravity suddenly reversed itself. Bound in ice the demon might be, but he still could work his magic. Taken by surprise, disoriented by the sudden gravity shift, Pharaun was unable to counter his fall with levitation magic. He slammed into the ceiling, knocking the breath from his lungs. Danifae and Jeggred crashed into the ceiling an instant later, but Valas had landed on his feet with catlike grace, and Quenthel was able to levitate before striking the rocks.

The demon lunged up at Pharaun, stretching as far as his ice-bound feet would allow. One of his pincers clamped onto Pharaun's foot and scissored down, slicing through boot leather and flesh until it grated against bone. Pharaun screamed in agony and scrambled at the rocks, trying to find a handhold as the demon pulled the drow wizard toward himself.

A moment later, something flashed past him: Valas. Magic lending him unnatural speed, the mercenary had sprinted across the jagged rock of the ceiling with a dagger in either hand to slash at the demon. One of the enchanted blades bit deep into

Belshazu's wrist, spitting blue sparks of magical energy as it cleanly severed the bone. The demon howled in wounded rage and flailed with his remaining pincer at his new target, but Valas darted out of range.

As Pharaun felt the severed pincer fall away from his bloodied foot he levitated away from the ceiling, pushing himself out of range of the demon. Still roaring, with foul-smelling black blood pumping from its severed wrist, Belshazu reversed the spell he had cast a moment before. Danifae and Valas fell back to the cavern floor, the mercenary at once clambering to his feet to menace Belshazu with his dagger. Quenthel and Jeggred floated down after Pharaun.

Pharaun, favoring his mangled foot, landed on the frozen pond behind the demon. Blood squelched out of his torn boot and spread across the ice, freezing to pink on the intensely cold surface. He fumbled a small metal flask out of a pocket of his *piwafwi*, uncorked it, and drained the contents. The healing potion took effect almost immediately, numbing his pain like a glass of lace-fungus brandy. In another moment his wounded foot was whole again. He tested his weight on it, and no more than a slight tingling feeling remained. Aside from the tear in his boot, he might never have been wounded.

From the slope where the others had landed came the low hiss of the vipers in Quenthel's whip. Their mistress's voice was equally impatient.

"Pharaun! Stop wasting time. Compel the demon to tell us what we need to know."

Pharaun gave a brief bow in Quenthel's direction, then turned to Belshazu, who had sagged into a crouch on the frozen pond, feet still bound by the ice. The demon was wheezing from his exertions and held his severed wrist tight against his chest. He appeared to be sulking—but by the blaze in his violet eyes

Pharaun could see that the demon had not been tamed. Yet.

Like a *sava* grand master, Pharaun put his final piece into play.

"Here's something else I think you should know," he told the demon. "My spell not only froze the pool, but also crystallized the water vapor in the air. That's what you can feel inside your lungs . . . thousands of tiny hexagrams, sawing away at your flesh. Tell us what we want to know, and I'll release you before they do any further damage. Keep stalling, and you'll die."

As Belshazu considered that, Pharaun carefully kept his face composed. He had no idea whether the ice crystals inside Belshazu's lungs could actually harm the demon—but it sounded good.

Belshazu roared in anger, but the roar ended in a wheeze. The demon gave Pharaun a pained look, then grudgingly nodded.

"I do not know of any gate," he growled.

Behind Pharaun, one of the vipers in Quenthel's whip gave a soft hiss of frustration.

"But there is a way to reach the Abyss from this plane," the demon continued. "There is a demon ship that will carry you there . . . if you can find it."

"A demon ship?" Quenthel echoed.

Belshazu glared at her.

"Have you heard of the Blood War?" Belshazu asked.

His voice was heavy with scorn, as if he expected the drow to be ignorant of the doings of his kind.

"Of course," Quenthel answered. "It is a contest between the Abyss and the Nine Hells—a glorious war that has raged for millennia."

"Glorious?" Pharaun scoffed. "More like loud, sloppy, and pointless. Neither side remembers what they're fighting about— let alone has the slightest hope of winning."

"The devils of the Nine Hells *will* be defeated!" Belshazu bellowed.

"In due time, I'm sure," Pharaun interjected dryly. "But for the moment, you were telling us about a ship?"

Still snarling, the demon wrenched his attention away from Pharaun and addressed himself to Quenthel.

"In ages past, my kind found a fresh way to launch our attacks against the Nine Hells. We built ships of bone bound with strands of spirit stripped from the manes who serve us, and hung with sails of flayed skin. These ships sail between the planes, blown by the winds of chaos.

"Centuries ago, one of these ships of chaos set out into the Plane of Shadow, seeking a new route to the Nine Hells. It sailed down the River of Shadows to a place where that river touches upon this plane, and there it was lost. Of its crew of thirteen, only one returned: a groveling mane. It babbled something about the uridezu who captained the ship being overcome and of a terrible storm. We subjected the mane to the fiery lash and the torments of boiling oil, but it was able to give us only one useful piece of information. Just before the ship was lost in the storm, it had visited a city of your world. The city's name meant nothing to us, but perhaps you will know it—Zanhoriloch."

Unlike Quenthel, who was listening avidly as the demon spoke, Valas seemed not to be listening; his attention was focused on cleaning the sticky black streaks of demon's blood from his dagger. Danifae stood behind them, an openly skeptical look upon her face, toying with a ring. Jeggred, bored, was licking the wound on his wrist.

"This information is useless," Quenthel said. "How are we to find this ship—assuming it exists? I've never heard of a city by that name."

"I have," Valas said. As the others turned to the mercenary, he gave a final polish to the kukri, then shoved it back into its sheath. "It's an aboleth city."

Pharaun rolled his eyes and said, "It just gets better and better, doesn't it? Those fish-folk are the last creatures I want to deal with."

Danifae suddenly stirred.

"Mistress," she said, "Pharaun's right. Shouldn't we be—"

"Silence," Quenthel spat. "I've noted your cowering—how you kept to the rear, like a whimpering male—and am tired of it. If I want your opinion, *priestess*, I'll ask for it."

Danifae did as she was told, pursing her lips shut in a tight, angry line.

"Zanhoriloch isn't far from here," Valas continued. "It's in Lake Thoroot."

"*In* Lake Thoroot?" Quenthel asked.

"Aboleths live underwater."

"How far?" the high priestess asked.

The scout frowned, thinking.

"If I can find the right tunnel," he said, "the journey would take no longer than it would for the heat to rise through Narbondel."

Quenthel considered that, then asked, "How big is this lake?"

"Enormous," Valas answered. "Big enough to cover a city, at any rate."

"Or a ship," Quenthel mused. "If the ship of chaos had just left Zanhoriloch when it ran into the storm, it may be at the bottom of the lake. If it is, the only ones who would know of its existence would be the aboleths." She glanced at Belshazu, and her expression hardened. "Assuming, that is, the ship is still intact. You said it was 'lost' in a storm, Belshazu? How badly damaged was it?"

Belshazu shrugged and said, "The mane said it was intact."

Quenthel's eyes narrowed.

"Then why didn't the demons try to recover it?" she asked.

Belshazu's eyes blazed.

"Weren't you listening, drow? I said it was lost—on this, the foulest of planes. How were we to find it?"

Pharaun, listening quietly, noticed that Danifae was staring at him. She'd shifted slightly, so that Quenthel was between her and the demon. When she had Pharaun's attention, she spoke to him in sign, behind Quenthel's back.

The demons know where the city is now. The minute you release this one—

Pharaun gave a quick flick of his fingers: *Yes.*

More than that, he did not offer. For all he knew, Belshazu could read the silent speech.

It was Valas, as usual, who asked the practical question, "Once we find the ship, and raise it from the lake, how do we sail it?"

Belshazu gave him a sly grin and replied, "The ship has a mouth. All you need do is feed it a soul."

Quenthel matched the demon's lascivious smile with one of her own. Seeing her glance in his direction, Pharaun had no doubt whatsoever about whom she'd most like to shove into the demon ship's gullet.

"And?" Valas asked, still focused on the practicalities. "Once the ship's been fed, what do we do next?"

"Sail it, ," Belshazu answered derisively. "It has sails, and lines, and a tiller. Catch the wind and go. Continue up the River of Shadows, and sail the breadth of the Shadow Deep. The river branches as it reaches the Abyss. Smaller streams empty into the pits that pock the Plain of Infinite Portals. One of those portals leads to the sixty-sixth layer. Follow the right branch, and the ship will carry you into the Demonweb Pits."

Pharaun said nothing. It all sounded highly doubtful to him. Quenthel, however, had a gleam in her eye. The serpents in her

46

whip lashed in apparent eagerness for their mistress to begin the search for the ship of chaos—at once.

"Our thanks, Belshazu," she told the demon in a purring voice. "And my apologies for the indignities this mage has subjected you to." She stared coldly down at Pharaun, and gave a terse order: "Release him."

Behind her, Danifae gestured rapidly at Pharaun, *No! The demon will only be waiting at the ship when we—*

With the speed of one of her serpents, Quenthel turned and, in one smooth motion, pulled the whip from her belt. Hissing with glee, the vipers lashed out at Danifae.

"I ordered you not to speak!" Quenthel shrieked.

Caught by surprise, Danifae was slow to react. She reared back—but not before the longest of the serpents grazed her cheek with its teeth. Its work done, the viper curled back, eyeing the livid red lines it had drawn in the drow's soft flesh. As its venom flowed through Danifae's body, she sagged to her knees, already gasping for air.

Quenthel stood staring coldly down at Danifae, stroking the head of the viper that had inflicted the near-fatal kiss.

"Don't worry," she told Danifae. "Zinda may be the largest, but her poison is the least venomous. You'll live—if you're strong enough." Ignoring Danifae's choking sobs, she turned back to Pharaun and said, "Well?"

Once again, Pharaun bowed—a little deeper—and he addressed himself to the more pressing issue. Carefully.

"I can speak the word that will release Belshazu, but he won't be able to return to the Abyss until the ice melts," he told Quenthel.

"Then speed it up," she spat back. "Fill the cavern with a ball of fire."

Pharaun cocked an eyebrow.

"Unfortunately, knowing we would be underground in confined

quarters, I did not prepare that spell," he offered, resisting the urge to say what he truly thought.

Quenthel was being even more stupid than usual—why, Pharaun asked himself, did the others persist in obeying her?

Jeggred was mindlessly, slavishly loyal to the nearest, highest-ranking female of his House, and Valas was getting paid to be there. But Danifae must surely have realized that her unfailing loyalty would go unrewarded. Especially with Lolth silent and presumably no longer watching the actions of her servants.

Valas cleared his throat.

"The ice will melt in time," he observed in a neutral tone. "What's a day or two of delay—to a demon?"

As Quenthel rounded on him, sputtering indignation at his "insolence," Pharaun at last realized what she must have had in mind. She hoped to curry favor with Belshazu. Like her sister Triel, Quenthel hoped to enter into unholy union with a demon, one day. And not just any demon.

Pharaun stared at Jeggred, who squatted at Quenthel's side, teeth bared in a silent snarl. Blessed of Lolth the hulking creature might be, but Menzoberranzan didn't need another draegloth. One fouling the air with its putrid breath was enough.

"I'm sure Belshazu will remember that you spoke for him," Pharaun reassured Quenthel. "I'm equally sure he'll . . . look favorably upon you . . . when the time comes."

The demon broke into a leer, tongue lolling as it stared up at the priestess. Its goatlike horns gave it the look of a satyr—if one discounted the misshapen body and the sole remaining pincer.

Pharaun shuddered.

"Very well," Quenthel said at last. "Speak the release word, Pharaun, and let Belshazu find his way back to the Abyss in his own time. When the ice melts."

"I will—as soon as the rest of you are safely out of here."

Careful not to get within range of the remaining pincer, Pharaun skated around the demon on the ice and climbed back up to where the others stood. He looked around, then asked, "Where's Ryld?"

Danifae, who had already fought off the worst of the poison and risen, shaking to her knees, answered, "We heard . . . a noise in the tunnel behind us. Just before . . . the demon freed itself. Ryld went to see . . . what it was."

"He should have come back by now," Pharaun said, a touch of worry in his voice.

Quenthel glanced at Jeggred and jerked her chin. The drae-gloth loped up the tunnel and returned, a few moments later, with the head of a broken crossbow bolt. He handed it to Quen-thel, his nose twitching.

"Blood," he grunted. "Ryld's."

"We should go after him," Pharaun said.

He started up the tunnel, but Quenthel caught his arm.

"You're not finished here yet," she said, indicating the demon. "And there's no point. The weapons master will either catch up to us or he won't. We've got to get moving, or we'll be trapped in this dead end. That bolt came from the bow of a surface elf."

"She's right," Valas said.

Grudgingly, Pharaun nodded. Even wounded, Ryld could take care of himself. He'd catch up to them eventually. Yet, since the warrior's absence had been pointed out, Pharaun felt it keenly. With Ryld gone, there was no one in the group to watch his back. Or to banter with. If Ryld was dead, Pharaun would miss him. Perhaps for days.

Quenthel glanced down at Danifae, who was still on her hands and knees.

"If you're quite finished lolling about, then get up," Quenthel told her. "We have a ship to find."

The vipers in her whip hissing with derisive laughter, Quenthel followed Valas out of the cavern. Jeggred growled one last time over his shoulder at Belshazu, then loped after his mistress.

As soon as he was certain Quenthel could no longer see him, Pharaun bent and offered Danifae his hand. She gave him a calculating look, as if deciding whether to vent her pent-up anger upon him, then she allowed him to help her rise. He supported her into the tunnel, then turned and spoke the words to a spell before hurrying after her.

Belshazu shook its remaining pincer at Pharaun's back.

"I will see you again, mage," it roared.

Pharaun chuckled as he scrambled up the tunnel and said, "When Hell unfreezes, Belshazu."

Which it was unlikely to do, since Pharaun had just cast a permanency spell upon the ice.

C h a p t e r

S I X

The surface world was cloaked in darkness by the time Ryld emerged from the tunnel. He had traveled for some time after leaving the others in the cavern. A full moon hung above the treetops, half hidden by clouds but still casting so much light that it impeded his darkvision. The snow that covered the ruined temple was covered with footprints, but Ryld was able to pick out those belonging to the cleric and warriors of House Jaelre. They led in one direction only—into the tunnel. The escaped cleric hadn't returned that way.

Ryld scanned the trees, searching for any sign that more of House Jaelre's warriors might be lurking in the forest. Seeing none, he crept out of the tunnel mouth.

A moment later he heard a soft, melodic whistle. It was a tune he recognized.

"Halisstra?" he whispered.

Halisstra negated the spell that had rendered her invisible and rushed over to embrace him.

"Ryld!" she exclaimed. "I thought you weren't coming back."

He tried to ask why she'd doubted him, but she pressed her lips against his, kissing him. For several long moments he returned her embrace, feverishly drinking in her scent and taste. She was alive! Then he remembered the warriors he'd killed—and the cleric who had gotten away.

"We can't stay here," he told her. "House Jaelre is on our trail. I ran into one of their scouting parties below."

"I know," she said, surprising him. "I saw three of them pass through the woods, just after sunset. I made some noise, and they were drawn this way. They didn't find me, even though they searched for a long time after finding my gloves."

"I'm glad," Ryld whispered fiercely. "No need to worry about them now, though. They're dead."

He heard her draw a sharp breath and thought she was reacting to his words. Then he realized that it was his grip on her arm that had prompted the gasp. She was wounded. Turning her arm, he saw a puncture just below the spot where the sleeve of her chain mail ended. The wound had been healed—probably by magic—but freshly so, since it still pained her.

"I think I got your gloves back," he said. "What happened?"

"Stirges. Dozens of them, but they're dead now."

"How?"

"I blasted them with magic, then made myself invisible."

"With your lyre?"

When Halisstra shook her head and grinned, Ryld blinked in surprise.

"How, then?" he asked. "Has Lolth reawakened?"

Halisstra laughed scornfully and said, "Let's check. Are you awake, Lolth? Can you see this?"

Smiling fiercely, she made a blasphemous gesture, flipping her hand palm-up, fingers curled in the sign for a dead spider.

Ryld cringed, but several heartbeats later, when nothing happened, he slowly allowed himself to relax.

Halisstra smiled and patted the hilt of the sword she'd taken from Eilistraee's cleric.

"I've found a new way to work my magic. I don't need my lyre—or Lolth—any more."

Ryld nodded, disturbed not so much by her blasphemy but by the fear of what would follow. Above them hung the moon—symbol of the god who had driven Lolth out of Arvandor. Was Halisstra about to be claimed by Corellon or one of the other surface gods?

Trying to ignore his own question, Ryld glared at the ruins of the creator god's temple.

"We should get moving," he said, more harshly than he'd intended. "This place is dangerous."

Halisstra stared at him a moment, then nodded and said, "Let's go."

🕷   🕷   🕷

With a quick motion of his hand, Ryld caught Halisstra's attention.

Be still, he signed. Then, *do you hear that?*

They had walked for the rest of the night through the forest without hearing anything but the pattering of the rain that was melting the slush underfoot, but from somewhere ahead came the sound of an animal's howl. It was answered a few moments later by a second howl, somewhere to the right, that ended in a series of brief, excited yips. The yips had a pattern, almost like that of speech.

There're at least two of them, Halisstra signed back.

Ryld nodded. He peered into the forest but the light of the rising sun, slanting in through a crack in the heavy cloud cover, was ruining his darkvision.

Halisstra reached for her sword as she signaled, *They're coming our way.*

Yes. And they're moving fast, but . . . He listened for a moment and heard a high-pitched yelp of alarm. *They're not hunting. They're fleeing from something.*

A grim look on her face, wet hair dripping onto the shoulders of her armor, Halisstra drew her sword. Curiously, she did not ready it but instead reversed the blade and held the hilt to her lips.

Levitate, she said with her free hand. *Hide.*

She pressed her lips to the hilt and blew, and a haunting music filled the air. An instant later she disappeared. The only way Ryld could tell she was still there was by looking at the ground. The spot where no rain was falling marked where she stood.

As the howls and yips drew closer, Ryld touched his brooch. He rose silently into the air through sodden tree branches, then paused at a height of about ten paces and readied his crossbow. A moment or two later, he heard a rustling in the underbrush. An enormous gray-furred animal that walked on four spindly legs burst into sight, running full out with its tongue lolling and eyes wide. It glanced from side to side as it ran—not with the terror of a wild creature but with a keen intelligence as if seeking somewhere to hide. It yipped once, was answered by a companion still some distance away in the woods, then was gone.

Ryld could have shot his crossbow but had not. He wanted to save the magical bolt for whatever was chasing the carnivore. He didn't have long to wait. A few moments later, he heard something big crashing through the forest with stumbling steps. From its gait, it sounded like a human, but by the snap of branches and the huffing grunts Ryld guessed that it was much larger. When it crashed into sight, smashing a slender tree in half with one careless swipe of its hand, Ryld saw that he'd been right.

It was a troll.

Twice the height of a drow and nearly five times as heavy, the troll had a mottled, gray-green hide covered in splotchy gray lumps. It loped along on misshapen, three-toed feet, its rubbery arms so long that its knuckles made drag marks through the slush on the ground. Greenish-black hair grew from its sloping forehead down its back in a tangled, dirty mane, and even in the steady rain its body emitted a foul smell somewhere between human sweat and the stench of rothé manure.

Ryld stared down at the troll as it paused, streams of drool sliding from the corners of a panting mouth filled with broken teeth. Once again, he refrained from shooting his crossbow. The bolt would do no more than annoy the troll and alert it to the fact that someone was there.

After a moment, having caught its breath, the troll got ready to run again. Then its head suddenly whipped to the side, and its nostrils flared.

"Halisstra! Watch out!" Ryld shouted—more to draw the troll's attention than to warn Halisstra, who was almost certainly watching the troll herself.

In that same instant, Ryld fired. The bolt whizzed toward its target but glanced off a branch just before striking the troll. Instead of burying itself in the monster's eye, as Ryld had intended, the bolt sliced a furrow across the top of the troll's head. A heartbeat later, the graze mended itself.

The troll, having scented Halisstra, raked the air in front of it with long sweeps of its clawed hands. It must have come uncomfortably close, for an instant later Halisstra became visible, her long sword slashing forward in an attack. Stupidly, the troll parried with its hand, and two of its fingers went flying. They lay on the forest floor, wriggling in the slush.

The creature struck with its other hand, raking it across Halisstra's chest. The magical chain mail stopped the claws from penetrating, but the force of the blow sent Halisstra stumbling backward. She slipped on the slushy ground and went down. Sensing an easy kill, the troll lunged, and only at the last moment did Halisstra manage to bring her shield up. The troll's teeth sank into the edge of the shield, crumpling it. Then the troll shook its head, wrenching the shield from Halisstra's arm. Pinned to the ground by the weight of the monster kneeling on her, she was unable to bring her sword into play.

Negating his levitation magic, Ryld plunged down through the branches. He landed perfectly braced in a ready posture, drawing Splitter in one smooth motion from the scabbard at his back. Putting all the force of his will into the blow, he swung the greatsword with both hands and felt it slice cleanly into the troll's neck, cleaving it instantly. The head flew into the air, eyes blinking stupidly, then it landed and rolled away. The headless body reared to its feet and spun around as Ryld opened its stomach with a second sword swing, spilling foul-smelling entrails.

The headless, disemboweled troll finally stumbled away into the forest.

Halisstra lay on her back on the wet ground, gasping, rain spattering her face. Worried that she might be in immediate need of healing magic, Ryld reached down to help her—

—and was slammed to the ground by an attack he should have anticipated. Rolling quickly away, he saw that the troll was back. The creature stumbled toward him, one hand holding its head on the stump of its severed neck, the other attempting to rake Ryld with its claws. Even as Ryld flipped himself up off the ground and back onto his feet, dancing out of the reach of those claws, he saw flaps of sinew burst out of the ropy muscles of the troll's neck and quest up like sentient worms to hook themselves into the head. Swifter almost than the eye could follow, they stitched the head back onto the body, while the entrails that had spilled from the troll's slashed belly sucked back into the stomach wound. Already the fingers that Halisstra's blow had sliced off earlier were starting to grow back. Knobs of pinkish-gray flesh pulsed outward from the severed digits.

Leaping forward, Ryld slashed at the troll's neck a second time, but the monster, unlike him, anticipated the attack. It ducked—startlingly fast—then lunged forward and wrapped a rubbery hand around Ryld's own. Ryld heard a bone in his hand crack and gasped at the incredible strength of the troll. Even with a hand that was missing two fingers, its fist was crushing his. The troll jerked Splitter out of Ryld's hand and cast it away.

Halisstra had struggled to her feet and was slashing at the troll's broad back, her sword making strange, flutelike noises as she swung it. The monster grunted with each stroke like a slave under the lash but otherwise ignored the deep cuts in its back. Whirling, it backhanded her away with a blow that sent her staggering. Ryld drew his short sword and thrust at the spot where the troll's heart should have been, but even though the blade buried itself to the hilt in the thing's rubbery chest the monster was not slowed.

A hand whipped out with the speed of one of Quenthel's whip vipers and wrapped itself around Ryld's neck. Powerful fingers tightened against flesh, choking off his breathing. Ryld felt a rush of magical energy flowing into his body from the dragon-shaped ring on his finger, as the ring hardened his flesh against the troll's claws—but too late. His windpipe had already squeezed shut. Abandoning his sword, still hilt-deep in the monster's chest, he

LISA SMEDMAN

drove stiffened fingers into what would have, on a drow, been a crippling pressure point—then he winced. He might as well have driven his fingers into solid stone.

Halisstra charged back into the fray and managed to slice one of the troll's feet from its ankle. It stumbled but quickly found its footing, balancing on the stump. Halisstra was rewarded with a rake of claws that snagged her chain mail, tearing a link from it.

Ryld, unable to breathe, shouted at her the only way he could.

Flee! I am finished!

"No!" she gasped. "I won't leave you."

She lunged forward, attacking the troll with a furious barrage of blows. Ryld, observing with the eye of a master, saw that Halisstra had opened her stance, inadvertently exposing herself to what would be a fatal rake of the monster's claws.

Though Ryld should have been watching with the detachment of someone who knows he is about to die and can do nothing about it, he felt a strange emotion fill him in that impossibly long moment that stretched between two fading heartbeats, a deep sadness and a sense of infinite loss. Not only because Halisstra was about to die, but because her death would mean the end of something Ryld had only just discovered: true friendship—perhaps even love. The kind that would cause a person to willingly sacrifice herself in a hopeless attempt to save another. As their eyes met, Ryld realized that he would have done the same for Halisstra—and he saw that she knew it. He also saw something he'd never seen in the eyes of a drow: trust.

At that moment a drow female burst out of the forest, her silver-white hair plastered against her face by the rain. She was naked, save for a heavy silver chain around her waist that was hung with a large silver disk and a curved hunter's horn. She moved at a full-out sprint, holding above her head a sword whose blade glowed with leaping silver flames. With a piercing, high-pitched shout that sounded like a single note in a song, strong and true, she slashed down with her sword.

The blade bit deep into the troll's shoulder, then flared. Silver fire spread instantly across the troll's body, blinding Ryld. He winced, expecting to be burned himself, but the wave of heat he'd been anticipating never came. The flames seemed to emit song rather than heat, dancing to their own rhythm as they licked over the troll's rubbery skin.

Bellowing, its flesh blackening under the magical fire, the troll sagged to its knees. Ryld, suddenly able to breathe again as the massive hand fell away from his neck, gasped in a lungful of air. Though fouled by the stench of burning flesh, it had never tasted so sweet. He watched, dumbfounded, as the troll's body crumpled in on itself, the magical, silvery flames destroying it in a matter of heartbeats.

"I thank you, my lady," he told the drow—obviously a mage or a cleric, and a powerful one. He bowed deeply before her. "You have saved both our . . ."

His voice trailed off as he saw the look on the woman's face. She was staring at Halisstra with a look of surprise—and bitter anger. Ryld finally recognized the symbol on the silver disk that hung from the chain at her waist. It was a sword, set against a haloed circle. The symbol of Eilistraee.

"That's Seyll's armor," the cleric said, eyes blazing as she stared at the chain mail Halisstra was wearing. "You're the one who killed her."

The stranger wrenched the horn from her belt and blew a single, prolonged note. An instant later, the horns of her fellow hunters answered.

Nimor leaned over the map of Menzoberranzan that had been laid on the floor of the mine, its corners weighted with jagged, fist-sized chunks of silver. He gestured with his rapier.

"The spider we hope to slay has two heads," the drow told the five others—three duergar and two demons—that had gathered around the map. "Cut off either, and the body dies." The point of his blade pricked the southern edge of the city. "One head is here: Qu'ellarz'orl, the plateau where the First House stands." He moved the rapier, pointing to a spot on the northern edge of the city where a smaller cavern bulged off the main one. "The other is Tier Breche, the cavern that houses three of the most important institutions in Menzoberranzan: Sorcere, Melee-Magthere, and, most importantly of all, the great temple of Lolth, Arach-Tinilith."

"Tough stones to crack, both one of them," said Horgar, who stood immediately to Nimor's left.

The gray dwarf prince came barely to the drow's waist but had wider shoulders than the slender Nimor. He scowled down at the map, absently rubbing his bald head with stubby fingers. His two guards—duergar like himself, one of them with a scar that stretched from chin to ear along the cheekbone—kept a wary eye on the pair of half-demons that stood on the opposite side of the map.

"Quite so, Crown Prince," replied Nimor. "Which is why I want the duergar to lead the assault on Tier Breche. A frontal assault down the tunnel from the north. Your troops will establish a siege wall, then, from behind it, use catapults to lob stonefire bombs into Sorcere and Arach-Tinilith, reducing them to a smoking ruin."

"Easily said," Horgar challenged, "but not easily done. That tunnel will be thick with jade spiders. We may be able to smash our way through one or two of them but not all."

Chuckling, Nimor reached into a pocket and pulled out half a dozen flat ovals of green jade, each pierced by a hole through which a silver chain had been threaded and inscribed with a name. Holding them by their chains, Nimor jiggled them so they tinkled together.

"Thanks to an associate who's managed to penetrate *deep* into Menzoberranzan, I'm able to guarantee you they won't be a problem," he told the duergar.

The scarred prince snorted and said, "And where will the tanarukks be while we're making our attack? Bravely bringing up the rear?"

This elicited a growl from Kaanyr Vhok, who bared perfect teeth and thumped the hilt of the rune-inscribed sword he held against his golden breastplate.

"My Scoured Legion could outfight your mushroom-men any day," he growled, glaring angrily across the map at the scarred duergar. "Why, even our orcs would be a match for—"

A tug on his arm from Aliisza stopped him in mid bluster. He glared at her but listened as she whispered in his ear, then slowly lowered his sword.

"Gentlemen, please," Nimor said. "Hear me out." He turned to Vhok. "The Scoured Legion will indeed be involved in the fight. You will take Donigarten, the city's food and water supply, then fall upon Qu'ellarz'orl from the east. That will cause the matron mothers to withdraw their defenders south, allowing the duergar to take up positions in the north. But not all of the duergar. One company, at least, must march together with the tanarukks, spread amongst their ranks to give the impression that our force as a whole is committed to an attack on Menzoberranzan's First House."

Vhok narrowed his eyes and asked, "We are to be a mere *distraction*?"

"Not at all," Nimor assured him, a twinkle in his eye. "You also have a chance at victory—an excellent chance. I've taken steps to take House Baenre out of the fight with a little surprise that I've got planned for its matron mother. Once Triel is eliminated, the other females of House Baenre will begin vying for her throne. The companies each commands will begin fighting each other—which will keep them too busy to bother about something so insignificant as defending their city.

"When the other noble Houses see Baenre in disarray, they'll sense its weakness and strike. One or more of them will try to usurp Baenre's position as First House. While they're busy fighting each other, Lord Vhok's troops can swoop in and seize Qu'ellarz'orl."

Vhok scowled and said, "An interesting theory."

"It's not just theory," Nimor countered. He paused to brushed rock dust off the sleeve of his immaculately tailored gray shirt.

"It's drow nature. We're like spiders reacting to the twitching of a web. When we think we have our prey at our mercy, we strike.

"Only this time," Nimor said, "the prey will be the drow themselves. Menzoberranzan will fall. I guarantee it."

※　　※　　※

Triel coldly regarded the prisoner who had been brought before her: a young male drow. He lay on his back on the floor of her audience chamber, wrists bound tightly behind him and ankles likewise tied above his bare feet. His black pants and shirt hung in tatters, the slashes revealing a myriad of lacerations that dribbled blood onto the floor. The hair on one side of his head had been burned down to stubble, and his face was covered in blisters. One eye was fused shut, its eyelid blistered and weeping, but the other glared up at Triel with undiminished defiance.

Triel crinkled her nose at the stench of burned hair and flesh and toyed with a perfectly balanced throwing dagger—the only one still in the fellow's bandoleer when he was captured. She could tell by the tingle it sent through her fingers that it was magic—as had been the blades that had killed four of her elite guard.

"This is an assassin's weapon," she observed, handing it to one of the females who stood on either side of her: two of the House guard who attended her at all times, magical shields and maces at the ready.

A third member of the guard—an officer—stepped forward to conclude her report.

"The intruder was captured on the fifth level, Matron Baenre," she said. "We believe he was trying to reach your private quarters."

Triel stared at the officer, who, despite all that was happening,

looked as if she was freshly turned out for inspection. Her adamantine chain mail was a glossy black, her long white hair neatly
braided. She stood at rigid attention, a polished mace hanging
from her belt and a hand crossbow strapped to the back of each
wrist. Five black spiders, embroidered into the shoulder of her
silver tunic, proclaimed her rank.

"How did he get inside, Captain . . . ?" Triel let the sentence
trail off, an obvious invitation for a name.

"Captain Maignith," the woman answered, meeting Triel's
eyes for precisely the amount of time that was appropriate. "He
didn't get in through any of the lower doors. I questioned the
guards—thoroughly. All were at their posts, and the wards are
still in place. He didn't slip past us. He must have gotten in from
above."

That said, Captain Maignith glanced at a second officer—a
lieutenant of the lizard riders—who stood several paces farther
back, as befitted a male. He wore tight-fitting, padded leather
breeches and a *piwafwi* trimmed in silver. He held his plumed
silver helmet in the crook of one arm and seemed to be having
trouble looking Triel in the eye.

"Matron Mother, I . . . My riders saw nothing on the outer
wall," he stammered.

Triel noted the shift of words with amusement. A magic
earring told her the lieutenant was speaking the truth—as he
believed it to be. She could hear none of the echoing quaver that
accompanied a lie.

She toyed with the handle of the whip of fangs that hung from
her belt, twin to the one carried by her sister Quenthel. The vipers
hissed softly in anticipation, sensing her desire. The lieutenant
deserved punishment—and would receive it, in due time.

Her hand fell away from the whip.

"Go and fetch your lizard," she said.

The lieutenant hesitated a moment too long, a mix of relief and puzzlement on his face. Then, suddenly remembering his place, he bowed deeply and backed from the room.

The captive smirked, obviously pleased with the concern his intrusion had caused.

Not liking the look in his eye, Triel drew a wand of braided iron that hung beside her whip. The tip of the wand was set with a tiny white feather, which she pointed at the captive as she spoke a command word. No visible force came from the wand, but the effect was instantaneous. The captive screamed—a sound of acute terror that filled the audience chamber—and drew his legs up to his chest. Had his hands been free, he would no doubt have wrapped them around his legs. He rocked back and forth, whimpering. When Maignith nudged him with the toe of her boot he screamed anew and rolled away, leaving a stain of pungent urine among the blood spatters on the floor.

Triel sighed, hoping she wasn't wasting her time. There were so many other matters in need of her attention. On the outskirts of Menzoberranzan, an army of duergar, tanarukks and other, lesser races were preparing to assault the city proper. Triel should have been in her war room, communicating with the officers who would hold the invaders at bay, but there had been an assassination attempt on her—not nearly the first, of course—and she needed to know who was behind it.

Had one of her sisters decided that she could do a better job as matron mother? Did Triel need to strengthen her defenses from within? Or had the assassin been sent by one of the other noble Houses? House Barrison Del'Armgo, perhaps? That seemed unlikely, since the second-ranking House was just as badly off as House Baenre just then. After the disastrous battle at the Pillars of Woe, Mez'Barris Armgo had come straggling back with what remained of her forces—and the sorry tale of how her troops had been driven up a side tunnel and lost one-quarter of their forces and all of their wagon trains.

As she waited for the lieutenant to return with his lizard, Triel walked to the thronelike chair that had once been her mother's. Shaped like an enormous spider and forged from solid adamantine, it balanced on eight curved legs. The chair had been imbued with powerful spells, not the least of which was a magical symbol that would instantly turn any attack directed at the matron mother back upon whomever had been foolish enough to initiate it. The chair was a symbol of Lolth, but even though the goddess had fallen disturbingly silent, its magic still functioned, since it was powered by wizardry.

As Triel settled cross-legged onto the chair—her two personal guards shifting to stay on either side of her—she thought of Gromph, and wondered, once again, where the city's archmage had disappeared to.

The door to the audience chamber opened, and the musty smell of lizard wafted into the audience room. The lieutenant walked in, leading his mount by the reins. The lizard squeezed in through the door, the sticky pads on its feet making faint sucking noises as they were lifted from the stone floor. With a body twice as long as a drow—three times as long, if the lashing tail was counted—it was a formidable sight. Its leathery skin glowed with a sparkling blue luminescence that faintly illuminated the otherwise dark room. As it scuttled past the captive, tongue flickering in and out, it twitched its head to the side, inhaling the man's scent. The assassin, still feeling the effects of Triel's wand, whimpered and cringed away from it.

Triel drummed her fingers on the cold metal of the throne.

"So," she said, making her observations aloud. "The assassin couldn't have climbed the outside of the stalagmite. If he had, the lizards would have picked up his spoor."

The lieutenant closed his eyes in relief.

"Which begs the question," Triel continued. "How *did* he get in?"

Beside the lieutenant, the lizard's tongue continued to flicker in and out, licking at the blood smeared across the floor. Its round, black eyes stared, unblinking, at the captive.

Triel smiled.

"Your mount appears hungry, Lieutenant," she observed. "Why don't you slip the muzzle and let it feed—on a non-essential part, of course."

Grinning, the lieutenant did as he was ordered.

The lizard twitched its tail in anticipation, its luminescent skin darkening momentarily to a deeper blue, but it waited for its master's hand signal before it sprang forward. Teeth cracked through bone with a loud crunch, severing the assassin's bound legs at the ankles. The assassin screamed once as his feet disappeared down the lizard's throat, then he fainted.

Grabbing the lizard's reins, the lieutenant pulled it back.

Triel looked dispassionately at the blood that was pumping onto the floor.

"Staunch those wounds," she ordered.

Obediently, Maignith stepped forward and tapped each of the assassin's severed ankles with the head of her mace. The magic possessed by the weapon caused the head to flare brightly, cauterizing the wounds. When they stopped sizzling, Maignith grabbed what remained of the assassin's hair and bent his head back. She slapped him awake.

The assassin's one functional eyelid fluttered, then opened. His burned face, once a throbbing red, had gone gray.

"Do you want to live?" Triel asked.

The assassin seemed to have recovered, at last, from the effects of the wand.

"You're going to kill me, no matter what," he croaked.

"Not necessarily," Triel answered. "You obviously have some talent, to get as close to my quarters as you did. Perhaps I'll recruit you for my House."

"With no feet?"

"We have regenerative magic," Triel answered.

"Not any more," the assassin said, wincing as he tried to smile. "Lolth is dead."

Triel shot to her feet, yanking out her whip, and shrieked, "Blasphemer!"

For a heartbeat or two, the vipers in the whip lashed, hissing their fury. How dare this male speak to her like that? She, who had been first in Lolth's favor and who was Matron Mother of House Baenre. A distant corner of her mind recognized that fear was driving her fury. The lack of a report from Quenthel was filling her with worry, increasing as each cycle passed. But if Lolth awoke from her silence and learned that Triel had not punished the male for his insolence. . . .

Then Triel realized she was being goaded. The assassin was trying to draw her closer to him. She couldn't see what attack he could possibly mount, wounded and bound with magical rope as he was, but she hadn't survived so many centuries by underestimating her foes. She stroked each of the vipers in turn to soothe them—and herself—then she tucked the whip away.

Lolth's grace might be out of Triel's reach—for the moment—but Triel had other magical abilities at her disposal. She used one of them, the power of her voice. Dropping into a husky, seductive tone that vibrated with magical energy, she began planting a suggestion in the captive's mind.

"You might as well tell me who sent you," she told him. "If it was a matron mother of another House, she's safe enough. I'm not about to waste my troops in striking back at her with this siege on. If it was one of my sisters, you have as much to gain by serving me as you do by serving her. So tell me . . . who hired you?"

"I am no mere hireling," the man gritted.

Ah, pride. Triel could work with that.

"Of course not. You're proud of who—and what—you are. Why don't you share this information with me? Surely telling me about yourself won't betray anything about the matron who sent you."

"I serve no *female*," the assassin spat. "Nor will any male, soon enough. The Masked Lord will see to that."

A ripple of tension passed through the room as the officers and guards reacted to the name. With an effort, Triel kept her temper. Instead she focused on the information he'd just let slip.

Vhaeraun's worship was strictly forbidden in Menzoberranzan. Admitting to it was tantamount to suicide—slow suicide, since its worshipers were typically tortured to death in an effort to root out the names of other blasphemers. The assassin had just signed his own death warrant, which meant that any promises Triel made to spare his life would be ineffective.

No, he *wanted* to die. And slowly.

Triel stared down at him.

"If you hope to be rewarded by Vhaeraun, think again," she told him. "You failed in your mission. You'll be lucky if your god lifts his mask to spit upon you. And your fellow conspirators are feeble and weak. Just look what they sent to do the job, a mere *boy*? They're not even worth my contempt."

The assassin's good eye blazed.

"Laugh while you can," he spat back at her. "You'll be weeping soon enough, when the Jaezred Chaulssin come to call."

Triel smiled to herself as she pondered the name. It was obviously an organization of some sort—perhaps one that had arisen during the slave rebellion that had been so recently put down.

Could they be some ragged refugees from the ruins of the city called Chaulssin?

"I've never heard of this Jaezred Chaulssin," she said disdainfully. "They're obviously as inconsequential as they are ineffective."

The captive gave a croaking laugh and said, "Hardly ineffective. My master brought an army to your doorstep."

Triel seized upon the information.

"Your master is a duergar then . . . or a tanarukk? Kaanyr Vhok?"

"Much more than that. Much more than that mercenary Vhok. My master has powers that you could only dream of. It was he who engineered your army's defeat at the battle of the Pillars of Woe."

Triel raised an eyebrow and asked, "Oh, did he?" She could guess who the assassin was referring to but needed confirmation. "Then no doubt he'd like me to know his name—to know which male dared attack Matron Mother Baenre in her own home. Or is he afraid of me, as all good little drow males should be?"

That goad, combined with Triel's magical suggestion, tipped the balance.

"My master is no mere drow," he said. "Nimor is—"

He bit off the rest, aware that he had already revealed too much.

"Nimor?" Triel growled. The name was unfamiliar. Then she realized who it must be. "You mean Captain Zhayemd of Agrach Dyrr, don't you? The traitor who led the army of duergar to our very doorstep?"

The prisoner nodded defiantly and said, "Your master, soon enough."

Triel thought about that for a moment. Zhayemd was clearly an assumed name—had the assassin's leader also assumed the

70

name of the Sixth House? She wondered how deeply Agrach Dyrr's treachery truly lay. Had Nimor persuaded the soldiers to attack their allies on his own, or had he the backing of the House itself? An important question, since Agrach Dyrr's household was under siege by forces of Menzoberranzan that could better be used to battle the duergar and tanarukks.

Triel decided to bluff.

"I knew your master was not an Agrach Dyrr," she told the assassin. "I had never seen him before—and I know all of the senior officers of that House. Matron Mother Yasraena and I are . . . allies. As much as any two matron mothers can be."

"Yasraena Dyrr is of no consequence."

Triel stiffened and asked, "What do you mean?"

"A male rules House Agrach Dyrr—the lichdrow. Vhaeraun has re-established the natural order of things, just as he will in all of Menzoberranzan, once this war is won."

Triel heard a slight intake of breath beside her, and remembered her lieutenant. Quick as a striking snake, she cracked her whip in his direction. Gleefully hissing, the five vipers sank their fangs into his dark flesh. The male officer stiffened, then gurgled faintly as his eyes rolled back. He crashed to the floor like a broken stalactite.

His lizard sniffed him once, then immediately began to feed, chewing on the head with loud crunching noises.

Triel glanced at Maignith.

"Not a word of this to anyone," she hissed.

Maignith bowed, then stared meaningfully at each of the guards on either side of Triel and said, "You can count on our silence, Matron Mother."

Triel returned her attention to the captive. She was delighted that he had at last succumbed to her magical suggestion—he was giving her even more information than she'd dared hope for.

Wetting her lips like a lizard scenting blood, she probed further.

"Was it the lichdrow who sent you here? Was it his magic that got you inside?"

"No . . . and no."

"Who got you inside, then?"

"Nimor himself. And though I have failed, he will not. Your defenses are as weak as cobwebs against him. He escorted me through the shadows and into your 'stronghold' with ease."

"Nimor is within these walls?" Maignith gasped.

The assassin smirked and answered, "He was."

Triel's eyes narrowed. Not at the fact that Nimor had been able to creep into the heart of House Baenre—the massive stalagmite that had been hollowed out to form the Great Mound—but that, having accomplished such a feat, he would have left it again. Why hadn't he stayed to attack her himself? Why leave a weaker vassal behind to do his bidding? Certainly he would have known that this man would be caught.

The assassin interrupted her musings with a pained laugh.

"You will see Nimor's power and majesty yourself soon enough, when he leads the final assault against this House. That is, if you live to—"

Triel realized that the glare of defiance—and self-will—had never left the assassin's eye, the entire time he was speaking. And his gaze had slid down to her chair more than once—but only when he thought she wasn't looking at him.

"Guards!" she shouted. "Shields!"

Instantly, the women on either side of her sprang into motion, thrusting their shields between Triel and the only visible threat: the assassin.

Even as the two shields clanged together, the audience chamber filled with a blast of magical energy. Searingly hot flame exploded outward from where the assassin lay, the roar of it slamming against Triel's eardrums with such volume that it nearly blotted out the screams of the guards whose bodies were blackening like overcooked meat.

The magic of their shields held fast, and the blast was deflected over, under, and around the chair on which Triel cringed. She felt the wash of its heat as little more than a flush of warmth; felt nothing of its blast save for the shields that were forced back against her chair. The throne itself had not reacted to the blast of the fireball the assassin had carried within himself. Triel could guess the reason. The attack was directed at the assassin who'd carried it into the room, not at the matron mother herself. Nimor's information—and his guess as to where Triel would question the failed assassin—had been flawless.

All this Triel realized in the instant of ear-ringing silence that followed the blast.

Maignith and the other two guards crumpled to the floor, burned beyond recognition. The lizard, too, was dead, curled and immobile in one corner of the room, its skin no longer glowing.

Of the assassin's body, nothing remained but bones, glowing red like coals and sending up wisps of oily black smoke.

Triel shivered, aware that she had come within a heartbeat of death. For a moment, she knew fear. No wonder the assassin had been so willing to talk. He had needed to keep her within range until the spell went off.

Triel heard running feet in the hallway outside, approaching the audience room door. She gripped the legs of her chair, clenching tightly to subdue the trembling of her hands. She stared over the blackened husk of her guard, wincing at the burned-meat smell, as a captain of her House guard ran into the room. The woman's eyes widened at once as she took in the blackened bodies on the floor.

"Matron Mother," she gasped. The captain was panting, as if she'd run some distance. "The enemy approaches the city!"

"From which direction?"

"Through the caverns to the southeast. Our patrols have skirmished with them at the Cavern of Severed Tentacles and at Ablonsheir's Cave."

"Was it tanarukks the patrols encountered or duergar?" Triel asked.

"Both, but most tanarukks"

"In what numbers?"

The captain shrugged and said, "Impossible to tell. But the armies seem to have combined and are making their way swiftly through the Dark Dominion. They'll reach the outskirts of the city at any moment."

Triel ground her teeth. Was it a feint—or an assault in force? Judging by their approach, the tanarukks and duergar were aiming to enter Menzoberranzan through one of the nine tunnels that lay between Donigarten Lake and the edge of the plateau, but which would they emerge from? And, should they succeed in entering the great cavern, what would their target be? Under ordinary circumstances, Triel would have expected the attackers to push north across the great cavern, cutting off Donigarten and the moss beds, the city's main water and food sources, to ensure that Menzoberranzan would have nothing to sustain it during their siege. But given the timing of the assassination attempt— which, had it succeeded, would have thrown her House into chaos—perhaps there was another target. House Baenre would be the first stepping stone to an assault on Qu'ellarz'orl itself. If she was right, the main force of the attack would come through the tunnels closest to the plateau.

Was there still time to plug the gap? She dared not commit the House guard. It would be needed to defend the Baenre compound if the enemy made it into the city. There was only one other House Baenre company close enough.

"Pull our troops back from the siege of House Agrach Dyrr," Triel ordered. "Send them into the caverns immediately below the eastern end of the plateau. Order them to hold them at all cost. And tell the other Houses to send their troops to defend the other caverns leading into Narbondellyn. House Barrison Del'Armgo especially. Our troops will be first to bear the brunt of the assault, but Del'Armgo must reinforce us. Leave Agrach Dyrr to the Xorlarrin."

The captain bowed and said, "As you order, Matron Mother."

As the captain hurried away, Triel chewed her lip, praying she'd made the right decision.

Where in the Nine Hells was Gromph when House Baenre needed him most?

Chapter

E I G H T

Glass.
Curved glass.
And outside it . . .
Gray stone.
Tunnel walls.
Close.
Outside curved glass.

Gromph Baenre, Archmage of Menzoberranzan, stared, unblinking, at the rough stone that lay just outside the wall of his prison. He was trapped inside curved glass. In utter silence. Inside a hollow sphere that lay on the floor of an unknown tunnel. Unable to move, unable to breathe, only sluggishly able to think.

He stared at his own reflection, distorted by the concave surface of the glass. His face was coarse but unlined despite his seven centuries, thanks to the amulet of eternal youth pinned to his *piwafwi*. His silver-white hair floated loosely around his head, unaffected by the gravity that existed only outside the sphere. His eyes were open and unblinking.

Growing weary of his own face, he stared at the tunnel walls instead, noticing a bright vein of quartz. Noticing how wide it was, how large the crystals.

Time passed.

A while later—ten cycles, a year?—Gromph felt something tickle his mind. An awareness. A presence. Turning his mind toward it, Gromph sought it out. Struggling like an exhausted man trying to lift his head, he concentrated his will.

Kyorli?

Nothing.

More time passed.

He stared at the vein of quartz, picking out a crystal within it. By concentrating on its facets—blurred though they were by the concave glass in front of his eyes—he could focus his thoughts.

What he knew was that he was inside a sphere of glass, the product of an imprisoning spell.

A spell cast by the lichdrow Dyrr.

He was far beneath the city, in an unknown tunnel, encased in a spell that prevented even divination magic from finding him.

Trapped.

More time passed. As it trickled by, Gromph tried to open his mouth, to force his eyelids to blink, to twitch his fingers.

Nothing.

Had he been able to draw a breath, he would have sighed. But even had he been able to move and speak—to cast a spell—it wouldn't have helped. The spell the lichdrow had cast on him was a powerful one, and Gromph knew it well. The only way it could be reversed was if a counterspell of equal power was cast on the sphere. And that spell could only be cast from *outside* the sphere, by someone else. If that wasn't difficult enough, the spell would only work if it was cast in the same location that the original imprisonment spell had been cast.

Gromph recoiled from the irony of it. He was the Archmage of Menzoberranzan, the most powerful wizard in all of the City of Spiders, privy to the arcane workings of more spells than most mages dared dream of. Yet even if he had been able to cast a wish spell, it wouldn't have done him any good.

After another length of measureless time had gone by, Gromph felt the tickle in his mind return. It felt closer, more insistent.

As before, it took an excruciating effort for Gromph to concentrate his will.

Kyorli? he sent. *Help!*

The mind-tickle disappeared. Had his body been capable of it, Gromph's shoulders would have slumped.

All at once the world spun in a crazy arc. The vein of quartz disappeared and Gromph found the position of his head and feet reversed—though in his state, up and down were concepts that had little meaning. He found himself staring into the eyes of an enormous brown rat twice the size of the sphere, its face distorted by the curvature of the glass. Pink paws rested lightly on the top of the sphere, and whiskers twitched as the rat sniffed the cold glass.

After a sluggish moment, Gromph realized his error in perception. The rat wasn't enormous, the sphere was tiny. The spell had shrunk him to less than rat size. His thoughts still sluggish, he at last noticed the kink at the end of the rat's hairless tail.

Kyorli! Help me. Take me home.

Go? the rat replied, more of a feeling than a word.

Yes, go. To the city. Go.

The world spun crazily by. Gromph could see stone walls

spinning past, could see them bump crazily up and down as the sphere, propelled by Kyorli's nose and paws, rolled along the uneven floor of the tunnel.

No, not a tunnel but a tiny fissure in the rock. No more than a rat-sized crack.

The walls continued to spin past. For a moment, the world opened up into looming darkness as Kyorli rolled the sphere across the floor of an enormous cavern. In the distance, Gromph saw a flash of lavender light: the visible spectrum of a *faerzress*. Then the patch of magical radiation was behind them, swallowed by darkness.

The sphere rattled on, Gromph suspended unmoving at its center, enclosed in absolute silence.

A short time later, the sphere bounced to a stop against a wall.

What's wrong? Gromph asked.

Kyorli's paws scrabbled against the sphere, turning it. Gromph found himself looking up at the wall of the cavern, where—several paces overhead—the tunnel continued through a wide crack.

Up! Kyorli "said." *City.*

The rat scurried up the wall, then down it again. Gromph's world tilted wildly as paws scrabbled uselessly against the outside of the sphere, spinning it around. After a moment, Kyorli scrambled back up the wall, entering the tunnel briefly, then came down again.

Gromph realized he'd been overestimating his familiar. Kyorli was only a rat—with no more than a rat's intelligence.

Try a different way, he suggested.

Kyorli stared at him, whiskers twitching. Then, bobbing her head in a rat's equivalent of a nod, she began moving the sphere again. Gromph found himself rolled back down the tunnel they'd just come along, across the cavern with the glowing *faerzress*, and down another tunnel.

When the sphere stopped rolling again, Gromph found himself staring at a river. Only a dozen paces wide but swiftly flowing. Gromph's hopes rose as he recognized it. He'd traveled through that tunnel once before, years past. The waterway was one of the subterranean tributaries of the River Surbrin. It eventually flowed into Donigarten, the lake that was Menzoberranzan's water supply.

But it flowed through an airless tunnel. If Kyorli tried to follow the sphere, she would drown. She could roll the sphere into the river and let the water carry Gromph to the city, but by the time she found her own way back to Menzoberranzan, the sphere might have been carried out of the lake again, down into the river's lower reaches. Gromph might wind up in an even worse position than before.

He considered the problem, though slowly. His thoughts were still a near-stagnant puddle. After several long moments, during which Kyorli disappeared from sight and reappeared again half a dozen times, a thought came to him.

The *faerzress*. The magical energies emitted by a *faerzress* were unstable, unpredictable in their effect. They might do strange things to Gromph, even kill him. But perhaps, if luck was with him, they might first mutate the effects of the spell that bound him.

Take me back to the cavern. The one with the glow.

The world spun around him as Kyorli complied. The glow reappeared, and the sphere rolled to a stop.

Closer.

The lavender glow grew larger, brighter.

Closer.

The glow expanded until it filled Gromph's peripheral vision.

Closer.

Kyorli hesitated, nose twitching.

Danger, she sent. *Too bright. Hurts.*

Yes, Gromph answered. *I know.* Then, giving his thought all of the authority of his will, he added one word more: *Closer.*

Kyorli gave the sphere a final shove, then scampered away, terrified.

As the sphere rolled and bumped along the uneven cavern floor, the glow spun closer. When the sphere came to rest, the glow surrounded it on every side. Still rigid, Gromph basked in the wash of magical radiation. The *faerzress* would either kill him or . . .

His muscles exploded with agony as sensation and movement returned. Chuckling with delight, he rose to his feet. The sphere rocked beneath him, forcing him to catch his balance. He reached into the pocket of his *piwafwi* and pulled out a small chip of mica. Tossing it casually at his feet, he spoke the word that should have activated a shattering spell. Nothing happened. He might be able to move and speak, but spellcasting was impossible while he was trapped within the sphere. He'd have to rely upon brute force to get to where he needed to be.

Experimenting, he threw his weight forward against the smooth surface—and wound up tumbling in a clumsy somersault as the sphere rolled in that direction.

It took some doing, but at last Gromph figured out how to coordinate his hands and feet, scrambling forward like a rat and maintaining his balance as the sphere rolled across the floor. More than once, a bump or crack in the floor sent him spinning in the wrong direction, but gradually, acquiring several painful bruises along the way, he made his way back down the tunnel that led to the river.

Kyorli, having overcome her fear now that her master was

no longer inside the bright wash of the *faerzress*, scampered along behind, from time to time correcting the course of the sphere with a nudge of her nose or paws. When they reached the swiftly flowing river, she fretted, running back and forth on its bank.

Master. Deep water. Swim?

No, Kyorli. Only I will swim. You return to Menzoberranzan the way you came, through the tunnel that leads up. Go to Sorcere, fetch any of the wizards there, and lead them to the shore of the lake.

The rat thought about that a moment, whiskers twitching. Gromph raised his hand, pressing his palm lightly against the inner surface of the sphere. Kyorli pressed her nose briefly to the spot, then turned and was gone.

Gromph drew a deep breath, preparing for the plunge into the river. Then he chuckled. No need to hold his breath—the magic of the sphere was obviously still sustaining him, or he'd have suffocated long ago in the tiny, confined space. Rocking the sphere forward, he plunged into the river.

Once again the world spun around him, then there was water, the bump of stone walls that sent him reeling, and the occasional flash of a luminescent fish. After some time underwater—how long, Gromph still had no way of measuring, but several miles of tunnel must have swept past—he was thrown against the bottom of the sphere. It was rising rapidly, like a bubble, then it burst up through the water, bobbing on the surface of a large lake.

He'd done it! He'd reached Donigarten!

Righting himself, Gromph attempted to continue as he had before, by rolling the sphere across the surface of the lake. But the sphere only spun in place. Realizing that he'd made a potentially fatal error, Gromph cursed. Unless Kyorli made it back to Menzoberranzan in time and swam out into the lake to help him, he would be at the mercy of the current. Gromph sent out a silent call but heard no answering voice. With a heavy sigh, he braced himself inside the rocking sphere, waiting to see where the current would carry him.

He'd surfaced near the northeastern tip of the island that lay at the center of the lake. Herds of rothé milled aimlessly on its banks. Behind the island, Gromph could make out the glowing spire of Narbondel. Someone had been casting magical fire into the enormous, natural rock pillar in Gromph's absence to mark the start of Menzoberranzan's "day," but for how long? Had he been gone for a month, a year?

As the sphere drifted closer to the island, Gromph once again tried to contact Kyorli but without success. Had the rat simply not had enough time yet to reach the city? Or was something else delaying her? When the lichdrow had imprisoned Gromph, an army of duergar, augmented by tanarukks, had been marching toward the city. Did Gracklstugh's forces block the approaches to Menzoberranzan? Even if they did, surely a rat could slip through their lines.

Gromph tried again.

Kyorli! Are you there?

From somewhere close at hand came a faint tickle of thought—Kyorli, swimming in the lake? Gromph reached out to it, but it was gone.

Something nudged the sphere, rocking it gently.

Kyorli?

Gromph opened his eyes in time to see a hand break the surface of the lake beside him. Enormous purplish fingers wrapped around the sphere, then pulled it underwater. The fingers, coated in a thin layer of slime, smudged the outer surface of the sphere, but through the streaks, Gromph could see a bulbous face with four writhing tentacles where a nose and mouth should be. The illithid's eyes were white and devoid of pupils, but Gromph could sense that it was staring at him as it sculled gently with its free hand, maintaining a position just below the surface of the lake.

Its voice forced itself into Gromph's mind, probing like an infestation of roots through soft, unresisting soil.

A mage, it observed. *How delicious!*

Halisstra's first impulse, as the priestess blew her horn, was to thrust her sword into the woman, but something made her hesitate.

Ryld, however, was quicker to act. He leaped to the still sizzling body of the troll, yanked his short sword from it, and sprinted toward the priestess.

The stranger was quicker, however. Dropping the horn, she sang out a single note and brought her hands together. As her fingers interlocked, branches whipped into place in front of her, weaving themselves together. Ryld crashed headlong into the barrier and was hurled back by it, at the last moment turning his fall into a controlled roll.

As Ryld sprang to his feet, Halisstra heard another woman's voice sing out from the forest behind her. She spun to face the new threat and saw someone moving through the forest. In that same instant dozens of crescent-shaped blades appeared from out of nowhere and began flashing in a tight circle around her and Ryld. The chest-high wall of spinning steel reminded her of the whir of the stirges' wings, overlaid by wet *thwacks* and *snaps* as rain-soaked branches and leaves were scythed down, leaving a ring of bare ground no more than four paces from where she and Ryld stood.

Ryld touched his brooch and sprang into the air, but his ankles were immediately caught by the bushes around him, animated by the first priestess's spell. He slashed at them with his sword but the enchanted bush was growing, sprouting new branches faster than he could sever them. For every branch he slashed through, three more sprang up to take its place.

At the same time, the barrier of spinning blades closed in. Halisstra tried to force a way through it using Seyll's shield, but two of the blades struck the shield at once, nearly ripping it from her arm. A third jarred into her elbow, grating against her chain mail sleeve. She yanked her arm back and shook numbed fingers.

Through the barrier of blades Halisstra caught glimpses of the priestess who had slain the troll—and the two others who had rushed to join her. Each was nearly naked, like the first, and held a sword in her hand. One of them—the one who was sustaining the barrier of blades—was small for a drow female and had dark brown hair. It took Halisstra a moment to recognize the woman under the black dye she'd rubbed onto her skin—dye that had started to run in the rain—but when she did, she cursed her ill luck. There would be no way that Halisstra could convince the priestesses she was an innocent who had "found" Seyll's armor.

Feliane, a moon elf, had seen Seyll die. Thanks to the magical charm Halisstra had placed upon her, she had readily believed Halisstra's story that she'd stabbed Seyll by accident, after slipping on a wet rock. But once that charm had worn off, Feliane would have realized the truth.

Ryld gave up slashing at the bush that held his feet and stared longingly at his greatsword, which lay just outside the barrier of whirling blades. He glanced at Halisstra and winced.

"If I had Splitter. . . ."

He didn't have to finish; Halisstra knew exactly what he meant. Had he been able to reach the greatsword, he could have used it to dispel the priestess's magic.

It was up to Halisstra, then.

"I *am* the one who killed Seyll!" she shouted at the priestesses over the whir of the spinning blades. "But you're making a mistake in killing me."

She laid Seyll's sword and crossbow on the ground, then yanked the chain mail tunic up and over her head. Tossing it beside the weapons, she removed the final thing she'd taken from Seyll's body: the priestess's magic ring.

Avoiding the advancing barrier of blades, she placed the ring on the ground as well and addressed herself to Feliane.

"As Seyll lay dying, she said she had hope for me still. She knew that guilt would force me to redeem myself for the treachery I had committed. That's why I came back, instead of returning to the Under dark, to beg Eilistraee's forgiveness for what I've done."

The whirling blades had passed over Seyll's weapons and chain mail without harming them and had come close enough to force Halisstra back into Ryld, whose legs were completely entangled in the bush that had grown up around him. He twisted at the waist and gave Halisstra a sharp look. She must have sounded very convincing.

Halisstra ignored him, concentrating instead on Feliane. Could she use her voice to overcome the priestess's resistance a second time?

The whirling blades paused in their advance. They were so

close Halisstra could feel the wind of them passing; one step forward and she would be cut to pieces.

"Prove yourself," Feliane said. "Swear to come up into the light, to serve Eilistraee and forsake Lolth. Swear it—by the sword."

Halisstra considered—but only briefly, one eye on the barrier of blades.

What harm could it do? she thought. Lolth is dead—or so close to death that it makes little difference.

Even if she did rise again, the Queen of Spiders appreciated and rewarded treachery—especially if it was directed against the goddess who was her chief rival. Halisstra could always turn her back on Eilistraee and be welcomed back into the fold.

Halisstra held out a hand to Ryld and said, "Loan me your sword."

Ryld gave her a quick, searching look, then complied.

Halisstra took the short sword from him and thrust its point into the ground. Then, as she had seen Eilistraee's followers do, she circled it, holding the hilt with her left hand. The barrier of blades didn't leave her much room, and so keen was Ryld's blade that when Halisstra brushed against it, the steel nicked her knee. She ignored the tiny wound and completed the circle.

"I so swear," she told Feliane.

Off in the distance, she heard the sound of a hunting horn. Another priestess, belatedly coming to join the others? The priestesses, also having heard it, exchanged nods.

The barrier of blades disappeared. In the abrupt silence that followed, Halisstra heard the snap of a branch. The first priestess negated her spell, loosening the branches that entwined Ryld. Angrily yanking himself free, he pulled his short sword out of the ground and assumed a ready stance as the priestesses approached.

What now? he asked in sign language.

I surrender to them, Halisstra replied.

That's suicide, Ryld signed. *I can't let you do that.*

Halisstra felt a flush of warmth and affection that, until recently, she would have described as weakness. To hide it, she let her expression grow ice cold.

"Let me?" she asked aloud. "You . . . a mere male? You've not only overstepped your place, you've just proven you're of no further use to me." She jerked her chin at the spot where his greatsword lay. "Go fetch your sword, Ryld, and go back to where you belong. Go back to the Underdark."

Ryld stared at her, a stricken expression on his face. For a moment, the rain he was blinking out of his eyes made him look as though he was crying—though of course, Halisstra knew that was something the hardened warrior would never do. Then Ryld walked over to where Splitter lay, his shoulders tensing as he passed the priestesses.

"You may go," Feliane told him as he picked up the sword. "Leave, and do not follow us, or you will invoke the goddess's wrath."

Ryld grunted and shoved the greatsword into the sheath on his back. Then, without a single glance back at Halisstra, he turned and strode away into the forest.

Halisstra, seeing that the priestesses were watching Ryld, briefly considered making a bolt for freedom, then she decided against it. Instead she stared at the spot in the forest that Ryld had disappeared into as the priestesses gathered up Seyll's weapons and armor.

Ryld will be better off in the Underdark, she told herself. *He wouldn't have been happy up here.*

Surrendering had been the only way to ensure his safety.

Feliane unfastened the silver chain at her waist and motioned for Halisstra to hold out her hands. Halisstra did, and the chain came alive, wrapping itself tightly around her wrists. Her strength seeped from her body and flowed out into the links of metal, leaving her as weak as sun-rotted adamantine. She staggered, fighting down the panic that was threatening to rise within her. What had she just done? She told herself to stay calm, and that she still had one weapon left. The time would come, when Ryld was far away and safe, that she could use the magic of the *bae'qeshel*.

Staring at Feliane's youthful, guileless face further reassured Halisstra. In Feliane she saw softness—a weakness she could turn to her advantage. Despite the way Halisstra had used her once before, Feliane actually believed Halisstra's pledge—that she had come back to redeem herself. All it would take was a friendly smile and a few words. Halisstra parted her lips—

—but the priestess who had slain the troll strode up to her and grabbed her chin, turning her head to the side. Belatedly, Halisstra noticed the priestess was humming. Halisstra tried to speak but found herself unable to make even the slightest noise.

"I will take this one back to the temple myself," the priestess said. "Eilistraee will decide her fate: the song . . . or the sword."

🕸   🕸   🕸

Ryld fumed as he strode away into the forest, wet ferns squelching under his boots. He had done what Halisstra had wanted, he'd walked away. Why then did he feel so impotent, so angry?

Because he'd saved himself and left her to die.

As a priestess of Lolth had ordered, he reminded himself. And he, a good male, always obeyed.

A *former* priestess of Lolth, he corrected himself.

Perhaps that was why she was so willing to die, to join the goddess who had gone before her.

Shaking his head bitterly, he curled his fingers into the blasphemous gesture Halisstra had used.

"Go ahead and let them kill you then, Halisstra, if that's what you . . ."

Was that what she wanted? Halisstra's face had been as frozen and expressionless as the black stone face that sealed the temple—or was it the tomb?—of Lolth. But Ryld had been able to sense the powerful emotions just beneath that cold surface. She'd proven that she cared for him, earlier, when they were fighting the troll. If all she'd been doing was using him, all that time, she could have saved her own life simply by fleeing, leaving him to die . . .

Just as Pharaun had done.

A thought occurred to Ryld then—a notion that was almost inconceivable, so foreign was it to the drow creed. Had Halisstra deliberately sacrificed herself so that he might live?

No, that couldn't be possible. She must have one final trick in her pocket—some hidden weapon or scroll that would allow her to escape, to rejoin him. But if so, why hadn't she given him some clue as to where to meet her again?

Because she was worried that the priestesses would hear it? Or was it because she expected Ryld to come to her? To help her escape.

Ryld, who had been slowing his pace all along, at last stopped. He stood, listening to the rain pattering down on the branches overhead, wondering if any of the priestesses had followed him. With all the noise the rain was making, he couldn't be certain they hadn't.

He *hated* the constant dribble of water from the sky. It trickled down his face, making him squint. It had turned his *piwafwi* into a heavy, wet blanket that clung to his shoulders and stuck to his thighs as he walked. It was making his armor squeak and would eventually cause his swords to rust. The rain was like a waterfall he couldn't step out of. He was trapped in it—just as he was trapped in the invisible webs Halisstra had woven around him with her smiles and kisses and sighs.

Pulling his wet *piwafwi* closer around him, he enveloped himself in its magic, becoming just another shadow in the overcast and dripping forest. He made his way back to the spot where they'd fought the troll.

Ryld circled the area, searching the rapidly melting slush for footprints to see which way Halisstra and the priestesses had gone, but found none. Cautiously he crept closer to the spot, expecting to hear their voices at any moment.

He saw the swath of chopped vegetation the barrier of blades had cleared and the blackened patch of ground where the troll had died, but no sign of the priestesses. He drew Splitter and spoke the words that would activate its magic, assuring himself that the priestesses weren't using an illusion or invisibility to cloak themselves.

Satisfied that he was alone, he strode into the clearing. Squatting, he studied the footprints left in the slush.

Halisstra stood here, he thought, and one of the priestesses there. The other two had stood there, and there . . .

And that was where the footsteps stopped. The priestesses hadn't left on foot, they'd used magic to spirit themselves away—and Halisstra with them.

She was gone, and there was no trail to follow.

Unless . . .

Yes, it's just possible, he thought as his eye fell on a footprint in the slush.

It was the track of the gray animal that had been fleeing through the forest. The beasts had been communicating with each other, at least, and might just communicate with him.

Ryld sheathed his sword, and began to follow the trail.

Valas peered down at the expanse of dark water below him. Lake Thoroot was even larger than he'd been told—so wide that the far side of it was lost in darkness. It reminded him of the wide, flat expanse of Anauroch, the desert they'd recently visited. The difference, however, was that the lake had steep cliffs hemming it in on every side, a waterfall that thundered into it from the cavern where Valas perched, and a high, domed ceiling overhead. Enormous stalactites hung from that ceiling. Some had points that touched the water; others were broken off like jagged teeth, making the cavern look like an enormous, fanged mouth. Valas shivered, hoping it wasn't an omen of what was to come.

A hand touched his shoulder. Turning, he saw Pharaun. Danifae was right behind him.

"What's wrong?" the mage asked.

"Nothing," Valas answered. "It's just the spray from the water-fall. I'm chilled."

Quenthel scrambled up behind Pharaun and Danifae—who backed away, one wary eye on the whip in Quenthel's belt. Quenthel was crouching to negotiate the low ceiling, her hands and feet spread wide to keep her balance on the slippery rocks. That and the hungry gleam in her eye made her look like a dark spider. Jeggred was one pace behind her, as usual, moving nimbly across the uneven ledge, his second, smaller set of arms held out for balance.

Quenthel peered into the vast cavern beyond the waterfall and asked, "Have we reached Lake Thoroot?"

Her voice was barely audible over the roar of falling water.

"It's just below," Valas answered with a nod. "About fifty paces straight down."

"Do you see any sign of the city—or the ship?"

Valas shook his head and replied, "Both are probably far beneath the surface."

But which part of the surface? he wondered.

For all Valas knew, Zanhoriloch was on the far side of the lake, though he wasn't about to admit that to Quenthel. They had entered through the only approach to the lake the scout was familiar with. The last thing he wanted was to exhibit any weak-ness or uncertainty, even after they found the ship and left the Underdark—and his expertise—behind.

One hand clutching the wet rock beside him, Valas leaned as far out as he dared, studying the wall below. The tunnel they'd been following was a wide one, with a natural ledge of rock on one side of the river. It had provided a welcome shortcut to the lake, an easy trek after their long, weary journey. But from there, things got tricky. The river burst out of the tunnel like a hori-zontal fountain, its spray soaking the rock for a great distance on either side. Through the mist, Valas could see faintly glowing streaks of green against the stone: patches of water-soaked, slippery fungi.

Valas felt someone looming behind him, and fetid breath told him who it was. Jeggred stared out at the lake, his monstrous body crowding Valas and nearly forcing him over the edge.

Elbowing Jeggred back, Valas shouted back to the others over the draegloth's head, "I'd like to scout ahead before we go any farther. Pharaun, I'll need magic to climb down, and that spell of yours that will allow me to breathe underwater."

"You're going alone?" the mage asked. "Shouldn't you take someone with you?" He glanced past Quenthel as if anticipating someone else to materialize behind her, then he sighed. "What about Jeggred?"

"No!" Quenthel barked, the vipers in her whip lashing. "Jeggred stays with me."

Sensing her anger, Jeggred scrambled over to crouch at her side.

"He can take Danifae," Quenthel said.

Before Valas could shake his head in protest, Pharaun butted in.

"Danifae will only slow him down—and I don't want to waste my time and talents preparing the same spells twice."

Valas glanced between Quenthel and Pharaun. Valas had to tread carefully, so as not to tip the scales—a balancing act that was growing wearisome. It would be a relief to get away on his own for a while.

"I'll go alone," he told them.

The Bregan D'aerthe scout took off his *piwafwi*, then set his haversack, bow, and quiver beside it. He also shed his chain mail—its weight would only drag him to the bottom of the lake—and his boots. He carefully removed from his enchanted vest any of his many talismans that might be harmed by the water, then put the vest back on. Next he lashed his daggers into their sheaths. The thread he used would prevent them from falling out when he was underwater but was thin enough to be broken easily in an emergency.

When he was done, he looked up at Pharaun and said, "Ready."

The mage nodded and pulled a small sheet of mushroom-skin paper from his pocket. Unfolding it, he handed its contents to Valas: a small blob of a black, tarry substance.

"Eat it," the wizard instructed.

Without asking what it was, Valas popped it into his mouth. It had a bitter taste, and it stuck to his teeth. With an effort, Valas forced his jaws apart, unsticking his molars.

Pharaun laughed and said, "You don't have to chew it. Just swallow."

Valas swallowed the substance, then stood waiting as Pharaun chanted the words to his spell. The mage ended by fluttering his fingers against Valas's chest, like a mother imitating a spider in a child's nursery rhyme. When Pharaun was done, the scout's fingers and toes felt gummy. He lifted one hand from the rock, and sticky strands of web followed it.

Pharaun reached into a pocket of his *piwafwi* a second time and pulled out a short length of some kind of dried surface plant.

"Ready?" he asked.

Valas nodded.

The mage grinned and said, "Then take a deep breath."

Valas did, and Pharaun blew through the stick at him, completing his second spell.

Valas's chest felt heavy, and water trickled from his nostrils.

"Go!" Pharaun shouted.

Valas didn't need any urging. The pressure of the water that filled his lungs was incentive enough. Scrambling over the edge, he scurried down the cavern wall like a spider, his sticky hands and feet allowing him to crawl along the sheer cliff face. Head-down, he hurried toward the water, eyes squinted against the spray. Above him, the waterfall arced out and over, obscuring his view of the tunnel he'd just left. It hit the water below in a thundering roar that grew louder as he descended.

The scout was still a pace or two above the surface of the lake when the urge to breathe overcame him. Expelling the water in his lungs like a vomiting man, he tried to draw air—and nearly drowned.

Sputtering, he at last reached the lake. As his head plunged beneath the cold, choppy surface he drew in a great lungful of water and felt relief.

He continued down, following the wall of stone until the churning water washed the stickiness from his hands and feet. Pushing off from the wall, he swam, allowing the current caused by the waterfall to carry him deeper. The water was cold—and dark. He swam through it for some time without seeing any-thing, relying on his keen sense of direction to keep him oriented toward the middle of the lake. Pharaun's spell would enable him to keep breathing water for more than a cycle—he could rest on the bottom of the lake, if he needed to—but he hoped it wouldn't take him that long to find some sign of where the aboleth city was.

After he swam, and rested, and swam a while longer, Valas saw a glow in the darkened water ahead. As he made his way toward it, the glow resolved itself into a pattern of tightly clustered, greenish-yellow globes that brightened and dimmed, brightened and dimmed.

Are those the lights of Zanhoriloch? Valas thought as he

stroked toward them, only to be disappointed as he drew near enough to see the lights more clearly.

The glowing globes turned out not to be the lights of the aboleth city but a school of luminescent jellyfish. There were hundreds of them, each the size of Valas's palm. They moved together, their tendrils contracting, then pulsing in unison, each pulse pumping up their light from greenish-yellow to yellow.

Valas started to turn away, disappointed, when he spotted a silhouette swimming between him and the jellyfish. The scout froze, not wanting to betray himself with movement. Drifting with the current, he hung in the water, watching.

The silhouette was the same size as a drow and had two arms and two legs, each of which ended in a wide webbed hand or foot. It also had a fluked tail—but no tentacles. Definitely not an aboleth then . . . but what race was it?

The creature swam beside the jellyfish, herding them with a staff it held in one hand. The head of the staff emitted crackling bursts of light whose frequency matched the pulsing of the jellyfish. Valas could just barely hear the sound that came from it, a low-pitched *thum, thum, thum,* like the sound of a muted drum.

Intent upon its glowing flock, the creature hadn't spotted Valas, which left the scout with a decision to make. He could approach and try to communicate, in the hope that the creature would tell him where Zanhoriloch was, or exercise his usual caution and swim away.

He touched his star-shaped talisman, reassuring himself that it was still pinned to his shirt. If necessary, he could always use its magic to escape.

He swam toward the creature.

As he drew nearer he could see that it had skin as dark as a drow's. Its head was bald, and its body glistened in the light of the jellyfish. A layer of greenish slime covered its skin. When Valas was perhaps ten paces from it, the creature must have sensed his presence. It turned with a sudden, whiplike flick of its tail. Seeing its face, Valas gasped. The high cheekbones and pointed jaw gave the creature a distinctively drow appearance. It even had red eyes, but no ears—or at least, only gnarled ridges around holes in its head that looked like the melted remains of ears. The thing's hands—one sculling back and forth, keeping the creature in place; the other holding the staff—had a thumb, but only two fingers, with a wide web of skin between them.

Valas opened his mouth, then remembered he was breathing water and was unable to speak. On a whim, he tried drow sign language instead. He chose a carefully neutral message. He still didn't know if the creature was a friend or foe of either the drow or the aboleths.

This is the lake of the aboleth, is it not? he asked. *Is their city nearby?*

He didn't expect an answer. The scout who'd told him about Lake Thoroot had said that only a handful of drow had ever ventured that way.

Valas was shocked, then, when the creature replied in sign— albeit a sign that was made clumsy by his awkward, webbed fingers, *You seek the aboleth? Are you insane? Go back, before they—*

The drow-thing convulsed as if it had been struck a blow. Releasing its staff it curled into a fetal position, webbed hands clutching its head, mouth open in a silent scream. Valas twisted around, reaching for his daggers as he searched for the threat, but before he could draw them a high-pitched scream pounded in through his skull.

Louder than any noise he had ever experienced, the scream shattered thought and forced his body into spastic jerks. He

ELEVEN

Halisstra sat cross-legged on the wet stone floor of a cave whose only exit was far overhead. The walls of the cave were covered with pictures, the paint daubed onto the stone itself, the lines following the natural contours of the rock. Life-size figures of drow strained toward the ceiling, hands extended overhead and eyes glowing with rapturous desire. All of the figures were adult, but each had an umbilical cord that snaked down toward the floor of the cavern like a root.

Halisstra's wrists were no longer bound, but she could no more escape the cave than the painted figures could step away from the rocky canvas that held them. The walls were at least three times her height and curved inward to meet the hole in the ceiling, making climbing impossible without the aid of magic. She had been carefully and thoroughly stripped of all magical devices and weapons, and the curse the priestess had placed on Halisstra prevented her from singing or even humming—from using any of her *bae'qeshel* magic.

After Ryld had gone, the priestess who'd slain the troll teleported Halisstra into the cave, then disappeared. The First Daughter of House Melarn had remained there for an entire day, at first restlessly pacing the cave, looking for a way out. When she finally accepted the fact that she was trapped, she sank, cross-legged, into Reverie. Once she'd emerged from her meditations, she'd watched the circle of sky above grow gray, then black. The rain had stopped but the sky was still overcast. Neither the stars nor the moon could be seen. Looking up, Halisstra could almost imagine that she was in the Underdark—that above the cave was a tunnel or passage. But the earth-and-bark-scented breeze blowing in through the hole destroyed that illusion, as did the low rumble of thunder in the distance. So too did the ferns that surrounded the opening like a fringe of hair. Beads of rain dripped from their sodden stems.

From outside came the sound of singing. The voices were those of the priestesses who'd gathered to decide Halisstra's fate. Their song was accompanied by the silvery tones of a flute and the rapid clash of swords, a staccato of metallic clangs marking the beat. Halisstra thought it might just be her imagination, but it sounded as if the song was reaching a crescendo. She assumed that one of Eilistraee's followers would appear in another moment and announce how Halisstra was to die.

Halisstra braced herself for the inevitable. One way or another—by the magic of their traitor goddess or the cold steel of a sword—she was going to be put to death. The priestesses would have come to their senses and realized that Halisstra had only been buying time when she swore fealty to Eilistraee. The time had come for Halisstra to pray and prepare for entry into the next realm—but pray to which god?

Halisstra knew hundreds of prayers to supplicate Lolth—prayers she could recite with her hands, using the silent speech—but they would go unheard, unseen. Lolth had vanished and was no longer listening to prayers. She wasn't even punishing blasphemers. The Demonweb Pits had been devoid of the souls of the dead, and Halisstra had to presume that Lolth's faithful were disappearing into oblivion, just as their goddess had.

Should Halisstra pray instead to Selvetarm, Lolth's champion? For all she knew, he might be locked in battle with Vhaeraun still and unable to hear her—or worse, slain. Was there any god who was still listening?

Halisstra shivered and drew her knees up against her chest, wrapping her arms around them. At least Ryld was safe. Her surrender had saved him. She started to rest her chin on her knee, then winced as it touched the cut from Ryld's sword. The wound was a tiny one, no bigger than the crescent of her thumbnail, but it burned like a fresh brand. It had broken open and was bleeding again, even though Halisstra's chin had barely touched it.

Outside, the singing stopped. Halisstra heard a rustling above and glanced up to see Feliane, kneeling in the ferns and staring down at her. The priestess had scrubbed her face clean of the black dye, and her skin was an unhealthy looking mushroom-white. Looking at it, Halisstra decided she must have been wrong about the sky being overcast; the moon must have been peeking through the clouds, because for a moment a faint, silvery radiance illuminated Feliane. Then it was gone, and Halisstra could see the priestess's face clearly again.

Well? Halisstra asked in sign. *What is my fate to be? The song—or the sword?*

"The song," Feliane answered.

Halisstra nodded grimly and stood. She wanted to meet death on her feet.

I'm ready, she signed, fingers moving in tense, sharp jerks.

Feliane's round face broke into a grin. On a drow, it would have been a gloat of triumph, but so innocent and naive looking was Feliane that for a moment it appeared like a warm smile. Halisstra pushed that foolish notion from her mind and stood, rigid, waiting.

Feliane began to sing in High Drow. From behind her, Halisstra could hear a chorus of women's voices, though Feliane's was the strongest.

> *"Climb out of the darkness, rise into the light.*
> *"Turn your face to the sky, your elf birthright.*
> *"Dance in the forest, sing with the breeze;*
> *"Claim your place in the moonlight among flowers and trees.*
> *"Lend your strength to the needy; battle evil with steel.*
> *"Join in the hunt; to no other gods kneel.*
> *"Purge the monster within and the monster without;*
> *"Their blood washes you clean, of this have no doubt.*
> *"Trust in your sisters; lend your voice to their song.*
> *"By joining the circle, the weak are made strong."*

Feliane extended her hand down into the hole, as if inviting Halisstra to take it. Her pale skin had taken on a moonlit glow.

It took Halisstra a moment to realize the import of the song and gesture. It wasn't an execution but an invitation. And not just to life, but to join the circle. To join the priestesses of Eilistraee.

Halisstra's eyes narrowed. It had to be a trick of some kind.

"Trust?" she said—out loud, surprised to find that her ability to speak had returned.

She didn't need to let the scorn she felt creep into her voice;

the word already held a negative connotation in the drow tongue, implying weakness, naiveté. She thought of the alliances she'd tried to build among her own sisters and how those alliances had been betrayed. She'd tried to reach out to Norendia, telling her sister about the bard who'd been teaching her darksong. A few cycles later, that bard had "fallen" from one of the city walkways to her death. Later that same cycle, Jawil, second oldest of the Melarn daughters after Halisstra, had made an attempt on Halisstra's life. When Halisstra had rushed to Norendia for help, she had been stabbed in the back. Literally. Thankfully, Halisstra's magic had proved strong enough to save her—and to kill her two sisters.

"Trust," she muttered again.

Behind Feliane, she could see the priestess who had slain the troll. The woman looked down, smiled, then stepped back out of sight.

Ideas flashed through Halisstra's mind, quick as lightning strikes. She could use *bae'qeshel* magic to charm Feliane into lowering her a rope then stun the rest of Eilistraee's priestesses with a painful burst of sound and escape. But each flash of inspiration left behind it a rumble of doubt, disturbing as the distant thunder.

Was escape really what Halisstra wanted—or had there been a faint echo of truth in the oath she'd sworn earlier? She'd been drawn to the World Above, though she hadn't been able to articulate the reason, either to Ryld or to herself. But now she was starting to understand. She'd always thought treachery and selfishness to be indelible hallmarks of the drow, but she was beginning to see that there could be another way.

The drow who lived on the surface not only trusted one another, they were also willing to extend that trust to her. Even knowing that she had killed one of their priestesses—that she might do the same to any of them. Their faith in her capacity for redemption was strong, even though there was only the word of a dying priestess to base it on.

Or was there?

From somewhere above came the sound of a flute, playing a few soft, tentative notes. It reminded Halisstra of the sounds Seyll's sword had made when she was fighting the stirges. And of that single, piercing note that had at last knocked them from the sky. Had that been Eilistraee's magic at work? Had Halisstra already been accepted by the goddess, even then?

Feliane waited patiently, hand still extended, as Halisstra wrestled with her doubts. The elf priestess's entire body was glowing silver. Her hair seemed alive with sparkling stars, her smile was as bright as a crescent moon. The goddess had filled her, transformed her. She stared down at Halisstra with a mother's love, urging her to accept it.

Trembling, Halisstra raised her hands above her head, just like the figures painted on the cave walls.

"I accept, Eilistraee," Halisstra said. "I will serve you."

She felt a tear streaking down her cheek, and angrily told herself it was just a drip from the ferns above—then she realized it didn't matter.

Feliane, too, was weeping.

The elf priestess began to chant, and Halisstra felt her body grow lighter. The stone floor dropped away from her feet as she floated upward, drawn by Feliane's spell. The fringe of ferns made the hole in the ceiling look too narrow to fit through, so Halisstra crossed her arms tightly against her chest, making herself smaller. As she rose through the opening, wet ferns brushed against her face, forcing her to close her eyes. Her body squeezed through them, slipping out of the cave, and she felt dozens of hands touching her, guiding her. The priestesses were all around the opening, lifting her from the cave, hugging her, singing.

"Climb out of the darkness, rise into the light . . ."

Opening her eyes, Halisstra looked up and saw the full moon through a break in the clouds. The goddess's face smiled down at her, weeping raindrops of joy.

"Eilistraee!" Halisstra cried. "I am yours!"

"The goddess welcomes you into her embrace," Feliane whispered in her ear. "Now you must prepare yourself for the trial she has set you."

🕷   🕷   🕷

Ryld frowned, puzzled, as he examined the footprints in the slush. He was still on the animal's trail—he was certain of that—but its footprints had suddenly changed. In one spot where the beast had paused, the track became more like the print a bare drow foot would make, but with deep gouges at the front of each toe that must have been claw marks. They reminded Ryld, at least a little, of the footprints of an orc but the stride, when the animal had continued from that spot, was all wrong. The beast had risen to walk on two feet, not four. The pattern of its footprints, however, was still more like the lope of a quadruped.

Short sword in hand, Ryld continued following the tracks. The animal-thing had tried to conceal its trail by walking along rocks or logs and wading up a stream, but Ryld had no difficulty following it. He was used to tracking opponents across the bare stone of caverns and tunnels. Even with it melting, the slush made tracking anything the work of a child.

Eventually he spotted a small structure deep in the forest. Made from rough-hewn logs, the one-room building had a slumped appearance, as if it was about to collapse at any moment.

Its door hung at an angle, attached to the frame by a single rusted hinge, and the roof was thick with moss and larger, leafy surface plants sprouted from it in spots. Firewood that had once been stacked against one wall lay tumbled across the ground, dotted with a sprouting of fungus, and a hole in the building's roof marked where a chimney had once stood. Surrounded by a litter of broken bottles and rusted pots that had obviously been dragged out by scavengers long before, the shelter looked utterly abandoned.

But something was moving inside it.

Ryld drew his *piwafwi* around himself and crept closer through the trees. He felt something soft under his boot, and the stink of fresh excrement rose to his nostrils. His lip curled. Even in the warrens of Menzoberranzan, people didn't defecate so close to their homes. Whoever was living in the little shelter was no better than an animal, the weapons master thought, angrily scraping his boot.

He looked up just in time to see a small black shape streaking toward him from the cabin. It was the same sort of animal he'd been tracking—but not the same one. As the beast sank its teeth into the wrist of his sword hand, Ryld's warrior's instincts took over.

He grabbed the creature by the scruff of the neck with his free hand and used its own momentum to slam it into a tree. Dazed, it staggered to the side, shaking its head.

Ryld whipped his sword around in a slash at the animal's throat—but it proved quicker than he expected. His blade slammed into the tree behind it as the beast rolled out of the way.

Yanking his sword free, Ryld rounded on the creature—only to see it rearing up on two legs. It held its forepaws out in an unmistakable gesture of surrender. Its mouth worked, forming words that were half yip, half speech.

"Wait!" it gasped in oddly-accented Low Drow. "Friend."

Ryld hesitated, but kept his sword ready.

"You can speak?" the weapons master asked.

The creature nodded urgently, then it closed its eyes as a shudder coursed through it. Bald patches appeared in its fur and spread, exposing pale skin, and its muzzle shrank and flattened. The quadruped legs rearticulated themselves with a soft crackle of cartilage, and paws transformed into hands and feet.

When the transformation was complete, a naked human youth stood where the animal had been. Were he a drow, Ryld would have guessed his age at about twenty, but humans matured faster than that. The boy was probably no more than a dozen years old. His hair was black and tangled, his hands and feet as filthy as those of an urchin from the Stenchstreets.

"What sort of creature are you?" Ryld asked.

The boy uttered a word that Ryld didn't recognize, speaking one of the languages of the World Above. Seeing that Ryld didn't understand, he switched to Low Drow.

"A blend of wolf and human," he answered. "I shift between the two."

"Wolf?"

"The furred animal that walks on four legs," the human replied.

The weapons master nodded.

"Where is the other wolf-human?" Ryld asked it. "The gray one."

He kept a wary eye on the structure and surrounding forest, furious at himself for having let his attention wane a moment before.

"There's no one here but me."

"Liar," Ryld spat. He stepped forward, menacing the boy with his sword. "Is the larger one your parent? Is that why you're trying to protect it?"

"I have no parents. They were killed in a hunt the year I was born," the boy explained. He not only stood his ground but glared back at Ryld, showing an amazing amount of mettle for a mere boy. "They were killed by your people."

Ryld considered that and said, "Is that how you learned to speak Drowic? Were you a slave?"

"My grandfather was, but he fought back."

"The gray wolf?" Ryld guessed. "That's your grandfather? Where is he?"

"He's not here," the boy replied, glancing into the forest in the opposite direction of the little building, though too casually.

The look told Ryld what he needed to know. The lie was as transparent as glass.

The weapons master reached down and grabbed the boy by the hair.

"I see," said Ryld. "Let's go talk to him."

He half-dragged, half-marched the boy to the shelter.

Pausing just outside the door, he held his sword to the chest of the squirming boy and called, "If you want the boy to live, show yourself. Give me some information and I'll spare his life, and yours."

There was no answer from inside the shelter, save for a low groan. As it sounded, the boy twisted in Ryld's grasp, trying desperately to squirm free. Ryld hurled him to the ground and slammed a boot into his chest. He raised his sword, too furious to care about getting information any longer.

"Stop!" a male voice gasped. "I'll tell you . . . whatever you want . . . to know."

Ryld looked up and saw a human with gray hair and a beard that hung to his chest, leaning in the doorway of the shelter with a dirty blanket wrapped around his shoulders. His face had a haggard expression, and his right calf was bruised and swollen to twice its normal size. The foot below it was a shredded, bloody mess, as if it had been impaled on spikes, then torn free.

The boy screamed something at his grandfather in a language Ryld didn't understand, but his gestures made it obvious he was urging the old man to flee.

The gray-haired man—he looked several centuries old, but was probably less than fifty—glanced down at his ruined foot.

"Run?" he asked the boy—speaking in Drowic, obviously for Ryld's benefit. "How can I?" Then he met Ryld's eye and asked, "What do you want . . . to know?"

"The priestesses of Eilistraee," Ryld said. "Do they have a temple in this wood?"

The boy suddenly stopped squirming and looked up at Ryld.

"You're not part of the hunt?" he asked.

A grim smile appeared on the older man's face.

"He's not. Or he wouldn't be asking." Then, to Ryld, he said, "Let my grandson go . . . and I'll tell you where the temple is."

Ryld removed his foot from the boy's chest. Instantly, the boy sprang to his feet. He stood warily, hunched over slightly with arms bent as if contemplating a shift into wolf form.

The gray-haired man chuckled, then waved at the boy.

"Yarno, leave him be. You can see by the look in his eyes. He's an enemy of the temple. And the enemy of our enemy . . ."

"Is your friend," Ryld completed.

The old man nodded and asked, "Have you any healing magic . . . friend?"

"Answer my questions, first," Ryld said. "And I'll see about healing you."

The old man surprised him by chuckling.

"Not for me," he said. "For you. Your wrist."

Ryld glanced down at the spot where the boy had bitten him. The boy's incisors had broken the skin, and a trickle of blood ran down the back of Ryld's hand.

"It's only a scratch," he said.

The old man shook his head.

"Tell him, Yarno. He . . . he doesn't know."

"Tell me what?" Ryld asked, suspicious.

"We're *werewolves*," the boy said. "Most of the time we shift forms because we want to, but whenever there's a full moon we become wolves whether we want to or not. We can't control ourselves when that happens. We attack everyone. Even our friends. When we wake up in the morning, we don't know what we've done."

"Your family is cursed?" Ryld asked, not bothering to inquire as to what a "full moon" might be.

"Not cursed," the old man said. "Diseased. And it's a disease that can be spread . . . through bites."

"They call us 'monsters,' " Yarno added in a pained whisper. "They hunt us."

Ryld nodded, understanding the boy's pain. Life as a werewolf in that forest would be much like living in the slums of Menzoberranzan. He recalled his own childhood, always dreading the next group of drunken nobles who found "sport" in raging through the narrow streets, blasting the screaming wretches of the Braeryn with bolts of magic, slashing as they rode past on their lizards, leaving their victims to bleed to death on the dirty stone of an alley.

The boy, Yarno, was staring intensely up at Ryld, his eyes filled with a lingering, unsalved hurt. Human the boy might be, but looking into his eyes was like staring into a mirror. Ryld's lips parted, and he nearly spoke the words aloud: I was hunted, too. I understand. . . . Then the boy's grandfather interrupted.

"I have belladonna," he said. "Yarno's parents planted it in the woods, hoping it would . . . spare their son. This was once their home." He paused to catch his breath, then went on. "The herb will make you sick, but if you eat it . . . you might avoid the disease."

Ryld nodded and sheathed his sword.

"Tell me where the temple is, and I'll see what I can do to clean your wound, and set those bones. Then I'll think about trying that belladonna."

TWELVE

Valas awoke to the feel of something soft and slimy stroking the left side of his face. Jerking his head back, he saw it was a tentacle—one of four that grew from the body of an enormous, fishlike creature with three slitted eyes.

Thrashing away from it through the water, Valas found his back up against the bars of a cage. He stared out through the front of the enclosure at the aboleth that was lazily withdrawing its tentacle. The creature had a body half a dozen paces long, with a wide fluked tail. Its rubbery looking skin was blue-green with gray splotches and covered in a thick coating of slime. Its belly was greenish-pink, with an enormous mouth that opened and closed like that of a fish. Three eyes—red and slitted—were lined up in a vertical row on its forehead. The tentacles, each half as long as the body, sprouted from a point just behind the head. They drifted lazily, leaving a smudge of slime in the water.

Valas could feel the slime on his face where the tentacle had touched him, and he could smell the clot of it that clogged his left nostril. He exhaled through his nose, blowing it violently away.

He checked his weapons and saw that his kukris were still in their sheaths. A quick glance told him his talismans were still pinned to his shirt. Reassured and ready, he looked around at his prison.

The cage was made from stout iron and had no door that he could see. Its floor rested on the bottom of the lake, on top of waist-high kelp that had been mashed flat by its weight. Beyond the cage, tiny glowing fish darted in and out of the gently waving strands. In the distance, stalagmites rose to meet the surface of the water, high overhead. The sides of those rock formations were punctuated by round openings through which aboleth swam. Valas realized the stalagmites must be the buildings of Zanhoriloch.

The aboleth was making no move to attack; it simply stared, like a visitor at a zoo. Valas spoke to it in sign, hoping it would understand.

Why am I a prisoner?

The answer came in a voice that sounded like bubbles erupting into water: "You trespass."

The words were spoken in Undercommon, a language comprised of a blend of simple words and phrases from several different Underdark tongues.

For good reason, Valas signed back. With his lungs filled with water, the scout couldn't speak. *I am searching for something. A ship of bone and flesh, made by demons.*

"You hunger for this knowledge."

Yes. Have you seen such a ship?

"I have not consumed it."

Valas frowned, puzzled. The slime the aboleth had smeared

across his face was back in his left nostril again. He pinched the other one shut and blew.

You have seen this ship—but not eaten it? he signed again.

The aboleth fluttered its tentacles in what might have been a sign of irritation—or the equivalent of a drow shrug.

"I have not seen it. Nor have I consumed any knowledge of it."

Consumed? Valas didn't like the sound of that.

How do you consume knowledge? he asked.

"From our parents, after we hatch. From other creatures, such as yourself. We consume them."

You . . . eat them? Valas asked. *Are you going to eat me?*

"That is not my privilege," the aboleth said. Then, "Do you have knowledge of this ship?"

Valas quickly shook his head and backed it up with an emphatic sign.

No. I was told that the aboleth knew of such a ship, so I came here to learn if it was real or rumor.

"Where are you from?" the aboleth asked. "How did you come here?"

Valas considered how to answer that. Was the aboleth trying to find out whether he had come to Lake Thoroot alone—or was it weighing the potential information stored in Valas's mind, prior to devouring him? He tried to think of an answer that wouldn't make him sound like an appealing snack, at the same time sizing up his chances of escape. The fact that he was in a cage—that the aboleth hadn't consumed him immediately—was promising. Valas thought that perhaps he was being saved for some other aboleth, one with more "privilege."

At least, that's what he hoped was true. If the aboleth left to report the results of its initial questioning to its superior, Valas could use the star-shaped amulet that was still pinned to his shirt to escape.

I am from Menzoberranzan, Valas signed. *I am a soldier in service to one of the Houses of that city. The matron mother used her magic to send me here, to inquire about the demon ship. Shortly she will use that same magic to summon me home again.*

Thus explaining my impending disappearance from the cage, Valas thought. And, hopefully, causing the aboleth to think that any search for me will be futile.

Once again, he noticed that his nostril had filled with mucus, and he blew it out. He scrubbed his face furiously with a sleeve, but it only served to spread the tentacle slime across his face. Growing worried, Valas stopped scrubbing. The image of the drow-thing that had been herding the jellyfish loomed large in his mind. Was his left ear tingling? He resisted the urge to reach up and touch it, fearful that it might already be melting away.

"You will not return to your city," the aboleth said.

Valas shuddered, fighting down the sick feeling that filled his stomach.

Am I to be made a slave? Does your city have no matron mother—no ruler whom I can appeal to?

A ripple passed through the aboleth's body. Valas wondered whether it was a sign of annoyance or pleasure.

"It has been many flows since Oothoon met with one of the dry folk. You are merely a servant among your people and do not warrant her attention. As for your question, you are a slave to Oothoon already. When your transformation is complete, you will begin to serve her."

This time, Valas did touch his ear. Its tip was still pointed, but it was definitely tingling, as was the left side of his face, and his left hand and wrist. The fingers of that hand felt sticky. Trying to spread them, he found that his forefinger was starting to fuse with the one beside it, and the little finger with the finger beside it.

A web of grayish skin was growing between the two malformed digits and was already up to the first knuckle.

How long will the transformation take? he asked, his left hand already clumsy.

"No longer than three *boorms*," the aboleth said. "When it is finished, I will return to release you."

With a powerful flick of its tail, it swam away.

Valas had no idea how long a *"boorm"* was. It might be as long as one cycle of Narbondel—in which case, he still might have time to make it back to the others if Pharaun's spell didn't run out first. Or, for all he knew, a *boorm* might be as short as a heartbeat. Glancing at his left hand, he shuddered. The sooner he started back, the better. The aboleth was swimming strongly back toward the city, no longer looking at him.

Valas touched the nine-pointed star on his chest and felt the familiar wrench of its magic. He found himself standing in the spot he'd chosen—a good hundred paces away—but the cage had been transported there with him. It landed on a fresh patch of kelp, raising a knee-high cloud of dirt and scattering a school of tiny, frightened fish.

Had part of his body touched the cage—was that why it had slid sideways between the dimensions with him? The cage was far too heavy to have been included in the talisman's magic, but it was the only explanation Valas could think of.

Sculling, he positioned himself exactly at the center of the cage, and tried again—a shorter hop. Once again, the cage came with him.

Valas frowned. The cage was obviously somehow enchanted to contain him no matter where he went. If his brooch had been more powerful, he might have used its magic to transport himself across the lake in a series of short hops—following the predominant current of the lake back to the waterfall that must be its source. But the brooch's magic was limited. After two more hops like the first one, it would fall dormant for a full cycle.

Meanwhile, the slime left by the tentacle was creeping across his face and up his left arm. He breathed in a deep lungful of water, then blew it out through his nose, clearing his nostrils. How much longer did he have? As least his mind was still his own, and he suspected that it was one thing he would probably retain. The drow-thing had exhibited free will. It had been able to warn Valas away from Zanhoriloch—for all the good that had done.

Time to try something else, the scout thought.

Valas plucked another of his magical items from his shirt: a short mithral tube no longer than his finger. Sculling with his left hand—the webs had already grown up to the second knuckle— he tapped the tube against one of the bars of the cage. A bright, clear note carried through the water, but nothing happened. Whatever door there might be in the cage was not responding to the chime's magic.

Slipping the chime back to a pocket, Valas reached for his last hope, a brooch set with a dull gray stone that was surrounded by a dozen tiny, uncut gems. Made by the deep gnomes, the brooch had the power to wrap its wearer in illusion, giving him whatever appearance he could imagine. It didn't actually transform the wearer, nor did it have the power to manifest more complicated illusions—like making a drow appear to be an aboleth, for example—but it would allow Valas to create subtle changes in his appearance.

He twisted the gem in its facing, and felt a warm shiver run through his body. Looking down, he "saw" webbed hands and feet and a fluked tail. The brooch's magic had worked, giving him the appearance of the drow-thing.

Everything depended on his guess: that the magic of the cage would be negated, once his transformation was complete. Kicking his legs, he propelled himself up toward the roof of the cage, praying that it would disappear.

His head struck bars with a crack that made sparks dance in front of his eyes. Grimacing, he drifted back toward the center of the cage.

That was it then. The brooch had been his final hope. Even the illusion magic of the deep gnomes was powerless against the cage that held him. He was trapped. All he could do was wait until his body caught up with the illusion he'd just created. Until he turned into a drow-thing himself.

I won't let it happen, he thought. I deserve a good clean death. A soldier's death. Not this.

He yanked out one of his kukris—the one that sent a jolt of magical energy through whatever it struck. The magic wouldn't affect him if he was holding the dagger—a precaution against accidental wounds—but if he shoved the hilt into the ground, he would be able to impale himself on the upturned blade. Reaching down for one of the bars that made up the floor of the cage, he used the dagger to prod at the floor of the lake, but the ground was too hard. The cage had landed on a patch of stone. He'd have to move it somewhere else.

Sculling up to the top of the cage, he peered back toward the spot where the cage had rested a moment before, but saw only a gently waving expanse of kelp, not the flattened patch he'd expected. Had he somehow gotten turned around? No, he could see Zanhoriloch in the distance. His sense of direction hadn't failed him. Yet he couldn't see either the spot where the cage had just rested or the place where it had been when he first found himself inside it. That was strange; the weight of the cage should have crushed the kelp flat.

Ah . . . there.

He spotted a square patch of kelp about thirty paces away—which made no sense. He'd just been looking at that spot a moment ago. Had the slime spread over his eyes, blurring them?

No. He could still see as clearly as he ever could.

Suddenly, he realized the answer: the cage was an illusion. An incredibly powerful illusion—one that manifested in all of the senses. Not only were the bars of the cage visible, but they *felt* real. They'd even caused his chime to ring when he struck it against them—or so he'd thought. But by closing his eyes—by concentrating so hard it almost hurt—he could feel the rocky ground beneath his feet. Sculling to hold himself down against it, he slid a foot along the ground—and encountered no resistance. Instead of his foot striking a bar, it slid along rough, bare stone.

Still concentrating, he continued sliding his feet along the ground until they encountered resistance: a strand of kelp. Its touch nearly broke his focus, so close was the feel to that of the tentacle that had left the slime of its foul touch on his face. Shuddering, he pressed on until he could feel kelp all around him, then he opened his eyes.

He'd done it. The illusionary cage had disappeared. He was free.

But for how long? He could no longer move his left hand properly. It had only two fingers, with a thick web of skin growing between them. His left ear felt strange, as did his left eye. It was starting to squint shut and the colors he saw through it were somehow wrong. Further confirmation of his fate came when he saw a clump of something lacy and white drifting away from him. It was the hair from the left side of his scalp.

He glanced back at Zanhoriloch and saw that the creatures of that city were still going about their business, swimming back and forth between their stalagmite towers, oblivious to his escape. No alarm seemed to have been raised, and none of the aboleth came swimming out to intercept him. A surge of joy filled him, but it was short-lived. With a sinking heart, he realized that his escape was only temporary. Soon he would be a drow-thing, transformed forever into a water-breathing creature. The entire lake would be his prison.

Even though he knew it was hopeless, since none of his companions had healing magic, and since they'd probably mistake him for a monster and kill him on the spot, Valas tied his kukri back into its sheath and began swimming against the current. He'd completed the first part of his duty as a mercenary: he'd escaped. Next he would carry back to his companions his report, even though it contained woefully little, save for a warning to avoid Zanhoriloch at all cost.

That report delivered, he would get one of the others to kill him. If they refused, he'd do the job himself.

THIRTEEN

Andzrel Baenre, weapons master of House Baenre, stood in the cavern directing his troops. Runners continually came and went through the half-dozen tunnels that connected to the cavern, carrying news of the battle for the approaches to Menzoberranzan. Soldiers from House Baenre were holding the northern exit from Ablonshier's Cave.

Faintly, from the connecting tunnel, Andzrel could hear the clash of steel on steel as drow sword met tanarukk battle-axe. A group of duergar had tried to force their way through a tunnel that circled past that exit, only to become tangled in the webs cast by the wizard attached to Andzrel's company. The latest report indicated that the webs were on fire. The half-orc, half-demon tanarukks, apparently, were trying to burn their way through—at the expense of their gray dwarf allies caught in the sticky strands. The reek of burned hair and flesh drifted down the tunnel.

In the caves to the west of where Andzrel stood, Baenre troops had forced a group of duergar back into a *faerzress* and hurled light pellets in after them. The resulting pyrotechnic display had apparently been quite spectacular, according to the slingers who had triggered it—slingers who had been struck blind as a result. More House Baenre fighters, waiting in the wings around a bend of the tunnel, had rushed past the slingers to deliver the coup de grâce to the blinded duergar.

Andzrel itched to be a part of it. To be crawling the jagged twists and turns of the Dark Dominion's narrow passageways, sword in hand, fighting his enemy face-to-face in the tight confines of the tunnels. Instead he was perched on a column of broken stalagmite, directing the troops that flowed past him into battle while he remained behind. He tried picturing himself as a spider at the center of the web—sensitive to the vibrations of battle coming from all directions and responding to them—but it didn't help. He wanted an excuse to draw his sword, for Lolth's sake, to engage the enemy in glorious battle as he had at the Pillars of Woe, when he'd snatched victory from the fangs of deceit.

But the defense of the tunnels was going too well. Alerted by Triel's warning, the matron mothers had poured troops into the Dark Dominions southeast of the city, forcing the enemy advance to grind to a halt. The duergar seemed to have withdrawn, leaving only the tanarukks to fight. And while the Scoured Legion might have thousands of troops, forcing an army through those narrow tunnels was like trying to shove a melon through the neck of a bottle. Yet they continued to send troops forward. It was almost as if they'd expected the tunnels to be undefended.

Sighing, Andzrel allowed his attention to wander. His eye settled on one of the wisps of smoke that had had been drifting in for some time from the tunnel to his left. It rose steadily upward, drawn by air currents that were surprisingly swift, toward a narrow crack that ran the length of the ceiling. Then it slipped inside the crack and was gone.

It was followed, a moment later, by another drift of smoke—one that was curiously shaped, with tendrils that looked like arms and legs. It, too, vanished into the crack. Then a third puff of smoke appeared, one with a bulge at the front of it that looked, for all the world, like a shaggy—

Suddenly realizing what he was seeing, Andzrel barked an order at the junior officer who stood beside him.

"Lieutenant! The smoke . . . shoot it!"

With a swiftness born of strict training and absolute obedience, the lieutenant whipped up his arm and fired his wrist crossbow in the direction indicated. A poisoned bolt whizzed through the air toward its target.

Instead of passing through the "smoke" and striking the stone behind it, the bolt sank into something soft, with a dull thud. An instant later, a tanarukk materialized out of thin air. It tumbled, arms and legs thrashing, toward the floor of the cavern, the battle-axe it had been carrying landing with a loud clang beside it. The tanarukk was dead even before it slammed into the stone floor, the virulent drow poison having done its work.

The lieutenant immediately fitted another bolt into the crossbow at his wrist and scanned the ceiling.

"Master Andzrel," he croaked, "where did it come from?"

Andzrel peered down the corridor from which the two-dimensional tanarukk had come. No more wisps of "smoke" appeared. The dead one seemed to have been bringing up the rear.

Short and stocky, with a prominent lower jaw and curving tusks, the tanarukk had a ridge of horn across its forehead that gave it a thick, unintelligent look. The trick it and its fellows had played on the drow, however, was anything but stupid.

LISA SMEDMAN

"The more important question, lieutenant, is where the tana-rukks were headed," Andzrel said, "and how many have slipped past us already. If I remember my geography correctly, that crack leads to the main cavern."

A runner emerged from a side tunnel.

"Good news, sir," the man panted. "We're not only holding them . . . they seem to be falling back. The enemy has all but disappeared."

As Andzrel cursed—surprising the runner, who'd obviously expected elation on his commander's part—the forefront of a company from House Barrison Del' Armgo trotted into the room. They were reinforcements sent in at last by the Second House, only after House Baenre's troops had secured the tunnels.

Leaping down from the broken stalagmite, Andzrel strode toward the captain who commanded them, a slender female in adamantine armor with white hair drawn up in a topknot.

"Captain!" he barked, foregoing the usual bow that was a ranking officer's due—and the Barrison Del'Armgo captain, being female, certainly did outrank him. "Turn your company around. March back to the main cavern at once."

The captain's eyes blazed an even deeper red as her cheeks flushed with anger. She jerked to a halt, and the soldiers following her did the same.

"Who in the Nine Hells do you think you are?" she said, glaring down at him. "You may be weapons master of House Baenre, but you're only a—"

"This isn't the time for arguments," Andzrel said in a tense voice, his intensity making up for his lack of height. "The enemy has slipped past us and are about to enter the city. House Barrison Del' Armgo lies directly in their path. Is your pride really worth your House, captain?"

The other captain hesitated, sword gripped in her hand, then she spun on her heel.

"Turn about!" she barked. "Back to the main cavern. Double speed!"

The look she gave Andzrel over her shoulder as she sped away behind her company, however, was as sharp as a dagger point. When the fight with the tanarukks and duergar was over, win or lose, Andzrel knew he would have a second battle to face.

He spun to face the House Baenre lieutenant and said, "You're in charge. Order half of our company to fall back to the main cavern, while the other half continue to hold the tunnels."

The lieutenant's white eyebrows lifted. "And you, sir?" he asked. "Where will you be?"

Then, realizing his impertinence, he dropped his gaze to the floor.

"I'll be making sure that Barrison Del' Armgo captain follows her orders," he said with a grin. He drew his sword. "And hopefully, I'll be giving the tanarukks a taste of this."

❁ ❁ ❁

Triel, flanked by her House wizard and the priestess currently serving as her personal attendant, stood on the balcony that encircled the Great Mound at the point where stalagmite and stalactite met. From far below, at the base of the Qu'ellarz'orl plateau, came the clash of troops in battle. A band of tanarukks had somehow slipped past the troops she'd ordered into the tunnels and had reached the mushroom forest. The wide caps of the mushrooms prevented Triel from seeing much, but every now and then one of the puffballs would explode as a sword or axe struck it, filling the air with a cloud of luminescent blue spores.

Among the combatants, Triel could pick out the silver uniforms of her own troops. The House Baenre company under Andzrel, together with a company from House Barrison Del' Armgo, were fighting a containing action, preventing the tanarukks from advancing farther into the main cavern. As the foot soldiers repeatedly charged the tanarukks, trying to drive them back through the fence, two squadrons of House Baenre's mounted troops made an assault on the enemy flanks, their lizards scurrying along the walls.

The enemy was gradually forced back against the wall of the great cavern. But just when Triel was certain they would either be shoved back into the tunnel like a cork into a bottle or smashed flat where they stood, the tanarukks closest to the tunnel mouth parted. Triel strained forward, expecting to see a tanarukk general stride through the gap in their ranks, but what emerged instead from the tunnel mouth made her chuckle.

It was a jade spider. Three times the height of a drow, the magical construct was one of those that guarded each of the entrances to Menzoberranzan. Made from magically treated jade, it moved with fluid grace. It was as captivating in its beauty as it was deadly.

"Now we'll see some fun," said the plump wizard standing next to Triel.

Triel acknowledged him with a curt nod. She didn't much care for Nauzhror, her first cousin once removed. He had only been promoted to the position of Archmage of Menzoberranzan because Gromph was missing, but he wore the archmage's robes with a stuck-up snobbishness, as if he'd earned them. Triel instead directed her comment to Wilara, the priestess who stood on her left.

"The spiders will put the fear of Lolth into them," she chuckled.

Wilara laughed politely along with her mistress. Her laughter ended abruptly a moment later, however, when the jade spider, instead of attacking the tanarukks, strode through the gap they'd created in their ranks.

"What in the Spider Queen's name. . . ." the priestess whispered.

Wilara's unfinished question was answered a moment later as the spider crashed headlong into the House Baenre soldiers. Plucking one of them from the ground with its mandibles, it scissored the soldier in half. Then, letting the pieces fall to either side, it continued to race forward, smashing its way through mushrooms and drow alike.

"Lolth help us," Nauzhror said in a strangled voice. "They've managed to get control of one of the constructs."

As the jade spider advanced, the drow fell back in confusion. One or two prostrated themselves before it—only to receive the same treatment as the first soldier.

The spider continued its relentless advance, and soon several drow lay in bloody heaps behind it. Within moments, the spider had carved a gap through both the mushroom forest and the troops—a gap the tanarukks were quick to exploit.

"Attack, curse you!" Triel cried as the enemy surged forward.

The drow soldiers were too far away to have heard her, but thankfully one of their officers—probably Andzrel, judging by the black armor and cloak—rallied them. They fell upon the tanarukks from either side and quickly closed the gap the spider had opened. But even as the enemy was driven back once more toward the cavern wall, the jade spider continued to advance. Leaving the struggling foes and the mushroom forest behind, it scaled the slope that led from Qu'ellarz'orl up to the House Baenre compound. It moved swiftly and in a few moments more was at the barrier.

It hesitated just outside the high fence that enclosed the

compound as if contemplating the magic that flowed through the barrier's glowing silver strands, then it turned toward one of the stalagmites to which the fence was attached. As the House guard on the balconies above watched in confusion, the construct scaled the stone as easily as a living spider, climbing to a point just above the fence. It leaped down over the barrier, then began moving toward the center of the compound.

Triel's eyes narrowed as she saw where it was headed. The jade spider was making its way to House Baenre's central structure—the great domed temple of Lolth.

Wilara gasped as she, too, calculated the spider's course.

"They dare attack our temple?" the priestess cried.

Nauzhror, with a sidelong look at Triel, exploded with appropriate rage.

"The insolence!" the interim archmage fumed. "May Lolth's webs strangle them!"

His familiar—a fist-sized, hairy brown spider—scuttled from one of his shoulders to the other, disturbed by the mage's violent motion.

Triel pursed her lips, saying nothing. The temple might be the target, but an attack on it was not the enemy's chief aim. There was little a single jade spider—or even a dozen of them for that matter—could do to harm the building itself. Triel was sure that the incursion was intended to be a demonstration, made where all could see it, that Lolth had turned her face away from her chosen people. The spider would have to be stopped—but anyone doing so outside the doors of a building consecrated to Lolth would incur the goddess's wrath.

In ordinary times, at least.

Triel longed to cry out to Lolth, to plead for the goddess to tell her what to do, but she knew what the answer would be: silence. The Matron Mother of the First House was on her own—and if the jade spider wasn't stopped, Menzoberranzan's weakness would be plain for all to see. The males of House Baenre, fighting so valiantly to force the enemy back into the tunnels, might falter. If they became convinced that Triel and the other ranking females had lost Lolth's favor for some fault of their own or that the goddess had turned away from all drow forever, they might even turn against their matron mothers.

That could not be.

"The enemy knows our weakness," Triel said in a tense voice. "They must believe that Lolth has fallen silent forever and hope to make it plain for all to see."

Beside her, Wilara stiffened. Then amazingly, she contradicted her matron mother.

"No," the priestess said, shaking her head and causing the long braid that hung down her back to ripple like a snake. "The goddess *will* answer. She *must*."

The vipers in Triel's whip hissed their annoyance, but Triel ignored them. Under the circumstances, she could allow Wilara's outspokenness.

"Lolth may awaken yet," she said, speaking as much to steady herself as for the lesser priestess's benefit. "My sister Quenthel has not yet given up, so neither should we. But in the meantime, we have to rely upon ourselves. And upon other forms of magic."

She turned to Nauzhror and asked, "Do you know the spell that will transform stone to flesh?"

"I do, Matron Mother," he answered, "but if we transform it to flesh, the statue will become a living spider. The problem remains. We just can't . . . kill it."

"Quite so," Triel said. As she spoke, she unfastened one of the wand cases hanging from her belt. "But by the time we're finished, it won't be a spider." She drew out a slender iron wand, tipped with a chunk of amber whose depths held the remains of a desiccated moth. "As soon as you cast your spell, I'll polymorph it into something else—something large and dangerous enough to have torn a hole through our ranks. Something our troops won't have any problem attacking."

Nauzhror smiled and said, "A deceitful plan, Matron Mother. One worthy of Lolth herself."

Glancing down, Triel saw that the spider had nearly reached the temple.

"Quit fawning," she ordered. "Teleport us down there at once."

Nauzhror spoke the words of his spell, and an instant later the balcony seemed to lurch sideways as he and Triel squeezed between the dimensions. In the blink of an eye they were standing in front of the doors to the great temple. Two dozen House guards who had been milling about uncertainly a moment before gasped as their matron mother suddenly appeared before them. Some bowed, and others glanced between Triel and the jade spider that was rapidly approaching, its stone legs *click-clicking* as it scurried across the cavern floor.

Nauzhror, his face paling to gray as the enormous stone spider rapidly closed the gap, began chanting a spell. He pointed a finger, from which an intense, narrow beam of red light sprang, but the trembling of his hand made the beam waver, causing it to miss the spider by several paces.

Triel grabbed Nauzhror's hand, steadying it. The beam connected—and jade became flesh. Triel activated her wand.

The spider shifted into the form she held in her mind: a two-legged creature with powerful muscles, enormous claws and mandibles, and a rounded, insectoid head. Its body was covered in chitinous plates, and feelers sprouted from cracks near its head where the sections met. Startled by its sudden transformation, the creature stumbled to a halt, feelers waving frantically as its mandibles clacked shut.

"Matron Mother," Nauzhror gasped. "An umber hulk?"

"Convincing, isn't it?" Triel said with a wry smile. She turned to the dozen or so soldiers who stood gaping nearby and ordered, "Soldiers of House Baenre, you have been fooled by an illusion. Defend me!"

To a man, the soldiers leaped forward, swords in hand. The transformed statue fought back, its mandibles tearing one soldier in half and neatly scissoring the head off another. Then a lieutenant of the House guard—a small male with white hair plaited in two braids that were tucked behind his pointed ears—leaped directly into the path of the umber hulk. He wore no armor, and his only weapon was a small crossbow strapped to his left wrist. He aimed deliberately as the umber hulk staggered toward him—still uncertain of its footing with only two legs, instead of eight—and he fired.

The bolt struck the umber hulk in the throat, in a spot where two of its armor plates met. It buried itself to the fletching in soft flesh—then exploded with magical energy. Sparks raced in brilliant streaks across the umber hulk's body, then shot up its feelers, sizzling them like burned hair. The umber hulk faltered, then fell.

The lieutenant—whom Triel belatedly recognized as one of her nephews, a male named Vrellin—dropped to one knee in front of her.

"Matron Mother," he said, never once lifting his eyes. "I failed to recognize the threat. My life is yours."

Closing his eyes, he raised his head, baring his exposed neck. Triel laughed.

The noise startled Vrellin. Uncertain, he looked up—but not quite into Triel's eyes. Vrellin was a male who knew his place.

"Matron Mother, do you mock me?" he asked in a strained voice. "Is my life worth so little you deem it not worth taking?"

Triel spread her fingers and brushed them across the lieutenant's head—a touch as light as a spiderweb.

"For what you have done, lieutenant, the goddess will reward you—in this life, or the next."

As she spoke, she wondered if that was true. Then something caught her eye in the distance, on the opposite side of the great cavern: streaks of dull red light, arcing up into the air and down again. They seemed to be coming from the rear of the Tier Breche cavern, from somewhere between and behind Sorcere and Arach-Tinilith.

She swore softly as she realized their point of origin— the tunnel that gave access to Tier Breche from outside Menzoberranzan—and what the source of the light must have been: pots of magical fire, capable of burning even stone, like those that had destroyed Ched Nasad.

Stonefire bombs.

Menzoberranzan was under attack on a second front. And, judging by the pinpoints of fire blossoming on the buildings in the distant cavern, the stonefire bombs were being used to good effect against Menzoberranzan's three most cherished institutions: Sorcere, Melee-Magthere—and Arach-Tinilith, the most holy of the temples to Lolth.

Tearing her eyes away, Triel glanced down at the base of the Qu'ellarz'orl plateau. The drow had finally beaten the tanarukks back into the tunnels All that was visible of the conflict were a few scattered corpses.

"Abyss take them," Triel swore under her breath. "It *was* just a feint."

Aliisza lounged on one of the plush carpets that had been thrown down on the floor of the cavern and sipped her glass of lacefungus wine. Kaanyr had been pacing back and forth across the cavern that served as his quarters in the field. He paused next to his "throne"—an enormous chair that had been lashed together from the bones of his enemies, a hideous piece of furniture he'd insisted on carrying with him on campaign. Snarling, he kicked over the enormous brazier that stood next to it.

"Abyss take Nimor!" he shouted, his skin blazing with radiant heat. "He promised the drow would be in disarray, unable to mount a coherent defense. Now my army sits stalled and impotent, while the duergar claim all the glory."

Glowing red coals scattered across the rugs, which began smoldering. Aliisza picked up one of the coals and juggled it back and forth across her palm. Its heat tickled her skin.

"So why not march your troops north and join the duergar attack?" she suggested, her black wings framing the question with a shrug.

"And give the drow an opportunity to attack us from the rear, and in territory they know well?" Vhok shook his head and added, "Your grasp of tactics—or lack thereof—astounds me. Sometimes I wonder just whose side you're on, Aliisza."

Setting her glass aside, Aliisza rose to her feet. She stood on tiptoe and locked her hands behind Kaanyr Vhok's head. Drawing his mouth down to hers, she kissed him.

"I'm on your side, darling Kaanyr," she murmured.

The half-demon broke off the kiss.

"This Nimor begins to annoy me," he grumbled. "He promised us the spoils of the noble Houses—an empty promise. Even without Lolth, Menzoberranzan is proving to be, as Horgar so aptly noted, a tough stone to crack. And if Lolth suddenly returns . . ."

He paused, lost in thought as he stared at one of the small fires that had erupted in the carpet at his feet.

"That group of drow you were spying on, back in Ched Nasad . . ." he said.

Aliisza was busy nuzzling the cambion's coal-hot neck.

"Mmm?" she purred.

"What were they doing?"

Aliisza pouted but asked, "Does it matter?"

"It might," Vhok said. "Which is why I have another little job for you. I want you to find them—and, more importantly, learn what they're up to. If I'm right, we may need to rethink our alliance."

Aliisza cocked her head and smiled—not at the treachery Kaanyr Vhok was hinting at, but at the thought of seeing Pharaun again.

He certainly was delicious.

FOURTEEN

Gromph felt the blood drain from his face as he stared, horrified, at the illithid. Were he not trapped in the gods-cursed sphere, he could have dealt with the creature in a summary fashion, casually flicking a death-dealing spell in its direction, but instead he was at its mercy. Every fleeting thought that passed through Gromph's mind would be heard by the illithid as if spoken aloud. None of Gromph's secrets—or the secrets of Sorcere—were safe, unless he could deliberately *not* think of them. That effort would only cause them to come bubbling to the surface of his mind. The only good thing about his situation was that the mind flayer's gently waving tentacles were on the other side of the glass. The illithid could no more reach in and attack Gromph than Gromph could send his magic out to blast the illithid.

The mind flayer's telepathic speech was another matter. It penetrated the sphere with ease.

Sorcere? Which building is it?

A fleeting image formed in Gromph's mind: Sorcere's sculpted stalagmite tower, standing proudly beside the other two edifices of the Academy: the pyramid of Melee-Magthere, and the eight-legged temple of Arach-Tinilith.

Gromph cursed, and quickly fixed his mind on something else, but it was too late. The illithid swam up until its head broke the surface of the lake. It glanced to its right, toward the northern end of the city, blank white eyes searching for the raised grotto that opened off the main cavern of Menzoberranzan. Its tentacles lifted slightly, and its mouth began to move.

A bright sparkle of magical energy enveloped the illithid, and the view of the lake and shore disappeared. With a sinking heart, Gromph realized that things were even worse than he'd thought. His captor was no ordinary illithid but one capable of sorcery.

Gromph immediately recognized the spot that the illithid's spell had carried them to. They were in the wide cavern that led from the Dark Dominions into Tier Breche. Exhausted duergar sprawled on the cavern floor, many of them wounded. Others, carrying enormous axes and battle-chewed shields, hurried through the tunnel, their officers urging them toward Tier Breche, which was filled with the flashes of exploding spells.

Still other gray dwarves busied themselves just inside the mouth of the tunnel, hurriedly assembling siege engines and shelters. The duergar labored without ceasing, even though an occasional ball of fire or ice or crackling electricity arced over and smashed into the ground near the siege walls they had set up just inside Tier Breche. Glowing pits of molten rock or ice-shattered stone attested to the force of those blasts.

Gromph could see everything but could not hear the shouts of the duergar—who nodded to the newly arrived illithid—nor could he smell the sulfurous explosions. The sphere enclosed him in a world filled only with his own breathing—which became rapid as he realized that Gracklstugh's army had not only reached Menzoberranzan but had established a foothold inside Tier Breche itself. The duergar were attacking the three buildings that were the most heavily fortified in the city, aside from the noble Houses themselves.

Hands pressed to the curved wall of his prison, Gromph strained his eyes, looking for the jade spiders that should have been guarding the tunnel. They were nowhere to be seen.

They serve a different master, now, the illithid said with a smirk. *As will the drow, soon enough. The army is already inside Menzoberranzan.*

Whose army? Gromph wondered. Not an army of illithids, surely, or the one who carried him would have said *"our* army." Had the duergar of Gracklstugh reached Menzoberranzan on their own?

The answer came swiftly.

Yes. And tanarukks march with them. The drow cannot stand against their combined might.

Gromph had no way of knowing whether or not that was true. If only he could get free of the sphere he could use his magic to drive the enemy back. But in order to free himself he needed to find a wizard who knew the precise spell required. And he needed to get inside Sorcere—specifically, to his quarters, where the lichdrow had cast his imprisonment spell. Unfortunately, both those things were on the other side of the duergar siege wall.

Gromph glanced up at the illithid and thought, Or . . . are they?

Deliberately, Gromph let his mind dwell upon that thought.

The reply was tinged with arrogance.

Of course I know that spell, but why should I use it to set you free? All of your secrets will be mine, in time. I will flay your mind, layer by layer, like the skin of a—

The illithid broke off in mid-sentence, suddenly glancing at someone who was approaching. Long, purple fingers closed tightly around the sphere. The illithid held it in both hands, hiding what it contained. It rubbed its fingers deliberately against the glass, smearing its surface with the slime that coated its palms. Gromph tumbled to his hands and knees as the illithid dropped the hand holding the sphere to its side. He scrambled forward to look out through the only clear spot that remained on the surface of the glass.

One of the duergar stood in front of the illithid, his face level with the sphere. Like the others of his race, the dwarf had pale gray skin, a snub nose that looked as if it had been flattened by a mace, and a bald head. He was dressed in mottled gray-and-black clothing the color of stone but wore a bronze breastplate so untarnished and free of dents that Gromph was willing to bet it was magical. He carried a greataxe whose double-bladed head swirled with ghostly patterns—likely the trapped souls of those it had slain, or so Gromph guessed.

The gray dwarf didn't have his head tilted up to speak to the illithid but kept his eyes level with the mind flayer's waist. The gray dwarf's gaze occasionally creeped down to the sphere, and he gestured repeatedly at Tier Breche.

Glancing up, Gromph could see the illithid's tentacles ripple as it shook its head. The gray dwarf, who obviously thought he was addressing another duergar, pointed at the sphere.

With a suddenness that surprised Gromph, the illithid bent over the dwarf. Its four tentacles lashed out, wrapping themselves around the duergar's face. The dwarf flailed with his axe, but the illithid had anticipated that move and countered it with magic.

The dwarf's body went suddenly rigid, the axe poised above his head. Tentacles flexed, and the duergar's head split open like a ripe fungus ball. One of the tentacles relaxed, and, while the remaining three held the head in a vicelike grip, it began scooping pinkish gobs of brain into the illithid's mouth. Gromph, sickened by the sight, turned his face away from the glass.

The other duergar turned, shocked looks on their faces. One or two reached for their weapons, took a look at the illithid's blank white eyes, then all of them suddenly relaxed. Gromph could only imagine how easy it was for the illithid to cloud the simple minds of a gang of duergar soldiers. He wondered what the duergar saw when they looked at the illithid—one of their own, most likely—and they were compelled not to think about their dead officer, his broken skull, or his half-eaten brain. One by one, the magic-addled gray dwarves simply went back to what they had been doing.

Finished with its meal, the illithid plucked the axe from the dwarf's hand, then let the body drop.

Now, it said, *you will tell me how to enter Sorcere.*

Gromph eyed the greataxe. It was obvious that the illithid cared less about the war than it did about personal gain.

You want magic, Gromph sent to the illithid.

Yes, the mind flayer replied.

You want to get inside Sorcere before the duergar do.

The illithid's next thought was more tentative, as if it was admitting a guilty secret.

Yes, it said.

Gromph smiled and replied, *You want to know if there's a back door into Sorcere, but if you try to get that information from me by force, it will take too long. By the time you find it, the duergar will be inside. You'll be left with whatever scraps they don't destroy or loot for themselves. But I can offer another alternative. Help me to get free of this sphere, and I'll reward you well. I'll willingly give you the magic you crave.*

What magic?

In my centuries of experimentation, I have developed powerful spells that other mages and wizards have yet to even imagine.

Gromph felt the tendrils of the illithid's mind-probing magic root even deeper in his mind.

Those spells are no longer in my memory, he told it. *They're in my private quarters, in Sorcere. In these.*

Gromph let his mind dwell on his office, on the enormous desk that dominated the windowless room. Made of polished bone, it had a number of drawers that opened onto extra-dimensional spaces. The front of each drawer was inlaid with a different skull. Gromph pictured himself sitting in his chair behind the desk and reaching down to a certain skull, then placing his fingers in its eye sockets. The drawer slid open, revealing a rack that held two bottles. Each was of cast gold, its sides set with a sigil-shaped "window" of moss-green glass, through which came a glow that originated from inside the bottle. Each of the sigils, in the drow script, represented the same word: "remember."

What are they? the illithid asked.

I call them "thought bottles," Gromph said. *Each contains a powerful spell—and all of the thoughts that led to its creation. Spells so powerful even I dared not use them, but so unique that, once created, I could not risk losing them, either. In order to avoid temptation, I created these bottles to hold them. Anyone who consumes their contents will gain not only the spell itself but every stage of the process that led to its creation.*

Once I am inside Sorcere, I will take them, the illithid said.

Not unless you free me, first, Gromph said. *The drawer will only open to my touch.*

The archmage let his mind dwell on an experiment he'd

conducted back when he'd first constructed and ensorcelled the desk. He'd deliberately left the door to his office lightly warded, then observed with clairvoyant magic as an apprentice forced his way into the office and tried to open the desk. No sooner had the drow placed his fingers inside the eye sockets than he stiffened and tried to scream. No more than a hoarse croak came from his throat, however, before a horrible wilting began. White hair broke off in clumps from his head like dried straw, and his eyes shriveled in upon themselves like heat-cured fungus and fell from their sockets. His skin chafed, then erupted in a series of cracks, from which brown dust—dried blood—trickled. Slowly he crumpled, shrinking in upon himself until all that was left was a pile of dusty clothes where a drow had once stood.

Impressive, the illithid said.

Thank you, Gromph answered.

Yet another fireball arced over the siege wall and landed a short distance away, scattering gobs of molten lava. The liquid rock slid off the illithid like water running down glass. The illithid had obviously cloaked itself in a protective spell.

Do we have a bargain, then? Gromph asked. *Will you free me and receive the thought bottles as payment?*

You must show me a way into Sorcere, the illithid said. *It is protected by wards that prevent magical entry, is it not?*

Gromph smiled and sent, *A good guess. But there's a portion of the building that is not protected by these wards, because it exists in its own pseudoplane: a vertical shaft that gives access to my office. If you could gate us into it, I'll show you how to find the door.*

Bring it to your mind, the illithid commanded.

Gromph fought down his irritation at being ordered about.

Of course, he answered. *Ah . . . what is your name, anyway?*

Sluuguth.

Assuming the illithid had told the truth, Gromph had a

weapon he could use against the creature. Certainly the mind flayer knew that too, which meant that Sluuguth had no intention of letting Gromph live. All that passed through Gromph's mind in a fleeting thought—hopefully too fleeting for Sluuguth to notice—then Gromph began to concentrate on the access shaft. He could feel Sluuguth mentally looking over his shoulder, studying the spot they were about to gate to with great care.

A circle of purple light shimmered into being next to them. Sluuguth fell into it and an instant later was levitating inside the shaft. It seemed to extend infinitely upward and downward and had walls of utter blackness that had a somehow palpable look to them. Had Gromph not been trapped in the sphere, he knew his nostrils would have been assaulted by the rank, foul odor of the pseudoplane, the stench of the malformed creatures that called it home.

Where is the door? asked Sluuguth.

Gromph indicated a patch of darkness that seemed more solid than the rest and sent, *Dispel its magic, then push.*

Sluuguth did as instructed. Previously invisible runes sparkled as light burst inside the diamond dust that had been used to inscribe them. When the light vanished, Sluuguth pushed open the door, revealing Gromph's office.

The chamber was a mess—the aftermath of Gromph's battle with the lichdrow Dyrr. The enormous desk at the center of the room was gouged in several places by the whirling blades the lichdrow had conjured, and the marble flagstone floor was cracked where Dyrr's staff had struck it. One of the bookshelves was a smashed ruin, and the scrolls that had tumbled from it had been trampled. As a sign of his disdain for the archmage's wizardry, the lichdrow had left them where they were after trapping Gromph in the sphere.

The perpetually burning red candles, set into wall sconces

made from skeletal fists, still provided illumination, and a plushly upholstered chair behind the desk had survived relatively unscathed. A harder wooden chair on the other side, where a visitor would sit, lay on one side, its legs splintered. Beyond it was a door of black marble, incised with glowing silver runes.

As for the spiderstone golem that had fought in an effort to defend Gromph, the only thing left of it was a severed stone arm, lying forlornly in a corner.

Still hovering in the shaft, Sluuguth pointed and thrust the tip of one finger into the room. Immediately, one of the office walls erupted in a triangle of flame as an invisible sigil released a fire elemental. Sluuguth's magic, however, was swifter. A bolt of energy leaped from his fingertip and struck the elemental, freezing it. The fire elemental hung, trapped from the waist down in the wall, its arms extended over its head. Only its eyes moved. White-hot flames blazed at Sluuguth as the illithid at last stepped into the room.

You didn't warn me about that, the illithid said, tentacles waving as it nodded at the frozen elemental.

No need, obviously, Gromph answered. *Now let's get down to business. Free me. Place the sphere on the chair behind the desk.*

Tentacles twitching as its face grimaced into what might have been a smile, Sluuguth laid the sphere on the chair cushion. Then, without further ado, it began to cast a spell. Its three-fingered hands began a series of gestures—Gromph thought he recognized a portion of the imprisonment-negating spell, but the somatic component seemed more complicated than it need have been—and sound crashed in on Gromph from all sides as the sphere broke apart.

For an instant he was twisting between dimensions, his body bursting free of the magic that had confined it, his ears ringing as if he were a clapper inside a bell—

—and he was sitting in his chair. Eyes gleaming in triumph, he started to lift a finger in the minute gesture required to activate a second invisible sigil on the wall. Interlocked ellipses would suck Sluuguth into a two-dimensional prison.

Stop.

Gromph's finger wouldn't move. Nor could he even imagine moving it any longer. Something had a vicelike grip on his mind and was crushing his will. Gromph could sense Sluuguth's foul-feeling, tentacled presence.

Heart suddenly beating faster, the archmage realized what must have happened. In casting the spell that gave Gromph his freedom, the illithid had woven in a second spell, one that had slowed Gromph's body. It had given Sluuguth just enough time to cast the mind-dominating spell that held Gromph in thrall.

Gromph sat motionless in his chair, awaiting the illithid's next command. Had he been able to, he would have groaned in frustration. He had been careful *not* to think about the sigils on the walls. The first one was meant to give Sluuguth a false sense of security after the illithid so summarily defeated the fire elemental—as Gromph knew it would. The second was meant to trap the mind flayer after Gromph was free. But the archmage's careful plan lay in ruins, as broken as the remains of the sphere that littered the floor at his feet.

Sluuguth moved to a position behind Gromph and loomed over his shoulder.

Open the drawer.

Gromph bent, inserted his fingers in the skull's eye sockets, and pulled. The drawer slid open, revealing the two thought bottles.

Take them out of the drawer, Sluuguth ordered.

Gromph did as he was told, placing both bottles on the desk in front of him. He braced himself. Surely the illithid would either end his life or at the very least imprison him, the desk's protective magic having been thwarted.

Instead Sluuguth gave him a further command: *Choose one.*

Gromph's fingers closed around the bottle closest to him. An instant later, at Sluuguth's command, they sprang open again, and he picked up the second bottle instead.

Consume it, Sluuguth ordered

With those words, Gromph knew the second part of his plan—which he had obviously been unsuccessful in *not* thinking about—had also failed.

Decades past, Gromph had created the thought bottles as a contingency, in case he ever became the captive of a creature who could read his mind. He'd been telling the truth when he said he had no idea what was in the bottles, but he'd left one tiny sliver of information within his own mind: the memory that if such a situation arose, he should offer them to his captor. But the *sava* board had been turned. Whatever was in the bottle his traitorous hands were even then uncorking was about to be unleashed on Gromph himself.

A part of Gromph's mind screamed in protest, but the tiny, trapped voice went unheard. Slowly, inexorably, the Archmage of Menzoberranzan raised the bottle to his lips, and drank.

FIFTEEN

Valas sculled just outside the turbulent swirl of water at the base of the waterfall, wondering how he was going to contact the others. Fully transformed, he was no longer capable of breathing air. His hands and feet had turned into webbed paws, and his tailbone had elongated into a fluked tail. After the last of his hair had fallen out, a grayish-green membrane had grown over his skin, which secreted a slimy coating that kept out the water's chill. Valas was trapped underwater, unable to climb back up to the tunnel where his companions waited.

At least he still had all of his equipment. He touched the thick leather belt around his waist, with its steel buckle shaped in the form of a rothé's head. Perhaps, with the aid of the magical strength it lent him, together with the increased nimbleness afforded by his enchanted chain mail, he could climb *inside* the waterfall, against its pounding force. But when he swam to the

Extinction

surface to take a look, he remembered that the waterfall arced out of the cavern above. For most of the climb, the falling water was a good three or four paces distant from the cliff—too far for him to duck his head into it while still holding on to the rock face.

Disappointed, he allowed himself to sink back under the surface of the lake. There was no way out.

Then he remembered his enchanted backpack.

Shrugging it off his shoulders, he moved it to his chest, putting the shoulder straps on backward and cinching them tight. He opened its main flap. Water rushed into the nondimensional space inside the pack. When it was full—holding the equivalent of perhaps thirty waterskins—he closed the flap. Many of the items the backpack held would be damaged, but that was a sacrifice that mattered little against his survival.

Valas swam directly under the waterfall, fighting the current with powerful strokes of his tail. The water falling from above thundered in his ears and forced him down, but at last he saw a more solid patch of darkness ahead: the base of the cliff. The current slammed him up against the rock before he was ready, but an instant later he found a handhold. To his surprise, he felt claws emerge from the ends of his fingers and thumb that helped him hold on. Muscles straining, he resisted the current that was trying to tear him away from the rock face. Valas began to climb.

The closer he got to the surface, the stronger the pounding of the waterfall became. Twice he slipped and was nearly swept back to the bottom of the lake, but he managed to hang on with one hand. By thrashing his tail, he forced himself back against the cliff each time. At last his head broke the surface.

He heaved himself up, scrambling for handholds and toeholds on the slippery cliff. As he climbed, he held his breath—or rather, held water in his lungs. When at last he could hold it no more, he exhaled through his mouth—a process that felt like vomiting, at least when he was no longer underwater—then he opened the flap of his backpack and plunged his head inside. He inhaled deeply, then closed the flap and continued to climb.

Gradually he drew near to the tunnel mouth. When he was perhaps a pace or two below its lip, Pharaun peeked out from above. The mage had obviously been alerted by magic to Valas's presence—there was no way he could have heard someone climbing the cliff over the thunder of the falls. The mage was casting a spell.

Valas—to Pharaun's eyes a "monster" rising from the lake—waved a webbed paw in a desperate attempt to fend off whatever magical attack was about to be launched at him. Shaking his head, he pointed to the kukris sheathed at his hip.

Pharaun, oblivious, touched his forefingers to his eyes and flicked them downward, releasing his spell. Valas felt a wash of magical energy tingle through his skin, and he flinched. Flexing his claws still deeper into the crevices to which he clung, he waited for death to take him.

Above him, Pharaun's eyes widened.

Lifting a hand, he signed rapidly, *Valas! It is you. What happened?*

Sighing water in a trickle over his chin, Valas realized he had been reprieved. Pharaun had recognized him by his kukris, after all—the spell had just been one that allowed him to see through the misshapen form Valas wore, to confirm the mercenary's identity. He signed one brief word—*Wait*—and inhaled once again from his bag.

Valas climbed up to where Pharaun crouched, and heaved himself over the edge into the tunnel. Slipping into the river, he grabbed a rock to hold himself against the current that threatened to carry him over the waterfall.

Quenthel, Danifae, and the hulking Jeggred were all still waiting by the river's edge. The vipers in Quenthel's whip lifted their heads and quivered in alarm as they saw Valas, and Jeggred sniffed the air and bared his teeth, but Pharaun told them that the drow-thing was, in fact, their companion. Danifae stared at Valas with an expression of open disgust, her perfect lips slightly curled, then she turned away.

"Well?" Quenthel demanded. "Did you find the ship of chaos?"

Valas shook his head. Using the silent speech, he told his story, ducking his head underwater each time he needed to breathe. Pharaun listened closely, looking grim as Valas told of his capture, then giving a congratulatory nod as the mercenary described his escape. Quenthel's expression, however, had not changed. Her lips remained tight, while her eyes blazed.

She turned on Pharaun, the vipers in her whip writhing, and said, "Your demon was lying. The ship isn't here."

Pharaun raised an eyebrow and asked, "*My* demon?"

"We're no farther ahead than when we started," Quenthel said. "You should have kept questioning Belshazu about gates. This rothé-dung story about a ship of chaos was obviously just a lie to throw us off the track."

"Off the track of what?" Pharaun asked, glaring back. "The only gate around here is the one in your imagination. And it was your bright idea to have me summon a demon in the first place."

Valas didn't like the look in the mage's eyes. Once again, Pharaun and Quenthel were on the verge of coming to blows. The Master of Sorcere let a hand drift behind his back and had his fingers flexed, ready to cast a spell. Jeggred crouched behind his aunt, clearly ready to spring at Pharaun's throat if any suspicious move was made. Danifae, meanwhile, folded her arms across her chest and stared defiantly at Pharaun—while simultaneously edging out of the path of whatever spell he was about to cast.

Valas, sick of their endless bickering and ready to die anyway, having delivered his report, slammed the flat of his dagger against the stone floor of the tunnel. Sparks exploded out from the blade like ripples from a rock hurled into a pond, crackling against both Pharaun's and Quenthel's feet. Each jumped back—Quenthel immediately drawing her whip.

"Insolent male," she sneered.

The vipers spat, their fangs dripping venom.

Valas could see she was itching to use the whip against him.

Please do, he signed. *It is the swiftest way.*

Quenthel frowned, confused by his reply, but Pharaun's mind proved the quicker again.

"There is no need for that, valued mercenary," the wizard said. "I can restore you to your proper, air-breathing, drow form."

Valas blinked, all thoughts of the viper whip driven from his mind.

You can? the scout signed. *But you don't have healing magic.*

"That's true, but I can—"

Quenthel spun—an awkward movement, forced to crouch as she was by the low ceiling—and said to the mage, "You can do nothing. You *will* do nothing. Valas will return to the lake and continue to search for the ship."

"He'll only be captured if you send him back," Pharaun objected. "He has no way to protect himself. The aboleth will eat him this time."

He paused, and a thoughtful look crossed his face.

"Just as," the Master of Sorcere went on, "they have eaten others who dared trespass in their waters. Including, perhaps, any manes who survived after the shipwreck. And if they did eat any of these petty demons and thus acquired their memories. . . ."

Quenthel at last understood.

"The aboleth would know where the ship of chaos sank," she finished for him even as her vipers writhed in anticipation.

Pharaun turned back to Valas and asked, "What is the name of the city's matriarch?"

Using sign, Valas spelled the name out phonetically: *O-o-t-h-o-o-n.*

Pharaun nodded, then stared out over the lake. It was clear to Valas what the mage was thinking. Pharaun intended to meet with Zanhoriloch's matriarch himself, to ask her for information. Pharaun had powerful spells, including one he seemed confident would shield him against the aboleth's mind magic. The scout was certain the mage could handle the situation, but then Valas had thought the same of himself.

Then came a surprise.

"I will go, too," Danifae said.

Quenthel started to object, then gave the Melarn battle-captive a long, pondering look. After one glance at the uncertain motions of the vipers in the high priestess's whip, Valas could guess the questions that must have been coming to Quenthel's mind.

Was Danifae offering to keep an eye on Pharaun to ensure that he remained loyal to Quenthel, in the hope of regaining her superior's favor? Or did she have some ulterior, even more selfish motive in mind? In the end it seemed not to matter, for Quenthel nodded.

Valas ducked his head for another breath, then he reached out and tapped on the mage's boot.

You said you had something other than healing magic that could help me, he reminded Pharaun.

Pharaun's lips parted in an "ah," and he nodded. He reached into a pocket of his *piwafwi* and pulled out a small brown cocoon. Crumbling it between thumb and forefinger, he let the fragments drift down onto Valas's head. Then, waving his hands over the flakes that stuck to the mercenary's wet scalp, he began a spell.

Kneeling, Pharaun leaned over Valas and shouted in his ear, "Exhale! Quickly!"

Valas did and an instant later felt a powerful wrench shudder through his body as the spell took effect. His tail sucked back into his rear like a snail retreating into its shell and his fused fingers sprang apart, the webs disappearing. Hair erupted on the top of his head, and the skin of his arms, legs, and chest tingled as the membrane that had been cloaking his body disappeared.

The scout was coughing violently, retching the last of the lake water from his lungs. Even though it hurt, he didn't care. Instead he was filled with relief. Pharaun had restored him to drow form—his body was his own once more.

Except for one small detail. Staring down at his hands, Valas saw that his scars were in all the wrong places.

"What spell," he wheezed as he climbed out of the river, "did you just cast?"

Pharaun, still kneeling, was directing a second spell upon him, one that required no arcane material component to cast. Valas saw the mage's shoulders slump as he completed it and knew it had cost Pharaun a piece of himself.

"I polymorphed you," Pharaun said when he was done. "I shaped your body into a pretty good likeness of its old self, if I do say so myself. Until something dispels it, that is. Be thankful that Ryld's not around, waving that greatsword of his."

Valas, still standing chest-deep in water, spread his fingers to admire their shape and nodded.

"I *am* thankful," he said aloud.

His eyes met Pharaun's, making it clear he was speaking not

about the absence of the weapons master but of the presence of the mage.

Pharaun nodded, then gave Quenthel a bow that just bordered on insolence.

"With your leave, Mistress, I will begin studying the spells I need. Then I—then *Danifae* and I—will set out for Zanhoriloch and speak to this Oothoon."

Chapter

SIXTEEN

Ryld shivered as he walked through the forest. Night was falling, and with it came a chill in the air. His *piwafwi* was still damp
from the rain of the night before, and a full day of steady walking
hadn't been enough to dry it. Overhead, above the branches of
the trees that crowded Ryld close on every side, the cloud cover
was breaking up. The sky was a mottled grayish purple, the color
of an old bruise.

The air around him darkened as the last of the sunlight faded,
but after a time, Ryld noticed it was getting brighter again. His
darkvision was giving way to the pale gray light that filled the
surface world at dusk and dawn—even though the dawn was still
a long way off. Confused, Ryld paused, and looked up through
the lacework of branches.

The full moon was rising.

As it peeked above the treetops, filling the air around him with a silvery light, Ryld was suddenly no longer cold. A flush warmed his cheeks, and he felt his blood quicken. The hairs on his arms stood erect, as if he had just shivered, yet at the same time he felt hot with fever.

"Lolth protect me," he whispered in a strangled voice, glancing down nervously at the bite mark on his wrist. "That brat *did* infect me."

The moonlight continued to grow brighter, and with it, Ryld's anxiety rose. Flashes of red swam before his eyes, and his pulse pounded in his ears. Already he could feel his control slipping. His clothing felt tight, constricting, heavy. He pulled it away from his throat, barely able to contain the urge to tear it from his body. He looked wildly at the forest that surrounded him, wanting to plunge into it and run and run and run. . . .

Struggling to maintain control, he plunged a hand into the breast pocket of his *piwafwi* and pulled out the sprig of belladonna that Yarno's grandfather had given him. It had dull green leaves and a single, bell-shaped flower. Ryld ripped off a leaf, stuffed it into his mouth, and chewed. A bitter taste filled his mouth, and his tongue went dry. He followed it with another leaf, then another, then the flower . . . then he threw the bare twig away.

He waited.

The urge he'd felt a moment before—the urge to tear off his clothing and run away into the woods—disappeared. Ryld felt light-headed. He tried to take a step, stumbled, and nearly fell. At the last moment he grabbed a tree for balance. All the while, the forest was becoming brighter, the moonlight flooding his vision. Something was wrong with his eyes.

Pulling his short sword clumsily from its sheath, he stared into its polished surface and saw that his pupils had dilated to the point where the red of the iris had all but vanished.

Grimacing, he lowered his sword, stood a moment, then remembered he hadn't sheathed it. He tried to shove the short sword into its sheath but missed, instead shoving it point-first into the ground as he stumbled. Unable to catch himself again, he fell flat out onto the soggy ground beside it. Above him, the trees seemed to have turned to pale gray shadows, wavering back and forth as though they were under water.

Lying there, watching the forest spiral in circles above him, Ryld wondered if he was going to die. The belladonna had halted his transformation into a werewolf, but at what cost? His heart was pounding at an alarming rate, and his skin felt dry and hot. He tried to wet his lips, but even that effort was too much for him. All he could do was lie on the forest floor, inhaling the smell of wet earth and rotting leaf with each halting breath.

His breath. That was the one thing he still could control.

Ryld cast his mind back to his training at Melee-Magthere. One of the tests initiates had been required to pass involved maintaining concentration in times of physical duress. The initiates had been instructed to strip off their clothing, sit cross-legged on the floor of the practice hall with their eyes closed, and focus on their breathing. At the time, Ryld thought the test was designed to teach them to ignore the cold of the stone floor—but he was wrong. One of the masters strolled between the rows of meditating pupils, dropping centipedes onto their skin. The insects were each as long as a finger and bit immediately when they landed, injecting a venom that raced like fire through the students' veins. Those initiates who cried out or gasped were given a sharp rap on the head. If they cried out a second time they were hit harder. A third, and they were told to leave Melee-Magthere and never return.

Ryld had been dimly aware of the student behind him gasping

a third time and listened with only a portion of his mind as he was ordered to leave. He heard the choked sob he made as he obeyed. Ryld forced his mind deeper into meditation, at the same time bracing himself for what he knew was coming next. When the centipede fell onto his thigh, he didn't flinch. As the centipede bit into his flesh like the stab of a fire-heated skewer, he told himself to remain calm, to breathe in through his left nostril, out through his right, in through his left nostril, out through his right . . .

Then the centipede scurried across his groin, its hundreds of legs tickling, its head moving from side to side as if it was looking for a second spot to bite. In the space between two heartbeats, Ryld nearly forgot how to breathe. He felt his heart begin to race, while instinct screamed at him to leap to his feet, to brush the foul insect away.

Then he remembered his life before Melee-Magthere—his life in the Stenchstreets, and the time, years before, when the nobles had come on their hunt. He was only six years old then, but he remembered lying there, blistered from the fireball that had left corpses strewn all around him. In order to survive, he'd been forced to lie utterly still, to play dead while the hunters claimed their trophies: teeth, ears, and occasionally an entire head. Ryld had learned then to control his breathing, to make it shallow and slow, inaudible above the sawing of blades through flesh. Thankfully, they did not deem any parts of a small, scrawny boy worth taking.

Remembering that trial, he found the strength to ignore the tickle of the centipede and its second painful bite.

When the ordeal was over, the masters nodded, silently acknowledging the fortitude of Ryld and the other five students who had passed the test. Ryld had been almost unable to walk for an entire tenday afterward.

Lying in the forest, riding the waves of the war between the belladonna and the disease, Ryld used what he'd learned that day. Focusing on his breathing, on the drawing in of air, the slow filling of his lungs, and the slow exhalation that followed, he slowed his racing pulse. He drove the heat from his skin, imagining it flowing from him with each breath. Slowly, his body returned to normal, and he shivered.

His eyes, however, continued to see the fantastic images the belladonna had limned on the world. The trees remained gray-white against a sky studded with impossibly bright stars. The moon, trailing brighter stars in its wake, hurt to even glance at. Wavering shadows danced in the forest. One of those shadows stepped out from the others and coalesced into the form of a woman.

"Halisstra . . ." Ryld breathed, then he saw that he was mistaken.

The woman was a drow but was not Halisstra Melarn. She was naked, her white hair hanging well past her hips. As she moved closer to Ryld, his fevered eyes saw that her skin was covered in evening dew. Drops of it covered her body, sparkling in the moonlight like stars against the sky-black of her skin.

She stood before him a moment, staring down with eyes that reflected the light like twin crescent moons. Then she touched the hilt of the sword he'd accidentally speared into the earth. Slender fingers traced a lazy circle around the leather-wrapped hilt. To Ryld's eyes the fingers looked as if they were dancing. Her lips parted, but instead of speech Ryld heard the notes of a flute. Its tune was somehow both welcoming and harsh at the same time, as if the flautist was of two minds about what tune to play and was able to play both at once. All the while, the woman stared deeply into Ryld's eyes, as if she was trying to see into his soul. Her hand closed around the hilt of the sword.

Something crackled in the forest. Startled, the woman looked up, just as a small black wolf burst from the underbrush. Teeth bared, snarling, it leaped for her chest. When it struck, the woman exploded into a million motes of starlight. The wolf continued its leap as if she had never been there. *Watching* it disappear into the forest once more, Ryld confirmed his earlier thought. It was all just an hallucination. The woman, the wolf . . . neither were truly there.

Something warm and moist nuzzled his ear. It was a nose. Then a warm, furry body lay down next to him. A tongue licked his cheek, and dark eyes stared into his.

Ryld didn't move and didn't speak. Instead he continued to concentrate on his breathing, forcing the last of the belladonna's poison from his body with each slow breath.

Eventually, he fell into Reverie.

When he became aware of his surroundings once more, it was daylight. He heard a crackling noise and smelled roasting meat, and rolled over to see Yarno squatting beside a small fire. The boy was holding a stick on which had been impaled the body of a small, four-legged animal. It had been gutted and neatly skewered, but Ryld could identify it by the tail. It was a rat. Yarno lifted the stick from the flames.

"You'll need strength," he said. "Eat."

Ryld sat up, shaking away the last of his lethargy. Rising to his feet, he moved his shoulders, his arms, his fingers. All were in working order; the poison was gone from his body. He squatted and accepted the rat.

"Thank you," he said. "I haven't eaten rat since I was a child."

Yarno studied him through narrowed eyes. Ryld realized the boy was trying to decide if he was being mocked. Ryld smiled and bit into the fire-seared meat, chewing it with gusto.

Yarno flicked back the lock of black hair that hung across his forehead and smiled.

"It's good, isn't it?" asked the boy.

"It is indeed," Ryld answered, wiping grease from the corner of his mouth with the back of his hand.

Yarno stood and scuffed soil over the fire with a dirty foot, turning his back to the fire and scraping the ground like a dog.

"Grandfather is feeling better now," he told Ryld.

"My masters taught me well," Ryld answered. "That—and I've had lots of practice binding wounds." He eyed the smudges of dirt that covered Yarno's pale, naked body, then added, "The first thing you need to do with a wound is clean it with hot water, as I did for your grandfather. Then bind it in a clean, boiled cloth. Remember that—it could save your life someday."

"I'll remember," the boy said.

Ryld wrinkled his nose, doubting it. Yarno seemed to attract dirt like a gutter attracted night soil. And he had fleas—as Ryld found out to his disgust a moment later when he felt the needle-sharp twinge of one of the vermin biting his chest. His memory of the werewolf sleeping beside him must have been accurate. How much else of the past night had also been real—and how much hallucination?

Ryld rose to his feet and glanced around at the forest floor. Aside from the paw prints of a small wolf and the footprints of a barefoot boy, he could see no other tracks.

"Yarno," he asked, "when you found me last night, was there a woman standing next to me?"

Yarno shrugged.

"What did you leap at?"

Yarno stared at the ground.

"I don't remember," he answered finally, shrugging again. "I never do."

Ryld nodded, understanding. Driven into a frenzy by the light of the full moon, the boy hadn't been in control of his actions—or his mind. Strange, then, that he had sought Ryld out and protected him—his bloodlust should have caused him to tear Ryld's throat out, instead. Perhaps the stench of belladonna had driven him back—but why then did Ryld remember the boy lying beside him, keeping him warm throughout the night?

He drew his short sword from the ground, cleaned the mud from its tip, then re-sheathed it.

"Which way is the temple?" Ryld asked.

Yarno pointed, then met Ryld's eye in what the weapons master would have taken as a challenge, had the boy been a trained swordsman.

"What will you do when you reach it?" Yarno asked.

"Rescue Halisstra," Ryld said. His eyes narrowed, and he added, "If she's still alive."

"And if she isn't?" Yarno asked. "Will you kill the priestesses to avenge her death?"

Ryld considered that for a moment, then smiled grimly.

"As many as I can, before I'm slain myself," he said.

"Good," Yarno said.

The boy's head lifted as if he'd heard something. He stared in the direction in which he'd just pointed.

Ryld, too, could hear it: the blare of a dozen or more hunting horns, muffled by distance, coming from the direction of the temple.

"I'd better get back," Yarno said, eyes wide with fear. "Grandfather needs me."

The boy shifted into wolf form and fled into the forest.

Ryld turned, and hurried the other way—toward the sound. As he wove his way between the trees, roughly shouldering branches aside in his haste, a single thought echoed in his mind.

SEVENTEEN

Danifae followed Pharaun through the round doorway in the side of the stalagmite, into a corridor that spiraled upward. The water she swam through was fouled by the slime of the aboleth that led them. Danifae could taste it each time she inhaled. A second aboleth followed close behind her, crowding her forward.

The corridor through which they swam was grayish pink and as shiny as the surface of a pearl. Deep lines were carved into it, revealing the dark gray stone underneath. Most were spirals or wavy lines. Danifae glanced at them, wondering if they were a form of written language. Then she remembered that the aboleth had no need for written texts. Whatever knowledge their minds contained was passed on to future generations when their hatchlings swarmed over them, tearing them to pieces.

She smiled ruefully, sorry that Lolth hadn't given the drow the ability to consume knowledge in that way. Still, there were other ways to find out what one needed to know. . . .

The corridor wound past several round doorways, then opened at last on a room that must have been near the stalagmite's core. Swimming into it, Danifae halted near Pharaun, letting the weight of her chain mail pull her to a standing position on the curved floor. The aboleth that had been following her swam into the room behind her and hovered in the water just close enough that it could reach her with its tentacles, if it chose. Danifae saw that the first aboleth had taken up a similar position on the other side of Pharaun.

On the far side of the chamber, enthroned within a niche in the wall, was an aboleth Danifae guessed was Oothoon. The creature rested on what looked like a nest of spongy kelp, occasionally using a tentacle to rip off a chunk and stuff it into the mouth in its belly. Its bluish-green, rubbery skin was dotted with white patches of freshwater barnacles, and its belly was a darker pink than those of the two that had accompanied Danifae and Pharaun into the room. Danifae searched in vain for a clue as to the thing's sex but found none—she thought perhaps the creature was male and female in one—though the others had referred to Oothoon as the aboleths' "matriarch."

She felt a tickle against her scalp, and an instant later a sparkle of magic crackled through the water, pushing the tickle back as the protective spell Pharaun had cast earlier was triggered. Danifae glanced at the mage out of the corner of her eye and saw him nod slightly. His boast had proved true. His magic was strong enough to keep the aboleth's mind probing at bay.

Oothoon stirred, rising slightly from the kelp nest. A chunk of something that had been trapped under the aboleth's massive body—it looked like fresh meat but left a smudge of green in the water rather than red—swirled in the current and floated gently to the floor. Aboleth flesh, Danifae decided, noting its mottled skin.

Ignoring it, Oothoon let one of her tentacles drift out toward Pharaun to hover a mere hand's breadth from his face. Another moved toward Danifae.

Pharaun's hand drifted slightly behind his back, where Oothoon wouldn't see it.

Steady, he signed.

Danifae stared at the taunting tentacle, tasting the rancid-grease odor that clouded the water around it. Fearing that even that slight exposure to it might transform her, she held her breath, not wanting to breathe the clouded water in. After a moment, Oothoon withdrew first the tentacle that was menacing Pharaun—then, when Danifae began to see spots before her eyes and was at last forced to inhale, the second tentacle. The creature's three eyes narrowed in what Danifae took to be a catlike smile.

"Why have you come?" Oothoon asked in a voice like rumbling bubbles.

Danifae let Pharaun do the talking. The mage used the drow silent speech, which Oothoon seemed to understand. The aboleth matriarch must have consumed a drow or two at some point in the past.

Centuries ago, a demon ship visited your city, Pharaun began. *After it left Zanhoriloch, it was caught in a storm and was lost on this plane. We are searching for it.*

"Why?"

Our leader, a powerful priestess of Lolth, wishes to find it. She wants to use it to sail to the Abyss, to meet her goddess.

Danifae glanced out of the corner of her eye at Pharaun, a frown starting to form on her brow. Quenthel had specifically ordered Pharaun to say nothing of herself—or of their quest. Was he telling the aboleth all that just to spite her?

No, Danifae thought, her eyes narrowing as she surveyed the mage. Pharaun knew better than that. He was up to something.

Once again, Oothoon's answer was a question: "Why does your leader wish to do this?"

Pharaun's expression grew troubled, and he replied, *She wants to consume Lolth.*

All four of Oothoon's tentacles began twitching at once. So too did the tentacles of their guards. Shared surprise, perhaps? Or humor at so audacious a statement? Danifae didn't let her mind dwell on the question. Instead she stared at Pharaun, wondering what he'd say next. He caught her eye and held it a moment in a silent warning to say nothing.

"Your leader is a fool," Oothoon said at last. "Her goddess will devour her, instead."

Our leader is no inexperienced novice but a most high-ranking priestess, Pharaun answered. *She knows a spell that makes it possible for her to slay a god. Any god.*

Hearing that outrageous lie, Danifae had to struggle to keep her face composed. Whatever mad scheme Pharaun was playing at, she didn't want to spoil it. He'd been crafty in his dealings with the demon Belshazu, after all. He was obviously up to more of the same.

"Who is this leader of yours?" Oothoon asked.

But when Pharaun began to spell out a word—*Q-u-e-n*—Danifae felt compelled to give the mage a warning nudge, disguising it as a swimming motion.

Don't! she signed, making the motion between strokes of her hand.

The mage continued as if he hadn't seen it.

—*t-h-e-l.*

"Quenthel," the aboleth said, repeating it aloud, then smacking her lips as if the sound itself tasted sweet. Her three eyes blinked rapidly. "I have never heard of her."

I'm not surprised, Pharaun answered. *We've come from a city of the Underdark that is many leagues from here.*

"Menzoberranzan?"

Danifae looked up at Oothoon in surprise and signed, *You've heard of it?*

"The one who escaped from the cage told Jooran the name."

And that aboleth reported it to you, Pharaun concluded, cutting Danifae off before she could question Oothoon further.

"Yes. I found it within Jooran's mind when I ate him."

Danifae shivered, wondering if Oothoon made a habit of eating everyone who came to the throne room. She let her hand drift down toward the morningstar that hung from her belt. If the aboleth made a lunge at her with its tentacles, she'd use her weapon's magic to beat them back. Then she reconsidered and let her hand fall from the mace. The fact that they'd been allowed to enter the aboleth matriarch's throne room with their weapons wasn't very reassuring. The aboleth obviously didn't fear magical weapons—or even Pharaun's magic, when it came to that.

A brief shiver of apprehension swept through Danifae. Was she going to get out of there alive? She realized she was depending upon Pharaun, and she despised herself for it.

Pharaun was signing again. Danifae had been distracted and so just caught the end of it.

. . . tell us where it lies, and I'll arrange for you to meet Quenthel, the mage told Oothoon.

The aboleth matriarch's three eyes blinked rapidly.

"To what purpose?" she asked.

Pharaun nudged the piece of aboleth flesh with his toe, then glanced up.

To eat her, he said bluntly.

Danifae's eyes narrowed. She hoped Pharaun was bluffing. Oothoon's tentacles writhed.

"Eat a drow priestess powerful enough to slay a god?" the aboleth asked in a voice that burbled with mirth. "You mock me!"

Not at all, Pharaun answered. *Quenthel's spells are strong, but each takes a long time to cast. She is weak, physically—as weak as any other drow. Knowing this, she keeps a half-demon at her side at all times for protection. If she can be separated from this demon—perhaps by some trick—she will be unable to defend herself. The magical items she carries are paltry ones: her only dangerous weapons are her hammer—which is magical and can smite at a distance—and her snake-headed whip, whose vipers have a poisonous bite.*

Danifae looked on in shock, astounded by Pharaun's audacity. He'd just told the aboleth everything she needed to defeat Quenthel. The only detail he'd left out was the fact that Quenthel no longer had access to Lolth's magic. He'd baited his hook with Quenthel's supposed god-slaying capabilities, and Oothoon, anticipating the acquisition of such a spell, was practically salivating as a result. Strangest of all, the mage had done it all in Danifae's presence. Did he realize that she would betray him to Quenthel—was he counting on it? Perhaps there was a deeper game the mage was playing at. . . .

Danifae shook her head. There was no guessing the mind of a man who had matched wits with a demon and won. She made a quick hand gesture, the sign that indicated she wanted to speak to him in private.

Pharaun frowned, then turned and addressed Oothoon.

The spell sustaining my companion is waning, he told the aboleth. *To recast it, I need to hold her hand for a moment. The spell will conjure up a small black cloud around our hands. Do not be alarmed by it, for it is harmless. Do I have your permission to proceed?*

The aboleth's three eyes narrowed—an expression the creature had doubtless picked up from the drow.

"You may."

The two guards tensed, watching Pharaun closely as he took both of Danifae's hands in his. A moment later, a sphere of darkness just large enough to cover their hands appeared and Danifae switched to finger-speech. With a rapid series of taps, she spelled out words against his palm.

Do you seriously intend to sacrifice Quenthel?

The fate of Menzoberranzan hangs in the balance, Pharaun tapped back. *I'm sure Matron Mother Baenre would consider it a worthy sacrifice. If she was in my place, she would do the same.*

Danifae could hardly argue with that logic. Instead she turned to a more pressing matter: herself.

You're asking me to take your side. To betray a priestess of my own faith. Why should I? I care nothing about Menzoberranzan.

What of Eryndlyn? Pharaun asked.

What of it? her fingers tapped back.

Would you like to return to it, one day?

That made Danifae pause.

I have visited Eryndlyn more than once, Pharaun tapped. *I know the plaza that surrounds the Five Pillars very well. With a simple incantation, I could send you there.*

There is nothing left for me in Eryndlyn, she replied. *No House, no family.*

Then where else?

Danifae was quick to catch on.

Quenthel would never permit it, she tapped out. *Not after losing Halisstra . . . and Ryld.*

No, Pharaun signed, shaking his head. *She would not—but I would. So the question remains, if not Eryndlyn—and certainly not Ched Nasad—where would you like to go? Llacerellyn? Sschindylryn?*

Despite herself, Danifae gasped. Sschindylryn was a city known for its many portals and known to Danifae as the adopted home of perhaps the only drow in all the Underdark who might be able to help her, who might be able to undo the spell that bound her to Halisstra. If indeed he could . . .

Seeing that Pharaun was studying her face—and irritated at herself for betraying her thoughts—Danifae composed herself.

For a moment, she'd almost believed him, but she knew better than to allow herself to hope. In her experience, promises—especially those made by a fellow drow—were seldom kept.

Still, there was a chance. During the fall of Ched Nasad, Pharaun had risked his life to rescue her. Danifae was still trying to puzzle out why. What advantage had that gained him? Maybe the rescue had simply been an impulse, a product of lust. That emotion might have been driving him still.

Had the moment come to switch her allegiance from Quenthel to Pharaun? Danifae turned the thought over in her mind. She'd cultivated an alliance with Quenthel because finding out what had happened to Lolth offered a chance to regain her magic, perhaps even to gain special favor from the dark goddess herself. Quenthel was the highest ranking drow among the Menzoberranyr, and if Danifae was doomed to serve, she preferred serving at the highest level possible. To be a battle-captive was one thing, to be the servant of a Houseless refugee from a crumbled city was another. Danifae's serving Quenthel had stymied Halisstra. The First Daughter of House Melarn could have killed Danifae on a whim, but once her battle-captive became Quenthel's plaything, Halisstra would be answerable to the Mistress of Arach-Tinilith.

After so many years of demurely bowing and murmuring acquiescence to others, Danifae was finally able to choose her own path, finally able to *act*—but she was far from free. There was still the Binding. She could still feel that unbreakable connection to Halisstra Melarn.

Quenthel was a powerful ally, and if Danifae played her *sava* pieces correctly, she might even wind up at Quenthel's right hand ... *if* the quest to find Lolth succeeded. Of which, given their lack of success so far, Danifae was less than certain.

But in Sschindylryn, if the old mage was still alive, she could be free at last. Free to—what? Where would she go? Even assuming Eryndlyn hadn't suffered the same fate as Ched Nasad, there was nothing left for her there. She could go to Menzoberranzan or some other city, but as what? A free drow, but one without alliances, without a House to protect her. But if she had a sponsor, a matron ... someone like Quenthel Baenre, for instance ... she might find a home at Arach-Tinilith. ...

Danifae decided to play her pieces carefully, starting with a lie.

I'll do it, she signed. *Quenthel will hear nothing of this from me. But make certain, first, that they really do know where the ship is—and that it's still seaworthy.*

Pharaun smiled and inclined his chin slightly in a token bow. Then he dispelled the globe of darkness, dropped Danifae's hand, and turned back to Oothoon.

Well? he asked. *Have you decided to accept my offer?*

The aboleth matriarch flicked a tentacle and said, "Give me Quenthel, and I will tell you where the ship of chaos is."

Danifae raised an eyebrow. Seeing it, Pharaun gave a slight nod. He'd obviously realized the same thing she had, they'd come looking for a ship, but neither one of them had mentioned precisely what sort of ship. Still, there was a chance that Valas might have done so.

Describe it, Pharaun signed. *Convince us that you know about it.*

The aboleth closed its eyes, as if calling up a distant memory.

"It was made of bone and moved upon the surface of the lake. The creatures that inhabited it were shaped as you are and seemed alive but were pale and bloated, and tasted of death—and of insects. The one that she-who-spawned-my-mothers consumed was infested with white, wriggling things."

Maggots, Pharaun signed, his face showing none of the revulsion that Danifae was certain was written plain across her own face.

"Yes. An uncomfortable experience—especially when the creature disincorporated into acidic vapor within her stomach. She-who-spawned-my-mothers nearly died and would not willingly eat one of those creatures again, had its mind held the secrets of the gods themselves."

Danifae seized upon that important point.

When did your ancestor consume the mane? she asked. *When the ship first visited your city—or after it was lost?*

"After," Oothoon answered. "The foolish creature came swimming back here when its captain was overcome."

Describe the captain, Pharaun signed.

"It was a land creature, with two walking legs and two holding legs," Oothoon answered, "and a long tail that constantly moved, like a strand of kelp in a shifting current. Its body was without hair, except for its snout. The demon's face resembled that of the tiny land creatures that scurry through the caverns, with a snout that was always tasting the air."

An uridezu, Pharaun signed, with a knowing look at Danifae. *Just as Belshazu told us.*

Valas could have mentioned that detail to the aboleth, Danifae signed quickly.

Pharaun shook his head and replied, *Valas doesn't know one demon from another. He wouldn't recognize an uridezu if one was staring him in the face, nor would he remember a demonic species Belshazu mentioned only in passing. Oothoon is telling the truth. Her ancestor did indeed consume the mane—and with it, knowledge of where the ship foundered.*

To Oothoon, he signed, *We know that the ship was lost in a storm. Was it destroyed?*

"When the mane swam away from the ship, it was still whole," Oothoon answered. "The storm immobilized it and killed the crew but did not damage the ship itself."

Danifae snorted. As if the aboleth matriarch would give them any other answer, after Pharaun had revealed their plans to raise the ship and sail it again.

And what of the demon? Pharaun asked.

"It, too, was immobilized by the storm."

The mage thought for a moment, then nodded, seemingly satisfied with Oothoon's replies.

Very well, he signed. *Tell me where the ship lies, and I will arrange for Quenthel to come to you.*

"No," Oothoon answered, glowering—and for a frightening moment, Danifae thought that the bargain was off, that the aboleth had decided to eat them, instead. "You will give me the priestess—and after I have consumed her, I will tell you the location of the ship."

Danifae snorted. Impasse. But to her astonishment, Pharaun nodded.

I accept, he told the aboleth.

As Oothoon gurgled in delight, the two guards nudged Pharaun and Danifae from the room. The audience was at an end.

Gromph was surprised by the contents of the thought bottle. He could hear the gurgle of fluid, but what slid over his tongue felt like fine sand. As he swallowed it, a curious taste filled his mouth—a strange blend of ancient, desiccated insect and the sharp tang of ground amber.

Memories burst into his mind with the suddenness of spores exploding from an overripe fungus. Included among them was a spell—one that needed no verbal component, merely a somatic one: the act of swallowing the last of the bottle's contents.

The illithid, sensing that something was wrong, leaped forward, one misshapen hand lashing out, but it was already too late. The last of the bottle's contents slid across Gromph's tongue and was swallowed, triggering the spell. A ripple of magical energy passed through the room quicker than thought, leaving Sluuguth frozen, eyes bulging in fury, tentacles halted in mid-lash a finger's breadth from Gromph's face. The thought bottle hung in mid-air where it had been knocked, and the duergar axe the illithid had been carrying was frozen between Sluuguth's outstretched hand and the ground. He'd dropped it in surprise the instant Gromph's thoughts told him what was about to happen.

Gromph stood up, steadying himself with one hand on his desk as the room blurred slightly. Unsticking oneself in time was always disorienting. He felt dizzy, slightly off balance, as if the world was solid but he was not.

With his memories restored, all was clear to him.

So *that* was why I erased everything but a single memory, the archmage thought, that I should offer these bottles to any creature who could dominate my mind.

It wasn't because he hoped to trick the creature into drinking their contents but because he expected it to read that thought and make him drink from one of the bottles first, as a safety precaution.

Just as Sluuguth had done.

Gromph wasted no time basking in his foresight, however. He had to move quickly. The time-stopping spell was a powerful one, but it was brief. It would hold for no more than a few heartbeats. Bending swiftly, he picked up the battle-axe.

After a slight tug—inertia made the weapon feel as though it was stuck in mud—Gromph grasped the axe firmly in both hands and swung. Its blade bit cleanly through the illithid's neck, severing it with a single stroke. Pulled by the blade, blood bulged at the exit wound, but the head itself remained on the shoulders.

As Gromph laid the weapon on his desk, the spell ended and time lurched forward again. Blood sprayed against the wall, Sluuguth's head flew from his body, and the illithid crumpled in a heap. An instant later, the thought bottle thumped against the wall and clattered to the floor.

Looking down into the blade of the axe, Gromph saw a frenzied swirling as the enchanted blade added Sluuguth's soul to those it had already stolen. The illithid's face stared out in horror from the flat of the blade, tentacles lashing. Eventually it turned transparent and was gone.

"What a useful weapon," Gromph said, setting the duergar battle-axe down again. He chuckled. "Perhaps I should hang it on the wall as a souvenir."

Kneeling, he chanted the words to a spell and passed his hands over the corpse of the illithid. His palms tingled when they passed over the illithid's out-flung hand. The gold signet ring on Sluuguth's middle finger was magical, imbued with protective enchantments. He slipped it off the illithid's finger and laid it on his desk.

His hands tingled a second time as they passed over an elongated leather carrying case that hung at Sluuguth's belt. Opening it, Gromph saw a tube inside. He eased out the tube—a length of hollow bone with a plug of wood at either end—and shook it. He heard the rustle of paper. Scrolls, perhaps? He would study them later, after taking the appropriate precautions.

Laying the tube down beside the ring, he completed his pass over the illithid's body. One of the pockets in Sluuguth's robe made his palms tingle a third time. Reaching inside it, Gromph pulled out a finger-length piece of quartz that had been cut into a prism. Tiny yellow sparks danced in its depths.

Gromph had seen similar devices before. They were magical constructs of the surface elves, who needed light to find their way through the Underdark. He spoke a word in their tongue—the surface elves were so predictable and almost always used the same command words—and the prism reacted as he expected it to, shedding a pale cone of candle-bright light. A second command word shaped the light into an eye-hurting, wand-thin beam of intensely white light. Had it not struck the wall of Gromph's office, it would have shone for some distance.

Squeezing his eyes shut against the glare, Gromph spoke a third command word, and the harsh light disappeared. The prism was as it had been before, still cool as stone against Gromph's palm.

"A useful trinket," he said, slipping it into a pocket of his *piwafwi*. "Handy to read scrolls by, if nothing else."

He almost ended his search there, but when he passed his hands a final time over the illithid's corpse he felt the tingle once more. Something was tucked deep into the pocket he'd just pulled the prism from. Digging into it, he pulled out a silver chain with a flat oval of green jade hanging from it. He recognized it at once.

"So *that's* where the jade spiders disappeared to," he muttered, slipping it into his own pocket.

Standing again, Gromph used magic to levitate the illithid's head—no sense touching those limp, foul-smelling tentacles if he didn't have to—and positioned it on the chest of the corpse. Then he pulled a pinch of dust from a pocket of his *piwafwi* and sprinkled it over Sluuguth's body. He chanted a brief spell and pointed a finger. A harsh sizzling filled the air as a beam of green energy sprang from its tip. It washed over the corpse, illuminating it in a blaze of crackling light. An instant later, all that was left of Sluuguth was a thin smudge of dust on the floor.

Crossing the room, Gromph picked up the empty thought bottle. One of its sides was dented slightly, but the sigil-shaped pane of glass was still intact. It could be reused. He removed the dent with a mending spell, then set it on the table beside the second bottle and cast a minor spell that caused the spray of blood that had landed on the desk to dry to dark brown dust, which he blew away. He placed the unopened bottle carefully in the drawer, then picked up the one that had been uncorked.

He turned to the wall, and, with a wave of his fingers, released the fire elemental that Sluuguth's spell had frozen in place. The elemental rushed out with an angry roar, filling the room with heat.

"Wher*rr*e is he?" it said, flaring as it twisted this way and that, looking for the vanished illithid. "He must bu*rrr*n."

"The illithid is gone," Gromph answered.

The elemental flared white-hot with anger.

"You said I had only to bu*rrr*n an intruder to be free," it growled. It pointed at the soot-smudged spot on the wall where the magical sigil had been. "Am I then to be put back in bondage?"

Shielding his face from the heat, Gromph said, "No. Your task has been altered, that's all. After you perform it, you are free to go." He showed the elemental the thought bottle. "In a moment, I will use this magical device. When I am done, you will relay the following information to me . . ."

A few moments later, Gromph found himself seated behind his desk, holding a corked bottle in his hand. A drawer containing a bottle identical to it was open, and a fire elemental hovered on the other side of the desk. Glancing at the wall, Gromph saw that the sigil that had held it had been activated. An intruder must have entered the office—Gromph cast a quick detection spell, but his magic revealed no trace of any creature, living or undead. Whoever the intruder was, he or she had left a gold ring and what looked like a spell tube on Gromph's desk—and an impressive battle-axe, leaning against the side of the desk.

Suddenly worried, Gromph realized that the last thing he could remember was being trapped inside the sphere, floating on the lake. He had obviously made it back to Sorcere somehow, found his way into his study, and escaped the imprisonment spell. But how?

Gromph stared at the golden bottle he held in his hand—one of his thought bottles. The answer must be inside.

"Master*rr*," the fire elemental said, drawing his attention.

Gromph looked up.

"The Gracklstugh army, together with an army of tanarukk, a*rrr*e attacking Menzoberranzan," the elemental announced, a tongue of bright red flame licking out of its mouth as it spoke. "The due*rrr*gar have set up a siege wall just inside Tier Breche and are attacking Sorce*rrr*e. At least one illithid was among their number—a so*rrr*cerer by the name of Sluuguth. He had in his possession one of the amulets that cont*rrr*ols the jade spiders. You defeated him."

That said, the fire elemental gave a roar of triumph as the invisible magical bonds that had held it fell away. It disappeared as abruptly as a blown-out candle.

"An illithid," Gromph whispered.

That explained, then, why he held a thought bottle in his hand. A tickle of memory returned. He'd created the thing—and the bottle that matched it—for use in the event of his capture by a mind flayer. His plan had been to offer it to the creature . . .

There, the memory faded.

Shrugging, Gromph placed the bottle carefully in the drawer beside the other one and pushed the drawer shut.

"Sorcere is under attack?" he muttered. "We'll see about that."

Gromph strode toward the balcony where two of his students stood. They were Norulle, a fifth-year student who had used a hair-growth cantrip to cause a long, dwarflike beard to sprout from his chin—hardly an appropriate affectation, given whom they were fighting—and Prath, a first-year student who was still only in his thirties, and whose stocky build and bulging biceps should have caused his House to enroll him in Melee-Magthere, instead. Both had their backs to the corridor down which Gromph hurried and were sheltering behind the ghostly image of a turtle shell the size of a table that hung in the air, just in front of the balcony.

Norulle flinched as a hail of arrows struck it, most of them exploding to splinters as the spell destroyed them. One arrow, however, sparkled with arcane energy. It pierced the magical barrier and snagged the sleeve of Prath's *piwafwi*. Barely glancing at it, Prath yanked it free and cast it aside. A moment later, a trickle of blood dripped from his hand. He shook it away.

The boy should have been a soldier, indeed, Gromph thought.

From outside came the sounds of battle: the shouted orders of the duergar below; the creak-and-thump of catapults being winched and shot; the crackling, explosive hiss of magical energy; and the frantic chanting of mages, casting retaliatory spells from the balconies above and below.

"Norulle, Prath—what's happening?" Gromph asked as he strode out onto the balcony. "Where are your instructors?"

Norulle whirled around in surprise, a wand clutched in one hand.

"Master!" he gasped. "You're here!"

Diamond dust glittered in Norulle's hair and beard. Someone had cast a powerful protective spell upon him.

It was Prath who answered Gromph's question, "Leandran's gone. He was hit square on by magic fire."

He pointed at a spot farther along the balcony—a smoldering crater in the stone floor. Through a hole at the center of it, Gromph could see the ground below. Smaller craters, also still smoking, pitted the wall behind that spot like splash marks. Each was ringed by a circle of frost. The two students had obviously used a cold spell to extinguish the blaze. Of Leandran, the school's Master of Abjurative Magic, there was no trace, save for the lingering stench of burned flesh.

A whistling sound drew Gromph's attention. He glanced to the side just in time to see an enormous clay pot arc up toward Sorcere and strike the side of the stalagmite, several dozen paces away. It broke against the stone, splashing liquid fire in all directions. The fire poured down the stone, burning everything in its wake: stone walls, a decorative arch of wrought iron above the balcony, and the balcony itself.

Figures on the balcony scurried away from the rush of flame— one of them a little too slowly. As some of the stuff poured down onto his *piwafwi*, his agonized screams filled the air. They were cut off a moment later when the wrought-iron arch, weakened by the fire, collapsed with a loud squeal of metal. Above the spot where it had been mounted, the wall continued to burn, and the flames soon ate a hole through the stone.

Gromph stared in the direction from which the pot of fire had come, at the protective barrier the duergar had erected. It stood just in front of the tunnel that gave access to Tier Breche from the Dark Dominion. The barrier appeared to be made of square-hewn lengths of fungus stem, stacked horizontally on top of each other, but had obviously been magically strengthened. The lightning bolts that one of the mages on a balcony above fired down into them did little more than chip off tiny pieces of the fungus, and the hailstones raining down from the ice storm another mage had caused to materialize in the air just above the barrier were melting before they struck it.

Yet another mage of Sorcere sent a cloud of acid billowing down at the barrier. The yellowish vapor swept over the fungus-log blockade and continued on down the tunnel beyond it. The barrier remained intact, however, and clay pots continued to sail into the air from the catapults behind it, whistling through the air to blast the walls of Sorcere with alchemical flame.

It didn't look as though Arach-Tinilith was faring any better than Sorcere. The walls of the spider-shaped temple were also dotted with gouts of white-hot flame, and the ground in front of the building was strewn with corpses. Many were squat and bald—duergar—but many more were drow. Dark elf soldiers had given their lives in defense of the cavern. Of the priestesses, there was no sign. Like their goddess, they had retreated behind walls of stone, leaving others to do the fighting.

Farther back in the cavern, the third building of the Academy—the pyramid-shaped warrior training school Melee-Magthere—remained unscathed. The catapults could not reach that far, it seemed.

Norulle leaned over the balcony, directing his wand at the enemy. Pea-sized gobs of fire erupted from its tip, enlarging as they streaked toward the siege fortifications below. By the time they struck the fungus-log walls, they were several paces in diameter. Yet even though each exploded with a roar that was audible even over the chaos of battle, the walls remained firm.

Gromph's eyes narrowed. The seeming invulnerability of the wall he could understand—the duergar must have carried the lightweight, fungus-stem logs with them in preparation for their siege, then used a spell to turn them to stone once they were in place. What he could not understand was why the duergar behind the walls were still able to work their catapults despite the searing heat of Norulle's fireballs and the cloud of acidic vapor that had swept over them.

He watched as one of the senior students appeared suddenly on the field of battle below, just in front of the duergar barrier, and cast a spell Gromph himself taught—the great shout. A wave of noise crashed against the duergar positions, causing the logs that made up the fortification to visibly tremble.

But still the attack did not falter. Arrows erupted from slits in the wall, one of them striking the student through the belly just as he teleported away.

"Master," Prath shouted over the ringing in Gromph's ears, catching Gromph's attention at last. "Should we perhaps send a swarm of vermin against them? Insects—or perhaps rats?

Gromph was about to ridicule that suggestion, but stopped.

" 'Out of the mouths of novices,' " he instead quoted, following the familiar saying with a chuckle.

Prath stared at him in confusion, a spark of hope in his eye.

"Was that the right spell to suggest, Master?"

"No," Gromph answered, "but it's given me an idea. Continue the fight—and keep your head down."

Stepping back into the corridor down which he'd hurried a short time before, Gromph closed his eyes. It took only a moment to locate Kyorli. Pouring his awareness into his familiar, Gromph could feel legs swiftly running and whiskers twitching as they sniffed the stone across which the rat was running.

Kyorli, the archmage sent. *Where are you?*

Running. Running quick to Sorcere! But the way is blocked.

Gromph was able, with a bit of concentration, to see through the rat's eyes. Kyorli was running through a tunnel, weaving through a forest of moving feet. The feet belonged to duergar, who were working in pairs, dragging away the bodies of their fellow soldiers. Two duergar, carrying the corpse of a slain companion, ran into a side tunnel.

Kyorli, Gromph commanded. *That tunnel. Look inside.*

Kyorli scurried to the tunnel mouth and peered in. Seeing through her eyes, Gromph saw what he'd expected: a duergar wearing a gray, hooded mantle and carrying a staff set with an egg-sized gem with a deep crack running down its center, symbol of the god Laduguer. The cleric stood in front of a dozen bodies that had been heaped on the floor of the tunnel, waving his staff over them as he cast a spell. A moment later the bodies began to stir. As one, the dead soldiers—animated with a gruesome semblance of life—rose to their feet and filed out of the tunnel.

Follow them, Gromph ordered. *Watch where they go.*

Kyorli did, from a safe distance. The undead duergar marched in a jerking line toward the mouth of the main tunnel. Reaching it, they took up positions behind the siege wall, oblivious to yet another cloud of acidic vapor that boiled down from the cavern above, blistering their undead skin.

Gromph had to admit the duergar were clever. With Lolth's priestesses bereft of their magic there was no one to turn an undead army back—or seize control of it. Once the magical fire had done its work they would march, unmolested, on Sorcere, Melee-Magthere, and Arach-Tinilith—then Menzoberranzan proper. And the only mage powerful enough to stop them was imprisoned far beneath the city—or so their commanders thought.

The view through Kyorli's eyes shifted suddenly as the rat was forced to scurry out of the path of a running soldier.

That will do, Gromph told his familiar. *Find yourself a place to hide. You'll be able to join me in Sorcere soon enough.*

Returning his awareness to his own body, Gromph strode with confidence to the balcony. He pulled from his pocket a small piece of engraved bone, and held out his palm to the two students who turned toward him.

"I need a small piece of raw meat," he told them.

Norulle glanced around. "But Master, there is none here," he said.

Prath met Gromph's eye and slowly nodded. Drawing a dagger that had been hidden up a sleeve of his *piwafwi*, he placed his left hand on the rail of the balcony and sliced off the fleshy tip of his little finger. Picking up the bloody piece—and ignoring the grimace of his fellow student—he offered it to Gromph with his good hand.

Gromph smiled.

"Well done, apprentice," he told the boy. "You'll go far. What House are you, by the way?"

Prath smiled through his pain, clenching the stub of his severed finger against his palm to staunch the blood, and answered, "House Baenre, Master."

"Ah." Gromph had never met the lad before—he must have been a child of the lowest of the noble ranks.

Prath wasn't quick-witted—any other student might have used a spell to summon a minor creature into his hand, killed it, and offered Gromph its flesh, instead—but he was loyal. Gromph could use that.

Smearing the blood on the bit of bone, Gromph cast his spell. With a flick of his hand, he hurled it in the direction of the wall that hid the duergar positions.

Then he shouted his command: "Break off your attack. Turn and fight the duergar, instead!"

Spells continued to rain down upon the fungus-stem wall. It took the other mages several moments to realize that the catapults had stopped firing. Then the undead duergar soldiers turned their backs on the wall. With unsteady, mindless motions they trotted into the tunnel that led to the Dark Dominion, weapons in hand. A moment later, the clash of battle echoed out of the tunnel, as they engaged their still-living companions in mortal combat.

Seeing that, the remaining warriors of Melee-Magthere burst

out of their pyramid. Rushing forward with swords raised, they clambered over the siege wall and immediately began tearing both it and the catapults apart. Others picked up the stonefire bombs the undead duergar had left behind and heaved them into the tunnel.

Gromph smiled grimly as he watched. Eventually he turned and looked out beyond Tier Breche, at the city below. Despite the toehold the enemy had gained—and lost—in Tier Breche, Menzoberranzan seemed untouched by war. The stalactites and stalagmites of the noble manors still sparkled, and a ring of magical fire was creeping up the great spire of Narbondel. Gromph frowned, wondering which of the wizards of House Baenre had been keeping it going in his absence. It seemed that he was not quite as irreplaceable as he would have liked. He'd have to speak to Triel about that.

Then, after making his report to his matron mother, he would see what he could do to put an end to the siege.

NINETEEN

As a dozen priestesses raised horns to their lips to signal the start of the night's hunt, Halisstra felt a thrill rush through her body. Part of it was a shiver. The wind was picking up, and a few flakes of snow had started to fall. Like the others, she wore nothing save for a heavy silver chain around her waist, hung with the silver disk that bore the symbol of Eilistraee.

Tipping her head back, she raised the hunting horn they'd given her to her lips, staring past it at the moon. She drew a deep breath and blew, adding her horn's strident voice to the others. There was an urgent rush of raw sound as each of the horns found its own note, then held it in perfect harmony with the others. The very air shivered and for several heartbeats was still. Then the wind resumed, stirring the tree branches overhead.

As if the goddess had given her a signal, Halisstra suddenly cut short her note at precisely the same moment that the other women did. She lowered her horn and stared expectantly as the leader of the hunt—Uluyara, the drow who had killed the troll the previous night—drew from the ground the sword they had been dancing around a moment before. Holding it straight out in front of her, the high priestess slowly turned in place.

Like Uluyara, Halisstra's only weapon was a sword, Seyll's long sword. Her hand gripped its hilt tightly, covering all but one of the holes. Through that single hole the wind blew, producing a faint, insistent note.

Feliane, who had stayed close to Halisstra throughout the dance, caught her eye.

"Use it well," she said, nodding at the songsword. The moon elf had dyed her skin black, once again, in preparation for the night's hunt. Too small and innocent looking to ever be taken for a drow at close range—especially with her brown hair—Feliane nonetheless gripped her own sword like someone who knew how to wield it.

"What do we hunt?" Halisstra whispered.

"Whatever monster Eilistraee causes to cross our path," Feliane answered, an enigmatic smile on her lips.

Uluyara began to spin faster. Her sword flashed in the moonlight as she whirled in tight circles: once, twice, three times . . . then she jerked to a halt, her blade quivering.

"This way!" she shouted.

Like a hunting lizard suddenly unleashed, she sprinted into the woods.

A rush of excitement swept through Halisstra as she leaped to follow the high priestess. All of the other priestesses did the same, and just behind her, Halisstra could see Feliane running swiftly, her eyes eager and bright. Urged on by an emotion that was part elation, part lust for the hunt, Halisstra wove through the trees, leaping over snow-dappled logs and clumps of fern, and shouldering her way through branches whose pine needles slapped her skin. She ran, following the others, and plunged after them down a gully. She splashed through a wide stream at the bottom of it, slipping on the ice that crusted the river stones under her feet. Then she was scrambling up the far bank, fighting to keep her balance as she climbed the steep slope with a sword in one hand and a horn in the other.

At the top she paused, uncertain which way to go. She could no longer hear the other priestesses in the forest ahead. The only sound was the noise of Feliane scrambling up the slope behind her. Then she heard a horn, coming from a distance and to her right.

"That's Uluyara," Feliane gasped. "She's found it."

Halisstra didn't stop to ask what the high priestess had found. Panting, sweating even though the air was cold, she plunged on into the forest, running in the direction from which the sound had come. As she ran, she noted to her disgust that, unlike her, Feliane wasn't even breathing hard. Like the other priestesses, Feliane was swift and sure of her footing on the snowy ground. Halisstra, accustomed to a noble's life in a city where one strolled along smooth streets and levitated from one avenue to the next, had never had cause to run and climb so hard or for so long.

This must be the "trial" Feliane had spoken of when I was lifted from the cave, Halisstra thought. That's why she's holding herself back, watching my every move.

Determined not to show herself to be wanting, aware that Eilistraee herself might be watching, Halisstra ran on, ignoring the pain that was pinching her side like a centipede's jaws.

At least the moon provided ample light to run by—to Halisstra, accustomed to the Underdark, the forest appeared brilliantly lit. But the trees were thick, the spaces between them filled with low bushes and ferns. Halisstra had long since lost sight of all the priestesses save Feliane. When Uluyara's horn sounded a second time, immediately in front of Halisstra, the closeness of it surprised her. An instant later, Halisstra burst through a tangle of tree branches that felt strangely sticky, into a moonlit clearing.

She spotted Uluyara, hunting horn still raised to pursed lips, but she could see none of the other priestesses. Nor could she hear them. Lowering the horn, Uluyara pointed at the far side of the clearing, then she backed slowly into the woods. Tree branches closed after her like curtains.

Halisstra stared in the direction in which Uluyara had pointed, but she saw only forest.

She turned to where Feliane should have been and began to ask, "What do I . . ."

Her voice trailed off as she discovered that Feliane, too, was nowhere to be seen. There was nothing behind Halisstra but tree branches, sighing against one another in the wind. As it blew across the clearing from the direction in which Uluyara had pointed, the breeze carried a familiar, musky smell.

Whirling back to face the clearing, Halisstra raised her sword—and not an instant too soon. In front of her crouched an enormous spider, easily half again as tall as she was. Its body was a mottled gray and black—perfect camouflage in the moonlight-dappled wood. Glossy black eyes reflected the moon as the creature reared up, jaws dripping venom.

For the space of a heartbeat Halisstra stared up at the spider, uncertainty making her sword waver. Years of subservience to Lolth screamed at her to throw her weapon to the ground, to grovel before the holy creature and selflessly offer unto it whatever Lolth would claim.

"A hungry spider must feed," was one of the first things she had been taught after being accepted as a novice at Lolth's temple.

"Give yourself to it joyfully, for in the end Lolth will consume us all. Better to suffer the torments of the flesh now than to face the wrath of the goddess later."

Lolth would surely have punished a priestess—especially one who had spurned her as Halisstra had—for so grave a transgression. But Lolth was dead. Or at the very least, not watching.

The moonlight reflected in the spider's eyes reminded Halisstra of one thing more: Eilistraee was watching. Or at the very least, she might have been. Halisstra smiled grimly, suddenly realizing why Uluyara and Feliane had disappeared.

The spider was her trial.

As the spider lunged down at her, Halisstra swung her sword with all her strength. Flashing in the moonlight, the sword described a clean arc, its blade exactly in line with the spider's bulging eyes. But instead of connecting with the meaty *thunk* Halisstra had expected, the sword continued to whistle through the air until it slammed into the ground. The spider had suddenly disappeared. Thrown off balance, Halisstra pitched forward. She managed to land on her knees and one hand by dropping the hunting horn. An instant later the spider reappeared—directly above her.

Halisstra rolled onto her back, swinging the sword into an upright position as she did, then she thrust upward at the belly of the spider. Just as it had done the first time, it disappeared.

"Goddess help me," Halisstra groaned. "A phase spider."

There was no way to predict where the spider would appear next—but at least for the moment, it was safely in the Ethereal.

Halisstra rolled violently to one side across the snowy ground, praying that she'd chosen correctly—that the spider was moving in the other direction, its ethereal legs passing right through her.

Halisstra's guess had been a lucky one. The phase spider

re-entered the material plane a pace or two away, allowing her the briefest instant in which to spring to her feet. Then it rushed forward again.

Grimly, Halisstra turned to meet it, knowing that she was in a fight she could not win—not even with Seyll's magic sword. All the spider had to do was wait her out, slipping into ethereal form each time she attacked, then skittering invisibly away to reappear somewhere else a moment later. One of those times Halisstra would guess wrong and it would wind up behind her. Unseen, it would inject its deadly poison and take its time as it sucked her dry.

There was, however, one thing she could fall back on: her *bae'qeshel* magic. Her voice shaking slightly, she chanted a song. It should have charmed the spider, rooting it to the spot in fascination, but nothing happened. The spider appeared, attacked, then disappeared again, forcing Halisstra to constantly whirl and defend herself with her sword. She cursed her luck, under her breath. Had she mispronounced a word—or were phase spiders simply resistant to the form of enchantment she'd attempted?

Dodging the spider once more she slipped on a patch of snowy ground and fell. The spider stepped on her sword, forcing Halisstra to release the weapon and roll to the side to avoid its jaws. When the spider disappeared once more, she sprang to her feet and snatched the songsword up again. To her dismay, she saw that the tip of the blade had been snapped off, rendering the blade useless as a thrusting weapon. But perhaps there was still hope.

Remembering how she'd used the songsword to augment the spell that had knocked the stirges from the sky, she quickly reversed the weapon and raised the hilt to her lips. The spell might not be enough to stun a creature as large as the phase spider, but at least she could try. Her fingers found the same holes that they had before, and she blew—hard and long, expecting the same shrill note—but nothing happened. The only sound the hilt-flute emitted was a sour *phht*. Slushy mud sprayed out of the hole.

Once again, the spider lunged, and Halisstra leaped away—but more clumsily. Frightened, she realized that she was tiring. The long sword felt heavy in her hand, its hilt gritty in her sweating palm. The next time the spider lunged forward, Halisstra was barely able to twist aside. Its jaws caught and held Eilistraee's symbol, yanking on the disk and pulling the chain tight around Halisstra's waist. Dragged forward, she flailed at the spider with her sword. Then the spider became ethereal once more, allowing her to stagger back.

If only she still had her clerical magic, she could have blasted the creature with a column of flame or held it at bay with a wall of wind. But those spells, like the charm she'd already tried, would in all likelihood also have failed. Lolth would hardly have granted one of her priestesses the power to kill one of her beloved, arachnid children, after all.

Eilistraee, however, would kill a spider without the slightest qualm. And if indeed the goddess was watching the battle—as Uluyara and Feliane almost certainly were—she just might grant her most recent convert the magic she needed to save her own life by restoring her spells to her.

Swept up in that revelation, that hope, Halisstra nearly missed spotting the phase spider when it re-appeared suddenly on a tree branch above her and dropped silently down in a direct line with her head. Only the slight creak of the branch warned her.

Just in time she threw herself to the side. Halisstra scrambled across the ground on hands and knees, dragging her sword behind her, then struggled to her feet again.

The spider, sensing that she was tiring, walked slowly across the clearing toward her, taking its time. Venom dripped onto the ground between its feet as its jaws opened and shut, anticipating the meal it would soon have.

Knowing it might be her only chance, Halisstra grasped the hilt of Seyll's sword in both hands and raised it above her head—not in preparation to swing it but instead to point it at the moon.

"Eilistraee, hear me!" she cried. "From this night on, I forsake Lolth and swear to be your humble servant. If you deem me worthy, I beseech you. Will you have me? If so, give me the magic I need to prove the truth of my words by slaying this symbol of Lolth. Give me the power to cast spells in your name—and to your everlasting glory!"

Her words rang out with the power and clarity of a song that was perfectly in tune and in harmony with her heart.

And she was answered.

The spell Eilistraee sent her looked like Lolth's flame strike, except that the vertical column of divine energy was silvery-white in color and seemed to rush down from the moon itself. It struck the phase spider when the creature was no more than a pace away from Halisstra, enveloping it in a beam of blindingly bright, absolutely silent light. One moment the spider was there, rearing up to rake impotently at the magical fire with its legs as it was enveloped in flickering white flames, the next, it was lying in a crumpled heap, bleached bone-white by the moonlight.

Eyes wide with wonder, Halisstra nudged the dead creature with the broken tip of her sword. The spider, burned instantly to ash by the cold magical moonfire, broke apart into pieces, which in turn collapsed, leaving only an outline of ash on the ground. A moment later, the wind blew it away.

Sensing someone staring at her, Halisstra glanced up, expecting to see either Uluyara or Feliane. Instead it was Ryld who gaped at her from the far side of the clearing. He was holding his greatsword in both hands, but the tip of its blade rested on the ground in front of him as if the weapons master had forgotten how to use it. His eyes were wide, his mouth open and panting. He'd obviously come at the run. After a moment, he seemed to remember how to speak.

"Halisstra," he whispered. "What have you done? You can never go back now. Never."

Halisstra stared at Ryld across the space where the spider had just died, conflicting emotions warring within her. She felt irritation at the fact that he had disobeyed her and followed her—and, at the same time, joy that he had cared about her enough to do so.

At last she sighed and said, "That's true, Ryld, but you can go back. You still have a choice, a choice between the Underdark and Lolth—who is obviously as dead as this spider—and Eilistraee, who smiles down upon us now. Which will you choose?"

Ryld stood silently for several long moments, then lifted his greatsword and shoved it into the sheath on his back.

"I choose you," he said, staring at Halisstra. "If you will have me."

Before Halisstra could answer, Uluyara and Feliane stepped out of the forest. Feliane was smiling at Halisstra, a look of rapturous joy on her face, but Uluyara kept a keen eye on Ryld, as if watching to make sure he wasn't going to draw his sword.

"If Eilistraee will have *you*, then you are welcome among us," Uluyara told him. "If not, then you will have to leave." A wry smile played about her lips. "Permanently, this time."

Ryld nodded and said, "Understood."

Uluyara turned to Halisstra.

"Come, priestess," she said. "There is much, yet, that you must learn. And much that you must do. This is only the first of the trials the goddess has ordained for you."

Halisstra bowed, acknowledging her new mistress. At the same time, her mind whirled at the wonder of it all. She'd fled from Ched Nasad as a homeless refugee, hoping to find out if her goddess was alive or dead, only to have her hopes dashed against the black stone monolith that sealed Lolth's temple. But in the alien forests of the World Above, she'd found something entirely unexpected, a new home—and a new goddess. In gratitude, Halisstra knew she would serve Eilistraee faithfully from that night forward. Whatever the goddess asked of her, Halisstra would give it.

Rising from her bow, she glanced at Ryld, silently contemplating the warrior. Would he do the same? Or would coming up into Eilistraee's light prove too much for Ryld, too far at odds with the ways he had always known?

Only time would tell.

Quenthel stared thoughtfully at Danifae's submissively bowed back. If the lesser priestess was to be believed, Pharaun was at last making his move. After endless petty insubordination, the infuriating male had finally worked up the courage to inflict the killing bite. Except that he didn't have the strength of will to kill Quenthel himself. Instead, he would let the aboleth do her in. That way, he could report back to the matron mother—honestly—that Quenthel had died at the hands of another, hostile race, in the pursuit of her quest.

A quest he obviously hoped to make his own, in order to steal what should rightfully be Quenthel's glory.

Quenthel stroked the sinuous bodies of her vipers, which shuddered softly as they shared her thoughts.

She must be telling the truth, Yngoth said, staring fixedly at the top of Danifae's lowered head. *I can see no reason for her to make up such a story.*

Nor can I, Quenthel thought back.

Danifae is your loyal servant, Mistress! said K'Sothra, squirming with delight.

Quenthel sighed and stroked the smaller viper's head. K'Sothra was pretty, but she wasn't very bright. She took everything at face value, completely missing the subtle nuances of deceit that usually lay just beneath the surface of so blatant a betrayal. But Quenthel thought that the naive snake might actually be correct. Danifae's motivation seemed clear as quartz crystal. The lesser priestess had everything to gain by betraying Pharaun's plans to Quenthel and nothing to lose. When Lolth reawakened, Danifae would no doubt attempt to claim a prominent place in Arach-Tinilith.

Quenthel shifted the whip to her left hand—smiling when Danifae flinched as the serpents passed over her head—and she curled the fingers of her right hand. She rested her fingertips lightly on Danifae's bowed head.

"You will be rewarded," she told the lesser priestess. "Now go. Return to Pharaun, before he suspects what you've been doing."

Danifae rose, smiling, and turned to leave the narrow cavern. Jeggred, who had been hunkered by the entrance the whole time, watching the tunnel beyond for signs of danger, flexed the claws of his fighting hands and glanced back over his shoulder at Quenthel. She gave a slight shake of her head, and Jeggred flattened against the wall to let Danifae pass.

"What about the mage?" the draegloth growled.

Quenthel saw that the hair on the back of his neck had risen. He'd listened carefully to everything Danifae said and was balanced on the knife edge of one of his rages. The slightest word from Quenthel would send him into violent motion back down the tunnel to where Pharaun sat by the waterfall, studying his spellbooks.

"I will deal with him myself," Quenthel told him. "Later."

Still growling softly, Jeggred settled back into a crouch, wrapping his smaller arms around his knees. Red eyes stared out into the tunnel, and slowly his hackles smoothed.

Quenthel sat for a moment in silence, brooding. The cavern she'd chosen for her Reverie was no larger than a servant's room, but it had a high ceiling that ended in a narrow fissure. Water seeped down one wall to puddle near her feet. It trickled out through the opening where Jeggred squatted, eventually joining the river she could hear flowing through the tunnel outside. A cluster of faintly luminescent, round fungi grew on the wet wall beside her, casting a dim greenish light. Quenthel reached out and popped one with a fingernail, releasing a sparkle of spores, then she contemplated her glowing fingertip.

Useful as Pharaun's spells were, his latest treachery had tipped the scales, turning him into a liability—one that needed to be eliminated. Yet killing him was not the simple solution it seemed.

Pharaun was a powerful wizard and a key player in the politics of the Academy. If it was learned that Quenthel had killed him, she would surely face the wrath of Pharaun's patron, her brother Gromph. Quenthel's sister Triel, Matron Mother of House Baenre, would not be pleased at having to choose sides between her siblings, especially as long as they were all weakened by Lolth's inattention. By all accounts, Pharaun's own matron mother, Miz'ri Mizzrym, was hardly fond of the mage, but he was a Master of Sorcere after all and still an important part of House Mizzrym's modest assets—and House Mizzrym was a close ally of the First House. The other masters and wizards of Sorcere would likewise be displeased to lose one of their own—especially one important enough to have been chosen for the expedition in the first place. Killing Pharaun would indeed be difficult, yet there had to be a way. . . .

Quenthel thought over what Danifae had told her. According to the battle-captive, the aboleth would only reveal where the ship of chaos was in exchange for an opportunity to consume a powerful spellcaster. Pharaun was obviously gambling that Oothoon would fail to realize that Quenthel's spells were no longer useful—that the aboleth would provide him with the location of the ship before his trickery was discovered. And the aboleth matriarch had obviously believed him. If not, she would have simply consumed Pharaun on the spot to acquire the spells the wizard carried inside his own mind.

You should turn the sava *board on him*, Yngoth suggested. *Offer Pharaun to Oothoon, in exchange for the ship.*

Easily said, Quenthel answered. *But not so easily done. I would have to meet Oothoon in person and first persuade the aboleth matriarch that I was not worth eating.*

Tell the truth, Zinda said. *Your spells are useless. Lolth is silent, perhaps forever. Perhaps she is dead.*

"No!" Quenthel cried aloud. "Lolth lives!"

Seeing Jeggred's sharp glance in her direction, she shut her mouth.

She must live, she continued silently. *If I didn't believe she was still alive, I would—*

What? Yngoth spat, his thoughts cracking Quenthel out of her despair. *Give up? Embrace death yourself? What god, then, would claim your soul?*

Anger making her steadier—she hated it when the vipers peered into her innermost fears—Quenthel spat her thoughts back at them.

No. Never that. It's just that revealing what has happened to Lolth would mean bargaining from a position of weakness. The aboleth would realize I was powerless. She might even decide to mount an attack on the drow, as other races have done.

Hsiv joined the debate with a chuckle in his voice. The first of the imps to be bound into her whip, he was often the one who helped guide Quenthel's thoughts back to a truer course.

The aboleths are an aquatic race, he reminded her. *They can't leave their lake.*

I know that, Quenthel retorted, not caring that the vipers would see through her lie. *But the aboleths might tell other races about Lolth's silence. If word of our weakness spreads, we're doomed. Ched Nasad has fallen, and now Pharaun is no longer able to contact Gromph. For all we know, Menzoberranzan—*

Menzoberranzan is far from Lake Thoroot, Hsiv gently reminded her. *And this is a little-visited region. Anyone the aboleth might tell would attack a drow city that is closer to hand.*

Quenthel barely heard him. All of the fears and doubts she'd kept bound tightly inside her ever since the group had fled from Ched Nasad erupted like spiders from a cocoon.

But that's just it! she wailed. *Who knows how many of our cities have been destroyed—or how many will yet be destroyed before this crisis is done? I've got to find Lolth—to tell her what's going on. Triel and the other matron mothers are all depending on me, and I'm not sure . . . I don't know how . . .*

Leave that to us, Yngoth hissed.

Quenthel wasn't listening.

The fate of every drow city in the Underdark is on my head, she moaned. *Things are hard enough without Pharaun and his stupid, petty power games. Doesn't he realize what's at stake? This could result in the extinction of our race!*

It could, Zinda agreed.

Yngoth quickly hissed the larger viper to silence.

You must focus on the matter at hand, he reminded Quenthel. *You must find out from Oothoon where the ship is—a task that will be easier than you think. The* sava *board has already been set up for you. All of the pieces are already in place.*

That brought Quenthel up short, and she asked, *They are?*

Yngoth's tongue flickered in and out in the serpent's equivalent of a smile.

To learn where the ship of chaos is, Pharaun must meet with Oothoon a second time. If he thinks you have been consumed, he may lower his guard slightly. And that may be his downfall.

Quenthel frowned and sent, *I don't understand.*

Listen, and you will, Yngoth continued. *You will tell Oothoon that Lolth is dead—*

Oothoon won't believe me, Quenthel interrupted. *I don't believe it myself.*

Your ring will prevent the aboleth from hearing your thoughts or from detecting your lies, Hsiv reminded her. *Then, once Oothoon has deemed you unworthy of eating, you will offer her Pharaun, instead. You will tell her that in return for her telling you where the ship of chaos lies, you will convince Pharaun that you have been eaten. Thus tricked, he will swim willingly into the jaws of death.*

The aboleth will eat him! K'Sothra cried.

And you'll be rid of Pharaun at last, Zinda added. *In a way that even Triel won't find fault with.*

How will I convince Pharaun I'm dead? Quenthel asked.

You won't, Yngoth answered. Twisting to stare at the entrance to the cave, the viper fixed its eyes on Jeggred. *He will. Take Jeggred with you—and tell him nothing of your plans. That way, his grief will be all the more convincing. Give him an order, and make sure he fixes it in his mind, that if you should be killed, he is not to take his revenge upon the aboleth. He instead must fight his way back to Pharaun and tell him what happened, so the others may carry word of your death back to Menzoberranzan. Tell Jeggred that he must succeed in doing this—at all costs—or the life of his mistress will have been forfeited for nothing.*

As if he'd somehow sensed that they were talking about him, Jeggred stirred and glanced back over his shoulder. His eyes narrowed, but he obeyed Quenthel's sharp gesture instantly, returning his attention to the tunnel.

Quenthel, meanwhile, was relieved to learn that there was a way out of her dilemma—one that would finally pay Pharaun back for his intolerable insubordination.

She stared at Yngoth expectantly and asked, *How am I to avoid being eaten by the aboleth?*

The viper bared its fangs in a menacing smile.

You still have your rod, Yngoth replied.

Quenthel nodded.

And that bottle of lace fungus wine you've been saving.

Yes, Quenthel answered. *But how in the Abyss are those going to—*

Listen, Yngoth said again. *And I will explain. . . .*

Quenthel listened avidly. By the time Yngoth was finished speaking, her lips were parted in a feral grin.

It might just work, she thought to the snake, sending a wave of excitement along with the thought. Then, on a grimmer note, she added, *It must.*

The other vipers, who had maintained a respectful silence as Yngoth outlined the plan, writhed in anticipation of seeing it carried out. Even Qorra, the serpent who almost never spoke, could hardly contain herself.

Oh! she said. *This will be such fun!*

☙ ☙ ☙

Jeggred waited just outside the audience room in which Quenthel was speaking with the aboleth matriarch, every muscle in his body tense. Quenthel was in there, alone, with two of them. She'd let one of the creatures—the one that wasn't Oothoon—move into a position behind her. Why had she allowed it to do that?

Jeggred didn't like the bloated fish-folk. They could not be trusted. Even with water filling his nostrils, he could smell the stink of deceit. He glanced, eyes narrowed, at a third aboleth, which had been ordered out into the corridor by its matriarch when Quenthel had told Jeggred to wait outside. Jeggred itched to rend its rubbery looking flesh, to see if its blood ran red. He could picture it . . . the blood would fill the water in a cloud. What a heady feast that would be—to inhale blood with each breath!

One of the trailing tentacles of the aboleth guarding him drifted close to his shoulder. Jeggred lashed out, clawing a furrow in its flesh.

Its three eyes blinking, the aboleth let out a burbling cry and yanked the tentacle away. It did not attack.

Jeggred, his pulse pounding in his ears, prepared to hurl himself after it, to close for the kill. Then, out of the corner of his eye, he saw that Quenthel had turned. She was signing at him furiously.

Hold your temper, she ordered. *We are their guests.*

Had it been a male who had spoken, Jeggred would have snarled back in defiance—then torn him to pieces. Instead, he bowed to his mistress.

As you command, Mistress.

As he signed, he snuck a glance at the aboleth he'd wounded. He'd been wrong about aboleth blood. It was green and didn't flow freely but oozed out like sap.

Satisfied the stupid creature was not going to retaliate, Jeggred returned his attention to Quenthel. He could have guarded her better if he'd been allowed to remain at her side, but an order was an order. He had obeyed, as he always did, without question. As a result, he could understand nothing of the conversation—Oothoon's voice was pitched too low for him to hear, and he could not see what Quenthel was signing, since her back was to him.

It didn't matter though. Jeggred didn't need to know what was being said. He could read Quenthel's emotions by the way she held her body. That stiffening of her shoulders was tension. And that furtive drift of her hand toward her wand was caution—perhaps even fear.

Strangely, the vipers in Quenthel's whip were drifting lazily with the current, completely relaxed. They, even more than Jeggred himself, should have sensed her rising tension. But instead the stupid things were off guard. Quenthel was wrong to put such stock in the bound imps, which were little better than slaves. Always asking their opinions—instead of trusting her own heart—made her weak.

The draegloth didn't like the feeling of that thought. He wasn't sure what to do with an idea like that, the idea that the Mistress of Arach-Tinilith, his aunt, sister to his mother the Matron Mother of the First House of Menzoberranzan, was . . . weak? He pushed the thought from his mind and found it quickly replaced by a growing unease.

Growling low in his throat—a low gurgle of water—Jeggred readied himself. Something was about to happen. He braced a foot against the far wall—one kick would send him into the room—and flexed his claws.

Quenthel drew her wand, and in a swift motion spun and aimed it at the aboleth behind her. A sticky glob shot out of the end of the wand, expanding swiftly as it raced through the water.

Simultaneously raking the aboleth beside him with one clawed hand, Jeggred kicked himself into the audience chamber—

—only to find his head and shoulders tangled in a sticky mass. Quenthel's shot had missed when the aboleth ducked swiftly aside. The viscous glob struck the doorway instead and completely blocked the opening.

Roaring with rage, Jeggred twisted his body around and braced both feet against the sides of the opening. Heaving, calf and thigh muscles nearly bursting from the strain, he tore his head free, then his shoulders. Ignoring the sting where hair had torn from his scalp, he clawed at the sticky barrier with a fighting hand. It got stuck, too.

Meanwhile, inside the audience chamber, Quenthel corrected her aim. A second glob erupted from the wand, and it struck the aboleth guard in the mouth just as its teeth were about to close on the drow priestess. Gurgling, the aboleth tried to spit out the sticky ball but could not.

The aboleth that had been out in the corridor with Jeggred had been motionless at first, but it soon moved in to attack. It reared above Jeggred, opening its mouth, attempting to bite. Jeggred raked its belly with his free hand, tearing a deep slash. Green blood oozed out—lots of blood—clouding the water Jeggred breathed. It tasted vile, like pungent seaweed—not at all as Jeggred had imagined.

The aboleth turned and bolted down the tunnel, retreating with powerful strokes of its fluked tail. Jeggred growled, knowing it had probably gone to summon more of the fish-folk.

He continued ripping at the sticky ball that blocked the audience chamber doorway. Each time, his hand got stuck—but each time he ripped off a few strands. Smelling real blood, the draegloth began to pant—then he realized that the blood was his own. His hand was raw where skin had been torn from it.

Inside the audience chamber, Quenthel held Oothoon at bay

with her rod. The aboleth matriarch stared for several moments, her three eyes unblinking, then she launched herself out of the niche. Mouth gaping, she sped across the chamber.

For some reason that Jeggred could not imagine, Quenthel seemed to be having trouble making her rod work. Only at the last moment did its magic come to life. A glob streaked toward Oothoon—and missed. As Quenthel flailed back in terror, the aboleth matriarch closed on her, and swallowed the high priestess whole.

For a moment, Jeggred could only stare in horror. His mistress was gone. Eaten. Dead!

Fury seized him. He tore at the sticky mess that held him, heedless of the skin that was being ripped from his hands and arms. Panting water in and out of his lungs—or perhaps vomiting it up and swallowing it again—he thrashed like a fish caught in a net.

All the while, Oothoon stared at him mockingly, one tentacle stroking a bulge in her stomach.

The sticky mass blocking the doorway tore but did not come free. Tipping his head back in frustration—and tearing out yet more hair that had become stuck in the viscous glob—Jeggred howled in rage and sorrow but at last came to his senses.

The Mistress was wise, he thought. She had foreseen this.

And she had given him an order—a final order that had to be carried out quickly, before the wounded aboleth returned with reinforcements.

Wrenching himself free of the sticky doorway, Jeggred swam as fast as he could down the corridor, looking for a way out.

C h a p t e r

T W E N T Y - O N E

Pharaun listened dispassionately as Jeggred gasped out his story. The draegloth was dripping wet and still making the transition to breathing air again. He sucked in great, gurgling breaths that might have been construed—were they made by a creature that was not demon-spawned—to be sobs.

"She's been eaten," Jeggred said, his head low and all four arms hanging dejectedly at his sides. "Mistress Quenthel is dead."

Pharaun regarded the draegloth coldly and said, "Thanks to you."

The comment normally would have caused Jeggred to leap forward, snarling for blood, but instead he stood as quietly as a rothé waiting for slaughter.

Danifae, standing in the tunnel beside the river, glanced at Pharaun.

"Is it even possible?" she asked. "Even without her spells,

Mistress Quenthel should have been capable of defeating the aboleth. Her armor and enchantments alone should have protected her from—"

"He said she was swallowed whole," Valas interjected. "She never had a chance."

At the mercenary's blunt words, Jeggred's shoulders slumped still lower. Hunkering down, the draegloth wrapped his smaller arms around his knees and stared blankly at the river.

Pharaun nodded to himself. As Jeggred had been relating what had happened in the aboleth city, Pharaun grew increasingly certain that the draegloth truly believed his mistress was dead.

Danifae touched his arm lightly and asked, "What should we do next, Master Pharaun? You're the leader now—it's your decision."

Pharaun noted how Danifae had glanced at Valas as she spoke, as if she was watching the mercenary for any challenge to Pharaun's leadership.

Valas, having noted the same thing, grunted, then shrugged.

"Yes," he said, meeting Pharaun's eye. "What now? Continue the search for the ship of chaos—or make our way back to Menzoberranzan?"

Pharaun's answer was immediate.

"We're still under orders from the Matron Mother," he told them briskly, "and I am still under orders from the Archmage of Menzoberranzan. Until we hear otherwise, we continue our quest to find out what's happened to Lolth. And that means finding the ship."

Danifae met his eyes and asked, "All of us?"

Pharaun stared at her.

"Since you didn't keep your part of the bargain," he said slowly, watching for Danifae's reaction, "what reason do I have to keep mine?"

Danifae's eyes blazed as she lost her usual control.

"But you promised!" she spat.

Jeggred, sensing the sudden tension in the air, looked up and growled softly. Valas glanced back and forth between Pharaun and Danifae.

"Promised what?" the mercenary asked.

Pharaun ignored the question.

"You made a promise, too," the Master of Sorcere reminded Danifae in a low voice. He patted the spellbook he'd been reading earlier. "When you slipped away to speak to Quenthel, did you honestly think I wouldn't listen in?"

Danifae's hands curled into fists at her sides. Pharaun almost expected her to stamp her foot and turn away, but after a moment her fingers slowly uncurled. She stared hard at him as if trying to guess his thoughts, then she tossed her long white hair and gave him a sulky pout.

"You meant me to betray you all along," she said. "You knew it would make Quenthel more sure of herself. She might not have met with Oothoon if—"

Pharaun interrupted her by clearing his throat. He inclined his head at Jeggred, who had risen to a fighting crouch.

"What are you saying?" the draegloth growled.

"Nothing," Danifae said smoothly, giving Jeggred a seductive smile. "Pharaun tried to get Oothoon to tell him where the ship of chaos was and learned nothing. He knew Quenthel would be able to succeed where he had failed, and so he was jealous. He was planning to discredit your mistress—to tell your matron mother, if and when he succeeds in making contact with Menzoberranzan again—that he was the one who found out where the ship is, not Quenthel."

Jeggred thought about that for a moment. Then his lips parted in a snarl.

"He would have lied," he growled, understanding at last. "Pharaun would have made the mistress look bad."

Pharaun waved a hand dismissively, thus concealing a gesture that activated a protective spell whose incantation he whispered under his breath.

"There's no need to get angry," he told Jeggred. "It's just . . . politics. You'd do the same, in my shoes. Any drow would."

Jeggred, unmollified, snarled at Pharaun and slammed his fighting hands into the mage's chest, but the gesture was half-hearted. His claws remained unflexed. The protective spell Pharaun had cast shimmered only faintly as it easily soaked up the force of the blow. The worst of it was the draegloth's foul breath, which he panted into Pharaun's face for several long moments as he tried to stare him down. Then the draegloth dropped back into a crouch, turning his back to resume his sulk.

Pharaun saw Valas, who had moved silently into position behind Jeggred, sheathing his kukris. Pharaun raised an eyebrow, then nodded his thanks at the mercenary. He had neither seen nor heard Valas draw the twin daggers—he was glad that the Bregan D'aerthe scout had chosen to back him and not Jeggred.

"As for the offer I made to you," Pharaun continued, turning to Danifae, "it still stands. It's just that it's not . . . expedient for you to leave us at the moment. With our numbers reduced, I may need you."

Danifae stood with her hands on her hips, an invitation and a challenge in one.

Interesting how quickly she begins to offer up her enticements, the wizard thought, now that Quenthel is gone.

"The question still remains," she said. "What do we do now?"

"We continue to try to get the information we need from Oothoon," Pharaun answered, stooping to tuck his spellbook back in his pack. "Or rather, *I* continue. I'm going back to Zan-horiloch. Alone, this time."

"Are you mad?" Valas asked, shaking his head. "You'll vanish down Oothoon's gullet, just as Quenthel did. Then where will we be?"

Pharaun shrugged and said, "Free to do as you wish, I suppose." He winked at Danifae, then added, "Which would mean you'd have to walk to . . . where you want to go. Perhaps your own mistress will return to claim you again, or maybe our valiant mercenary would escort you." He laughed and patted his backpack. "Don't worry. I've prepared a little magical surprise for the aboleth. My memories won't be added to Oothoon's."

Danifae gave him a mock pout and said, "See to it that they aren't."

🕷   🕷   🕷

Pharaun wasted no time in making his preparations. He pulled a leather glove onto one hand in preparation for a spell he would cast once he arrived in Zanhoriloch and made sure his wands were close at hand. He then cast two protective spells in quick succession. The first would shield him from any attempts the aboleth made to dominate his mind. The second created eight illusionary images of himself that mirrored his every move.

All nine Pharauns nodded their farewell and smiled as Valas saluted them. The one that was second from the left—the real Pharaun—cast the spell that allowed him to breathe water. Mirrored by the others, he stepped into the river, and, as soon as the cold water closed over his head, he spoke the word that would teleport him to Oothoon's audience chamber.

His arrival took the aboleth matriarch completely by surprise. Oothoon was resting in her niche, admiring a large black pearl held in the tip of a tentacle. As Pharaun and his eight illusionary doubles materialized suddenly in the room, she startled, then coiled her tentacle tightly around the pearl, drawing the precious object closer to her body.

Another aboleth was just outside in the spiraling corridor, guarding the entrance. It blinked its three eyes in startled surprise to see nine drow suddenly appear in the audience chamber but reacted with the swiftness of a trained soldier. A powerful stroke of its fluked tail propelled it into the room. One of the illusionary Pharauns disappeared in a sparkle of magical energy as the aboleth tore through it in an attack as savage and swift as that of a shark.

As the aboleth guard turned for a second attack Pharaun raised his gloved hand and flexed it, swiftly fingering an evocation with his other hand in the silent speech. An enormous ebony-skinned hand appeared in the water. Fingers open, it met the guard head-on, then wrapped itself around the aboleth. It squeezed tight, smashing the aboleth's tentacles against its body. The guard, nearly blinded by a finger that covered two of its eyes, gurgled with rage and gnawed at the palm of the hand, which was pressed up against the mouth in its belly. The hand, however, was made of magical energy, not flesh, and so the guard's attempts to bite it were futile. The aboleth thrashed helplessly in the hand's firm grip, slime from its body clouding the water around it.

Pharaun gave a quick mental push, and the hand carried the guard out of the room and down the corridor.

All that happened in the space of a few heartbeats. Immediately after shoving the guard away, Pharaun turned—together with his mirror images—and cast a powerful enchantment at Oothoon. A wash of magical energy stirred the water around the aboleth matriarch, and an instant later Pharaun saw Oothoon's tentacles relax. Still wary, he spoke to Oothoon in sign, testing the effects of his charm. If the spell had worked, she would be not just willing but eager to chat with her "old friend" Pharaun.

I apologize for the abrupt intrusion, he signed, *but I wanted to find out how our little plan went. I have heard that Quenthel came to you, and that you consumed her. Now will you keep your part of the bargain and tell me where the ship of chaos lies?*

Oothoon glanced at the corridor, bereft of its guard, then back at the mage.

"Your 'priestess' had no magic."

Pharaun had anticipated that response.

I suppose you learned from her memories that Lolth is . . . unavailable, he signed. *In time, however, the goddess will awaken, and you will have full use of the spells you just acquired.*

"I did not consume Quenthel. She was not worth eating."

Pharaun blinked.

But the one who accompanied her came back to us and told us you consumed her. He saw you swallow her whole.

"The four-armed one saw what I wanted him to see," Oothoon said, tentacles quivering and mouth open in what Pharaun took to be a wide grin.

That made Pharaun pause. He had heard that aboleths had mind magic capable of creating illusions. It seemed that Oothoon had used just that talent on Jeggred. Was she dulling Pharaun's senses with an illusion even then? Were the audience chamber and the corridor beyond not as empty of guards as they seemed?

Pharaun had with him a vial of ointment that, when rubbed on the eyes, would instantly reveal the truth once the words of the spell that activated its potency were spoken—but using it meant reaching inside a pocket of his *piwafwi* and closing his eyes briefly. If there were illusion-cloaked guards nearby, it would be the ideal moment in which to overpower him.

No, he'd rely on the magic he'd already protected himself

with. Seven of the mirror images he'd created were still hovering in the water next to him. If a surprise attack came, there was only a one-in-eight chance that he would be the one who was targeted.

Oothoon, meanwhile, seemed relaxed. The aboleth matriarch rested easily in the niche, the only sign of unease the fact that the pearl was cupped protectively against her belly. Oothoon hadn't called for more guards to replace the one Pharaun had incapacitated and hadn't made any threatening moves. Pharaun was probably worrying needlessly. His charm spell had obviously taken hold. He decided to test it further by asking a question the aboleth wouldn't answer unless charmed.

Where is Quenthel now? Pharaun asked.

"Gone in search of the ship of chaos."

You told her where it was?

The aboleth matriarch just stared at him—but the silence was answer enough.

Pharaun glanced quickly around the chamber and at last spotted the missing pieces of the puzzle. There, clinging to the doorway, was a handful of sticky strands that looked like the remains of a broken web. He also spotted, peeking out from the kelp on which Oothoon's belly rested, the neck of a wine bottle. Not everything Jeggred had seen had been an illusion: Quenthel had used her wand—deliberately—to block him on the other side of the doorway. Later, after she'd gotten the information she wanted from Oothoon, she'd dissolved the barrier with alcohol.

Together, Quenthel and Oothoon had played an elaborate and illusion-enhanced ruse on Jeggred—and Pharaun. Oothoon had been waiting for her reward all the time. The aboleth matriarch knew that Pharaun, as soon as he heard of Quenthel's "death," would return—

—and be consumed.

LISA SMEDMAN

Pharaun's hands rose to cast a spell, but before he could complete his incantation, the pearl Oothoon had been holding appeared just in front of him—the real him, not one of his mirror images—as if out of nowhere. In the instant before it struck his chest, Pharaun realized what must have happened. The aboleth matriarch had put it in her mouth and had spat it at him, masking the action with an illusion.

The pearl struck his chest and exploded in a rush of sound that drove the water from his lungs and made his ears ring. Stunned, unable to gesture or speak, he hung limp and alone in the water, his mirror images dissipated by the force of the blast. Though he was weak, dizzy, too stunned to move, a part of his mind was still able to note the irony of what had just happened. He'd been about to stun Oothoon with a spell, only to have the aboleth lay him low with precisely the same form of magic. What he'd mistaken for a "pearl" was none other than one of Quenthel's magical beads of power.

It looked as though Oothoon hadn't succumbed to his charm spell, after all. Nor had the aboleth matriarch been fooled by his mirror images—an illusion Oothoon had obviously seen through, since she managed to pick the right Pharaun to spit the bead of power at. She'd been teasing him with the truth, knowing he'd soon be as helpless as a flutter lizard in a web.

Launching herself out of the niche, Oothoon streaked toward the spot where Pharaun hung helpless. Jaws open wide, she sucked Pharaun into her mouth. Still stunned by the blast of the bead, Pharaun didn't even have the strength to scream as the jaws snapped shut. Darkness enveloped him, and razor-sharp teeth sawed into his body.

Chapter

TWENTY-TWO

Halisstra stood near one of the trophy trees, the hilt of the songsword raised to her lips. After she'd killed the phase spider two nights before, the priestesses had let her keep the broken sword, as well as Seyll's shield and chain mail. They'd also given her back her House insignia—which Halisstra had tucked into a pocket, instead of pinning to her *piwafwi*—and her other enchanted rings and devices. She also still had her magical lyre, though she felt as disinclined to use it as the other things from the Underdark she had set aside. Instead she practiced on the songsword, fingers dancing as she tried to create a tune to suit the mood of the snow-dappled woods and the clouds drifting lazily overhead, as white and fine-spun as hair.

Ryld sat cross-legged on a log a short distance away, sharpening his short sword. His eyes were squinted against the morning sunlight even though he'd chosen a spot in deep shade. He sat with his back against a large boulder, under a canopy of tree branches that hung no more than a handspan above him. He was obviously still struggling with his unease of open spaces, of having nothing but the sky over his head.

After a while, the arrhythmic *rasp . . . rasp rasp . . . rasp* of Ryld's sharpening stone grated on Halisstra's nerves, forcing her to lower the songsword.

"Ryld," she said in exasperation. "If you have to do that here, could you at least work in time with my music?"

Startled, Ryld looked up.

"Fine," he said. He crawled out from under the overhanging branches, stood, and shoved the short sword back into its sheath. Scowling at the forest, he asked, "How long do you intend for us to stay here?"

"A tenday, a month . . . a year, if need be," Halisstra answered. "Until I learn everything I can about Eilistraee's worship."

"A lifetime, you mean," Ryld said sourly.

"Perhaps," Halisstra said with a shrug, then added, "There's no one forcing you to stay, you know. You could go back to Menzoberranzan or try to find Quenthel and the others—or go to the Abyss itself, if you like."

Ryld gave her a stubborn look and said, "I want to stay with you."

Seeing the look in his eye—a human might have called it "love"—Halisstra's temper cooled.

"I'm glad," she said. "And not just for my own sake but for yours, as well. The Dark Maiden will embrace you, if you only let her. Eilistraee can show you a joy you've never known. We drow have been confined to the Underdark for too long, and it's time we took our rightful place in the sunlight—and held it, by the strength of our swords if need be."

Ryld didn't answer but instead stared up at the trophy tree.

Following his gaze, Halisstra saw that he was looking at a deep, sword-shaped niche in the trunk in which two heads rested, one on top of the other. They were skeletal, with only a few clumps of black hair clinging to them, and the jawbone of the top skull had fallen away. They were human, by the shape of them, though the mouth and jaw of the bottom skull protruded slightly, and the canine teeth were overly large. The sight of them seemed to be making the hardened warrior uneasy, which was strange, since Ryld had undoubtedly seen far more gruesome sights in his career as a weapons master of Melee-Magthere.

Ryld wrenched his gaze away.

"Why Eilistraee?" he asked. "Why not worship . . . Kiaransalee, or Selvetarm? His faith, at least, I could have had some part in. Or do you think Lolth's champion has suffered the same fate as his mistress?"

"Selvetarm guards Lolth still," Halisstra answered. "Vhaeraun did not defeat him."

Ryld's eyebrows raised and he asked, "How do you know?"

"Last night, Uluyara led the priestesses in a spell-song. The scrying they performed penetrated deep into the Abyss, and Uluyara was able to look briefly upon the stone that sealed Lolth's temple. Selvetarm was squatting in front of it in his spider form, wounded, but with sword and mace still in hand. He may have defeated Vhaeraun—or perhaps just temporarily driven the other god off. Uluyara was only able to get the briefest of glimpses before the water in her font boiled away."

Ryld cursed softly under his breath.

"Last night?" he asked. "So that was what all the singing was about. Why didn't you tell me this sooner?"

Halisstra shrugged and said, "What difference would it have made? You're not thinking of reporting back to Quenthel, are you?"

Ryld gave her a sour smile.

"I couldn't—even if I wanted to," he said. "She'd brand me a deserter and have those vipers of hers sink their fangs into me. I'd be dead before I could get a single word out in my defense. I just wish you would keep me informed." He paused, then frowned. "How did Uluyara know that Lolth's temple was sealed?"

"I told her," Halisstra said. "I told her everything. About our trip to the Abyss in astral form, about Lolth's silence, and about the battle between Vhaeraun and Selvetarm—I even told her about the fall of Ched Nasad. Everything."

Ryld nodded slowly and said, "I shouldn't be surprised, given your conversion, but I am. Revealing so much to priestesses who, until a short time ago, you would have counted as your enemies, seems like . . ."

Perhaps realizing he was speaking to a priestess, he lowered his eyes. As he hesitated, either uncertain how to finish his sentence or else unwilling to continue it, Halisstra guessed the rest.

"Like a betrayal?" she asked. "A traitorous act? Well so be it. Lolth is dead—or will soon be."

"And you've aligned yourself with what you think will be the winning side," Ryld said. He nodded. "I suppose that's a sensible move to make."

Halisstra sighed, wondering why Ryld just couldn't understand.

"It's more than mere tactics," she said, trying to explain. "Eilistraee is the only deity to offer the drow any hope. With Lolth missing and her priestesses unable to mount a defense, the cities of the Underdark are going to fall, one by one. Soon hundreds—if not thousands, or even tens of thousands—of drow will come streaming up out of the Underdark, looking for refuge. Eilistraee's priestesses will offer it to them. They'll help guide our people up into the light. They'll teach the drow to take their rightful place in the world—to not just *survive* up here, but thrive. We'll be able to reclaim our birthright. Just look how much the Dark Ladies of Eilistraee have done so far, in terms of clearing this forest of monsters and making it fit to live in again. We're creating a new home on the World Above, one in which the drow can live in harmony with one another. A home we'll defend with our magic—and our swords. What more noble cause can there possibly be than that?"

Ryld, staring at the trophy tree again, muttered something under his breath. Halisstra thought she heard the words "just like clearing the slums," then decided she must have been wrong, since the phrase made no sense.

"Ryld," she said slowly, "are you sure you—"

Quiet! Ryld warned, switching suddenly to silent speech. *I hear voices in the woods. Human voices. They're coming this way.*

Halisstra, worried, reached for the horn on her belt. Should she sound it to warn the priestesses? That was what she'd been sent out to the perimeter of the temple grounds to do, after all: stand guard. Uluyara had warned her that human adventurers sometimes ventured deep into the Velarswood—adventurers who made no distinction between the worshipers of Eilistraee and the drow of the Underdark. Humans slew any ebony-skinned elf they met on sight.

But blowing the horn would also alert the humans to Halisstra's presence—and they were close. Better to assess the situation from hiding and deal with the humans herself, if possible. Ryld would back her up—and provide an additional element of surprise.

Take cover, she signed to him. *I'll challenge them. You wait.*

Nodding, Ryld slid his greatsword silently out of its sheath, at the same time flipping up the hood of his *piwafwi*. He stepped back into the branches and stood utterly still, becoming no more than another shadow. Halisstra, meanwhile, quickly sang under her breath, casting a spell that rendered her invisible. Then she waited, songsword in hand.

The humans were either bold—or stupid. They came through the woods with heavy, snow-crunching footsteps, not bothering to lower their voices, which, when Halisstra could finally hear them clearly, sounded strained. Occasionally they grunted, as if carrying a heavy load. As they passed by the base of the trophy tree and came into sight through the underbrush, Halisstra saw two of them, both human males with axes in sheaths on their backs, carrying a body on a cloak they held stretched between them.

The body of a female drow.

And not just any drow, but one who wore the moon-and-sword emblem of Eilistraee on a chain around her neck, and a cluster of miniature swords that hung from a ring on her belt like keys.

"Who are you?" Halisstra called out, dropping her invisibility spell. "What's happened to this priestess?"

She held her songsword at the ready—not because the men looked threatening but because, if the priestess was still alive, healing magic might be needed, and quickly. Stepping closer, she touched the woman's throat, but saw that it was too late for any spells she might have offered. The priestess's skin was cold, and the rhythm of life had stilled. Her closed eyes would see no more.

Both of the humans were thin and muscular, with pale blond hair and darker skin than most humans, suggesting there had been a drow somewhere among their ancestors. The older of the two men inclined his head to Halisstra. It was as much of a bow as he could manage while still holding on to the cloak that sagged with the priestess's weight. When Halisstra nodded back in acknowledgement, the two men gently eased their burden to the snowy ground.

"We two are from Velarsburg," the older man said. "I am the lumberman Rollim, and this is my son Baeford. We were cutting timber near the Howling Hills when we heard a woman calling for help. We followed the voice—some ways through the woods, from which I figure it must have been a magical sending—and found this Dark Lady outside a cave. She looked near death—she was breathing shallow, and fast. She couldn't speak, but she could still sign. She said she'd been attacked in the Realms Below and needed to get back to the temple."

Halisstra contemplated the dead priestess. She was a stranger, but Halisstra could guess her mission by the tiny swords that hung from the ring on her belt. She was one of the priestesses who traveled as missionaries into the Underdark, carrying the faith of Eilistraee to the drow who dwelled below. The tiny swords would have been handed out to the faithful, to serve as "keys" that would ensure them safe passage to the temple.

"Did she tell you what attacked her?" Halisstra asked.

Rollim frowned and replied, "Not 'what,' Lady, but who. When she was telling her story, she used the sign for 'she.' The sign that means 'drow female.' "

Halisstra winced.

"Did you see any sign of this other drow?" she asked.

"None," Rollim said. "There was only the Dark Lady's footprints—and we didn't dare go into the cave. The other must still be below."

"Stabbed in the back," Halisstra muttered, staring down at the priestess. "How typical."

Behind the two men—both had their backs to the spot where Ryld was hidden—she saw dark hands briefly flash: *Or else abandoned to fight alone.*

Even though Ryld's face was no more than a shadow under the hood of his *piwafwi*, Halisstra could see he was scowling.

"Not stabbed," Baeford interjected. "There wasn't a mark on her." He glanced apprehensively down at the body of the priestess. "It must have been magic that killed her."

Rollim ran a heavily callused hand through his hair, which was damp with sweat and dotted with sawdust. "A normal injury, we might have been able to do something about—we could have splinted a broken bone or stanched the bleeding of an axe cut. But this—" he shuddered—"She died as we were lifting her onto the cloak."

Halisstra nodded. "You did well to bring her here," she told them. "I'm sure the priestesses will reward—"

"They already have," Rollim said. He raised his right hand, palm up, toward the sky in a reverential gesture, then let it drop to his side. "If it wasn't for the Dark Ladies, Baeford wouldn't be alive today. He had the pox soon after his birth and nearly died, but Eilistraee healed him." He glanced at the dead priestess, and his expression grew grim. "I only wish we'd been able to repay that kindness."

Baeford—whose face did have pock marks—shuffled his feet nervously.

"Lady," Baeford asked, "shall we carry her to the sacred circle?"

He looked as though the last thing he wanted to do was pick up the body again.

"No," she answered. "I'll take her. You may go."

"You'll carry her alone?" Rollim asked, eyebrow raised.

He bowed hurriedly when he saw Halisstra's frown. She still didn't appreciate a male questioning her authority.

"As you wish," Rollim quickly said. Then, to his son, "Come, Baeford. We've done all we can."

As they left, Ryld slid silently out of the branches.

Should I follow them? he signed.

Halisstra shook her head.

"No. There's something amiss here, but though the younger one could sense it, he doesn't know what it is. Whatever it is, they weren't the cause of it."

She knelt beside the body and studied it, shifting it slightly to observe the woman's back. As Baeford had said, there were no obvious signs of injury. The priestess's skin was unbroken, and her tunic and boots showed only normal travel wear. Just as all of Eilistraee's priestesses did—especially when venturing into the Underdark—she wore a chain mail shirt. Its links were undamaged, and her sword was still in its scabbard.

On an impulse, Halisstra grasped the hilt and tugged. The sword slid out of its scabbard easily, its blade keen and bright—had it been used, it might have been sticky with blood. As Halisstra reached once again over the dead woman to resheath the weapon, her face came close to that of the priestess. Detecting a faint but acrid odor, she bent closer and sniffed. The smell was a distinctive blend of the sulfuric fires of the Abyss combined with rotten spiderweb.

Halisstra swore softly, "Eilistraee protect us."

"What is it?" Ryld asked, tense.

"She was killed by a yochlol," Halisstra said. "I can smell its stink on her skin and hair."

Silver flashed as Ryld drew his greatsword. He assumed a ready position, eyes darting around the forest.

"Do you think it followed her?" he asked through gritted teeth.

"I doubt it."

As she spoke, Halisstra pried open the dead woman's mouth. The priestess's jaw opened easily. She had not been dead long. As Halisstra had suspected, the smell was stronger when the woman's mouth was open. The yochlol must have assumed gaseous form and flowed into the priestess's lungs, choking her and rendering her unable to retaliate with either sword or spell. Which meant that the yochlol had gotten close to her—close enough to take her completely by surprise. It had done so either by using a spell to dominate her, or by the simple subterfuge of assuming one of its most innocent-looking forms, that of a female drow.

A "drow" who had, Halisstra guessed, pretended to be a petitioner seeking to join in Eilistraee's worship. The yochlol must have toyed with the priestess, secretly gloating at what was to come while accompanying her to the cavern that led out onto the World Above. Then it struck.

"This was no random attack," Halisstra concluded. "The yochlol chose its victim deliberately."

"Do you think the demon was summoned?" Ryld asked, his brow creased in a worried frown. "If it was. . . ."

The warrior didn't finish his question, but he didn't have to. Halisstra knew full well what was on his mind. The yochlol were demonic creatures that served the Queen of the Demonweb Pits. The handmaidens of Lolth could only appear on the prime material plane if summoned by her priestesses. It was possible, however, that one had already been on the prime when Lolth fell silent and had subsequently broken free of its mistresses.

It was also possible that Lolth had returned from wherever she'd gone to, and that her priestesses were once again able to use their spells.

"Uluyara will want to know about this," Halisstra said. She moved to one end of the cloak on which the priestess lay, and grasped its two corners. "Let's get the body to the temple—at once."

TWENTY-THREE

Sculling to keep herself just beneath the surface of the lake, Quenthel waited until the spell that allowed her to breathe water ended. When her lungs began to feel tight and hot, she exhaled the last of the lake water from them and let her head break the surface. Then, treading water and coughing slightly, she touched the brooch on her chest. She rose smoothly into the spray-filled air beside the waterfall, at last drawing level with the tunnel.

Jeggred was sitting just inside it brooding, staring out across the lake. When he saw her his eyes widened. Letting out a howl of delight, he leaped to his feet, cracking his head against the low ceiling and splitting his scalp. Oblivious to the blood that flowed freely through his thick white hair, he broke into gulping laughter.

"Mistress!" he barked.

Quenthel landed lightly on the ledge beside him. Crouching

low, she scrambled into the tunnel. Jeggred leaped forward, his massive fighting arms wide as if he were actually about to *embrace* her, of all things. Quenthel's stern look—and the twitching of her vipers—warned him off, and instead he groveled at her feet. Not daring to touch her, he kissed the cold stone in front of her feet, whimpering softly.

Quenthel half-hoped Jeggred would ask how she'd managed to escape the aboleth. She would have relished relating how clever she'd been. But, being a draegloth, he was far too literal-minded for that. His mistress had been eaten, but now she was alive again. That much was enough. That—and the comfort of having someone to give him commands again.

Curling her fingers like a spider's legs, she touched them momentarily to his shoulder and watched his mane ripple as he writhed with pleasure. Then she turned to more pressing matters.

"Where are the others?" she asked.

Jeggred pointed behind him, back down the tunnel, and said, "In another cavern. That way."

Stooping to avoid the low ceiling, Quenthel set off in the direction indicated. Jeggred trailed behind her, ducking his head subserviently and silently pointing each time she glanced at him for directions. After a while, the ceiling became higher, and they were able to walk upright. They were going back the way they had come, still following the river. Up ahead Quenthel could hear voices, one male, the other recognizable as Danifae's by the audible pout of the words. Quenthel remembered a larger cavern, just ahead. By the echo of their voices she guessed they were probably standing inside it, talking.

"Why were you alone?" Quenthel asked Jeggred. "Did the others leave you behind after Pharaun failed to return?"

When Jeggred didn't answer immediately, she glanced back at him. The draegloth had a confused frown on his face.

"The wizard did return," he answered.

Quenthel ground her teeth, irritated, and felt her whip-vipers writhing against her hip. Sometimes her nephew could be so thick-headed.

"I know he came back the first time he went to speak to Oothoon," she said. "I was talking about the second time he—"

Hearing a third voice—one she recognized—Quenthel stopped so abruptly that Jeggred bumped into her from behind. So surprised was she by the sound of the voice, she didn't even think to draw her whip and lash the draegloth for this transgression. Instead she swore softly under her breath—a curse that would have invoked the wrath of Lolth, had the goddess been able to hear it—then she rushed forward, scrambling up the incline that led away from the river tunnel, toward the cavern from which the voices came.

The entrance to the cavern was a narrow one, and Quenthel had to squeeze past a mushroom-shaped stalagmite to get inside. Through the opening she saw Valas and Danifae sitting on a natural shelf of rock, sharing a bricklike loaf of pressed fungus. A moment later she saw the third speaker, standing a little apart from them and holding a small spherical object in front of one eye as he chanted the words to a spell.

Quenthel's ears hadn't lied. It was Pharaun, alive, whole, and without a single aboleth tooth mark anywhere on him.

"Ah, Mistress," the Master of Sorcere said, stopping in mid-incantation and lowering the glass sphere. "I was just casting a spell to help me look for you."

Quenthel stood frozen in the cavern entrance, mouth hanging open. Even her serpents had stopped their usual writhing and were rigid with surprise, eyes staring, unblinking. Then, as Valas and Danifae looked up—and gaped back at her—Quenthel realized how foolish she must have looked.

Pharaun tucked the sphere inside a pocket of his *piwafwi*.

"You're wondering why I'm still alive," he said, addressing the question she hadn't dared to ask. "The answer is simple: a contingency spell that I prepared before visiting Zanhoriloch. I was expecting something like that little surprise you gave the aboleth matriarch, though I'm surprised you were willing to part with one of your beads of force. Still, it served its purpose, I suppose."

"What contingency spell?" Quenthel asked, still not understanding.

Valas, having quickly recovered from the shock of seeing Quenthel alive, bit off a chunk of fungus loaf and chewed. Danifae sprang to her feet and clambered down the shelf of rock toward Quenthel, exclaiming her relief and joy at the fact that her mistress was alive. Quenthel stared at Pharaun, ignoring both the lesser priestess—who was kneeling before her in a bow—and Jeggred, who was crowding close behind her to stare over her shoulder.

"You see?" Jeggred grunted, his foul breath hot in her ear. "He came back."

"Before teleporting to Zanhoriloch I cast a number of spells," Pharaun explained at last. "One of them was a contingency that would teleport me back to these tunnels if certain events occurred. I made the condition simple, and specific. The spell was triggered the moment an aboleth—Oothoon, as it turned out—tried to eat me."

Oothoon ate him? K'Sothra asked.

Be silent! Yngoth shot back. Then, to Quenthel, the viper said, *Tell him you knew this would happen—that you were counting on his resourcefulness.*

Quenthel smiled and said, "I expected no less of you, Master Pharaun. You are truly resourceful."

Pharaun returned the smile with eyes just as cold as Quenthel's. The looks they exchanged made it clear that knives had been drawn—and would be plunged home when the time was right.

"Thank you," Pharaun said, acknowledging her false compliment. "You are wiser . . . Mistre*ss* . . . than I thought. How clever of you to escape the aboleth. Your 'death' was in fact a ruse of the highest order. You have the very mind of a demon, when it comes to trickery, and I commend you for it. No doubt you managed to get the location of the ship out of Oothoon, in return for my life?"

Quenthel frowned. Had the mage deliberately hissed when using her title? It was almost as if he suspected the idea had come from her serpents all along. Which it only partially had. The vipers had made a few suggestions, it was true, but it had been Quenthel who had pulled everything together, who had seen the pattern those suggestions wove.

Of course it was your idea, Hsiv soothed.

We are but your servants, added Yngoth.

You are a priestess of the great Spider Queen, and we bow to your wisdom in all things, Zinda said.

Quenthel nodded and absently stroked the largest viper's head.

K'Sothra twisted around to look at Hsiv and said, *But she—*

Silence, the elder viper interrupted.

Yes, silence, Quenthel snapped, her irritation rising to the surface once more. *I can barely hear myself think, with all of you talking at once.*

She squeezed the rest of the way into the cavern, Jeggred following close behind.

"I did discover the location of the ship of chaos," she told Pharaun and the others. "It went down in the Lake of Shadows." She turned to Valas and asked, "I assume you've heard of this lake?"

The Bregan D'aerthe scout chewed a moment—annoying Quenthel, who was used to more prompt answers. Her hand fell to the handle of her whip, and she was just about to draw it and threaten to flog an answer out of him when he stood, wiping the last crumbs of fungus loaf from his mouth. Why couldn't he be like Danifae who, she was pleased to see, had scurried back a pace or two? The lesser priestess was suitably cowed by the vipers, which were nearly spitting in anticipation of tasting flesh once more.

"It's a large lake," the scout continued, obviously sensing the high priestess's impatience, "about the same size as Lake Thoroot. The two are connected by an underground river."

"Flowing in which direction?" Quenthel asked.

"Toward Lake Thoroot, from the northwest."

"How far?" asked Pharaun.

"About the same distance away as the Fireflow," Valas said, and Pharaun's eyes lit with recognition. "By surface and tunnel, that's about a tenday's march from here. The river might be longer, especially moving upstream."

Quenthel nodded, pleased to see they were getting somewhere at last.

Turning to Pharaun, she said, "We'll set out for the Lake of Shadows at once. Prepare your water-breathing spells."

Pharaun's eyebrows rose and he asked, "You intend that we *swim* there?"

"Of course," Quenthel said.

"That won't work."

Quenthel squeezed her whip handle so tightly the serpents spat venom.

"Why not?" she asked through gritted teeth.

"For one thing, if we use an underwater route, the aboleth will follow us," Pharaun said. "We're too tasty a treat to let go, and we'd end up fighting them all the way. For another, as our able scout mentioned, if the connecting river flows *from* the Lake of Shadows *to* Lake Thoroot, we'll be swimming against the current. That could make the journey much longer than a tenday, and there will be no place for me to stop and re-study my spell along the way. When its magic runs out, we'll all drown."

Quenthel was furious—but even through her rage, she could see that the mage was right.

Why didn't you think of this? she thought furiously at her whip vipers.

A hissing match ensued, in which each of the vipers berated the other four for not realizing something so obvious.

At last, Hsiv answered. *Our apologies, Mistress. It will not happen again.*

Valas cleared his throat and said, "There is more than one approach to the Lake of Shadows. Chosing the wrong one, farther from the ship, could cost us days . . . even tendays. Did Oothoon mention anything else about the ship of chaos, Mistress? Anything that might help me to find it in such a large body of water?"

Quenthel, still glaring at Pharaun, started to shake her head. Then she remembered a passing comment the aboleth matriarch had made.

"Only one thing," she said, "that the air above the lake was thick with bats. That's what gave the lake its name . . . the shadows they make against the cavern ceiling."

"That's not the only reason, Mistress. There are . . . oddities there," Valas said. "It's said to be a gateway of sorts to the Plane of Shadow. Anyway, I know where the Lake of Shadows is, and I know of two different ways to reach it that are reasonably safe."

Finally, Quenthel thought then asked, "What are they?"

"The lake is connected to the surface by natural chimneys in the rock—that part of the Surface Realms that lies just above it is known for the bats that fly out of the holes in a cloud every night. We could descend through one of the chimneys—but that would mean climbing up to the World Above again and traveling through the forest."

Quenthel considered that—briefly. She wasn't about to subject herself to a cold, snowy trudge through bright sunlight again.

"We're not going back to the surface," she decided.

That's wise, Hsiv's voice breathed in her ear. *House Jaelre's warriors will still be looking for us.*

"We want to avoid House Jaelre's warriors," Quenthel explained to Valas. "They either killed or captured Ryld Argith, the best warrior we had. We don't want to lose anyone else."

Valas's eyes narrowed slightly, and Quenthel wondered if he was silently questioning her order. To remind him of his place, she drew her whip—but held it by her side.

Ha! K'Sothra chortled. *That pricked his pride.*

Valas glanced at the vipers.

"As you command, Mistress," he acquiesced. "We'll keep to the Underdark. But that leaves only one other means of reaching the Lake of Shadows—and it's a dangerous one."

"Go on," Quenthel prompted.

"There is an ancient portal that gives access to a lake. It's a march of about four cycles from here, northward through a series of connecting tunnels and caverns. The portal was constructed centuries ago, but I have heard from a reliable source that its magic is still active. Reaching it, however, might prove difficult."

Quenthel nodded, unperturbed by Valas's grim tone. Everything in life was difficult—only those who rose above difficulties were worthy of Lolth's favors.

"We'll make for the portal," she told the mercenary. "Pack your things, everyone. We'll set out at once."

"This portal," Pharaun said slowly. "What makes it so difficult to reach?"

"It lies directly under the ruins of Myth Drannor." Valas said nothing more, as if that was explanation enough.

"Myth Drannor?" Pharaun groaned. "Not again. I have no desire to stare down a beholder a second time."

"We wouldn't be facing a beholder, this time," Valas said. "Which is probably just as well, since we don't have our 'best warrior' here to dispatch it, like he did the last one."

"What *would* we be facing?" Pharaun asked.

Valas muttered something too low for Quenthel to hear, but Pharaun's reply was loud enough for her ears to catch.

"Too bad our spiders have lost their venom," he said, glancing at Quenthel and Danifae.

Valas nodded gravely.

Furious at the deliberate slight, Quenthel drew her whip. She snapped it, and the serpents hissed loudly, splattering venom on a stone floor that had been hastily vacated by Danifae.

"You will address your answers to me," she told Valas. "House Baenre has paid for your services, mercenary, not Sorcere."

"I beg your pardon, Mistress," he said, bowing deeply and addressing her in a suitably chastised voice. "Ah . . . what was your question?"

Pharaun turned abruptly away, suddenly interested in placing his spellbooks back into his pack.

What creatures might we face? Hsiv prompted.

Quiet! Quenthel thought back. *I can ask my own questions.* Then, out loud, she added, "What will we have to fight, this time?"

Rising from his bow, Valas met her eye.

"Wraiths," he said. "Dozens of them."

That made Quenthel pause. Wraiths were dangerous creatures;

shadowy, incorporeal. Their slightest touch could drain a living creature's vitality in an instant, and even magical healing would not restore it. Those drained entirely by wraiths became undead themselves, rising as twisted caricatures of their former selves to feed on their own kind. Few ordinary drow had seen a wraith—let alone several dozen of the shadowy creatures—and survived to speak of it.

And that was what Quenthel had been reduced to after all, an ordinary drow. Had Lolth not been silent, Quenthel could have used her magic to drive the creatures back from her, blowing them away like rags in a wind, but without it, she was as powerless against them as any other drow. The thought of facing several of the creatures without being able to turn them made her shiver.

Then she reminded herself that the fate of the drow race hung in the balance. She *had* to find the ship of chaos—it offered her the only chance she had to reach the Abyss and find out what had happened to Lolth. And that meant reaching the Lake of Shadows. Then, once Lolth restored her magic to the drow, Quenthel could return to Menzoberranzan in triumph. She might, perhaps, even depose Triel and claim the throne of the most powerful House in the city.

Yes, Hsiv thought. *You were meant to rule. You must succeed.*

Ignoring him, Quenthel returned her attention to Valas.

"Tell me more about the portal," she ordered. "How do you know of it?"

With a slight bow, Valas answered, "I heard about it from a rogue—an odd little fellow who hailed from Gracklstugh. He learned of a vault under Myth Drannor that supposedly had treasure the surface elves left behind during their Retreat. He found a way to get there through the Underdark, but the vault was empty—except for the wraiths. They killed his four companions and nearly killed him too, but he escaped by leaping into a portal. It led to a narrow ledge overlooking the Lake of Shadows. Fortunately, he wore a ring that allowed him to levitate out of the cavern—otherwise he'd be there still."

Quenthel listened, nodding.

"Did any of the wraiths follow him through the portal?" she asked.

"No. According to the rogue, it would admit only living creatures."

Quenthel thought a moment then asked, "Did he see anything that might have been the ship of chaos?"

Valas shook his head and replied, "Nothing that he mentioned to me. But the Lake of Shadows is wide—as large across as Lake Thoroot—and deep. If the ship sank, there'd be nothing to see."

"This rogue told you there were 'dozens' of wraiths?" she asked.

Valas nodded and said, "Those were his very words."

"An exaggeration, no doubt. What race was he?"

Valas frowned.

"The rogue?" he asked. "He claimed to be human, even though he was no taller than a duergar."

"Humans," Quenthel snorted. "A cowardly race. There were probably less than half a dozen wraiths, all told. With Pharaun's spells—and our magical weapons—we'll easily be able to fight our way through."

Valas opened his mouth—perhaps to protest that even half a dozen wraiths were too many—but he closed it a moment later.

Quenthel, meanwhile, took mental stock of the resources she had at hand. Valas, whose speed and stealth would allow him to get behind the wraiths and dispatch them with his magical daggers. Pharaun, with his arsenal of powerful protective spells. Jeggred, who would protect Quenthel at any cost, hurling himself headlong at the wraiths, if the need arose. And Danifae . . .

Quenthel paused, considering. What good was the battle-captive, really? Oh, she groveled sweetly when threatened and gave pleasure readily enough, but Quenthel sometimes noticed a look in Danifae's eyes that she didn't like. Not at all.

Still, Danifae was a competent enough fighter, when she had to be. The morningstar she carried was no mere boy's weapon. If it came to it, Danifae could be abandoned to the wraiths, if the need arose to sacrifice someone. Truth be told, Quenthel would rather be rid of Pharaun—though she had to admit that his expertise with demons was going to come in handy, once the ship of chaos was finally located.

No, she'd have to make sure that Pharaun survived the encounter with the wraiths. Which meant making sure that if Danifae's life was threatened, the mage didn't try to defend her.

"We'll get by the wraiths," Quenthel told the others. "We'll reach the portal." Then, silently, so only the serpents could hear, she added, *Or at the very least, some of us will.*

Chapter

TWENTY-FOUR

Gromph strode through one of the main corridors of Sorcere, followed closely by Kyorli, who scurried along behind him, and Prath, staggering under a load of spellbooks that Gromph had hastily assembled. Since the duergar had been driven back from Tier Breche, and the tunnel sealed, most of the students were heeding the call of their respective Houses. Apprentice mages ran this way and that down the corridor, arms laden with spellbooks and magical devices, bleating like a milling herd of rothé as walking chests scuttled along on spider legs behind them.

As he hurried along, Gromph held a circle of copper wire close to his lips.

"Wizards of House Baenre," he called, speaking through the enchanted wire. "Attend me at once in the scrying chamber."

The wire hummed, sending a tingle through Gromph's fingertips. Then it glowed a dull red and crumbled. Flicking flakes of copper from his fingers, Gromph pushed open the heavy double doors of the scrying chamber and stepped inside.

Like the rest of Sorcere, the walls of the large, circular chamber were lined with lead sheeting and plastered with a stucco made from gorgon's blood and spellstone dust. Runes had been embossed upon the surface and limned in gold to further prevent against unwanted intrusion or observation. No spellcaster, no matter how powerful, could teleport past them or probe the minds of the students and masters inside.

It was possible, however, to see *out* from there, thanks to an enormous crystal ball that floated at the center of the room. Into the sphere had been magically bound one eye of the eagle that resided in a gilded cage just below the crystal sphere. As Gromph and Prath entered the room, the eagle flapped its wings and gave a *scree* of excitement, blinking its one remaining eye. The sphere above it turned, rotating to face the two drow. The eagle's second eye, which filled the crystal ball from side to side, fixed them with a hungry stare.

Or rather, it fixed upon Kyorli. Snapping its beak, the eagle *screeed* a second time and hurled itself against the bars of its cage. The rat, taunting it, sat back on her haunches no more than a pace from the cage and groomed her whiskers, ignoring the frenzied wing flapping of the eagle.

Kyorli, stop it, Gromph ordered. *Come here.*

Obeying the telepathic command, Kyorli dropped to all fours and scurried back to her master. Climbing swiftly up Gromph's *piwafwi*, she settled herself on his shoulder, tickling his ear with her whiskers. Prath, meanwhile, stooped to place the spellbooks he'd been carrying on the floor.

"The eagle is hungry," Gromph told Prath. "Find it some raw meat—but don't go slicing off any more fingertips. You're going to need them."

Prath grinned.

"I thought you might need more, Archmage" he said, reaching into one of the bags that was slung over his shoulder. "So I stopped by the kitchen on the way back from the components storeroom. The cook gave me this."

Pulling out a waxed rag, he unwrapped a fist-sized chunk of meat. At Gromph's approving nod he held it up against the bars of the cage. The eagle tore into it greedily, ripping off bloody chunks with its hooked beak and eventually wrenching a large piece inside. It settled upon that portion, content, and soon reduced it to no more than a smear of blood on the bottom of the cage.

Gromph, meanwhile, greeted the House Baenre wizards who straggled into the room, directing them to the circle of chairs that surrounded the cage and the crystal ball. He was pleased to see Julani, a Master of Evocation. His fellow instructor bowed, touching long, supple fingers against his chest. The next two to arrive were a pair of tenth-year students. Grendan was a handsome male with a natural flair for illusion. Gromph wondered how much of his good looks were natural and how much had been augmented by magic—especially since the smell of singed hair still clung to him. Judging by the burns in the hood of his *piwafwi*, the student must have been splattered by one of the duergar's incendiary missiles.

His companion, Noori, was equally beautiful—naturally so—with arched eyebrows and white hair that cascaded past her shoulders in soft waves. She was high-born, a cousin to Gromph and Triel, but she had eschewed the worship of Lolth to enter Sorcere and study divination magic instead. Remembering that, Gromph wondered whether or not Noori might have had a premonition, so many years before, of Lolth's demise. She certainly seemed to have been able to keep out of the way of any harm during the recent fighting. There wasn't a mark on her—not even a soot smudge.

The final mage to enter the room was Zoran, an irritating, second-year student who was continually making poor choices in class, using magic in frivolous, inappropriate ways. Gromph winced, seeing him—especially when he noted the wand of wonder in the boy's belt. Zoran was tiny, even for a male, and had a receding chin, made more pronounced by the fact that his hair was pulled into a topknot at the crown of his head. He must have been injured in the recent battle. Gromph didn't remember him walking with a limp before.

As the four mages settled themselves into chairs, waiting quietly for his instruction, Gromph opened one of the scrying chamber doors and peered each way down the corridor. Seeing no one else, he slowly closed them.

"Is this all?" he asked Julani. "Is there no one else from our House?"

The Master of Evocation shook his head.

"Only Nauzhror," he said, "who sends his regrets. He was . . . too busy to attend. The rest are dead—or badly injured and removed to Arach-Tinilith for healing."

A slight tightening of Julani's eyes told Gromph that he too knew how little "healing" there was left to go around.

Gromph sighed. So few House Baenre mages left—and only one of them a master. Gromph cast a lock spell upon the doors, motioned Prath to also take a seat, then seated himself in the thronelike chair that controlled the crystal ball.

"I invite you to join me in looking upon the enemy," he told the other wizards. "Observe."

With a flick of his fingers, he nudged the crystal ball with an unseen hand, causing the eye to turn to face the south wall. The bird in the cage below fell silent and still, wings folded and talons gripping its perch. Concentrating, Gromph peered through the eagle's eye.

The walls of Sorcere seemed to melt away, and in an instant he was looking at Arach-Tinilith. His penetrating gaze swept past its spider-shaped bulk and on through the walls of the cavern, through stone and tunnel and stone . . . until at last it came to rest in a cavern in which four individuals stood. One was a drow male, dressed in immaculate gray clothing. The fellow next to him was a cambion known, at least by reputation, to them all. The other two were both duergar, squat and gray—one with a scar that ran the length of his cheek, the other cradling a stone scepter.

Leaving the eye focused on that scene, Gromph pulled his awareness back into this own body. Inside the crystal ball, the figures gestured and talked—in angry tones, judging by the way the duergar tapped the scepter against one palm as the half-demon loomed over him, his pointed, sharklike teeth exposed in a snarl. The drow, meanwhile, kept turning back and forth between the half-demon and the two drow, speaking rapidly and with placating gestures.

The other wizards stared into the scrying device, their expressions thoughtful.

"These are the leaders of the army that has besieged us?" Julani asked.

He had rested his elbows on the arms of his chair, and his steepled fingers were laced with angry sparks.

"I recognize Crown Prince Horgar of Gracklstugh and his bodyguard, and is that Kaanyr Vhok?" Grendan asked.

"The same," Noori said. "The tanarukks that harry our southern approaches are his Scoured Legion."

"That leaves but one," Gromph said.

"The one in the middle—the drow," Prath said, clenching his

fists. "That's Zhayemd—the bastard from House Agrach Dyrr who betrayed us at the Pillars of Woe."

"His real name is Nimor," Gromph said. "Nimor Imphraezl."

"Is he a wizard?" Julani asked.

"I don't think so," Gromph answered. "Though there is a strong aura of magic about him; I think he's more than he appears to be. And he certainly has enough magical devices. I can detect an aura of magic on his weapons, several items of his clothing, his rings . . ."

He paused for a moment, contemplating the two rings the man wore. One Gromph recognized as a protective device, but the other—the slim black ring that seemed no more substantial than a band of shadow—was quite unusual. Gromph had never seen anything quite like it.

Suddenly Gromph realized what it must be. Ever since Triel had told him that Nimor had somehow spirited an assassin into the inner most corridors of House Baenre's great mound, Gromph had been puzzling over how that might have been accomplished.

That black ring on Nimor's finger must be a magical device that conveyed the ability to shadow walk. That would make him a difficult character to corner, indeed. It was a good thing the wizards were striking from a distance, unseen—otherwise Nimor might have just shadow walked away.

Shaking his head, Gromph continued, "Our matron mother has learned that Nimor belongs to an organization known as the Jaezred Chaulssin. Unfortunately we know little about this group, save for its name."

Zoran toyed idly with his wand of wonder, spinning it between his fingers.

"So we know his name. So what?" he asked insolently.

Gromph resisted the urge to fry the boy where he sat.

"A name is power," he said, speaking to the others. "It helps us to define our target. A target that seems to be the lynchpin holding two otherwise unfriendly armies together." He gestured at the figures in the crystal ball. They had not yet come to blows but were still arguing. "Remove the lynchpin—and the alliance will come apart. The duergar and tanarukk will fall upon one another, and victory for Menzoberranzan will be assured."

Julani glanced at Gromph and asked, "What do you suggest?"

"A concerted attack," the archmage answered. "All of us, casting our deadliest spells at once. Nimor will undoubtedly resist them, but some, certainly, will get through."

Prath rose from his chair, unlacing the lid of a wand case at his belt.

"Are we going to teleport to the cavern?" he asked.

Gromph patted the air, motioning the impetuous young mage back to his seat.

"We don't need to teleport anywhere," he said. "We can cast our spells from here."

Grendan raised a perfect eyebrow and asked, "How?"

"Through this," Gromph said, pointing at the crystal ball. "Since its creation, I've imbued it with a few . . . extras, the knowledge of which you must swear to keep secret."

"Ah," Julani said. "So *that's* why you summoned only House Baenre mages." He placed the tips of curled fingers to his chest, over his heart. "May Lolth's poison consume me, should I divulge whatever I am about to hear."

Gromph stared at each of the mages in turn, and one by one they nodded their agreement and spoke oaths of silence.

"This is not just a scrying device," Gromph told the others. "Once primed, it can be used to cast spells at a particular target—in this case, at Nimor. It will work not only for spells that can carry as far as the eye can see but also for those that are limited by distance. Now then, which spells are your most potent?"

One by one, the other mages described which spells they would cast. Gromph rejected some suggestions and approved others. When it was Noori's turn, she spread her hands.

"I don't know if my spells will be any use," she said humbly. "They tend to be divinations."

Gromph smiled and said, "On the contrary, Noori, you will contribute the most useful spell of all. In order to use the crystal ball, we must first cast a spell that will pinpoint the individual we wish to attack. Which is where you come in. Please cast a location spell on the drow."

With a slight bow that didn't quite hide her smile, Noori rose to her feet. She pulled a scrap of fur from her pocket and used it to polish the crystal ball. As she did, Nimor loomed larger inside the crystal ball, his face and chest filling it.

At a nod from Gromph, Noori resumed her seat. As she did, Gromph thought he saw Nimor follow her with his eyes. Had the drow sensed that someone was scrying him and glanced around in an effort to locate the source? Little matter; soon enough he'd be ducking spells.

Gromph pulled a pinch of sand out of a pocket of his *piwafwi* and flicked it into the air in front of him, chanting the words of a minor creation spell. A tiny hourglass appeared on top of the eagle's cage, and the sand inside its uppermost globe began trickling away.

"Cast your spells when the last grain of sand falls," he told the others. "Make sure your conjurations all end at precisely the same instant."

After taking care to make sure his protective devices were still on his person and tucking Kyorli safely into his sleeve, Gromph began his own spell.

He chose a necromantic spell, one of the most powerful in his arsenal. Slowly, one eye on the hourglass, he rasped out words whose raw power scratched the inside of his throat, making it bleed. Dimly, he was aware of the magical conjurations of the other wizards.

Julani held both hands in front of him, the first two fingers forked in the gesture that would summon a powerful lightning bolt, and Grendan was kneading the air with his fingers, creating a hypnotic weave of shifting color. Prath had chosen an evocation that would summon a magic missile—a feeble spell, but probably the best the first-year student could manage. Zoran, meanwhile, slumped lazily in his chair, a grin tweaking the corner of his lips. Gromph longed to give the insolent boy a magical thrashing—but dared not interrupt his own spell. The hourglass was nearly empty.

As the last of the sand trickled out, Gromph spoke the final word of his spell—and heard the others do the same. His pointing forefinger turned momentarily skeletal as a thin ray of bone-white erupted from its tip and lanced into the crystal ball, streaking toward Nimor's chest. In that same moment, lightning erupted from Julani's fingers, filling the air with the boom of thunder and the stench of ozone. Grendan's hypnotic pattern rushed toward its target. Zoran had said he was going to cast a spell that would send Nimor into fits of laughter, incapacitating him, but instead he drew and fired his wand of wonder. A useless stream of gems erupted from its tip. Meanwhile the three magic missiles Prath had conjured up glanced harmlessly off some magical defense that surrounded Nimor, just as Gromph had expected.

No, they ricocheted—straight back at the boy. Which was impossible.

Gromph tried to shout a warning, but all he managed was, "Ward yourselves! The spells—"

Then his own death spell came hurtling back at him. The bone-white ray, chill as the grave, struck him in the chest, the precise spot he'd aimed for on Nimor. His enchanted *piwafwi* soaked up the spell, its hood, cuffs, and hem instantly crumbling away like ancient, rotted cloth. Even so, the spell rocked him to the side as if he'd been kicked in the head by a rothé. He tumbled out of his chair, winding up in an undignified heap on the floor.

As he fell he heard Prath grunt as his three magic missiles struck, punching deep, bloody holes into the boy's chest. In the same instant, twin lightning bolts struck Julani, passing through his body in less than a heartbeat to explode out of his hands, feet and the top of his head, killing him instantly. Grendan, meanwhile, went slack-jawed as the hypnotic pattern he'd conjured appeared in the air in front of his face. Beside him, Zoran flung up his hands as the stream of gems from his wand rushed back at him, thudding into his chest. One caught him in the head, knocking what little sense he had out of it, and he fell out of his chair, unconscious.

Lifting his head, Gromph was just in time to see the crystal ball turn a solid white. It fell with a crash to the floor, knocking the eagle's cage over and cracking in two. Inside the cage, the eagle *screeed* in anguish as its missing eyeball—split in two and weeping blood—returned to its socket.

Gromph looked at the destruction his plan had wrought and was furious with himself. His experiment had turned out most disastrously for House Baenre. Julani was dead, and Prath— judging by the sound of his labored, gurgling breathing—would soon die without magical intervention. Grendan would be a drooling idiot for some time to come, and Zoran . . . well, being knocked unconscious was precisely what he deserved for using so whimsical a weapon in such dire circumstances. Noori was unscathed but had only divination magic at her disposal. Besides, she was too busy fussing over her lover to be of any use, even were her spells more powerful.

Gromph had half expected Nimor to have magic that would protect him from spells, but only a handful of the spells should have been turned—not all of them. And certainly not those spells, like the hypnotic pattern, which targeted the air next to Nimor, and not the drow himself. Whatever device or spell protected Nimor must have been the result of a unique enchantment—one beyond the capabilities of most mortal wizards.

Gromph knew of only one spellcaster capable of such powerful magic: the lichdrow Dyrr.

Easing himself off the floor, Gromph was relieved to see Kyorli, unhurt, scurry out of his sleeve. As Gromph rose to a sitting position, a sharp object dug into his hip. He assumed it was one of Zoran's useless gems but then realized it was something in the hip pocket of his *piwafwi*. He reached into the pocket—and to his surprise found a prism of quartz. Tiny yellow sparks as bright as miniature suns danced inside it, evidence of the light-producing magic that was trapped in its depths.

How had it gotten into his pocket?

He stared at it absently, half-listening to the gurgling, bloody breathing of Prath. All the while, he was thinking furiously. He alone must deal with Nimor—but how? Any spell that targeted the strange drow would only bounce back at its caster—even a spell that affected an area, rather than Nimor himself, couldn't take him down. Yet Nimor must have a weak spot. One that seemed, on the surface, to be his chief strength . . .

Shadow walking.

Glancing at the prism, Gromph began to smile. Carefully, he tucked it back in his pocket. The insignificant little magical device—a trivial construct of the Surface Realms that was designed to serve no more noble purpose than to illuminate darkened corridors—would rid them all of Nimor Imphraezl.

Without having to cast any spells on him.

TWENTY-FIVE

A chorus of nearly fifty voices filled the air as Eilistraee's priest-esses, seated in a circle around a waist-high, rust-red boulder, gave worship to their goddess through evensong. Halisstra sat among them on one side of the crater that had been formed when a boulder fell from the heavens, centuries gone by. The crater was bowl-shaped and dozens of paces wide, its sides smoothed by a dusting of snow.

The evensong was one of thanksgiving for the forest that sustained them; for the sun that even then was setting behind the trees, filling the sky with rosy pink light; for the moon that would illuminate the darkness, reminding the drow that even at night the goddess still watched her children; and for the ground beneath their feet, which gave up its iron needed to forge the Dark Ladies' swords.

"Up from the earth, and into the flame," Halisstra sang,

together with the other priestesses, "I temper my heart, in Eilistraee's name."

Though the evensong was a joyful one, it had an undercurrent of rage that night. Upon hearing of the death of a member of their faith at the hands of a yochlol, priestesses from all over the forest had gathered to pay tribute to the woman who had fallen. More priestesses were still emerging from the forest to join in the circle. Clad in chain mail and bearing shields they sank down beside the others, sat cross-legged with drawn swords placed across their knees, and joined in the song.

When it was done, Uluyara rose and walked down the slope to the boulder. Placing her left hand on it, she raised the sword she held in her right hand to the heavens, invoking the goddess.

"Eilistraee, hear me," she cried. "Breena's death shall be avenged. We shall hunt down the servants of the Spider Queen and put them to the sword! Dark Maiden, give us strength."

As one, the seated priestesses raised their own swords and shouted, "By song and sword!"

Belatedly, Halisstra joined them, thrusting her own sword at the heavens. She glanced, nervously, at the priestesses on either side of her, worried that they might think her tardiness showed a lack of faith—or that they might cast a critical eye on the blade's missing tip. But they were caught up in the moment, sighting along their own blades at the sky above.

"Whether they try to run on the surface or hide in Lolth's dark depths, we shall hunt them down," Uluyara continued, the fire in her red eyes matching that of the setting sun. "We will have our vengeance upon them and will dance in delight as they fall. Lady of the Dance, give us strength!"

Halisstra was ready.

"By song and sword!" she shouted, thrusting her songsword into the air at the same time the others did.

"We will tear through their web of lies and deceit and destroy all who prevent the dark children from claiming their rightful place in the light," Uluyara continued. "Lady Silverhair, give us strength!"

"By song and sword!" the priestesses replied.

Then, all at once, they stood, and Halisstra scrambled to join them.

"Lolth will be defeated!" Uluyara cried. The blade of her sword was glowing with a cold, white light. "Eilistraee, give us strength!"

"By song and sword!" the priestesses shouted, raising their swords a fourth and final time. Then, reversing their weapons, they drove them point-first into the ground and shouted, "Lolth must die!"

Halisstra had shouted the first response together with the other priestesses but was taken by surprise when they thrust their swords down, instead of up. A heartbeat behind the others, she thrust Seyll's songsword into the ground, forcing its blunted tip into the earth.

"Lolth must die!" she shouted—suddenly realizing that her voice was all alone in the abrupt silence.

She glanced up and found that all of them were staring at her—especially Uluyara. The high priestess had driven the point of her own sword not into the earth but into the boulder beside her. For a moment, the boulder reminded Halisstra of a slain spider, the red streaks of rust emulating blood. As Uluyara tossed back her hair, the silver radiance cast by the blade of her sword caught it, making it sparkle like moonlight. She beckoned Halisstra forward.

Deciding after a moment's hesitation to leave the songsword in the ground where she'd thrust it, Halisstra approached the high priestess. Uluyara reached out for her hand, and when Halisstra gave it to her, she placed it on the hilt of the sword in the stone.

"This one holds a special place in Eilistraee's heart, though she has but recently renounced the Queen of Spiders," Uluyara told the others. "May the Lady of the Dance bless her and guide her sword well. Eilistraee give her strength."

Halisstra, her palm damp with nervous sweat, spoke the ritual response: "By song and sword."

As she said it, the sword she was holding quivered slightly. Then, seemingly of its own accord, it slid deeper into the stone. Halisstra, still holding its hilt, followed it down, pushing it into the boulder until its hilt struck the stone with a dull clank.

"By song and sword!" the other priestesses cried.

Then, as one, they broke into song, whirling their swords above their heads. A moment later, they were dancing in a circle around the stone.

Halisstra, still gripping the sword tightly, felt Uluyara place a hand on hers.

"Come," the high priestess said. "Join the dance. When it is done, there is something I'd like to discuss with you."

Halisstra nodded and allowed herself to be led into the swirl of dancers. On the way she plucked the songsword from the ground and waved it over her head. As she moved gracefully among the other priestesses, sword flashing, she could feel Eilistraee looking down from the heavens. Not just at the dance, but at her, personally. Filled with wonder, Halisstra realized the goddess had something in mind for her, something momentous. Would she be able to rise to the challenge? She who, like the yochlol, had so treacherously betrayed and slain one of Eilistraee's priestesses?

As she danced, Halisstra could sense another set of eyes, watching her. Not those of a goddess but of a mortal. She searched the trees that fringed the crater, looking for a familiar patch of too-deep shadow, for the tiny flash of white that would mark the eyes that were observing her. At last she found it, high among the branches, and knew that it was the spot where Ryld was levitating.

Seeing him—or rather, seeing the subtle signs that he was there—Halisstra felt a chill course through her blood. Males were forbidden from observing the evensong ritual. Spying on one so emotionally charged was to court disaster. Any moment, one of the priestesses might spot the weapons master and punish his transgression by striking him blind, deaf, and dumb. For all Halisstra knew, Eilistraee herself might punish him, smiting him with the cold fire that had killed the phase spider.

Those grim thoughts filled Halisstra's mind as she followed the dancing women in their circle, for a few moments losing track of Ryld as her back was turned to him. Then, as she came around to the other side of the circle once more, she snuck a glance at the spot where he was—carefully, so as not to attract attention to him.

Ryld was gone.

Lost in thought as he approached the tiny cabin in which he and Halisstra had been quartered, Ryld didn't react, at first, to the faint, musky odor that came to his nostrils as the wind shifted. Instead his thoughts were on the dance he'd been spying on and Halisstra's conversion, heart and soul, to a goddess who would condemn her to forever live in the World Above. Only at the last instant—as a patch of shadow in the bushes to his right suddenly shifted—did he jerk back. By the time he drew Splitter from the sheath on his back, a black wolf had leaped onto the trail in front of him, blocking it. Instead of attacking, however, it cocked its head and gave Ryld a sly grin, tongue lolling from its mouth. A ripple passed through its body, causing the wolf to stagger, and

Ryld heard the sound of cracking cartilage as the animal became a dirt-smudged boy.

"If the wind hadn't shifted, I'd have had you," Yarno said.

Ryld grinned in acknowledgement and sheathed his sword. Then, hearing female voices in the forest behind him, he frowned down at Yarno.

"You shouldn't be here," he told the boy. "If the priestesses find you within their sacred grove. . . ."

The boy's eyes narrowed, and he asked, "How many have you killed?"

It took Ryld a moment to realize what the boy was asking. The question was one he was often asked by the students at Melee-Magthere—and one he always declined to answer. "The proud spider gets caught in its own web," he would quote, reminding them that hidden prowess with weapons was a weapon in and of itself. But Yarno was talking about the priestesses—which reminded Ryld of his promise to the boy.

"They didn't kill Halisstra," he told Yarno.

The boy scratched his ear.

"You rescued her?" he asked. "Then why are you still—"

Hearing footsteps approaching on the trail behind him, Ryld tried to shoo the boy away.

"Go," the weapons master said. "Hurry. If they find you . . ."

Seeing Yarno tense, Ryld whirled around, drawing Splitter a second time. Relief flooded through him as he saw it was only Halisstra—whichever of the priestesses she'd been talking with must have turned down a different trail. She halted abruptly as she saw Yarno and frowned—and Ryld groaned as he realized what was happening. Out of the corner of his eye he could see the boy shifting back into wolf form—the worst thing Yarno could have done in that moment. If he'd stayed in human form, Ryld might have passed him off as a scatterling, but . . .

"Monster!" Halisstra gasped.

In that same moment, Yarno leaped toward her. Fortunately, Ryld was swifter. Dropping Splitter, he caught the werewolf by his haunches and slammed him to the ground.

"Stop," Ryld grunted through gritted teeth. Yarno wriggled in his arms, teeth bared in a threatening growl as he struggled to snap at Halisstra. "That's Mistress Melarn. The one I came to rescue."

Halisstra, meanwhile, yanked her hunting horn from her belt and raised it to her lips. Still hanging onto the struggling Yarno, Ryld twisted his body like an eel and lashed out with his feet, tripping her.

Halisstra fell, dropping the horn. She scrambled for it.

"Don't blow it!" Ryld exclaimed.

Halisstra glared at him as she recovered the horn and backed out of range of his feet.

"Are you mad?" she asked as she climbed to her feet. "That's a shapeshifter."

Once again, she raised the horn to her lips.

"He won't hurt you," Ryld gritted. To prove it, he released Yarno and sprang to his feet. "Go!" he ordered. "Flee!"

Without waiting to see if Yarno obeyed, Ryld whirled toward Halisstra and grabbed her arm, forcing the horn away from her lips.

Yarno stood panting a moment, glancing between Ryld and Halisstra. Then—with one final snarl at the priestess—he leaped away into the bushes.

Halisstra yanked her arm out of Ryld's grasp and glared at him. Behind the glare was a hint of distrust.

"You knew that boy was a . . . an animal . . . thing?"

"Yarno is harmless," Ryld said, returning Splitter to its sheath. "Let him go."

"He's a monster. Eilistraee has commanded us to clear this wood of vermin like him."

Ryld winced.

"He's a boy," he sighed. "Just a boy."

Halisstra shook her head, not understanding.

"Then why do you care if he lives or dies?" she asked.

Ryld opened his mouth, trying to find the words.

"Because he . . ." the weapons master fumbled, confused himself. "He reminds me of myself at that age."

"How is that possible? You're a drow, and he's . . ." Halisstra paused, uncertain what to call the boy.

"He's a 'werewolf,' " Ryld said, supplying her with the word. "And hunted. And frightened. Just like I was, once."

For a heartbeat or two, Halisstra stared into his eyes, and Ryld thought she had understood. Then she lifted her horn.

"He may look like a boy, but he's a monster," she said firmly.

"And you're a First Daughter," Ryld replied, grabbing Halisstra's hand. "Always one of the hunters—never one of the hunted. You never had to survive in the Stenchstreets."

Halisstra paused, and Ryld realized she might not know exactly what the Stenchstreets was.

"But you're a noble drow too," she said. "Aren't you?"

"I have no House," Ryld answered. "I never have."

He sighed, wondering what he was doing. Was he really choosing to stand against Halisstra—the woman he loved—for the sake of a boy he'd only just met. For a werewolf? What kind of drow was he?

The kind who remembered what it was like to be a small boy and frightened.

Ryld let go of Halisstra's hand.

"Summon the hunt then, if you must," he told her. "But know that, if you do, I'm leaving."

Halisstra's mouth gaped.

"You're asking me to choose between you," she said, "and my sacred duty to the goddess."

"I'm asking you to choose between what is wrong and what is right."

"Strange words, coming from the mouth of a drow." She stared off into the moonlit forest, hefting the horn in her hand. Then, slowly, she lowered it.

Relieved, Ryld took Halisstra's hand and bowed low over it, brushing the back of it with his lips.

"Thank you," he said.

Halisstra yanked her hand free—and for a terrible moment Ryld thought he was going to be chastised—but instead Halisstra lifted his chin and kissed him fiercely. She wrapped her arms around him, pulling him close.

Closing his eyes, Ryld felt her lips brush his ear—and heard a whisper so faint he was certain it hadn't been meant for him.

"Eilistraee, forgive me. I love him."

Then, taking him by the hand, she led him to the ancient ruin the priestesses had set aside as their shelter.

As soon as they were inside, she kissed him again. Her lips pressed into his with a fierceness uncharacteristic of her. They had kissed before, it was true, but not like that. All she had permitted him, before that night, were brief, almost chaste brushes of his lips against hers. Obedient male that he was, he had not dared ask for more. But that kiss . . . that was the kind of kiss his fantasies had been filled with. Eagerly, he returned it, barely keeping in check the hard, insistent heat that was threatening to overwhelm him.

"I want you," Halisstra said, breaking away from the kiss just long enough to gasp out the words. "I want to take you. Here. Now."

At these words, Ryld felt self-control slide completely from his grasp. Breathing rapidly—where had his warrior's training fled to?—he slid Splitter from his back and tossed the greatsword aside, then rapidly began shucking his armor.

Halisstra was stripping off her own armor and clothing. Then she was kissing him again, one hand pressing against the back of his head, the other snaking tight around his waist, making the process of undressing even more difficult. For one panicked moment, Ryld had a vision of himself as a fly, caught in a spider's web. Halisstra's arms were tight around him, pulling him closer, her mouth devouring him. Her teeth bit passionately into his neck, then his chest, then the hard muscle of his stomach, and onward.

For several long, dizzy moments Ryld flung his head back and stared sightlessly at the sagging ceiling of the ruin. Dimly he was aware of the rough floor rushing up to meet his back, of a corner of his vambrace digging with blissful pain into his shoulder.

Halisstra was on top of him. For just a moment, her hair seemed streaked with silver as she tossed it back behind her shoulders, and Ryld was reminded of the woman who had appeared to him in the belladonna-induced fever dream. Sparkles of moonlight rushed down and exploded into his mind, obliterating everything else.

Much later, Halisstra touched his shoulder and whispered, "Ryld? Are you in Reverie? I wanted to speak to you about something."

Ryld opened his eyes. He could tell by Halisstra's tone that he wasn't going to like whatever it was she was going to say. She sounded formal and firm, her tone reminiscent of the way a priestesses would address a male. He braced himself, waiting for the whiplike reprimand that must soon come. She must have spotted him earlier, spying on the sacred song and dance, and she was going to chastise him for it.

"I'm going back to the Underdark," she told him. "I'm going to find Quenthel Baenre and the others and rejoin their quest."

Startled—but not showing it, in case it was a test—he stared deep into her eyes. Her face, like his own, was perfectly neutral. No, not completely. Something shone in her eyes—something more than reflected starlight. An echo of the passion they'd shared.

"Why?" he asked.

Halisstra visibly relaxed.

"Uluyara has asked me to go back there. Eilistraee's priestesses need to know if Lolth truly is dead. The information is vital to their cause—and I'm the only one who can obtain it for them."

Ryld nodded. The warrior part of his mind acknowledged the wisdom of Uluyara's command. Halisstra would make an excellent spy. Moreover, she was merely a foot soldier in Eilistraee's order. If Quenthel killed her, she would barely be missed. The traitor priestesses' war against Lolth would continue with barely a ripple. Deep inside, however, he boiled with anger at Uluyara's willingness to sacrifice Halisstra.

"I'm not asking you to come with me," Halisstra said.

Realizing that he had let his anger show—and that Halisstra had misread it—Ryld said what was on his mind.

"One tiny slip, and Quenthel will kill you, as fast as a striking serpent."

"That's something I'm willing to risk."

"I'm not," he said. "That's why I'm going to come with you."

Halisstra touched his cheek.

"Thank you," she whispered.

Later still, when Ryld had indeed slipped into Reverie, Halisstra stared at him. He sat cross-legged, his eyes closed. His hands were crossed on the scabbarded blade of Splitter, but otherwise he looked like a vanquished warrior, his armor strewn about him and his weapons cast aside.

Sighing, Halisstra leaned back against a wall of the ruin and settled into Reverie herself. Her muscles were already loose and relaxed, and so it took but a moment for the familiar wash of memories to claim her.

She drifted with them, observing with detachment as her mind skipped from one to the next, like a stone skipping on water. Memories of the first day of her service in the temple of House Melarn and her instructors caning her palms until they bled after she mispronounced the words of the daily prayer. And of the satisfaction Halisstra had felt the next day, when she was called to lead the prayer—and did so with a precision that earned a brief smile from the priestess who had beaten her. Memories, too, of the footraces she and her sister Jawil had run, as children, along the roads of Ched Nasad—and the terrifying plunge after Jawil had pushed her over the edge in retaliation when Halisstra at last won a race. Only the fact that Halisstra had "borrowed" an aunt's House insignia—one that provided levitation magic—had saved her. Later, Jawil had said that she'd known about the insignia all along.

Those older, well-visited memories jostled against newer, fresher, somehow *cleaner* ones. Of the night she had been lifted from the cave and embraced by the priestesses of Eilistraee. Of the fierce joy she'd felt after defeating the phase spider. Her mind even drifted over brand-new memories that were only then being engraved upon her soul.

All of the other males Halisstra had lain with had been eager, yes, but an undercurrent of fear ran just beneath the surface of their lust. Perhaps it was because they knew they were being taken by a priestess of Lolth and feared that Halisstra, like the spiders she held sacred, might casually kill them and cast them aside. When she had first started kissing Ryld, Halisstra had seen a fleeting trace of that fear in him, but then it had disappeared. At some point during their lovemaking, he had surrendered—not to fear, or even to Halisstra, but to something larger. It was not so much that she had taken him. Instead he had given himself.

That realization acquired, Halisstra's mind drifted on to other recent memories. One of them, harsh and insistent, rose to the fore: Seyll. Or rather, her death at Halisstra's hands. Strangely, that image was garbled. Halisstra's memory of Seyll, dying, blood leaking from her side into the stream in which she lay had somehow become confused with that of Seyll in the moment just before she died, when the priestess had turned and was reaching out with both hands, preparing to help Halisstra cross the stream. In that false recollection, Seyll was reaching up toward Halisstra and speaking—whereas in truth, Seyll had actually been lying so still that Halisstra had thought her already dead. And the words were wrong—they were not the words of hope that Seyll had offered after Halisstra had dragged her "body" from the stream and begun stripping it of its weapons and armor. Instead they seemed to be a message, and an urgent one.

Halisstra, still deep in Reverie, leaned forward to hear it.

You will need the sword, Seyll whispered.

Halisstra, her eyes still closed, patted the floor beside her and her fingers came to rest upon the broken-tipped songsword, nested in its scabbard.

"I have it," she whispered aloud.

In the dream-memory, Seyll shook her head.

Not that one. Blood bubbled from her lips as she spoke. *Only with the Crescent Blade can you defeat her.*

"Defeat who?" Halisstra asked. "I don't—"

It was lost on the Cold Field, Seyll interrupted, her voice gurgling as her breathing became ragged. She was close to death, almost unable to speak. *The priestess was carrying it . . . and was slain. The . . . worm has it now.*

Halisstra puzzled over that one: was it "worm" Seyll had said—or "wyrm?" She decided it must have been wyrm. Dragons were known to covet treasure—especially magical weapons. And judging by the reverential way in which Seyll had said the words "Crescent Blade," magical was exactly what the sword was.

Seyll was still speaking—so faintly that Halisstra could barely hear her.

Find the Crescent Blade . . . and use it . . . to defeat her.

"Defeat who?" Halisstra cried.

From beside her came a swift, rustling noise. Her Reverie broken, Halisstra opened her eyes and saw Ryld in a ready crouch, Splitter in hand. He glanced swiftly around the darkened room, then at Halisstra, eyebrows raised in a silent question.

"It was nothing," she answered. "I was in Reverie. It was just a dream."

Ryld relaxed and slid the greatsword back into its sheath. His eyes lingered on her, and Halisstra remembered that she was still naked. He did not look respectfully away, as was the custom for a drow male. Instead his eyebrows raised a second time, and a fire danced in his eyes.

Halisstra shook her head.

"Later," she told him. "I need to speak to Uluyara about something."

Leaping to her feet, she hurriedly clothed herself, then slipped out into the night.

Chapter

TWENTY-SIX

Gromph strode up to the captain who stood surveying the silent battlefield, arms folded across his blackened mithral plate mail. Andzrel's eyes held a satisfied glint as he took in the shattered mushroom forest and the tanarukk corpses that littered the ground like felled stems.

"Drag the bodies back to the corrals," the Baenre weapons master told the soldiers who were inspecting the fallen tanarukks. "We can feed them to the lizards."

As he spoke, he cleaned blood from his sword with a scrap of cloth. He inspected his blade, smiled, then shoved it back into the scabbard at his hip.

"I wouldn't put that away just yet," Gromph said. "You'll be needing it."

Andzrel turned, a surprised look on his face.

"Archmage!" he gasped. "Where in the Abyss have you been?"

"Not quite as deep as the Abyss, but close enough," the archmage quipped. "I'll tell you all about it later." He glanced around. "How do things fare here?"

"Everything is under control," Andzrel reported. He gestured at the mouth of a tunnel in the wall of the great cavern. In front of it was a heap of tanarukk dead. "We've driven the enemy back into the Dark Dominions. They're pulling back from the city, regrouping. And Tier Breche?"

"Quiet, for the moment," Gromph answered. "The enemy has also been driven back on that front and the approach well sealed. I expect the duergar will eventually rally, recombine with other units somewhere out in the tunnels, and resume their siege elsewhere. Before they have a chance to do that, however, I need your help with something."

"Something other than corpse disposal?"

Gromph nodded.

Andzrel grinned and said, "Name it."

The archmage glanced at one of the bodies that lay nearby. Part orc, part demon, the tanarukk was a stocky monstrosity covered in patches of coarse hair and scabby-looking scales. A long jaw jutted out from under its abbreviated snout, and the tusks that curled over its upper lip were chipped and yellow. Its low, sloped forehead gave it a stupid appearance—accentuated by the flat glaze of death in its dull red eyes.

"I need to get through the enemy lines," Gromph began. "And I'll need an escort. A soldier, rather than a mage." He nudged the dead tanarukk with his foot. "Tell me, Andzrel, have you ever been polymorphed?"

"Once," Andzrel answered. "Years ago, into a lizard. As a joke, by a prideful upstart who thought that saddling me up and riding me would teach me my place. After I took a bite out of him, he didn't think it was so amusing anymore and changed me back."

Gromph smiled. He remembered well the day that Nauzhror had limped into Sorcere, demanding a cushion because he was unable to sit down. A "riding accident" he'd called it—until one of the other students had used a spell to peer through his robe and had spotted the bite wound on the buttocks. The pompous young Nauzhror had been the butt of many a joke after that.

"I'll try not to give you cause to use your tusks on me," Gromph told Andzrel with mock gravity.

$$\math459 \quad \math459 \quad \math459$$

The tanarukk soldiers retreated in disarray through the tunnels, snarling and nipping at each other whenever a narrowing of the walls caused a bottleneck. The air was filled with the clank of weapons and armor, the tang of blood from the wounded who had been rudely shoved aside and abandoned to die—and with the shouts of the sergeants who tried to bring order to the chaos.

Two tanarukks shuffled along behind the rest, taking care to keep apart from the jostling masses, neither giving provocation nor accepting it. One had a more pronounced forehead than his fellows and bristle-stiff patches of white hair. The other was broader across the shoulders and clad in chain mail that seemed slightly stiff. The blade of the battle-axe he carried was streaked with blood. The white-haired one seemed to have lost his weapon and carried a small scrap of fur—a trophy scalp, to all appearances—in one hand. He drew his companion to the side of the tunnel, out of the way of the marching hordes, then whispered a spell while twisting the fur in his hand. He nodded at a narrow fissure to their left.

"He's down this way," Gromph said. "Or at least he was a moment ago. I've lost him again."

"Where does he keep disappearing to?" Andzrel asked, irritated.

The stoop-shouldered posture of his tanarukk body was giving him a backache. He longed to get this mission over with and be back in drow form. And his tanarukk body *stank*. Gromph had no such problems, however. He'd used a glamer to change his appearance. If he'd polymorphed himself, the material components he needed to work his spells—like that scrap of bloodhound fur, for example—would have been changed into items more suitable to a tanarukk.

Or at least, that's what the archmage had told Andzrel. The Baenre weapons master suspected, however, that Gromph just didn't want to endure the stink of tanarukk sweat on his own skin.

"I don't know what Nimor's up to," Gromph answered. "Reporting to his masters, perhaps. But he keeps returning to this spot. It must be one he knows well."

Slipping away from the other tanarukks, the pair squeezed through the narrow tunnel. It extended horizontally for some distance, then sloped up to a small cavern, one whose entrance was guarded by a duergar. The gray dwarf lifted his axe as the pair approached.

"We've got an urgent message for the drow Nimor," Gromph said, adopting the low, grunting voice of a tanarukk.

"Oh yeah?" The duergar snorted. "So does every other bloody tanarukk in Vhok's useless excuse for an army. Well, Lord Nimor's not here."

Gromph ignored the taunt. He sniffed loudly as he scanned the apparently empty cavern.

"He's here," the disguised archmage said. "I can smell him."

"No he's not," the duergar replied with a frown. "Get back to your ranks."

Andzrel balled a fist with knuckles that were ridged with scales and raised it under the duergar's nose.

"We know he's in there," he growled. "Let us by."

The duergar suddenly grew larger and broader—until he was half again as tall as Andzrel's tanarukk form. He squeezed the handle of his axe, causing a shimmer of magical energy to pulse through it.

"Don't make me use this," the giant gray dwarf warned.

"Nimor will want to hear this message," Gromph insisted. "Tell him it's from the spy he sent into Menzoberranzan."

"What spy?"

"Sluugguth," the other tanarukk said.

The duergar's face paled to a lighter shade of gray, and he said, "Oh . . . the illithid."

Gromph frowned.

"Sluugguth doesn't like it when his messengers get delayed," he growled. He pulled a length of silver chain from his pocket. From the end of it hung an oval of jade. "He told us to bring this to Nimor as quickly as we could," he said. "He said it's important."

At last, the duergar nodded. Shrinking back down to his usual size, he stepped aside.

"Go on in," he told Gromph, but he held up a hand as Andzrel tried to follow, and added, "But *you* have to leave your weapon outside."

Gromph and Andzrel exchanged a look. That was going to be a problem. As soon as Andzrel's "battle-axe" left his hands it would no longer be affected by the polymorph spell and would turn back into a drow sword.

"I can deliver the message on my own," Gromph told Andzrel. "You wait out here . . . until I'm done."

Andzrel nodded.

Gromph entered the cavern. Once inside, he could see that the space was more of a natural chimney, with a high ceiling. Up near the top was a ledge on which Nimor squatted, eyes closed, apparently in Reverie. He was in an unusual pose, with his arms drawn against his chest and his fists touching his shoulders, which were hunched. His posture reminded Gromph of a sleeping bat turned wrong way around.

Wondering if Nimor, too, was cloaked in an illusion, Gromph reached into a pocket for the small stone jar he carried there. He was just about to scoop out a little of the paste it held when Nimor's eyes opened. They immediately locked on the oval of jade that spun gently at the end of the chain in Gromph's hand. The magic in the amulet was still potent—though the jade spider it had once commanded had been reduced to a heap of rubble, at Gromph's orders, before he and Andzrel set out into the Dark Dominion.

Nimor stepped off the ledge, levitating down to where Gromph stood.

Gromph withdrew his hand from his pocket, abandoning the spell he'd been about to cast. There was no time for true seeing, he had to be ready to mount a magical defense if one was required.

"Where did you get that, soldier?" Nimor demanded as he landed lightly on the floor next to Gromph.

Gromph smiled to himself. The illusion was holding.

"From Sluuguth," he answered, holding up the jade spider amulet.

At the same time he reached into a pocket and carefully grasped the item it contained—the prism—by the end that protruded from the oiled sheath he'd constructed for it. He'd made some magical alterations to the prism before embarking on his quest to find Nimor, weaving new spells into the magic the device already contained.

"Sluuguth got busy and couldn't bring the amulet himself, so he sent me," Gromph continued.

Nimor started to reach for the silver chain, then stopped.

He eyed Gromph warily and asked, "Busy with what?"

"That wizard that Lord Dyrr captured—the one from House Baenre. He escaped from the sphere."

"Gromph?" Nimor waved a hand dismissively. "Old news. Gromph's dead now."

Gromph shook his head vigorously and said, "No, he's not. Sluuguth says he's up to something that could hurt our army . . . some spell."

"Where is he?" Nimor demanded.

Gromph scratched the bristles on the top of his head and frowned. Fortunately he didn't need any help looking stupid with the illusion of a tanarukk cloaking him.

"Who? Sluuguth . . . or Gromph?"

Nimor's eyes narrowed in irritation, and he said, "Gromph."

"Oh . . . yeah. Sluuguth said to show you this," Gromph answered, as if just remembering.

As he spoke, he slid his hand from his pocket. The prism he held came out of its oiled sheath with a jerk and emerged from the pocket without any of the sovereign glue that coated it sticking to the fabric.

So far, Gromph thought, so good.

Nimor glanced at the prism.

"What's that?" he asked.

Gromph's gamble was still holding up. Like most drow, Nimor was unfamiliar with the magical items of the World Above.

"It's a scrying device," he told Nimor. "You can see Gromph in it."

Nimor folded his arms across his chest and said, "You look into it. Tell me where he is."

"All right," Gromph said with a shrug.

Again, all was going according to plan. He'd factored the

drow's suspicious nature into his plans. He stared into the prism, angling it this way and that.

"Can't see anything," he said. Then he suddenly held it still. "Oh, there he is . . . but is Gromph the skeleton or the drow with the rat on his shoulder?"

Nimor reached for the prism and said, "Let me see that."

The moment had come. As Nimor's fingers touched the prism, Gromph let go of the end he held and dropped his illusion, revealing himself.

At the same time, he shouted, "Andzrel! Now!"

Behind him, Gromph heard a thud and a grunt—the sound of the duergar guarding the door being felled by Andzrel's weapon. An instant later, as a wide-eyed Nimor backed away, flicking one hand to try to rid it of the prism that was stuck to it with magical glue and drawing his rapier with the other hand, Andzrel burst into the cavern, battle-axe held high. Unused to his tanarukk form, he swung it awkwardly, but even so his charge looked formidable.

Nimor, seeing that he was cornered, did exactly what Gromph had expected him to. He shadow walked.

But even as Nimor began to slip into the Plane of Shadow, a smirk on his lips, the contingency spell Gromph had woven into the prism was triggered. It, in turn, triggered the prism's tertiary power, causing the prism to flare with a blinding flash of light. For an instant, it was as if the sun of the World Above had been teleported into the cavern, bathing its walls in the most intense light Gromph had ever experienced. Nimor screamed—a howl of anguish and a bellow of rage in one. Then both the light and the sound of Nimor's voice winked out.

Gromph heard the *swoosh* of a blade through the air and the clang of metal against stone as Andzrel's battle-axe split the air where Nimor had been standing. Unable to see, trying to blink away the aftereffects of the brilliant flash, Gromph patted the air around him with his hands. His outstretched hands encountered only air. Nimor seemed to have completed his "escape" into the Shadow Plane.

"Andzrel!" Gromph called. "Can you see? Where's Nimor?"

Someone moved closer to him. A gnarled hand touched his arm.

"I can't see very well." Andzrel's voice came from right next to Gromph. "But my darkvision's starting to come back. Nimor's gone. What about you?"

Gromph's eyes were streaming with tears. He seemed to be having trouble seeing Andzrel—seeing anything.

"I'm . . . still blind. That flash of light seems to have had a greater effect on me than it did you—perhaps because the magic protecting Nimor recognized the spell inside the prism as mine and turned it back on me directly. No matter. It should be a simple matter to restore my sight."

Gromph touched a finger to each eye and cast a spell that should have dispelled his blindness—but though he felt the tingle of magic under his eyelids, his darkvision did not return. He was as unable to see in the dark cavern as any creature from the Surface Realms.

And that worried him. With Lolth's priestesses unable to contact their goddess, finding a restorative spell would be difficult.

"So where is Nimor now?" Andzrel asked.

"In the Plane of Shadow," Gromph answered. "And you know what that means."

"Actually, no, I don't," Andzrel answered. "My apologies, Archmage."

Gromph chuckled and said, "It means he's stuck there. In order to complete his shadow walk, Nimor needs either a patch of shadow—if you're in the World Above—or darkness to step into. A *deep* patch of darkness. That's something he isn't going to find any time soon, with a prism stuck to his hand that glows with the light of the sun."

"Well that's one piece gone from the *sava* game," Andzrel said in a satisfied voice. "What's next?"

"Back to Menzoberranzan," Gromph said. "You lead, and I'll follow."

🕷   🕷   🕷

Gromph stood at the base of Narbondel, one hand on the natural pillar's cold stone. It loomed large in Kyorli's eyes. The rat peered up at the darkened pillar from her perch on Gromph's shoulder, whiskers tickling his ear. Behind him, Gromph could hear Nauzhror muttering to himself. The younger wizard had relinquished the archmage's robes to Gromph with great reluctance and had insisted on being present at the lighting ritual. Like a spider, he sensed that Gromph had a weakness—even though he hadn't discovered what it was yet.

Turning to face the pillar, Gromph lifted both hands above his head. As he chanted the words to his spell he felt a familiar, tingling rush of power flow into his hands. When the magic reached its zenith, he slapped both of them against Narbondel, directing the magic into it. The cold stone warmed under his palms and a faint crackling filled the air. Like flames climbing a burning curtain, the magical heat and light slowly began to rise through Narbondel. Gromph couldn't see it with his own eyes, but through Kyorli's he saw a muted version of it, a circle of light emitting sparks of every color from deepest red to brightest purple, rising slowly against black stone. A beautiful sight—and one that would inspire hope in those who yet held the enemy at bay in the Dark Dominion, when they returned from the tunnels.

By memory, Gromph turned in the direction of House Agrach Dyrr.

"Can you see that, lichdrow?" he whispered. "I've escaped your imprisonment. Soon, I'll be coming for you."

Later, Gromph sat in his private office in Sorcere, drumming his fingers on the desk in front of him. Kyorli sat on his shoulder; Gromph still needed the rat's eyes in order to see. He had consumed a potion that should have restored his eyesight fully, but all he could see was a series of shadows and blurs. Had it been a combination of his own permanency spell and the magic that protected Nimor that had wreaked such destruction? With time and research, he would know the answers—but with two armies still hovering on the outskirts of Menzoberranzan, time was a luxury he didn't have.

A tickling at the back of his neck alerted him to the fact that someone was watching him—something that should have been impossible within the magically warded walls of his office. It seemed to be coming from the axe he'd hung on the wall—the one his forgotten illithid visitor had left. For a moment, Gromph wondered if the observer was one of the souls trapped within it, but when he bade Kyorli to turn and take a look, he saw no movement, no face in the axe blade.

As the archmage turned away from the axe, a familiar voice whispered at him from out of the thin air—the voice of the one drow Gromph had ensured would be able to penetrate the wards of his office..

Going to Lake of Shadows, Pharaun's voice whispered in his mind. *Aboleth said ship of chaos is sunk there with uridezu. Will sail ship to Abyss and appeal to Lolth directly.*

At twenty-five words, the message was precisely at the limit of the sending spell Pharaun had used to contact Gromph. The arch-mage sat in silence, contemplating his reply. It needed to be equally brief . . . and informative.

"Your mission is more urgent now. We *need* Lolth. Duergar and tanarukks besiege Menzoberranzan. Lichdrow Dyrr is a traitor." Gromph paused, then added in a wry voice, "An uridezu? I wish you luck."

The sense of being watched vanished, leaving Gromph sitting alone in his office. Slowly, he shook his head, wondering if that would be the last time he'd ever hear from Pharaun.

TWENTY-SEVEN

Uluyara listened in silence as Halisstra described what she had seen in Reverie. When she finished, Uluyara whispered a brief prayer, then raised a hand reverently to the night sky. Lowering it, she stared hard at Halisstra, her red eyes reflecting the moonlight.

"Lost, all these years," she said. "Our best scryers, joined in spell-song, could not find the Crescent Blade—and now a novice thinks she can succeed where they failed."

Halisstra, hearing a tone she didn't like in Uluyara's voice, bristled.

"I'm only repeating what Seyll said," she countered. "This was no hallucination. I'm sure it was her spirit who spoke to me. I think she was trying to tell me that I'm going to have to face down Quenthel Baenre in combat and that I'll need this Crescent Blade—whatever it is—to defeat her when I do."

Uluyara stared into Halisstra's eyes, as if weighing her words.

"If this is an excuse to delay rejoining your former companions," Uluyara said, "you might have picked something a little less dramatic than a search for the Crescent Blade. I'd rather you were honest with me and simply tell me you're not ready yet. If you've changed your mind, or are afraid—"

"Afraid? How dare you! I am the First Daughter of a noble House!" Halisstra spat.

Then she remembered who she was talking to—and remembered that her House was no more—and she threw herself onto the ground at Uluyara's feet.

"My apologies, Dark Lady," she whispered, tensing in expectation of the lash that would have immediately scoured her shoulders, had it been one of Lolth's high priestesses to whom she had spoken so boldly. "I was of a noble House and am not used to having my courage questioned. I was taught, long ago, to cocoon my fear up tight and never let it unravel. I assure you that I'm *not* afraid—and I'm not making this up. I don't even know what the Crescent Blade is. Please, enlighten me."

Uluyara sighed and said, "Rise, priestess." When Halisstra had, she continued, "This past day has been a difficult one for both of us. I was the one who first brought Breena up into the light. She was like a daughter to me. Her death . . ."

She paused to stare out into the darkened woods. From the direction her eyes yearned toward came the sound of women singing, the voices of the three priestesses who were laying out Breena's corpse on a bier high above the forest floor where it would be washed by the tears of the moon. The death song seemed to float on the breeze, accompanied by the clean scent of freshly fallen snow.

At last Uluyara tore her eyes away and began her story.

"The Crescent Blade was forged centuries ago, after Eilistraee plucked a pebble from the heavens and tossed it down to the earth below. By the time it struck the ground, it had grown to the size of a boulder and was glowing as brightly as a forge. It was so hot that no one could approach it without a protective spell. The boulder was weeping metal—moon metal, for that was where it came from. If you look up at the moon, you can see a hole. That is the spot from which Eilistraee plucked the stone."

Halisstra peered at the moon, which had just risen above the trees. Its face was pocked with dozens of dark, circular holes. She glanced from one to the next, wondering which was the one.

"There," Uluyara said, pointing. "The smaller hole within that larger, darker one. See how what remains of the larger hole forms the shape of a crescent?"

Halisstra closed one eye and sighted along Uluyara's arm, then nodded as she spotted it.

"The moon metal shed by the boulder was collected and forged into a sword with a crescent-shaped blade," Uluyara continued. "With each heating, with each hammer stroke against the anvil, with each quenching, enchantments were laid upon the blade. It was made holy, giving it a keener edge against evil. It was made quick as thought, allowing it to strike twice for each stroke of an enemy blade. It was enchanted with moonlight, just as my own sword is, allowing it to pass through armor—or even stone—as easily as through flesh. By the blessing of Eilistraee it can also fend off evil magic, casting a protective circle around the one who holds it.

"The final enchantment laid upon the Crescent Blade," Uluyara continued, "is perhaps the most powerful of all. If the arm of the priestess wielding it is strong and her aim is true, the blade will sever the neck of any creature."

Uluyara paused, and her eyes bored deep into Halisstra's.

"*Any* creature," she repeated. "Be it a drow, a demon . . . or even a goddess."

All at once, Halisstra understood.

"So that's what Seyll was trying to tell me," she whispered. "I'm to use the Crescent Blade not to kill Quenthel Baenre but to kill Lolth herself."

Uluyara stared at her for a long moment before she said, "Impossible as it sounds, it is so."

"But I . . . But she . . ."

Overcome by the enormity of the idea, Halisstra found herself unable even to protest. She, Halisstra—a former priestess of Lolth only recently brought into Eilistraee's light—was to slay the most powerful deity known to the drow? With a sword? The notion was insane. Laughable, even. She'd witnessed first hand a battle between gods, when Vhaeraun and Selvetarm confronted each other outside Lolth's temple in the Demonweb Pits. None of the mortals present—even Pharaun—could have affected the outcome of that battle if they tried. But Halisstra supposed Eilistraee must know what she was doing—that she must have chosen Halisstra for some reason.

Though really, Halisstra couldn't see why. She knew only a handful of *bae'qeshel* spells—mostly simple healing magic—and was still struggling to relearn the clerical spells that Lolth had once granted, and that Eilistraee was slowly revealing to her in new forms. Halisstra was like someone who had been laid low by an illness and who was only slowly learning to walk again. And Eilistraee expected her not just to walk but to run. To fly, even.

As Uluyara had said, impossible.

Or was it? Lolth might not be dead, but she was inactive—and inattentive. When Halisstra had blasphemed against her, nothing had happened. Even killing the phase spider by invoking Eilistraee's moonfire had failed to arouse her wrath. Lolth's yochlol handmaidens might have killed one of Eilistraee's priestesses, but from the goddess herself there had been no direct sign. According to Uluyara's scrying, Lolth's temple was still sealed by an enormous black stone. A stone that resembled a face—and had a neck.

A neck made of stone—a material the Crescent Blade could cut through easily, as easily as a normal blade through bare flesh. With a single, well-aimed stroke of the Crescent Blade, that neck could be severed. As long as the blow was struck by one of Eilistraee's faithful.

Would that really kill Lolth?

Halisstra shook her head.

"Why me?" she asked Uluyara. "Surely Eilistraee could have found a more worthy priestess. You, for example."

"It is not I who was chosen," Uluyara said. Then, after a moment's thought, she added, "You, out of all of those who worship Eilistraee, are unique for the simple reason that you are the only one Quenthel Baenre and the others will trust. If they do succeed in reaching Lolth's domain and you are among them, you'll be in the perfect position to end the Spider Queen's dark reign and release her children from the clinging webs that hold them back from their birthright."

"If it truly is Eilistraee's will, I will try," Halisstra said slowly. Then she realized that the first step in her monumental quest had yet to be taken. "Seyll said the Crescent Blade was lost on the Cold Field. Where is that?"

"It lies about three days' march to the southeast of here, at the edge of the great wood," Uluyara said. "It is a dangerous place. Centuries ago it was a battlefield, and the foul magic once unleashed there permeates it. The ghosts of the dead soldiers who once fought there roam it still—and are at their most dangerous in winter. When the chill of the air matches the chill of the grave they rise to fight again—and sweep away everything in their path."

Halisstra, going over Seyll's message again in her mind, was only half listening.

"Is the Cold Field home to a dragon?" she asked, remembering the warning about a wyrm.

Uluyara shrugged and said, "None has been sighted there, but it is possible. The battle was said to involve dragons. The Cold Field was scoured by their magical breath, and its soil remains infertile to this day. One of these dragons might have laired there in the centuries since."

"How did the Crescent Blade come to be lost?" Halisstra asked. "Seyll said 'she' was carrying it. Who? A priestess?"

The look Uluyara gave Halisstra was a peculiar one. She stared as if she'd suddenly realized something about Halisstra—something of import.

"She who carried the Crescent Blade was a priestess of the first rank," she said. "One of our Sword Dancers. She came, originally, from the same city as yourself. She came from Ched Nasad."

Halisstra nodded. She was surprised to hear that someone from her own city had also wound up at that temple, so far from home.

"What House was she?" Halisstra asked.

"House Melarn."

Halisstra blinked, and asked, "What . . . what was her name?"

"Mathira."

Halisstra frowned. She didn't recognize the name, at first—but then a memory bubbled up from her childhood. A memory of the day she'd noticed that one of the portrait busts in House Melarn's great hall was "broken." The chisel work that obliterated the features of the stone head and the name carved into its base had been roughly done, so it was still possible to make out the first letter: an M. When Halisstra noticed the damage, she asked her mother whose bust it had been and how it came to be broken. Her answer was a stinging slap across the face—a slap so hard it had split Halisstra's upper lip. She could still remember her surprise—and the taste of her own blood. Some questions, she'd learned, were better not asked.

Which had made her all that much more keen to have an answer. And so, years later when she had become a priestess, she'd used one of the spells granted by Lolth to satisfy her curiosity. Under the spell's magic, the name on the ruined bust had blazed clearly: Mathira. Discreet inquiries had uncovered a sliver of information about the woman, that she had fallen into disgrace and been forced to flee Ched Nasad a decade before Halisstra was born. What her "traitorous act" had been, however, Halisstra had not been able to discover. Eventually, having reached the end of the thread of family scandal she grew bored and let the matter drop.

"So," Halisstra said, half whispering, "Mathira must have fled Ched Nasad because she'd turned to the worship of Eilistraee."

"And she came here," Uluyara finished for her. "She rose through the ranks of the faithful to become a Sword Dancer, and was the priestess who carried the Crescent Blade onto the Cold Field—and lost it.

And it was up to Halisstra to find it and to use it as Eilistraee intended, to kill Lolth.

It was all too much to be mere coincidence. Halisstra saw the hand of Eilistraee in every step of it. Who else but a goddess could guide the lives of mortals in so subtle a fashion, weaving together a plan that spanned centuries? Halisstra was certain that, were she to try to back out of the quest, Eilistraee would find a way to steer her feet back onto her ordained path.

The thought terrified her. At the same time, it also gave her hope that she might succeed. She had to trust in the goddess—even though trust was something she had only just learned. It still came only with difficulty.

One question, however, remained.

"How do I find the Crescent Blade?" she asked.

Uluyara stared up at the moon and for several long moments said nothing. Then slowly, the words came.

"You have magic that we do not—'dark song magic,' you called it. Perhaps that is what is needed to bring the Crescent Blade back into the light."

Halisstra nodded and said, "There is a spell I was learning, before I left . . . before Ched Nasad was destroyed. The bard who was teaching it to me said it could be used to locate any object I could visualize. If I'm able to cast it, I might use it to find the Crescent Blade. If, that is, you could tell me where I should begin my search. Where was Mathira when she disappeared?"

"She was last seen in Harrowdale," Uluyara answered. "From there, she was to travel south to Scardale, then on to Blackfeather Bridge. She could hardly go missing along so well traveled a road, and so we assumed she veered from it and became lost. Mathira's business was urgent and perhaps caused her to choose a shorter route—to travel to Blackfeather Bridge in a direct line across the Cold Field, instead of circling around it by road."

Already Halisstra was deciding how to use her spell to best advantage. She'd travel to Harrowdale, orient herself in the direction of Feather Falls, and march in as straight a line as possible, casting her spell every eight hundred paces—the limit of its range.

"How big is the Cold Field?" Halisstra asked, picturing something the size of a large cavern.

"Unfortunately, the Cold Field is widest from northeast to

southwest," Uluyara said. "It's open ground—so no more than a two-day march at a steady pace. But it will be far from easy. You'll be lucky to reach the other side of it alive. Luckier still, if the ghosts that inhabit that bleak place haven't driven you mad long before you leave it."

"Won't any of the other priestesses be coming with me?" Halisstra asked.

"Most have already left to search for the yochlol that killed Breena. The one or two who remain have other, equally pressing matters to attend to. I don't know if they can be spared."

Halisstra's eyes narrowed, and she asked, "You don't really expect me to find it, do you?"

"It isn't that, child," Uluyara answered softly. "It's just that some journeys must be taken alone." Her gaze drifted up toward the treetops. The singing had stopped. Breena's body had been laid to rest.

The night air was cold, but Halisstra felt a fire begin to smolder inside her.

"I'll find the Crescent Blade," she vowed. "On my own. I don't need help from anyone."

She turned and strode into the forest, back to the shelter she shared with Ryld. Uluyara might not have faith in Halisstra, but there was one greater who did.

Eilistraee.

TWENTY-EIGHT

Valas waited, a kukri in each hand, at the end of the tunnel that Pharaun had bored through solid stone with his magic a moment before. Perfectly smooth and slightly oval in shape, the tunnel was not quite high enough for Valas to stand fully upright. He stood with shoulders hunched, his hair brushing the magic-warmed stone.

Pharaun, a pace behind him, chanted softly, holding the tiny seeds that were the spell's material component between forefinger and thumb. The mage had prepared well over the course of the four days it took them to reach the portion of the Underdark that lay beneath Myth Drannor. He'd already cast the spell several times, extending the tunnel until it was more than a hundred paces long. If the rogue who'd told Valas about the portal had been accurate in his estimates, the distance between the corridor behind them and the vault they hoped to reach was close to that figure. The next spell should see them through the intervening rock.

As Pharaun completed his spell, flicking the seeds at the tunnel's end wall and pointing with his forefinger, Valas braced himself. The stone before him shimmered, then seemed to melt away in front of Pharaun's finger, revealing a large room about ten paces ahead. A rush of stale air came back along the tunnel, carrying with it the smell of dust and desiccated flesh.

Quiet as a spider, Valas crept forward and peered into the ancient treasure vault. It was, as the rogue had described, immense. Circular in shape, it was perhaps a hundred and fifty paces across and fifty paces high, with a domed roof whose ceiling was inlaid with intricate mosaics. Those, wrought in polished pebbles—many of them semi-precious stones— depicted a number of the surface elves' gods, bows in hand with arrows nocked. Portions of the mosaic had fallen away in spots where tree roots had grown down through the ceiling, bulging its masonry inward. Chunks of stone and a scattering of earth lay on the floor below. The gods that remained in the mosaic frowned down into the empty room as if angered by its decrepit state.

At floor level—about five paces below the tunnel in which Valas crouched—were three doors, set at equal distances from each other. The one immediately below Valas and to his right looked as though it had been blasted off its hinges. That was how the rogue and his companions had entered, after negotiating a corridor filled with more traps than a spider's nest had eggs. Wisely, Quenthel—or rather Pharaun, who had subtly persuaded her—had chosen not to try that route.

Valas stared into the darkened room, listening intently. Of the wraiths there was no sign, but that was not unusual. Wraiths could pass through walls, and they might appear at any moment.

Nor was there any sign of the bodies of the rogue's companions. Again, that was not surprising. Risen again as wights, they probably left through the ruined door in search of fresh meat—only to be cut to pieces by the blade traps that lined the corridor. Their stench, however, lingered in the still air . . . or did it?

Glancing up at the ceiling again, Valas saw a skull nested in one of the tangles of tree root that bulged down into the room. The vault must have been built under a graveyard. The surface elves were known for planting trees atop the graves of their dead. With all of the moldering corpses that lay just above the ceiling, it was no wonder wraiths were drawn to the place.

Pharaun crept up behind Valas and stared down into the vault.

See anything? the Master of Sorcere signed.

Transferring both daggers into one hand, Valas shook his head and replied, *I see no sign of the wraiths—or of the portal.*

If it's here, you soon will, Pharaun signed back.

The wizard began whispering the words to a spell. He passed a hand through the air, palm toward the room. After a moment, a circle at the center of the room began to glow a faint purple.

There, he signed, pointing.

Valas made a mental note of the spot, then continued watching and waiting. Since magic had disturbed the air of the vault, the wraiths would likely appear that much sooner. Assuming, that was, that the rogue's story had been accurate.

The fellow had claimed the vault still held treasure— something Valas hadn't told his companions, since it might have distracted them from their mission—but the room was clearly empty. Perhaps the rogue had been lying about the wraiths, as well. Neither the sudden appearance of a magic-hewn tunnel in one wall of the vault nor the divination Pharaun had just cast had brought them out into the open. If wraiths had once haunted that place where the gods frowned in stony silence, they seemed to have gone.

But that didn't mean Valas wouldn't take precautions. Hanging around his neck on a delicate gold chain was an amulet crafted by the surface elves and shaped like a golden sun. He pulled it out from under his armor and kissed it, then let it hang free against his chest, ignoring Pharaun's raised eyebrows. If any wraiths did turn up, it would protect him.

For a while, at least.

You and the others should make a run for it, he signed. *With a running start and a leap, you should be able to levitate down onto the portal without touching anything in the room. I'll use my amulet to make the jump. With luck, the wraiths—if there are any—won't even know we're here.*

You're forgetting that Danifae can't levitate, Pharaun signed.

Valas groaned—softly. Was he the only one capable of tactical thinking?

Use one of your spells on her—the one that enables you to leap around like a flea. She'll be able to make the portal in one or two jumps. He paused, then added, *Just make sure she goes last. She'll be the clumsiest—if there are wraiths here, it will be her noise that attracts them.*

Pharaun frowned at that but made no comment. Instead he raised a hand to his lips and pointed back down the tunnel, where Quenthel, Danifae, and Jeggred waited.

"We're through," he breathed, his spell carrying his whispered words to Quenthel. "The portal looks clear—and active. Come quickly, but quietly."

Valas, still intently watching the room below, heard a faint clink of armor from the far end of the tunnel—Danifae and Quenthel moving along it—and the faint *click-click* of Jeggred's elongated toenails on the stone. He gritted his teeth, praying that his companions would learn the value of moving silently—and learn it *soon*. Then he heard the clicking pause and the sound of a low growl.

His patience at an end, Valas spun around, an oath on his lips. He saw Quenthel moving toward him, leading the others down the corridor. Danifae was just behind her, but Jeggred was lagging several paces to the rear and was looking back over his shoulder, still growling.

Mistress! Valas signed angrily. *Tell Jeggred to keep—*

Before he could finish, the relative silence was split by a fierce roar. Jeggred launched himself back down the tunnel, bellowing his battle howl as his claws scrambled on the floor. In another instant, Valas saw what had triggered the draegloth's attack.

Two twisted caricatures that had once been duergar, with claws as long as Jeggred's own and mouths filled with needle-sharp teeth, were stalking up behind them. Rotted clothing hung from them in tatters, and their hair was a tangled mass, crusted with dirt. Their eyes blazed with the malevolence with which all undead regarded the living. Unlike the drow they'd been stalking, the two wights moved in utter silence. Seeing they had been spotted, they ran forward to meet Jeggred's charge.

Jeggred crashed headlong into the first wight, smashing it against one wall with a powerful swipe of his fighting arm, then ripping its belly open with a rake of the claws on one foot as he stomped on it. As the pungent odor of death and rot filled the air, the second wight darted under Jeggred's other arm and casually slapped Jeggred's chest. The draegloth grunted and clutched one of his lesser hands against him—the first time Valas had heard him express pain aloud—and he staggered slightly. An instant later, however, he recovered. Roaring fiercely, the draegloth grasped the wight's face with a fighting hand and, wrenching violently, tore the head from its neck.

The first wight was still moving, crawling furiously after Jeggred with its rotted entrails dragging along behind it. Before it could reach him, Danifae rushed forward, morningstar in hand. There wasn't much room to swing the weapon in the low-ceilinged corridor, but she managed an abbreviated downward smash. The spiked ball of the morningstar connected with the wight's head in a blaze of magical sparks, filling the air with a sharp ozone tang. The wight dropped and laid still.

Pharaun stared at Danifae with a look of open admiration. He held a tiny leather pouch in one hand, which he'd drawn from his pocket as the wights attacked.

"Well done," he said, tucking it back into a pocket of his *piwafwi.*

Quenthel looked past Danifae.

"Are there more?" she asked Jeggred.

Jeggred stood panting, head turning from side to side as he searched for the scent of additional foes. As his chest rose and fell, Valas noted the wound the wight had inflicted on the draegloth. It was little deeper than a scratch, but it was causing Jeggred to wheeze as if each breath was painful. After a moment, Jeggred shook his head.

"No more," he concluded. "Just these two."

Valas cleared his throat.

"Wights are the least of our worries," he reminded the others. "We should get moving. The portal is just ahead, at the center of the vault, about seventy-five paces into the room. Pharaun's marked it with a spell. Quickly now, and one at a time. Take a run and leap out from the end of the tunnel, then levitate down. Touch nothing in the room. You first, Quenthel, then Jeggred, while Pharaun casts a spell on Danifae. Then Pharaun, followed by Danifae. I'll go last."

That said, he flattened against the wall and motioned the

others forward. As he did, he scanned the vault one last time, searching for signs of movement, in case any wights had entered it while his back was turned.

They hadn't.

Quenthel moved forward to glance down into the room, then, after communing silently with her whip vipers, she nodded. She backed down the corridor, then sprinted past Valas and leaped into the air. A heartbeat later Jeggred rushed after her, arms flailing.

As the pair drifted down through the empty room toward the portal, Valas glanced up at the ceiling. Were the gods in the mural scowling a bit more fiercely? He stared back at them a moment, then decided it must have been his imagination. Meanwhile, Quenthel had ignored his instructions and was hovering above the portal. Jeggred, floating in the air beside her, kept glancing back and forth between his mistress and the portal, a confused look on his face.

Valas turned to warn Pharaun that something was delaying the pair, but the mage was just completing the spell he was casting on Danifae, tracing an invisible symbol on each of her knees with something he held pinched in his fingers. Finishing, he gave Danifae a quick smile of encouragement, then he turned and sprinted down the corridor past Valas, leaping into the vault.

He levitated to a halt just above Quenthel and Jeggred and motioned furiously for them to go through the portal. Quenthel, however, shook her head.

"You first," she ordered.

Pharaun, hovering in the air, folded his arms across his chest. "Come on, Danifae!" he shouted up at the tunnel. "We're all waiting."

Valas shook his head. The scuffle with the wights had already caused enough noise to wake the undead, and with all the shouting they'd never hear if more approached. Impatiently, he beckoned Danifae forward.

As she crouched on the lip of the tunnel, he noticed that her legs were articulated the wrong way. She leaped—in a jump that carried her halfway across the room. She looked confident and to all appearances was about to land easily on the bare floor—but then, when she was still about a pace above the floor, she suddenly stumbled and pitched over to one side. As she did, Valas heard a noise that sounded like pebbles shifting.

Danifae wound up on her hands and knees—but not on the floor. Instead she seemed to have landed on something that held her at arm's length from it. Something invisible—or something cloaked by an illusion. Something that kept shifting.

Pharaun, too, saw her stumble. One of his hands whipped into a pocket of his *piwafwi*, and a moment later he was smearing something across his eyes as he chanted a spell. As Danifae struggled to her feet on the shifting surface—causing that pebble noise again—Pharaun's eyes widened.

"Danifae!" he shouted. "You're standing on a rotted chest that's spilling gems—but more importantly, there's a wand just to your right. Grab it!"

Quenthel's head snapped up, and she asked, "A wand?"

Danifae began patting the still-invisible pile on which she stood. Valas, meanwhile felt a growing sense of unease. Someone, or something, was watching. Once again, his eyes flicked up to the ceiling.

The scout saw that his intuition had been right. The eyes of the gods in the mural *were* different. They'd been dull, flat stones a short time before, but had begun too glow red, like angry coals.

Then they blinked.

"Venom's kiss," Valas swore under his breath. Then, as two

pairs of glowing red eyes detached themselves from the ceiling and drifted down into the room, he shouted. "Pharaun! Quenthel! Above you—wraiths!"

Jeggred was the first to react. Grasping Quenthel's shoulders, he gave her a shove that forced her down into contact with the floor. Her feet touched the portal and she disappeared. The draegloth then turned and tried to do the same to Pharaun but the mage twisted out of his grasp, kicking Jeggred. The blow forced the draegloth into the portal, and he too disappeared.

Valas grunted. Jeggred's actions had been too deliberate—and too disrespectful—to have been anything but Quenthel's orders. Quenthel had obviously briefed him well in advance about what to do should wraiths attack—and her tactics were sound. She and Pharaun were vital to the quest, but the others could be sacrificed. Pharaun, however, had guessed what was coming—and had decided, wisely or not, to stay and fight.

The mage yanked from his pocket the tiny pouch he'd been reaching into earlier. With a serpent-fast motion, he pulled from it a pinch of diamond dust and flung it into the air. As a pair of wraiths swooped in to attack him—their location revealed only by their glowing eyes—Pharaun shouted his incantation. Unable to stop themselves in time, the two wraiths plunged into the diamond dust. As they struck it they wailed—a hollow, anguished sound that raised the hair on the back of Valas's neck. Their eyes winked out as the powerful spell snuffed out the necromantic magic that had sustained them.

Unfortunately, there were, as the rogue had correctly warned, more than just those two. Dozens of glowing red eyes erupted from the ceiling and descended into the room like tiny, paired embers falling from a burning building.

Seeing that, Pharaun glanced quickly between the wraiths and Danifae. What he was thinking was plainly written on his face.

Should he save his own skin by escaping through the portal—or should he stay and protect her?

The wizard began to levitate down toward the portal, then paused abruptly and stared hard—not at Danifae but at something near her feet. Instead of fleeing, he reached into his pouch for another pinch of dust.

The hesitation nearly cost him his life. Unseen, one of the wraiths swooped down behind him and, with a hollow death-rattle of laughter, swept through his body. As its glowing red eyes erupted out of Pharaun's chest the Master of Sorcere shuddered, his face slate gray.

Three more of the wraiths descended with murderous purpose toward Danifae. Raising her morningstar, she braced herself to meet them, even though she must have known the futility of it. The magical weapon might account for one of the ghostly undead, but the other two would almost certainly kill her a heartbeat later.

Acting purely on his soldier's instincts, Valas touched the nine-pointed star pinned to his chest and stepped between the dimensions. He materialized beside Danifae just as the ball of her mace whistled past his head, exploding with sparks as it struck a wraith. Losing her balance as her weapon met no resistance, Danifae stumbled.

Seizing the opportunity, the other two wraiths rushed forward. Before they could close with Danifae, however, Valas leaped into the air, his magical boots propelling him upward. Arms wide, he drove the points of his kukris into the wraiths. As Danifae's mace had, the blades passed through the bodies of the wraiths without stopping. The one in his right hand exploded with magical energy, but the one in his left merely tore a rent in the keening wraith's mistlike body.

Unable to avoid following through on his knife thrusts,

Valas found both arms engulfed by wraiths. A shudder passed through him, and he fell back to the ground in a barely controlled landing, stumbling on the invisible, shifting gems. He thought his heart was going to falter and stop as the ache that chilled him to the bone was drawn upward into his chest. Then it was gone, absorbed by the amulet that hung around his neck, which suddenly felt much heavier.

Having driven the wraiths away from Danifae, Valas expected her to make her escape. Surely she was smart enough to realize that Pharaun had paused not for her but for the wand which only he could see. Three more wraiths were nearly on them, and others were descending through the ceiling every instant. But instead of fleeing toward the portal, Danifae dropped to her knees and began patting the ground.

"Protect me," she barked up at Valas, not even bothering to look up.

Valas considered for a heartbeat—battle-captive or no, Danifae was a priestess of Lolth, and her word was his command—then he shook his head.

"No time," he bellowed. "Jump!"

Ducking just in time as a wraith swooped past, he called upon the magic of his star-shaped amulet and stepped between the dimensions a second time, arriving at the portal. He paused just long enough to observe Danifae suffer the same fate as Pharaun, her face blanching to a pale gray as the wraiths swept through her body. Meanwhile Pharaun had managed to dispatch another wraith with his dust—leaving his pouch empty.

Glancing up at a wraith descending through a tangle of exposed tree root, Valas suddenly realized something. The surface could be no more than a few paces above the ceiling. After a quick calculation of the time, he realized he had overlooked one of the most powerful weapons of all. He pointed up at the ceiling with one of his daggers—goring a low-flying wraith in the process—and shouted to Pharaun.

"There's daylight above—use it!"

"Ah!" Pharaun exclaimed, understanding instantly.

One hand darted to his pocket. He barked out a spell, flicking a pinch of seeds into the air. Even as he did, six wraiths dived down toward him and another four at Valas, eyes blazing. Then, like a cork being pulled from a wine bottle, a portion of the ceiling disappeared as the spell bored a tunnel through it. Daylight streamed into the vault. Valas had a brief glimpse of red eyes, streaking toward him less than a palm's breadth away—and the eyes were gone. Squinting against the glare of the shaft of light, he looked around the vault. The wraiths, driven off by the sunlight, had vanished.

He closed his eyes and breathed a deep sigh of relief. Then he glanced down at his sun amulet. The metal had lost its bright gold sheen. It was left a dull, lead gray. All of the rays were drooping.

Valas tucked the amulet inside his tunic, out of sight. It had done its duty.

So had he.

"I'm leaving," he told Pharaun and Danifae. "You two can stay and fill your pockets with treasure if you like."

He glanced down at the floor and saw the magic that had limned the portal in light had faded. No matter, he remembered where it was. As he stepped forward onto the portal, Pharaun, the vault—and Danifae, who had risen to her feet and was glaring at him with eyes that blazed more furiously than the wraiths' had—all disappeared.

The air around Valas was cooler and more humid, a welcome change from the vault's oppressive atmosphere of death and dust. He had the sense of enormous distance in front of him and a stone wall at his back. Shaking his head to clear the slight dizziness that traveling through the portal had produced, he saw Quenthel and Jeggred standing nearby on a narrow shelf of rock that was splattered with bat guano. Far below the ledge a vast, dark lake stretched as far as the eye could see, illuminated by beams of winter sunlight that shone in through crevices in the rock above. The ceiling of the cavern was high overhead, but even from a distance Valas could see the thousands of bats that clung, sleeping, to it. When dusk fell the air would be thick with them.

"Where's Pharaun?" Quenthel asked urgently, confirming Valas's earlier guess about himself and Danifae being little more than wraith fodder, in her eyes.

Jeggred, meanwhile, sniffed at the rock face, prodding it with a finger.

"We can't go back," he growled. "Pharaun didn't follow us—and we can't go back."

"Pharaun's still in the vault," Valas told them.

The vipers in Quenthel's whip gave Valas a baleful look.

"You left him?" Quenthel spat.

"Why not? The wraiths are defeated—no thanks to you," Valas grumbled—then realized he'd spoken out loud.

Stepping back a pace, he lowered his eyes, but the reprimand he'd expected did not come. Quenthel's whip was still in her belt, and her attention was entirely on the wall behind him. Her body radiated tension as she waited, silently staring at the wall, as if willing Pharaun to step through it.

A few moments later, Pharaun obliged by emerging from the portal, together with Danifae, whose legs were articulated normally again, Pharaun's spell having ended.

Jeggred growled softly at the mage, but Quenthel silenced him with a curt wave of her hand as she spotted the object Danifae held in her hands. It looked, to Valas's unschooled eyes, like a forked twig, plated in silver, but Quenthel seemed to recognize it at once.

"A wand of location," she said, holding out her hand in silent demand.

"It is indeed, Mistress," said Danifae, her face expressionless. "The rogues who were in the vault before us must have dropped it."

She handed the wand to Quenthel, bowing her head.

Quenthel stroked Danifae's hair in what Valas, had he not known Quenthel as well as he did, would have taken to be a sign of affection.

"At last, Danifae, you've proven your usefulness. This will make finding the ship of chaos much easier."

So fixated on the wand was Quenthel that she missed something that Valas did not: the look on Pharaun's face. Once again, the Master of Sorcere was plotting something. Valas, neither wanting to know nor caring what it might be, turned away and stared, brooding, out at the lake. Then, spotting something in the distance with his keen eyes, he stiffened.

"What is it?" Pharaun asked, peering in the same direction. "More wraiths?"

Valas shook his head, and pointed to a distant spot where bats were frantically circling above a disturbance in the water.

"Something's stirring up the bats . . . something big. And it's headed this way."

Ryld trudged along the open, treeless plain, following Halisstra's trail. She'd forbidden him from accompanying her, saying the quest for the Crescent Blade was something she had to undertake alone—but she hadn't forbidden him from *following* her. Not in so many words.

And so he'd bade her farewell when she left Eilistraee's temple, then set out after her as soon as she was out of sight. He'd been able to trail her closely during the three days she'd traveled through the forest, but when she struck out across the Cold Field, he'd been forced to fall back and follow only under cover of darkness. Even with his magical *piwafwi* there was no way for him to hide on the flat, featureless plain in full daylight.

He followed the faint traces of Halisstra's passage: a blank spot on the frosted ground where a pebble had been kicked out of place; a patch of lichen that had been scuffed off a rock; and a concave fragment of bone, recently kicked over, the frozen dirt clinging to its underside still fresh.

Flicking the fragment of skull aside with the toe of his boot, the weapons master stared across the desolate landscape, looking for Halisstra. As far as he could see the frozen ground was studded with crumbling pieces of bone, rusted lance heads, shield bosses, and chunks of chain mail so rusted the links had fused into a single, solid mass. It was as if the remains of the armies that had fought there centuries past had been seeded into the ground in the hope that they would one day rise again. Yet nothing grew there, save for a few faint traces of lichen on those rocks that hadn't been melted to slag by the fiery breath of dragons.

A bitterly cold wind began to blow, plucking at the ends of Ryld's *piwafwi* like the ghosts of the dead. Shivering, he peered into the gloom, searching for Halisstra. She must have still been far ahead of him; he couldn't see her. Ryld wondered if the ground had swallowed her up, just as it had the fallen armies, then he realized his nerves were getting the better of him. That was the way of the place, though. The combination of the moldering death beneath his feet and the vastness of the sky above him made him feel vulnerable, exposed. If the dead truly did walk that barren landscape, there was nowhere to make a stand against them—no cavern wall to place his back against.

Running a hand across the crown of his head—his close-cropped hair had almost grown out and would soon need to be shaved back again—he trudged onward, eyes constantly flicking down to search the ground for Halisstra's trail. After a few paces, however, he stopped. There, some distance ahead of him in the direction Halisstra had been heading—was that someone moving?

Not someone—some*thing*. The figure was definitely drow-shaped but seemed to be lacking its lower half. Ryld could clearly see a head, shoulders, and arms silhouetted against the spot on the horizon where the moon was rising behind the clouds, but below the waist there was nothing but a trail of dark fog, twisting in the wind like smoke from an extinguished candle. He didn't need to see its legs, however, to determine which direction the thing was moving in. It sped briskly along, stopping every now and then to stoop down low over the earth. With a shudder, Ryld realized it too was following Halisstra.

He drew Splitter from the sheath on his back and sprinted forward. The ground beneath his feet blurred as his magical boots propelled him along at several times his normal running speed. To attempt stealth on the featureless plain was futile. All Ryld could count on to tip the balance in his favor was speed. That, and the magic of the greatsword in his hand.

Within moments he was close enough to the creature to see it clearly. The thing had once been human. It wore a soldier's surcoat over chain mail—the surcoat emblazoned with a stylized tree—and an ornate silver helmet topped with a plume of white hair that spilled over the creature's shoulders, marking the soldier as an officer. The helmet shone in the cloud-shrouded moonlight, and the links of the officer's chain mail still clinked. At least part of the creature was corporeal, then, though Ryld was doubtful it could be wounded by a normal weapon. Ryld was thankful he had Splitter; its enchantments would help even the odds.

Ryld was still two dozen paces away—and closing the distance swifter than a charging rothé—when he heard the low muttering. He couldn't make out the words, but the emotion attached to them made him stagger. It was as if he'd run into a pool of chest-high water. Waves of disappointment, sorrow, and loss crashed one by one into his chest, slowing him to a stumbling walk.

The undead officer stopped, then slowly turned. It was a human male, with a dark mustache that framed a drooping mouth, and eyes creased with sorrow. Every aspect of the apparition cried out despair, from its drooping shoulders to the listless way it held its dagger.

A dagger that was thrust, hilt-deep, into its own chest.

As the eyes of the undead officer met Ryld's, the tide of emotions rose above the weapons master's head, drowning him in despair. With it came a voice—a telepathic voice, for the officer was still muttering, and the movements of the ghost's mouth bore no relation to the words that pounded into Ryld's mind.

It is finished, the voice moaned. *Our army is defeated. It was our duty to die in defense of Lord Velar, yet we few did not fall. We cannot return to him in disgrace. Only one course remains open to us—one path that leads to honor. We must take our place beside those who have already fallen. Like them, we must die.*

The words echoed in Ryld's mind.

Die . . . die . . . die. We must die. We must take our place beside the others. It is your duty. You must die . . .

Rooted to the spot by the intensity of the command, Ryld tried to obey. He turned Splitter, holding it by the blade and placing the hilt on the ground between his feet. All he had to do was lean forward, and his agony would be at an end. His honor, hanging in tatters like the banners of his fallen army, would be restored.

Letting his head droop, Ryld stared down at his hands—and the point of the blade he held between them. He leaned forward until the magically keen blade punched through his breastplate to prick his chest, and felt the eyes of his commanding officer watching him approvingly. All he had to do was allow his weight to fall forward, and the defeat of the army of Lord Velar would be . . .

Ryld's eye was caught by a ring on the finger of his own left hand. Shaped like a small, twisting dragon, it was obviously an insignia of some sort. The army of Lord Velar had been laid low by dragons—what was a ring shaped like one of those foul creatures doing on his finger? It was just plain *wrong* . . .

No . . . the ring was the only thing that was right. It marked Ryld as a Master of Melee-Magthere and triggered in him a realization.

He was not an officer in some army that was defeated centuries before he was born. He was Ryld Argith, Weapons Master of Melee-Magthere, citizen of Menzoberranzan.

Shaking his head violently, Ryld threw off the last of the magical compulsion. He let Splitter fall from his hands and drew his short sword—a weapon that had been enchanted with just such a foe as this in mind. The weapons master leaped forward, plunging it into the undead officer's chest.

His blade met resistance, just as if it had been thrusting into solid chain mail and living flesh, and the thrust did the job. Glancing down at the sword that was buried in its heart—beside its own dagger—the undead officer let out a groan. Ryld yanked his short sword free and danced back out of range.

A wisp of dark mist spurted from the puncture the sword had made in the undead officer's chest. The smokelike substance that was its lower body began to swirl. Within the space of a few heartbeats its stomach, chest, arms, and neck dissolved into dark mist.

The head was the last thing to disappear. As it did, the undead officer's lips curled into a smile, and its eyes brightened.

Thank you, it whispered.

A heartbeat later, it was gone.

Shuddering at his close escape, Ryld stared at the sword in his hands. The blade was unblemished; its plunge into the undead officer didn't seem to have tarnished it. He peered carefully in each direction to make sure there were no more of the foul creatures. Seeing none, he returned his short sword to its sheath, then picked up Splitter and sheathed it as well. He resumed his journey, following Halisstra's trail.

The sooner she finds this sword she's looking for and leaves the Cold Field, the weapons master thought, the better.

🕷   🕷   🕷

Halisstra sank, exhausted, into a crouch, feet crunching the dusting of snow that had fallen just after the moon rose. She'd been searching for a night and a day—and on into a second night—without pausing for rest. She'd tried to cast the spell that would help her to locate the Crescent Blade several times, but though she was certain she'd committed the words of the song to memory correctly, she might have confused the melody slightly. Either that, or the darksong was still beyond her limited reach. She'd felt none of the tingling certainty that should have led the way to the object she was seeking. The only thing she'd felt was the incessant cold wind sweeping across the desolate plain.

She sat in the darkness, peering through the gloom at the object she'd just pulled from the breast pocket of her *piwafwi*: her House medallion. When she converted to Eilistraee's faith, she'd decided to set it aside with the rest of her past, but something had made her hesitate. The brooch was magical, after all, and gave her the ability to levitate—but there was more to it than that. She sensed that it was not only a link with her past but with her future as well.

Setting the brooch beside her on the snowy ground, she drew Seyll's songsword from its sheath and raised the hilt of the weapon to her lips. How did that melody go again? It seemed strange to be playing a song from the *bae'qeshel* tradition on an instrument forged for a priestess of the Lady of the Dance . . . or did it?

Wasn't the raising of the skills and talents of the Underdark to the World Above the very end for which Eilistraee strove?

For a time, Halisstra concentrated on her fingering, trying the melody in different keys and pausing, from time to time, to warm her fingers by blowing on them. Though she tried to concentrate, her mind kept drifting, and her eyelids felt heavy. After more than a cycle and a half of constant searching, she was desperately in need of the release that Reverie could give. She longed to let it claim her, to drift among her memories until they soothed her, but she couldn't give up her search. Exhausted though she was, she would master the spell before she rested. But the bitterly cold wind seemed to snatch away the notes and fling them into the night, scattering her efforts like dead leaves in a wind.

Lowering the songsword, Halisstra stared at the scraps of bone and rusted metal that protruded through the snow all around her. Centuries before an army had taken the field against a foe who counted dragons among their allies. Knowing that they would almost certainly be defeated, those soldiers had nonetheless marched bravely into battle—and been slain.

Centuries later, at the urging of a dead priestess, Halisstra was about to face even more impossible odds. It was madness to think that she could defeat a goddess. Even armed with the Crescent Blade—assuming she could find it—Halisstra would surely be defeated. Lolth's power was unimaginably vast and all encompassing; no one could escape her web of destruction and vengeance. Halisstra was foolish to even think of trying.

Perhaps it would be better if she *didn't* find the Crescent Blade.

Suddenly Halisstra sensed someone looking over her shoulder. Someone whose breath came in thin, chill gasps.

Startled, she sprang to her feet, songsword in hand. She whirled but saw no one. Quickly, she sang the spell that would allow her to see invisible creatures. The few flakes of snow sharpened as the air took on a magical shimmer, but still she saw nothing.

Then a ghostly figure materialized right in front of her.

It was a drow female, but one who had been horribly disfigured. Long white hair clung in straggling clumps to a scalp that was puckered with deep pits, and her face was terribly burned. Where the nose had been was nothing but a gaping hole, and the eyes were likewise missing. Skin had bubbled in enormous blisters on the face and on those portions of the arms and legs that were bare. The torso, thankfully, was hidden by a chain mail tunic, but the metal links were corroded and loose as though the armor had been hurled into a lake of acid.

Halisstra clutched the broken songsword, heart pounding, wishing desperately that she held a better weapon. The ghostly figure, however, made no threatening moves. Instead it stooped and reached for something on the ground: Halisstra's brooch. As it did, a medallion that hung from its waist by a metal chain swung forward. Like the chain mail, the medallion was blackened and pitted, but Halisstra could see a faint trace of the design it once bore: Eilistraee's symbol.

Halisstra glanced at the corroded sheath at the figure's hip—a sheath that was curved like a crescent moon. Slowly, she lowered her sword.

"You're Mathira Melarn," she whispered.

The ghost nodded.

"I'm looking for the Crescent Blade," Halisstra told the ghost. "Will you help me?"

Once again the figure gave a slow, mournful nod.

"Where is it?" Halisstra asked.

The ghost opened its mouth, but all that came out was a gurgling groan. The tongue was missing, burned away by the acid that had consumed the rest of the woman's body. The wyrm that had killed her must have been a black dragon. Halisstra shuddered at the thought of the agonies its acid spittle must have wrought upon the priestess in the moments just before her death.

Can you sign? Halisstra asked.

In answer, the ghost let Halisstra's medallion fall to the ground and raised hands that were lumps of pitted flesh, the fingers burned away to skeletal stubs. Then, turning stiffly as if still suffering the agonies of her wounds, she motioned with one arm in a gesture whose meaning was clear enough: *Come.*

Halisstra glanced at her House insignia and saw that the ghost's touch had left it pitted and blackened. Not wanting to touch it, Halisstra left the medallion where it lay and followed the ghost.

Chapter

THIRTY

When Ryld saw the metal object peeking out of the snow, he thought it was another bit of battlefield debris. Corroded and pitted with black spots, the brooch looked centuries old. Then the shape of the piece caught his eye. Quickly he stooped to pick it up, then winced as something on the brooch stung his hands. Holding the brooch by the edges, he sniffed, and caught an acrid odor. Acid?

Turning the brooch over confirmed his guess. Only portions of it looked ancient. The clasp on the back was undamaged, and sections of the metal were still brightly polished. It was no battlefield remnant.

He peered at it more closely, trying to make out what design had been on the front of it. When he at last confirmed his guess, he shuddered.

It was Halisstra's brooch—the insignia that marked her as a

LISA SMEDMAN

noble daughter of House Melarn. Something must have surprised her, out on the wind-blasted plain. Had she been wearing the brooch on her *piwafwi*? If so, she might have been injured when whatever had aged the metal had struck her.

Searching the ground carefully, Ryld saw none of the usual signs of a struggle. Two deep footprints and a mark made by the hem of a *piwafwi* showed where Halisstra had squatted for a time, and a confused overlapping of footprints showed where she had whirled rapidly around, but there were no other prints in the snow.

Had she been attacked from above? Ryld imagined a black dragon swooping down on Halisstra, blasting her with its acid breath, and shuddered. But, no, that didn't seem to be the answer. Aside from Halisstra's footprints, the snow was undisturbed. Flapping wings would have stirred it up with their downdraft, and a black dragon's breath would have left spray marks in the snow.

It must have been a ghost—perhaps one similar to the officer Ryld had encountered—or some other noncorporeal creature that had startled Halisstra. Whatever it was, it seemed to have done no more than destroy her brooch. Halisstra had moved away at a walking stride in a straight line to the south. The trail she'd left was as before, normal and unremarkable.

No . . . not quite. About a pace to the right of Halisstra's footprints was an irregular line of dimples in the snow, as if something had dripped onto it—but not blood, Ryld saw with relief as he stooped to examine them. There was no trace of red, and the droplets were very small. Bending closer, he sniffed and caught the same faint, acrid odor. Cautiously, he touched a callused fingertip to one of the holes, held it there a moment, then jerked it back when he felt a slight sting.

Acid.

Wiping his finger, he considered. If Halisstra had run into a malevolent spirit, it certainly had a strange way of manifesting itself. Ryld had once encountered a ghost that left smears of blood on the ground wherever it walked—the ghost of a man whose throat had been slit. Had the spirit that confronted Halisstra—assuming that's what it was—been killed by acid?

Whatever had made the droplet trail in the snow, Halisstra had followed it. Her footprints overlaid the holes in several places. Grimly, Ryld followed the trail.

It didn't lead far. After about five hundred paces, Ryld spotted a black, gaping hole in the snowy ground. About three paces across, it looked as though it had been punched open from below. A scatter of rock and loose earth encircled it. Halisstra's footprints led to the edge of the hole, paused—then continued, as if she had descended into its depths. The trail of droplets also led to the hole's edge.

Drawing Splitter, Ryld crept forward, studying the ground. The hole sloped down into the earth at a gentle angle. Scuffs in the snow showed where Halisstra had placed her feet on the slope, but the droplets ended at the hole's edge. Whatever had led her to the hole hadn't gone inside.

Squatting at the edge of the hole, the weapons master used the point of his sword to prod the debris that had been thrown up around it. The soil was frozen solid. The pit had been created some time ago.

Cocking an ear to the hole, Ryld listened, but if Halisstra was moving around down in the black depths it was impossible to hear her above the moan of the wind. Snow had started to fall again. The flakes landed feather-light upon his head, then melted, sending trickles of icy water down his neck. His breastplate was cold even through the padded tunic he wore and his vambraces creaked each time he moved his arms. At least the tunnel would provide shelter from the wind and snow.

Clambering over the lip of the hole, Ryld cautiously descended the slope. Frost on the floor of the tunnel made the footing tricky for the first dozen paces or so, but after that it widened out, and the floor was clear. As his eyesight adjusted to the darkness inside, he saw that the tunnel forked. One path led off to the left, another straight down.

Knowing that Halisstra's only means of levitating had been her brooch, Ryld chose the left fork. He was relieved to see, after a pace or two, six pebbles that had been set on the ground to form a triangle, pointing out of the tunnel. Halisstra had indeed gone that way—and she'd left a marker to guide herself back out.

Ryld walked briskly for some time, following a more or less horizontal course for some distance but not in a straight line. Instead the tube snaked back and forth in a series of wide, gentle turns, often doubling back over itself again. At each of those junctions Ryld paused and searched carefully and found a triangle of pebbles. Thanks to Halisstra's marks he was able to make good time.

Eventually the cave veered off in a fairly straight line for nearly a thousand paces, only to abruptly bend downward at a steep angle. There, Ryld paused. He'd been trying to decide what would have created such a sinuously curved tunnel. He'd once seen Pharaun use a spell to bore a path through stone, but the end result had been lance-straight and oval, with walls whose stone looked highly polished. The tunnel he'd followed Halisstra into was round, and rougher, with occasional jagged-edged niches that looked like something had taken a bite out of the wall, and its floor was littered with patches of loose stone. Bending to examine one of those, Ryld saw that the stones were rounded, like river stones, but pitted. Mixed in with them were fragments of metal—scraps of armor from the battlefield above—that looked as if they had been tumbled in a stone-polishing drum filled with acid instead of water. The edges of the metal were smooth, yet the metal itself was deeply pitted and crumbled when Ryld stepped on it.

Ryld stood again and tightened his grip on Splitter. The cave hadn't been created by magic; it had been bored through the rock by a living creature.

He'd been praying that it was an ancient pathway, and not freshly made, but the lingering smell of acid in the air told him otherwise. The fact that the odor was getting stronger the farther along he went didn't bode well. And if he was right in his guess about what kind of creature had made the tunnel, Halisstra shouldn't have been facing it alone.

Cautiously, Ryld picked his way down the slope ahead. He moved slowly at first, aware that any tiny avalanche of stone caused by a misstep could alert the creature below to his presence, but halfway down his ears caught a faint noise: the sound of a woman singing. His heartbeat quickened as he recognized the voice as Halisstra's. She was casting one of her bardic spells—but why? Was it merely in preparation for what was to come, or was she already under attack? Grimly, he hurried forward, not caring that his feet were skidding on the ever-steepening slope.

Ahead, the bottom of the tunnel opened into a larger space, a cavern that looked as though it had been formed by the tunnel coiling back upon itself several times in succession as the creature created a nest for itself. The patch of floor that Ryld could see was dotted with puddles, and the acid smell was strong.

Moments later, he neared the bottom of the slope and saw that his guess had been correct. At the far end of the cavern was an enormous purple worm, larger even than Ryld had expected— perhaps thirty paces long. It was coiled like a snake, its head lifted and mouth gaping wide, acid dripping between teeth the size of daggers. Halisstra stood just in front of it with her back to Ryld, songsword in hand, staring the monster down. The charm spell she was singing seemed to be working. The worm swayed in time with the tune, its tiny eyes fixed and staring. Ryld felt a fierce admiration. Halisstra was the epitome of a drow female: strong and fearless, capable of handling any threat.

Wary of disturbing her magic, Ryld halted at the bottom of the slope. He managed to do so without making any noise, but when he stepped forward into the room his ankle twisted as an acid-weakened stone crumbled underfoot. His foot slipped into a puddle of fresh acid—fortunately, his boot leather protected him—but the slight splash alerted Halisstra to the fact that she was no longer alone in the cavern. Her head jerked quickly around—just long enough to see who it was—and a startled look passed across her face. All the while she continued to sing without pause, but the momentary loss of eye contact with the purple worm broke the spell. Whipping its head from side to side, sending acidic spittle flying in all directions, it shook off the effects of the charm spell. Then it struck.

Lunging downward, mouth gaping wide, the worm descended on Halisstra. She barely had time to lift her sword and thrust upward with it as her head and shoulders disappeared into the worm's mouth.

Ryld leaped forward, shouting to draw the creature's attention. He saw the broken point of the songsword thrust jaggedly out at an angle through the worm's cheek, just below one eye, but the creature seemed unaffected by the wound. Even though Ryld ran forward with all the speed his magical boots were capable of, the worm was quicker. Like a curtain falling the mouth continued to descend upon Halisstra, engulfing her to the chest, waist, and knees. Then the terrible purple-black jaws struck the ground on either side of Halisstra's boots—and clamped shut.

Ryld closed with the creature a heartbeat later. He swung

Splitter with all of the strength his sinewy arms could muster, intending to cut off the monster's head, but in that instant he heard Halisstra's muffled scream from inside the worm's gullet and saw a bulge moving down its throat. Worried that he would slice Halisstra in two as well, he twisted the sword aside in mid-swing. The blade struck a coil of the worm, cutting deeply into its purple hide and exposing the pinker flesh beneath.

The worm writhed in agony, uncoiling with such swiftness that it crashed into Ryld, hurling him backward. Anyone other than a master of Melee-Magthere would have been knocked flat, but Ryld had been trained to keep his footing. One of the first things he'd learned as a novice was how to roll his body with a blow and use feet, knees, and elbows to spring upright again.

As the worm continued to thrash he rolled nimbly back, then leaped forward again to strike a second blow in another portion of the worm's body. As the monster's head whipped around in an attempt to bite him, Ryld did the unexpected. He leaped backward, and levitated.

The worm's mouth crashed down into the spot where Ryld had been standing, teeth splintering on the stone floor. An instant later the head reared up again, mouth gaping as it lunged upward. Instantly negating his levitation magic, Ryld plummeted to the ground, landing lightly on bent legs and bounding aside. That brief glimpse into the worm's mouth and throat—which were empty—told him that his fears had been realized.

The monster had swallowed Halisstra whole.

Rage seized him then, stronger and fiercer than any battle had ever provoked before. He found himself howling in an anguished voice, eyes hot with tears.

"Halisstra!" he cried.

Rushing forward, he slashed at the worm's throat. If only he could kill it quickly, there might still be time to cut Halisstra free before the worm's digestive acids killed her—she would be disfigured, but she would live. And that was all that mattered.

Howling with each sword stroke, Ryld slashed deep rents in the worm's body. The creature had enough intelligence—instinct at least—to jerk its head and neck back, keeping them out of range of the sword, but with each fresh wound to its side it slowed. Encouraged, Ryld pressed his attack home, aware that each passing moment was lessening Halisstra's chances. Stupidly, the worm lowered its head, giving Ryld a clear swing at its throat. Moving forward, he obliged it—then realized a heartbeat later that it had been a clever feint.

Even as Ryld leaped in to attack, the worm whipped its tail forward, revealing a stinger in its tail that Ryld hadn't seen before. The stinger glanced off the bottom of Ryld's breastplate and plunged into his stomach with the force of a knife blow, burying itself in his gut. Nearly blinded by the sudden rush of pain, he flailed backward, pulling himself free of the deadly barb. For two or three staggering steps he managed to hang onto Splitter, but with the pain of the wound came a rush of agony that felt like fire, sweeping in an instant from his wounded gut to the tips of his fingers and toes. In that terrible moment, Ryld knew that he had been poisoned. Suddenly too weak to hold his greatsword, he let it fall.

He heard the clank of metal striking stone dimly, through ears filled with the sound of a labored, pounding heart. The pain was as intense as if someone had filled his gut with boiling water. He crashed to the ground, barely managing to break his fall with one outstretched arm. Clenching his stomach with his other hand he slowly forced his head up, intending to look the worm in the eye before it swallowed him whole.

At least, he thought as the poison pounded in his temples, he would pay with his own life for having caused Halisstra to lose hers. He would die beside her—a slow, painful death was exactly what he deserved.

To his surprise, he saw that the worm was not pressing its attack but had drawn back against the far wall. He must have wounded it more grievously than he'd thought. Then, to his horror, he saw a bulge form in the worm's side—and disappear. A bulge that could only have been made by a creature moving inside it.

Halisstra! She was still alive!

He saw that the tip of the songsword was still protruding from the worm's cheek and he realized she had nothing to save herself with.

Ryld tried to rise, tried feebly to reach for Splitter, but found that his body no longer obeyed his will. Each breath only increased the roiling agony in his gut, and the air around him seemed to have become tinged with gray. The arm he was using to support himself collapsed, and the floor rushed up to strike his face. The stone, he noticed dully, felt cool against his burning cheek.

Chapter

T H I R T Y - O N E

Pharaun peered in the direction Valas was pointing and at last saw what had prompted the mercenary's warning. Far across the Lake of Shadows, a storm was churning the surface. The water twisted in an enormous circle, as if flowing down a drain. Above the whirlpool was a waterspout that must have been a hundred paces high. The top of it bobbed up and down against the ceiling, scattering clouds of bats with each touch.

The storm was still some distance away but was approaching rapidly. Pharaun measured its progress as it passed through one of the beams of sunlight, and estimated its advance at the speed of a riding lizard running full out. Already he could hear the low rush of spinning water. That the storm was magical he had no doubt. Had it always been there—or had something triggered it? Their use of the portal, perhaps?

The others had spotted it as well. Quenthel stared at the

storm with a clenched jaw, the serpents at her hip softly swaying. Jeggred turned his head from side to side, sniffing the humid air. Danifae took one look at the storm, then glanced out of the corner of her eye at Quenthel, Valas, and Jeggred in turn. Pharaun noted where those glances lingered: on the amulets each wore that would allow them to either levitate up through one of the holes in the cavern ceiling or—in Valas's case—step through the dimensions to escape the storm.

Catching her eye, Pharaun held his hand up in a reassuring gesture and signed, *Wait.*

Then he turned to Valas and asked, "Did the rogue who told you about the portal mention anything about this?"

Valas shook his head. "He didn't linger here. As soon as he reached the cavern he levitated straight up and out." As he spoke he glanced up at the nearest of the sunlight-limned holes in the ceiling as if measuring the distance to it. Then he gave a resigned sigh and stared grimly at the approaching storm.

Quenthel, meanwhile, had turned her attention to the wand Danifae had recovered from the treasure vault and was experimenting with different command words. Jeggred, crouching beside her, pawed at her sleeve and muttered something—and received a backhanded slap for disturbing his mistress. The draegloth prostrated himself at her feet, whimpering his apologies. Quenthel ignored him and continued to try to find the wand's command word.

Pharaun rolled his eyes. At the moment, the storm was a more pressing problem than trying to find the ship of chaos, but Quenthel's muttering was getting on his nerves.

"It's probably a word in the duergar tongue," he told her. "Try 'treasure,' or 'seek' or something like that. And turn the wand around—you have to hold the forked end for it to work."

Quenthel's serpents hissed with irritation, but she did as

he suggested, turning the wand and switching to the guttural tongue of the duergar. Meanwhile, the storm whirled ever closer. The sound of it had grown loud enough that they had to raise their voices slightly, and its breeze stirred Pharaun's hair.

Danifae shifted nervously.

"If we're still here when the storm hits, we'll be smashed against the rocks," she said.

"Or drowned," Valas muttered, glancing below at the waves that were already starting to lap against the bottom of the cliff.

"You're forgetting my teleport spell," he told them. "One quick incantation, and we'll be back in the World Above. The only question is, where to go?"

Valas squinted against the swirl of mist that was starting to strike the ledge.

"In a few moments," the scout said, "anywhere is going to be better than here."

Beside him, Quenthel gave a gasp of satisfaction as the wand came to life in her hands. The end of it trembled and jerked back and forth like the head of a lizard that smelled blood, and a loud whine filled the air. As Quenthel moved the wand in a wide, horizontal arc the whining noise rose, then fell—then rose again as she swung the wand so that it pointed at the waterspout.

As the storm grew nearer, filling the air with a spray of water and an even louder roar, she shouted exultantly, "There! The ship of chaos is inside the whirlpool!"

Pharaun squinted at the storm.

"Yes," he told Quenthel. "I can see it now."

And there really was something there—a dim, dark shape at the eye of the storm. For once, the high priestess seemed to have gotten something right. Belshazu had told them the ship was lost in a "terrible storm" and they were looking at just that—a storm that had raged for centuries.

The ship of chaos might have been whole when the surviving demon swam away from it, but after centuries of being buffeted by wind and water it seemed unlikely that it would still be intact. The storm had yet to hit them fully, but already the wind of it was tearing at Pharaun's *piwafwi* and pelting him with spray. Just being at the outer edge of the storm was like being struck, repeatedly, by water thrown from a bucket. Pharaun pulled his *piwafwi* tighter around him, making sure it covered the backpack in which his spellbooks were stored.

"We've got to get a look inside that whirlpool," Quenthel shouted, oblivious to the drops of water striking her face.

"And how do you propose we do that?" Pharaun asked. "Dig our claws into the rock and hang on, as Jeggred's doing, then dive into the eye of the storm?"

To his surprise, Quenthel nodded vigorously.

"Yes," she replied. "Valas can do it."

The mercenary's eyes widened.

"Dispel your polymorph spell," Quenthel shouted back. "Valas can swim into the whirlpool and take a look."

Valas's eyebrows rose even higher.

"Swim?" he protested, staring at the violently spiraling water. "Through *that?*"

He folded his arms across his chest, ignoring the angry twitching of Quenthel's serpents as she drew her whip. His eyes—which for once he did not lower under her glare—said it all. He'd rather die by her lash than embark on such a suicidal mission.

Danifae, meanwhile, gripped Pharaun's arm.

"We're wasting time," she whispered. "Leave these fools behind. Cast your teleportation spell."

Pharaun plucked her hand free—earning a wrathful glare from the battle-captive—and he reached into a pocket of his *piwafwi*. Pulling out his last pinch of seeds, he held them tightly between thumb and forefinger, wary lest the storm pluck them away. Squeezing past the others, he walked to one end of the narrow ledge to a spot he judged to be well beyond the portal.

"I've got a better idea," he told them all.

Releasing the seeds, he barked out the words of his spell and stabbed a finger toward the rock. A tunnel opened in the wall—at an angle, running in the direction the wind had carried his seeds. Stepping inside it, he motioned for the others to join him.

They needed no urging. The storm was upon them, whipping their hair and *piwafwis* and soaking them with sheets of water. Stumbling along the slippery ledge, they hurried inside, Quenthel and Jeggred shoving their way past Danifae and causing her to slip on the bat guano that had been soaked by the storm. Pharaun reached out to steady her, but Valas was quicker. Grabbing Danifae's arm, he shoved her forward into the tunnel.

Pharaun tried to convey his apologies in a glance, but Danifae ignored him. Sighing, he waved the others to the back of the tunnel, then pulled out his cone of glass. Pointing it at the open mouth of the tunnel, he hurriedly cast a second spell. A blast of bitterly cold air erupted from the glass cone, turning the water that was spraying into the tunnel into pellets of hail. A sheet of water crashed full-on into the ledge outside—and was instantly turned to solid ice, sealing the tunnel. Pharaun held the spell for a moment or two longer, until the ice wall had thickened sufficiently, then he lowered his hand.

Turning to Quenthel, he bowed, then swept a hand in the direction of the plug of ice.

"Won't you step up to the viewing platform, Mistress?" he asked. "I'm sure the ship of chaos will be along directly."

Quenthel stared at him for a long moment as if trying to decide whether or not she was being mocked. Her whip vipers snapped at each other, then relaxed. Nose in the air, Quenthel strode past Pharaun and stared out through the ice, leaning this way and that as she tried to see beyond the water that crashed against the other side of it. The air inside the tunnel was bitterly cold, and her breath misted in the air. She shivered in her wet clothes. Even so, the high priestess peered with rapt attention—then stiffened.

At that, the others crowded forward. Even Jeggred loped up to crouch and peer out past his mistress's legs.

"That figure," Quenthel gasped. "What is it?"

Pharaun leaned forward for a better look. The wall of ice he was staring through was half as thick as his forearm was long, and beyond it was the waterspout, several paces thick at that point and filled with whirling spray. Dimly, at the very eye of the storm, he could see a twisting shape. It was proportioned like a drow, with head, arms, and legs, but twice the height of the tallest female and with a whiplike tail. It appeared to be naked, its skin a pale gray. Pharaun thought it was flailing against the wind, raking the air around it with wide sweeps of its claws, but then he realized that it was spinning in place. The creature itself wasn't moving—not a muscle. It looked as though it had been rendered immobile by magic, by a spell that must have been cast centuries before.

Beside him, Danifae gasped.

"The uridezu," the battle-captive whispered.

Pharaun nodded.

"And the ship!" Valas exclaimed, standing on tiptoes to peer down over the lip of the ledge outside and pointing.

Pharaun looked down at the point where the waterspout met the whirlpool. The ship was indeed there, its hull stuck fast in the water that formed the inner wall of the whirlpool and its masts angled in toward the eye of the storm. It was difficult to make out details through the wall of ice and the spray whipping horizontally past outside, but Pharaun could see enough to confirm that it must, indeed, be the ship of chaos.

The hull was bone-white in color, as were the three masts, from which hung tattered sails.

Quenthel laughed, shattering the tense silence.

"I've done it!" she said. "The ship of chaos is mine." Abruptly, she turned to Pharaun. "Prepare a binding spell."

"The demon already appears to be 'bound,' " observed Pharaun, nodding at the scene outside the ice wall. "Albeit not in the conventional manner. My guess is that it was caught in a temporal stasis spell—a powerful one that I'll have to break once I've imposed a binding of my own. And there's the little problem of the storm."

Quenthel flicked wet hair out of her face, then glowered down the ship of chaos, still whipping around in circles in the whirlpool.

"We're not teleporting away," she told him, a dangerous light in her eye. "Not now, when we're so close."

"No," Pharaun sighed. "I suppose not. But to be quite frank, I'm not sure what to do next. The storm's obviously magical. If a spell created it, the incantation was powerful—and permanent. Even I couldn't control that volume of water—which means any spell I cast won't be powerful enough to dispel the storm."

Valas scratched his head, then said in a thoughtful voice, "Could we sail the ship out of the storm?"

"Possibly," Pharaun said, thinking aloud. "Or rather, the uridezu could. But assuming I'm able to dispel the magic that froze the demon in time there's still the matter of binding it to my will."

"That's easy," Quenthel spat. "Just pull the demon out with one of your grasping-hand spells."

Pharaun sighed. The spell Quenthel had mentioned was

unnecessary. The binding spell itself would draw the demon to the deck. The problem lay in the ship itself. Pharaun had pictured it wrecked on shore or perhaps resting quietly at the bottom of the lake—not half awash and buffeted by spray and wind. Drawing a pentagram on the deck of the ship would be an impossible task.

There was an alternative to using a magic diagram, but it presented its own problems. He could render the demon's image in miniature, either on vellum or in the form of a statuette. The latter could easily be done—he had wax and an opal in his enchanted pockets—but as soon as he placed the statuette on the deck, one sweep of a wave would wash it overboard. And how, in the name of the silent Spider Queen, was he going to come up with a length of chain?

Then he remembered the amulet that had protected Valas from the wraiths. Its chain—having faded to the color of lead, a most suitable material indeed—still hung around his neck.

Pharaun nodded at the amulet and said, "I believe I'm correct, Valas, in assuming your amulet is no longer functional?"

Valas gave Pharaun a wary frown but nodded.

"May I have the chain it's hung on?" Pharaun asked, holding out a hand.

Valas complied—taking care to keep the amulet hidden inside his tunic as he slid it off the chain. Pharaun could guess why. Judging by its sun shape, it had been created by surface elves. And not just any surface elves, but those who worshiped Labelas Enoreth, Lord of Longevity. If Quenthel saw the mercenary wearing it, her fury would be unbounded. She'd rather have lost a valuable ally to the wraiths than admit that an amulet created by "sunspit" was anything other than an abomination.

As Valas handed Pharaun the chain, Danifae leaned closer to the wall of ice, her breath fogging in the chilled air.

"Careful," Pharaun cautioned. "Don't touch the ice with your tongue."

She gave him a disdainful look, then indicated the storm outside with a jerk of her chin.

"If you're going to try to bind the demon, you'd better get started," she told him. "The whirlpool is starting to move away."

Nodding, Pharaun squatted and began his preparations. From the pockets of his *piwafwi* he took a lump of beeswax he'd picked up in Menzoberranzan, months before, from a trader from the World Above; and a black opal the size of his little fingernail, shot through with veins of red. He warmed the beeswax by working it with his hands, then he sculpted the softened lump, modeling the arms, legs, tail, and snout of an uridezu demon. The statuette was crude, but it would suffice. Slicing open its chest with a fingernail, Pharaun pushed the opal inside, then pinched the wound shut. He wrapped Valas's chain around one of the statuette's legs, securing it there by joining two links together.

"There," he said, nodding in satisfaction at the chain that bit slightly into the wax statuette's ankle. "That should hold him long enough to get us to the Abyss."

Chapter

THIRTY-TWO

As the worm's mouth closed around her, Halisstra squeezed her eyes shut. She gasped as a wave of acid splattered against the exposed portions of her body—her face, neck, and hands—then regretted it as the stench of acid filled her nostrils. Rivulets of agony trickled through her hair and down her neck, searing her chest and back as they found their way under her chain mail and padded tunic.

Clinging to the hilt of the songsword, she twisted violently against the rippling, sucking force of the worm trying to swallow her down. She managed to get her feet braced against the worm's lower jaw, but when she tried to lever the mouth open her boots slipped. The worm swallowed her, wrenching her hands away from the hilt of the sword.

As the worm's throat muscles constricted, forcing her down its throat, Halisstra began to pray. To open her burning lips would mean swallowing acid, which would further increase her torment, so she prayed silently, fervently, begging Eilistraee to help her. Despite the fact that she could feel her skin erupting into blisters, she didn't attempt a curative spell—that would only delay the inevitable—instead she pleaded for something that would help her to escape.

The worm thrashed back and forth, bending Halisstra violently this way and that. She heard dull, muffled thuds that must have been Ryld hacking at the worm with his sword, but then the creature twisted suddenly and they stopped. The motion forced the air from Halisstra's lungs—and she dared not try to inhale. Instead she forced her hand down, scraping it against her acid-slimed chain mail to touch the amulet hanging from her belt, next to her empty sheath.

Eilistraee, she prayed. *Help me. Send me a weapon.*

Something nudged against her hand—something hard and smooth. Grasping it, Halisstra realized it was the hilt of a sword—obviously the weapon of some other unfortunate victim of the worm. She wasted no time in using what the goddess had provided. Forcing her elbow back against the pulsing wall of the worm's gut, she brought the point of the weapon to bear and felt it slide into the worm's flesh. Then she began to saw.

Her entire body was covered in acid. The worm's digestive juices had seeped under her armor and clothing and onto her skin. She could feel blisters erupting and could feel the acid flowing into the rupturing skin with each move that she made. Head pounding from a lack of air, she sawed desperately, her movements made short and jerky by the fact that the worm's gut was pressing her arm against her side. Flashes of red danced before her eyes, but still she continued to saw. It was either that or die.

The wall of gut in front of her ruptured. Riding a wave of acid, Halisstra fell through the wound in the worm's side, dropping the sword. She lay for a moment on the hard stone, drawing deep, shuddering breaths and watching the worm thrash itself across the cavern. The creature was wounded in half a dozen places: deep gashes that had probably been made by Ryld's greatsword. As the worm shuddered and at last died, Halisstra rolled feebly over, out of the puddle of acid.

"Ryld," she gasped, sighting him.

As her pain-dulled mind registered that he was lying on his back on the cavern floor, she forced herself into a sitting position, nearly fainting at the pain of her heavy chain mail as it rubbed against her acid-burned flesh.

"Ryld," she said, her voice cracking. "Ryld!"

The weapons master's chest still rose and fell beneath the breastplate he wore, though the breaths were shallow. Just below the edge of his breastplate his tunic was torn—a round blood-stain told her that it was a puncture wound. The worm had injected him with its venom.

He needed her magic—and quickly—but she could not aid him without first healing herself. Time was of the essence, so she used *bae'qeshel* magic, a darksong that would close her wounds. The worst of her pain was relieved—though it returned, in lesser form, a moment later as the acid that had soaked into her clothing began to eat at her skin again. As rapidly as she could, she stripped off her chain mail and pulled off her soggy tunic and boots. Her tunic came off easily, peeling away in wet, rotted chunks. As she stripped down, she noted that the spell had knitted her ruptured skin back together but had left a pattern of overlapping burn marks. Startled by the sight of them, she began to raise a hand to her face—then immediately dropped it as she heard Ryld softly moan. It was no time for vanity.

Scrambling across the floor to him, she laid a hand over the site of his wound and felt a shudder pass through the flesh under the blood-soaked tunic. Closing her eyes, she chanted her prayer.

Eilistraee, aid him. Slow the poison that rushes through his veins. Grant him just a little time, yet, to live.

She lifted her free hand, imagining herself outside, under a clear sky, reaching up toward the moon. When she felt the familiar tingle of magic she swept her hand down, placing her palm upon the hand that still covered Ryld's wound. She felt a rush of magical energy flow through her and into Ryld—energy as cool and as bright as the moon. As the last of it drained out of her she shivered, suddenly cold and exhausted.

Halisstra knelt, anxiously watching Ryld's slow, labored breathing, wondering if her spell had worked. Uluyara had been right—Halisstra had been mad to think she could find the Crescent Blade, when the combined efforts of Eilistraee's faithful had failed. Halisstra wondered if the ghost that had led her to the worm hole had truly been Mathira Melarn. It seemed more likely that it was just some malevolent spirit seeking to lead others to experience the same gruesome death that it had. Stupidly, like a rothé being led to slaughter, she had followed the ghost to the edge of the worm hole, then entered, despite her realization that it would be a purple worm she'd be confronting and not a dragon after all. She had proceeded anyway, blind faith causing her to believe that the Crescent Blade would be inside the worm's lair.

If it was, she hadn't seen it. In the moments before Ryld had startled her, breaking her spell, Halisstra had gotten a good look at the cavern floor. She'd even gotten the worm to shift this way and that, enabling her to search beneath it.

She'd seen nothing.

Sighing, she stared down at Ryld. In pursuing her quest, she'd come close to forfeiting her own life. That, she had no quarrel with. As a drow, and a former servant of Lolth, she was used to such sacrifices being demanded of her and all around her. The goddess consumed her followers like flies, then cast their empty husks away. But Halisstra had expected more of Eilistraee. A little mercy—if not for her, then for innocents like Ryld. She hadn't expected her quest to cost him his life as well.

Then she saw a slight change. Ryld's face, which had been swiftly draining of color a few moment before, seemed slightly darker, less gray. She could see his breathing begin to steady, though it still sounded wet and tight. The spell had worked—there was still hope.

"Eilistraee, forgive me," she quickly whispered. "Forgive me for doubting your mercy."

Squatting, she hooked one hand under Ryld's shoulders, the other under his hips, intending to carry him, if need be, all the way up to the surface, then back across the Cold Field to the nearest town. Eilistraee willing, she would be able to locate one of the priestesses—someone who knew a healing spell that would flush the poison completely from his body—before the poison-delaying spell she'd cast ran out.

As she started to lift Ryld his eyes flickered open, startling her. He looked confused for a moment, but slowly recognition dawned.

"Halisstra," he croaked. "Is it really you?"

At first Halisstra thought he was still groggy from the poison. Then she realized, from the way he was staring at her, that he truly did not recognize her. She touched her face and found it cratered with overlapping scars. Her hand trembling, she reached up still farther, and found that most of her hair had fallen out. Only a few ragged strands remained. The *bae'qeshel* magic had closed the wounds caused by her burns—but it had left her with terrible scars.

She told herself not to worry about it—the priestesses would certainly have a spell that would smooth her skin and restore her hair. Getting Ryld back was the thing to concentrate on.

"It *is* me, Ryld," she told him. "Do you think you can walk? Otherwise I'll have to carry you back across the Cold Field."

"I can walk . . . if you help me up," he said. Then he looked around. "Splitter—where is it?"

The poison having been slowed, Ryld struggled to his hands and knees—still shaky but looking stronger than he had just a moment before. Halisstra knew he would no sooner leave his enchanted greatsword behind than he would sacrifice an arm or a leg, but he was still weak.

"I'll find it," Halisstra told him. "You stay here, and save your strength."

She approached the worm carefully, worried that it might not yet be dead. Its body was unmoving, however, coiled in a limp tangle. Easing its mouth open, she yanked Seyll's songsword from its cheek and let the acid drain from the finger holes in the weapon's hilt. Then she searched for Splitter.

The greatsword lay close to the spot where Halisstra had hacked her way out of the worm's belly, its hilt protruding from under a coil of the worm. She stooped and yanked it free—then spotted something lying half in and half out of the wound. It was the sword she'd used to cut herself free. Its blade was bright and untarnished—obviously magical, since it had been protected from the acid's corrosive effects—and curved. Curved.

Halisstra realized what weapon it must be.

It was the Crescent Blade.

Eyes wide with awe, ignoring the acid that was stinging the soles of her bare feet, she picked up the sword, then backed out of the pool of acid. The hilt should have been slippery with the worm's digestive juices but its leather wrapping felt dry and clean—further evidence that it was a magical weapon. Silver had been inlaid along the length of the blade, giving the metal its sheen. The inlay spelled out words in the drow tongue that began to glow slightly as Halisstra held the sword.

Ryld, rising unsteadily on his feet, moved closer to take a look as Halisstra read the inscription.

" 'Be your heart filled with light and your cause be true, I shall not fail you,' " she recited. Her brows puckered in a doubtful frown. "Even in the Abyss?" she whispered.

When she looked up, she saw Ryld staring at her.

"So that's why you wanted the Crescent Blade," he said softly. "To try to kill Lolth?" He shook his head. "That's something even Vhaeraun failed to do. How can you hope to succeed where a god has failed?"

"I don't know," Halisstra answered honestly.

Part of her felt manipulated—despite nearly being devoured by the worm, it felt as though the Crescent Blade had just fallen into her hands. That made her wary, uneasy. But at the same time, another part of her felt elation. She might be no more than a piece on a *sava* board, being moved this way and that by an unseen hand, but that hand belonged to a goddess. Eilistraee, for good or ill, had taken a personal interest in her—something Lolth had never done. The thought filled Halisstra with a heady pride.

"Eilistraee is watching over me," she told Ryld. "It feels as if all of this has been preordained—and I have a sense that it's my destiny to at least try to follow the path the goddess has set me on. If I do succeed in killing Lolth, we'll at last be free of her clinging webs. All of us. The drow can come up into the light, without fear of her retaliation."

"And if you fail . . ." Ryld began, then weakly coughed.

Halisstra took his arm and helped to steady him. They didn't have time to stand there contemplating her chances of success. Not with the poison only temporarily held at bay.

"Do you have any spare clothing?" she asked.

He nodded at the backpack on the floor and said, "In there. A tunic and some boots."

"Good," she said.

A tunic and boots alone would be little protection against the bitter winds of the World Above, but Halisstra knew she could use her spells—if sparingly—to gain temporary respite from the cold. She dug out the clothes and put them on, helped Ryld slide Splitter back into its sheath, and strapped the Crescent Blade and songsword across the top of her backpack and slipped it onto her back.

"Come on," she said, slipping one of Ryld's arms over her shoulder. "The sooner we get you back to the temple, the better your chances of living long enough to watch me die trying to kill a goddess."

C h a p t e r

T H I R T Y - T H R E E

"Ready?" Pharaun asked, looking up from the circle he'd been drawing on the floor of the tunnel.

Only a pinch of powdered amber remained in the pouch he was holding—just enough to complete the circle in which Quenthel and Jeggred stood. The two were crowded close together, Quenthel stroking Jeggred's tangled mane in a calming gesture.

Valas and Danifae stood outside the circle, back where the water dripping from their soaked *piwafwis* wouldn't mar the pattern. Without levitation magic, they had no way to land safely on the storm-tossed ship, so they would remain in the tunnel.

"Get on with it," Quenthel said, forcing his mind back to the task at hand. "Cast the spell."

Pharaun stepped into the circle beside her, taking care the hem of his *piwafwi* didn't disturb the powder, then he crouched to sprinkle the last pinch of amber that would complete the pattern on the floor. Standing again, he stared out through the ice wall at the ship of chaos, locking the position of its upper deck in his mind.

"*Faer z'hind*!" he cried.

As his spell took effect, the stone floor vanished from under his feet. An instant later he, Quenthel, and Jeggred were falling through the air toward the deck of the rapidly moving ship. The wizard checked his descent by levitating, but the water stinging his eyes made it difficult to see. He'd aimed for a pace or two above the deck—the only sane option, with the ship rising and falling so violently and listing at such a sharp angle—but without anything solid under his feet he was in danger of being hurled into the eye of the storm. He floundered about, trying to find the deck with his feet as sprays of water lashed him and the wind tore at the hood of his *piwafwi*, nearly strangling him. A gust of wind caught him, slamming him into the main mast and knocking the air from his lungs. Desperately, Pharaun grabbed at the closest thing to hand: one of the lines that formed the ship's rigging.

The line compressed as his hands tightened around it. Inside the line was something soft and wet—and warm. An instant later, as something pulsed through it, Pharaun realized that the line was made not of rope but of a strand of intestine. He curled his lip, hoping the line wouldn't rupture. Pharaun didn't relish the thought of being spattered by its contents.

He wedged one foot against the base of the mast, the other against the tilted deck, and he glanced up. Jeggred and Quenthel had halted their fall a pace or two above him. The draegloth had grabbed the mast and was hugging it with his fighting arms. Rigid as a statue, muscles bulging, he easily held himself in place against the wind that tore at his mane. Quenthel clung to his back, supported by the draegloth's smaller arms.

Quenthel stared down at Pharaun, her hair writhing in the

wind like the vipers that thrashed furiously in her whip. She shouted something, jerking her head up at the demon that floated at the eye of the storm, far above the mast to which they clung.

Pharaun had no idea what Quenthel was saying, but the need for urgency was certainly clear.

With his feet securely braced, he released the line with his left hand and reached into his pocket for the twig he'd used to collect a spiderweb, so many days before. Pointing it at the deck of the ship, he chanted a spell.

A spray of web filaments erupted from the twig and struck the deck. Several twisted away in the howling wind, but the majority of them stuck. They formed a sticky smear across the bone-white deck—a smear that gradually built in thickness as yet more web pulsed out of the twig. By the time the spell was spent, the mass of spiderweb was nearly half a pace deep, mounded in an oval that resembled a cocoon.

Letting the twig go—it was instantly snatched away by the wind—Pharaun fished a wad of bitumen out of a pocket and popped it into his mouth. He swallowed the gummy mass down, gagging slightly as the spider hairs embedded in the bitumen scratched the back of his throat, then he curled his fingers into the shape of a spider and tapped fingertips lightly against his chest. Immediately his hand grew sticky—gummy enough to pluck at his sodden *piwafwi* when he pulled it away.

Tentatively, still holding the line of intestine, Pharaun moved one foot away from the mast and felt his boot stick to the deck. Then, walking slowly and with one hand touching the tilting deck, he worked his way over to the patch of web.

Standing erect was impossible—the ship was canted at an acute angle, sailing in crazy circles around the inside of the whirlpool with its hull half in and half out of the water and its masts pointing at the eye of the storm. The deck shuddered

LISA SMEDMAN

under Pharaun's feet like a live thing as the ship twisted around and around in the whirlpool, its planks groaning like a chorus of undead. The wizard heard what sounded like a weight shifting in a space under his feet, but there was something more to the sound that he couldn't quite put his finger on.

Forced to stand at an angle that made his knees and ankles ache, Pharaun fought to keep his balance. To fall then would ruin everything. Meanwhile, the wind howling through the lines above added a ghastly harmony, and the *flap-flap* . . . *flap-flap* . . . *flap-flap* of the tattered sails pounded like an off-kilter heartbeat.

Pharaun opened the pouch he'd hung around his neck. The statuette inside it had held up well under the buffeting the storm had given the pouch. The only damage was that its tail had been bent slightly. The length of chain Valas had provided was still fastened securely around one ankle, and the pin was still in place at the end of the chain.

Working quickly, Pharaun reached down—nearly falling into the web as the ship bucked on a wave and only recovering his balance at the last moment—and mired the statue's feet in the outer edge of the web, sticking it to the deck. Then, carefully, he pushed the pin into the deck. It slid home into the bone-white boards as easily as if it was piercing a stick of wet chalk.

Pharaun began the binding. Staring up at the demon that hung far above the mast, he chanted the words of his spell, hands raised above his head with thumbs and forefingers forming interlocking circles. Slowly, he drew his hands down toward the deck—and chuckled with delight as he saw the demon begin to descend toward the ship. Compelled by the spell, it was pulled down past the top of the mast, down past where Quenthel and Jeggred clung, down toward the spot where Pharaun stood. Still twisting in the fierce wind, the demon seemed to grow larger and more fearsome as it descended, but that was just a product of the unholy aura that surrounded it. In fact the demon was only a little larger than Pharaun himself. It was, however, powerfully muscled, with claws like yellowed daggers on hands and feet and a tail that looked powerful enough to smash a stalagmite in two. Its face resembled a rat's, and its skin was a mottled, dead-looking gray. As it descended to Pharaun's eye level, guided by his hands toward the statue on the deck, Pharaun noted that one of the demon's ears had a half-circle bitten out of it. The wound had festered, and a maggot protruded, unmoving, from the rotten flesh—another victim of the spell that had frozen the demon in time.

Squatting, Pharaun touched the statuette, then ripped the finger-and-thumb links apart. As the symbolic chain parted, a flash of multi-colored magical energy exploded from the opal, melting the statuette.

For a moment Pharaun was blinded—but the sweet tang of melted beeswax told him his spell had succeeded. Blinking away the spots of light that dazzled his vision, he peered at the demon that stood before him, its ankle secured to the deck by a thin length of lead chain. The demon was still frozen in time, but its red eyes blazed with fury. Despite the stasis spell that held it, the demon seemed to know it had been bound.

Pharaun waved at Jeggred and Quenthel to join him on the deck. At a nod from Quenthel, who was still clinging to his back, the draegloth obeyed. He leaped down from the mast and anchored himself on the steeply sloping deck by thrusting his hands into the sticky mass of web. Pharaun immediately cast another spell, tossing a pinch of ground diamond into the air. A dome of force shut out the storm, enclosing the three of them, together with the demon, in welcome silence. Sprays of water crashed onto the invisible barrier and ran down it in streams, but inside, all was quiet.

Quenthel clambered off Jeggred's back, but she continued to hold onto his mane, steadying herself against the rise and fall of the deck. She stared at the demon, the serpents in her whip tasting the air next to it with flickering tongues, and she wrinkled her nose. Even with its body held in stasis, the demon stank of sulfur and rot.

"It's small," she noted derisively. "Not even a match for Jeggred."

The draegloth, mired in the web up to his elbows, grunted his agreement.

"Don't let its size fool you," Pharaun cautioned, wrinkling his nose at Jeggred's panting breath, which was almost as bad as the stench from the demon. "One bite from those needle teeth, and you'd be paralyzed."

Quenthel tried to back up a step but a lurch of the ship caused her foot to land squarely inside the sticky web. She fell sideways, arms flailing. She landed in an undignified sprawl in a thicker patch of web and immediately erupted into muffled cursing.

"Dispel this!" she spat, struggling to rise from the tilting deck and only getting herself further mired. "Dispel it at once."

Her serpents, too, were stuck in the web and spat violently at each other in frustration. Jeggred tried to help, but was unable to free his hands from the web. Frustrated, the draegloth turned to growl at Pharaun, instead.

With an effort, Pharaun fought down his mirth. It wouldn't do to laugh, not with Jeggred's hackles raised—even though the sight of a priestess of the Queen of Spiders being caught in a web was too good to be true. Instead he inclined his head in a bow.

"As you wish, Mistress. But you're going to need something else to anchor yourself to the deck, or you'll slide right off the ship. Allow me, if you will, to provide an alternative."

He pulled out a second wad of bitumen and broke the gummy mass in half. He passed a piece each to Quenthel and Jeggred, and when they had swallowed them, cast the spell that would allow them to cling like spiders to anything—even a spray-sodden deck. He then dispelled the web.

Clambering to her feet, purple-faced with suppressed rage, Quenthel looked around the ship.

"I see no mouth," she spat. "Belshazu lied."

"That wouldn't surprise me in the least," Pharaun said dryly.

Indeed, having had a chance to look around, he could see that Quenthel seemed to be right. The deck of the ship was a flat expanse of bone-white board, devoid of a cabin or any raised structure. There were rails at the edges of its deck to prevent crew from falling overboard, but the only other thing rising above the desolate flatness of the deck, besides the three masts with their tattered, patchwork sails, was a tiller at the stern of the ship. Seeing no hatches, he wondered if the ship had a hold—or if its hull was solid bone. He'd heard a faint noise, a moment before, that might have been cargo shifting, but it was probably just the sound of the storm.

"We'll have to ask the uridezu where the mouth is," he said. "Let's just hope I can dispel the stasis."

That said, he set to work. Dispellings were among the first spells wizards learned at Sorcere, and a quick incantation and a brief gesture were enough to dispel simple spells. But a temporal stasis was tricky. Only the most powerful mages could cast it. That the demon was indeed held by such a spell was readily apparent. Peering into its open, snarling mouth, Pharaun could see red, blue, and green glitters on its tongue—a dusting of the powdered gems that had triggered the spell.

A greater dispelling was certainly needed—one that was tightly focused, so it wouldn't negate the binding spell. Taking a deep breath, Pharaun began his incantation.

Quenthel must have seen the unease in his eyes, for she

drew her whip. Beside her, Jeggred absently picked at the deck's caulking with a claw, scratching out chunks of black, congealed blood.

Extending the finger on which he wore his magical signet ring, Pharaun touched the demon between the eyes. The ring flashed a bright silver as the symbol of Sorcere activated, lending its power to the spell.

As the dispelling took effect, a shudder ran through the demon's body. Pharaun jerked his hand back. Quenthel and Jeggred also tensed, but for several long moments, nothing happened. The only sounds were the muted splash of water against the dome that still held the elements at bay and the faint, curious hissing of the whip vipers.

Sighing, Pharaun shook his head. The dispelling had failed.

"Try again," Quenthel ordered.

"Repeating the spell won't help," Pharaun told her as he stepped forward to inspect the demon more closely. "The mage who froze the demon in time must have been an extremely powerful—"

He'd half turned as he answered Quenthel, but out of the corner of his eye he saw the demon blink—and that was what saved him. With a shriek of centuries of pent-up rage, the demon leaped forward, claws lashing at Pharaun's throat. Pharaun threw himself backward, but his boots were still stuck to the deck. He crashed onto his back, banging his head. Blinking away stars, he managed to focus his eyes just in time to see the demon at the apex of a full-out leap. Still confused from the blow to his head, Pharaun wondered why he was moving away from the demon, then realized that his fall had jerked his feet out of his boots; he was sliding rapidly down the sloping deck. In that same instant, the demon jerked to a stop in mid-air, then crashed facefirst into the deck on the spot where Pharaun had just been lying.

Groggily, Pharaun realized that the chain around its ankle had tripped it.

He also realized that he was still sliding down the tilting deck. He slapped sticky hands down onto the boards, jerking himself to a halt just before he hit the edge of his dome of force. Meanwhile the demon leaped to its feet and fell upon the slender chain that held its ankle, gnashing at it with yellowed teeth.

Quenthel backed up a pace, her whip held at the ready and an undecided look on her face. Then she gave a grim chuckle.

The demon gave up gnawing on the chain to glare at her.

"You dare laugh?" it said in a voice that squeaked like twisting chains, its tiny red eyes bulging. "I will feed you to the maw."

Pharaun sat up, rubbing a tender spot on the back of his head.

"That's just what we'd like to talk to you about," he told the demon. "The ship's mouth. Tell us where—"

He never got the chance to finish. Jeggred, hackles raised by the insult to his mistress, chose that moment to leap forward. Howling with rage, he raked the demon with his fighting hands, tearing deep slashes in its chest and thighs.

Pharaun sprang to his bare feet—which, thankfully, were still sticky from his earlier spell.

"Jeggred, stop!" he shouted. "That's what it wants!"

Already he could see what the demon was doing—it fell back under Jeggred's attack in a move that left its bound leg exposed. The demon could neither harm nor remove the chain that bound its ankle itself, but if a careless swipe of Jeggred's claws did the job. . . .

Quenthel, for once, thought quickly. She lashed out with her whip—not at the demon, which was probably immune to her serpents' poison—but at Jeggred, instead. Her vipers snapped a hand's breath over his bare back, splattering his mane with their venom.

"Jeggred!" she shouted. "Leave him."

The draegloth glanced back over his shoulder, suddenly aware that his mistress was angry. Instantly he cowered on the deck, ignoring the raking kick the demon gave him.

Foiled in its escape bid, the demon hunkered down, whiskers twitching.

Pharaun clambered up the steeply sloping deck.

"Now then, demon," the Master of Sorcere said, "to get back to my question about the ship's mouth. I want to know where it is and what we need to feed it to get this ship going. You're going to sail us out of this whirlpool and into the Plane of Shadow."

"And you will free me?" the demon asked, its watery eyes blinking.

"Yes," Pharaun lied. "As soon as we reach the Abyss."

The demon's whiskers twitched.

"The mouth is in the belly of the ship," it said.

"In the hold?" Pharaun asked.

The demon nodded.

"How do we reach it?"

"Use her wand," the demon said, flicking a finger at the forked wand in Quenthel's belt. "The hatch is hidden by magic, but the wand will show you its location."

Pharaun's eyes narrowed. He didn't like the sly smirk in the demon's eye. A wand of location was easy to recognize by its distinctive forked shape, but it was almost as if the demon wanted Quenthel to use it. Was there some additional property of the wand that Pharaun had missed—something the demon hoped to turn to its advantage?

"Just a moment, Quenthel," Pharaun told her. "We'll use my wand, instead."

Reaching into the slender case that hung from his belt, he drew one of his four wands and waved it in a slow pass in front of him, level with the deck of the ship. A hatch that had been previously hidden by magic suddenly became visible, its edges limned with a faint purple glow. The ring-latch that would open it was recessed into the hatch itself, flush with the deck. Nodding, Pharaun tucked the wand back inside his case.

Quenthel chuckled and reached for the latch, then paused as her whip vipers hissed a warning. She glanced at Pharaun, parted her lips as if to speak, then decided against whatever order she'd been about to give.

Instead she turned to Jeggred and commanded, "Open it."

Obediently, the draegloth bent forward.

"Jeggred, wait," Pharaun barked.

He had no love for the draegloth, but Pharaun was still suspicious of the demon's motives. Waving Jeggred back, the wizard motioned for the demon to open the hatch, instead. It was just within the demon's reach. By straining, the uridezu was able to hook its fingers into the latch.

Be ready, Pharaun signed to the others behind the demon's back, reaching for a different wand. *Something's going to come out.*

He was right. As soon as the demon yanked open the hatch, a wave of rats scurried out, tittering and squeaking. And no ordinary rats but gaunt, half-rotted caricatures of life—a swarm of tiny undead.

With a speed born of long practice, Pharaun fired his wand. A lightning bolt exploded from it and careered along the deck, turning nearly a dozen of the creatures instantly to charred flesh and blackened bone.

Quenthel and Jeggred were equally quick to react. Quenthel lashed at the rats with quick flicks of her whip, and Jeggred batted whole handfuls of them away with powerful sweeps of his fighting arms.

Pharaun chuckled as he blasted the last of the swarm with his wand. Was that the best the demon could do—summon up a few undead rats?

The laughter died in his throat. He'd been expecting a complicated trick worthy of a *sava* master and had felt somewhat disappointed when the demon had done nothing more than send a swarm of undead rats against them. Then Pharaun realized the demon's real plan—one so simple it had slipped under Pharaun's guard. The undead rats' attack on Pharaun, Quenthel, and Jeggred was just a diversion. All the demon needed was for a single rat to survive. That animal's true target, as directed by the imperative telepathic commands of its demonic master, was the chain.

The soft lead chain.

An instant later the rat's sharp teeth parted the chain, and the demon was free. Whirling in place, it lashed out with its tail once—knocking Jeggred headlong down the slanting deck, through the dome of force and out into the whirling sea—then again, sending Quenthel tumbling after him.

It turned to face Pharaun, whiskers quivering.

"Wizard," it squeaked. "You are mine."

Pharaun made no answer as his free hand plunged into his pocket, whipping out a glove. As the demon bared its fangs, then leaped for his throat, Pharaun was silently thankful it had chosen a simple frontal attack, rather than to use its magic—it would give him the instant he needed to cast his spell.

Demons really *were* predictable.

Sometimes.

Chapter

THIRTY-FOUR

As the mouth of the tunnel came into view, Ryld's heart sank. Fresh snow lay ankle-deep on the slope that led up to the surface, and enormous flakes of white were falling into the tunnel so thickly it was impossible to see more than a few paces beyond the opening. How were he and Halisstra ever going to find their way across the Cold Field in that curtain of white? Without landmarks to guide them, they were likely to wander in circles until the cold finally claimed them.

Over and above that small problem, Ryld was already tiring. His House insignia allowed him to levitate, so that Halisstra could tow him through the air like a child's floater, but the concentration required to sustain the brooch's magic was wearying him. Allowing it to lapse, he sank gently to the ground and contemplated the snow falling into the tunnel.

Halisstra shivered, making him aware of just how woefully

inadequate her clothes were to ward off winter's bitter chill.

"Do you have any magic that will keep you warm?" Ryld asked.

She nodded and answered, "Eilistraee will grant me a spell that will help me resist the cold, but . . ."

"But what?" Ryld prompted.

Halisstra sighed and said, "It only lasts a short time. I'd have to recast it—several times—to keep warm all the way to the edge of the Cold Field. And that would mean not being able to recast the spell that's keeping *you* alive."

"Then leave me."

The look Halisstra gave him needed no words.

"How long do I have?" he asked instead of arguing.

"The spell I cast on you should last the rest of the night, at least—until just after the sun rises," she told him. "I'll use my magic sparingly until then and count on the sun to keep me warm afterward. That should leave enough magic to slow the poison a second time. Let me know—immediately—if your pain worsens. The spell's duration isn't that precise. It could wear off suddenly, without warning. If the poison returns full force to your body, the shock could kill you. The fewer times I have to recast the spell, the better."

Ryld nodded.

Halisstra shivered, then added, "Let's get moving. I'll be warmer if I'm walking."

Once again Ryld levitated. Halisstra trudged up the slope and onto the open plain, boots squeaking in the fresh snow, towing him behind her, then she broke into a jog. After no more than a dozen steps Ryld was unable to see the worm hole behind them. Ahead lay a thick veil of falling snow that hid the landscape from sight. No stars or moon could be seen overhead. The sky was a solid, sullen gray. Thick flakes landed on the weapons master's close-shaved scalp, melted, and froze again.

For a time, the rapid pace Halisstra set kept her warm. But by the time the snow had deepened to calf level, she was shivering. She pressed on until her teeth began to chatter, then at last she paused and whispered a quick prayer to Eilistraee, her breath fogging in the bitterly cold air. When it was done she breathed easier. Gradually her shivers subsided.

As she'd predicted, the soothing effects of the spell didn't last long. Halisstra was able to continue for some time more, her jog slowed to a walk by the deepening snow, but then she began to shiver again. When she raised a hand to her lips, blowing on it, Ryld saw to his dismay that her fingertips had a grayish tinge. The surface elves had a word for it: frostbite. Ryld was coming to understand why they'd chosen such an odd term. His own fingers and toes—and the end of his nose—felt raw, as if invisible creatures were gnawing on them.

"That spell doesn't last long enough," he observed.

"No," Halisstra agreed, her teeth starting to chatter again. "It doesn't."

Ryld squinted at the thickly falling snow that formed a curtain on every side. Though the sky was getting lighter, he could no longer see the battlefield debris that littered the ground due to the snow. A moment later, however, Halisstra's boot crunched down onto a piece of frozen bone, snapping it, reminding him that they were still on the Cold Field.

"We're not going to make it," Ryld said. "Not without help."

He paused as pain twisted his gut, making him gasp.

Halisstra's eyes widened.

"What's wrong?" she asked. "It can't be the spell ending—it's too soon."

Ryld allowed himself to sink to the ground and stood for a time with his hands on his thighs, breathing away the pain.

When he felt steady again, he answered her question.

"It's the strain of levitating. I'm weak. Your spell delayed the poison, but by then the venom had already done a fair bit of damage, by the feel of it." He nodded at the Crescent Blade strapped to her backpack. "I'm expendable, but you have a job to do. If you're going to make it off this plain, you've got to save your magic for yourself. Leave me."

Halisstra didn't argue. She merely stared at Ryld, her eyes watering. Lips pressed in a tight line, she took his hand and squeezed it. He nodded at her, encouraging her, and she started to turn away.

Then she stopped.

"No," she said, turning back to him again. "There must be a way. Let me think. There must be a spell I can use—something that will help me to move more quickly."

Ryld nodded, staring dully at the falling snow. The flakes drifted straight down from the sky; there wasn't a breath of wind. Strange, then, that patches of falling snow seemed to be swirling, taking vague shape and breaking apart again . . .

With a start, he realized what he was seeing.

Halisstra, he signed, not daring to speak out loud. *Ghosts. We're surrounded by them.*

"We m-m-may be among them, s-s-soon enough," Halisstra said through chattering teeth. "It's nearly d-d-dawn. C-come closer s-so I can c-c-cast—"

Quiet, Ryld signed. *They can hear you.*

One of the ghosts had glanced briefly in their direction as Halisstra spoke. As it did, it seemed to solidify a bit. Ryld recognized it as a soldier, his face so smudged with soot it was almost as dark as Ryld's own. The front of his wooden shield was burned nearly to charcoal. The ghost remained corporeal just long enough for Ryld to recognize the emblem on the back of its tunic—the tree of Lord Velar's army—then it dissolved into a swirl amid the snowflakes.

Ryld could see dozens of the ghostly figures, moving in the same direction he and Halisstra had been. He caught only glimpses of them—like the first soldier, they seemed to be shifting between solid and mistlike form—but those glimpses were enough to tell him that it was an army in retreat. Shoulders slumped and eyes staring dully at the ground, the soldiers listlessly dragged their weapons behind them. Every now and then a ghostly animal of the Surface Realms would race past, the rider on its back whipping it frantically. Whenever that happened the foot soldiers would glance fearfully over their shoulders as if looking to see what was pursuing the rider, and some would break into a run. After a few stumbling steps, however, they slowed to a trudge again, some of them falling and failing to rise, their ghostly forms sinking into the snow.

The army of ghosts took little notice of Ryld and Halisstra. The soldiers seemed to sense, somehow, that the drow were also walking wounded—that they too were trying to retreat from that cold, lifeless plain. One of the soldiers—a standard-bearer who still carried an iron pole topped with a pennant emblazoned with the tree emblem—crumpled to the ground right in front of Ryld, taking no notice of him. Though the pennant brushed Ryld's arm as it fell toward the snow, the pole itself made no mark in the smooth white surface. Like the standard-bearer's body, it sank into the snow without a trace.

Ryld noticed that the snow in front of him was slightly humped. Curious, he reached into its cold depths and felt a skeleton, and beside it a cold metal pole, its surface flaked with rust. Like the ghostly officer Ryld had met earlier, the soldier had acted out the final moments of his life, crumpling once again in the same spot where he had died, centuries gone by.

Ryld, feeling the pain in his gut start to grow, wondered if he was about to join him.

Halisstra touched the symbol of Eilistraee that hung from her belt.

"The s-s-spell," she said, shivering violently, then switching to sign language. *I should cast it soon.*

Ryld's attention, however, was focused on a ghostly rider racing toward them on one of the surface mounts—a "horse," Ryld suddenly remembered it was called. The horse's feet did not disturb the snow, yet Ryld could hear—faintly—the sound of hooves striking the ground. The horse was still strong, still capable of running swiftly—and was corporeal, at least for the moment. And that gave him an idea.

Grasping the fallen standard-bearer's pole, he wrenched it up out of the snow and stood as straight as the wracking pain in his gut would allow.

"In the name of Lord Velar, halt!" he shouted. "I bear a message that must reach your commander's ears."

For an anxious moment, Ryld thought his ruse wasn't going to work. The standard in his hands was ancient and rusted, the pennant long since rotted away. But the officer seemed to see it as it once had been. Immediately, the ghost pulled up its mount. Fully corporeal, the dead man stared down at Ryld. Its horse mirrored the ghost's apprehension as it flared its nostrils and—perhaps catching scent of a dragon that was long-since dead in Ryld's time—whinnied nervously.

The undead officer's eyes narrowed, however, as it glanced between Ryld and Halisstra.

"You aren't soldiers," the ghost said. "You're not even human."

"We're drow," Ryld said quickly, silently praying that his race had not been at war with those humans in their day. "Dark elves from the Realms Below who have come to fight beside Lord Velar."

"You're too late. Look around you. Lord Velar's army is defeated. The dragons . . ."

The ghost shuddered, unable to go on.

"Yes, I know." Ryld raised his left hand, drawing the officer's eye to the dragon-shaped ring of Melee-Magthere on his finger. "I am quite familiar with dragons, and I know how terrible a weapon they can be. I have knowledge that can help Lord Velar defeat them—if I can reach him in time. Loan me your horse, and this defeat may yet be turned into a victory."

Behind Ryld, Halisstra stood shivering, her arms tucked tight to her chest.

The officer gave one last nervous glance over his shoulder, then swung down out of the saddle.

"Take her," the apparition said, thrusting the reins into Ryld's hand. The ghost drew its sword and turned back toward the direction from which it had ridden. " 'Better to die proud than live in shame,' " it said, reciting the words like a quote.

The ghost officer strode away, dissolving into a swirl of mist amidst the thickly falling snow.

The horse, however, remained. As it shifted its weight, its legs ploughed a furrow in the snow. Reaching up to stroke its neck and steady it, Ryld found that he could smell the sweat and dust that clung to its hair. The animal's body gave off a welcome heat—one that Halisstra, shivering violently, could use to stay alive.

"Can you ride it?" he asked her—a bit belatedly, he realized.

Halisstra gave a shiver that might have been a nod.

"I've r-r-ridden lizards. This beast sh-shouldn't b-b-be any more d-difficult. Wh-what is it?"

"It's called a horse. I saw one for sale in the Bazaar in Menzoberranzan a few years ago. Heard it fetched a pretty penny but only lived a couple days," he said, then realized again that time was of the essence. "Sit in the saddle, and I'll—"

A wave of pain flowed through Ryld's gut, forcing him to gasp.

Halisstra gave him a worried look.

Ryld, irritated by his lack of control, forced the pain out of his awareness. He gave Halisstra a tight smile as he handed her the reins.

"You ride," he said, "and I'll hold on, levitating behind. The animal will be able to move faster that way. With luck, we'll reach the forest and make contact with the priestesses before the spell you cast on me runs out."

"Not luck," Halisstra chastised. "With the b-blessing of the g-g-goddess."

She gave him a brief kiss—with lips that seemed as cold as those of the dead—then she limbed, still shivering, into the saddle.

THIRTY-FIVE

An instant before the demon reached Pharaun, the spell activated, and an enormous glowing hand interposed itself between them. The hand slammed into the demon, smashing it down against the deck and dragging it across the bone-white boards away from Pharaun. Squeaking with fury, the demon tried to squirm free, but the magical hand was too strong for it.

As the uridezu struggled, unable to move, Pharaun cautiously approached and grasped the two ends of the broken chain. Holding them together, he cast a cantrip, glad that he had been forced to use that form of binding. A pentagram, once broken, had to be redrawn entirely, but a chain used in a binding spell could always be restored with a simple mending—assuming one had the magic to actually restrain the demon, first.

The instant the chain mended itself, Pharaun stepped back and dispelled the magic hand. The demon leaped to its feet, eyes slitted with fury. As it yanked, futilely, on the chain, Pharaun turned to look for Quenthel and Jeggred. He spotted them a moment later—they'd managed to escape from the whirlpool by levitating and were floating in the eye of the storm. Unable to reach the ship, they were rapidly being left behind. Quenthel shouted something at him, but Pharaun couldn't hear her over the crash of waves and the howl of the wind. Her message was plain enough, however, from the waving of her arms. She wanted Pharaun to use his magic to fetch them back to the ship.

Pharaun made a show of cupping his ear and shrugged theatrically. Then he turned away, chuckling. He stared at the demon, which once again had lapsed into surly submission.

"Now then, demon," he told it. "You said the mouth was in the ship's hold?"

The demon snarled and said, "Go see for yourself."

Pharaun took a step toward the open hatch, watching the demon out of the corner of his eye. When it tensed expectantly, he paused.

"I think not," he said.

Instead he pulled from his pocket the jar of ointment and rubbed a little of it on his eyelids. When he opened his eyes, he saw that his caution had been well founded. There was indeed a hatch on the deck, but it didn't open onto stairs and a darkened hold. The edges of the hatch were actually a wet pucker of flesh resembling lips. Inside, where the stairs had appeared to be, were rows of jagged teeth. Beyond those, the hold was filled with bones and skulls. Red light flickered around them, shining up through the eye sockets like the glow of angry coals.

The mouth was breathing, exhaling a rank smell that was a combination of burned flesh and charred bone, overlaid by the stench of rot—worse, even, than Jeggred's breath. Wincing, Pharaun pinched his nose shut and backed carefully away from it.

He was glad that he'd had the good sense to have the demon open the hatch. He was certain that if he'd opened it himself, he would have been sucked into the mouth and consumed—utterly.

Too bad he hadn't instructed Quenthel to open the hatch, instead. That would not only have produced an amusing result—but also a practical one. In order for the demon to sail the ship out of the storm, the mouth had to be fed something.

Pharaun paused. Or did it? For all he knew, a ship of chaos could sail for years on a single meal. Centuries, even. But could it sail from one plane to the next without feeding? That was something he'd have to find out. A bluff was in order.

He folded his arms against his chest and looked the demon in the eye.

"We've wasted enough time," he told it. "Get the ship under way. Set sail for Plane of Shadow."

The demon mirrored Pharaun's action, crossing its own arms.

"Stupid mortal," it said with a disdainful smirk. "You know nothing. We can not travel that far. Before the ship can enter the Shadow, it must feed. Permit me to gate in a worthless mane, and I will stoke its fires."

Pharaun returned the smile. The demon had unwittingly told him what he needed to know. He wasn't about to allow it to cast any spells—it wouldn't be manes stepping through the gate, but another uridezu.

"The fires are stoked enough for the moment," Pharaun told it. "We'll sail out of this storm first and see about feeding the ship. Remember—the sooner you complete the task I've set for you and get us into the Abyss, the sooner you'll be free."

For a few heartbeats, the demon tried to stare Pharaun down. Then its whiskers twitched, and it looked away. It lifted its foot, indicating the thin length of chain that bound it to the deck.

"Someone must take the tiller," it said.

"I'll do it," the Master of Sorcere said. "Just get the ship moving." Then, noticing the sly look in the demon's eye, he added, "And no tricks. I want smooth sailing—or at least, as smooth as possible in this storm." He paused as spray from a breaking wave crashed over him, re-drenching his already sodden *piwafwi*. He pointed at his bare feet, still stuck firmly to the sloping deck, thanks to his spell. "As you can see, I don't wash overboard easily."

Pharaun turned and made his way against the wind and spray—one slow, sticky step at a time—to the stern of the ship. The tiller, he found, was, like the rest of the ship, made of bone. Not of powdered and compressed bone, like the boards that made up the deck, but of a single bone—an enormous radius, by the look of it, nearly ten paces long. It was slender and light enough that it must have been hollow, Pharaun decided, as he twisted it in its socket. It probably came from a dragon's wing. Gripping the handle, Pharaun glanced down over the stern and saw that the rudder was an enormous sickle blade.

"Get us under way," he shouted at the demon.

The uridezu snarled, then raised clawed hands above its head. As it swept its hands forward in the direction of the bow, the tattered skin sails above stopped luffing in the wind and belled out, straining at their lines. The ship began to move more rapidly in its circuit around the inside of the whirlpool. The demon continued to move its hands, plucking at the air with its claws, and with each motion the lines that controlled the sails either tightened or loosened, trimming the sails.

Experimentally, Pharaun moved the tiller to the left. A lurch sent him rocking backward as the ship turned in the opposite direction. He clung to the tiller as the bow swung around until it was pointing straight up at the cavern ceiling. Sails straining and boards creaking, the ship began climbing the inside wall of the whirlpool. After a few moments the bow came level with the surface of the lake and began climbing into the waterspout itself.

The ship teetered, then pitched violently forward. For a few terrible moments Pharaun fought to hang on to the tiller as the wall of water smashed into him, but then the ship was free of the waterspout and floating, level at last, on the surface of the lake. Shaking his head to free his face of the sodden hood of his *piwafwi*, Pharaun grinned at the demon, still fastened securely by its chain to the middle of the deck.

"Smooth sailing," the wizard said, chuckling as the ship glided across the choppy surface of the lake, away from the storm.

He flicked wet hair back out of his eyes, glanced up at the ledge where they'd first entered the cavern—some distance away—and turned the ship in that direction. He'd collect Danifae and Valas first and retrieve Quenthel and Jeggred from the eye of the storm later.

Then the fun of deciding what—or who—to feed to the ship would begin.

$$\mathbf{\mathscr{S}} \qquad \mathbf{\mathscr{S}} \qquad \mathbf{\mathscr{S}}$$

Halisstra clung grimly to the reins as the horse galloped across the open plain. She could see little through the thickly falling snow, and prayed the animal would neither slip nor plunge its foot into a hole. It was apparent just looking at the beast how fragile the swift mounts of the World Above were compared to the riding lizards of the drow. Surely but one little twist could snap a leg, sending a rider tumbling to the ground.

Should that happen, at least Ryld would be protected from injury by his levitation spell. He clung to the hem of her *piwafwi*, trailing behind her like a cloak as she rode.

Above them, the sky was getting lighter by the moment. Dawn had come and gone and the sun was rising steadily in the sky—a faint glow behind the sullen, flat gray clouds. It had grown light enough for her to see for some distance—at least in the rare moments when the snow lessened and anything could be seen at all. Which was hardly a welcome thing. The fully risen sun marked the time that the spell Halisstra had cast on Ryld would end. Any moment the poison might rush back upon him full force, like a tide overcoming an already drowning man.

Halisstra stiffened. Was that dark line up ahead the forest? If so, they had reached the edge of the Cold Field at last.

Twisting in the saddle, she gave Ryld a reassuring grin—only to have that grin falter as she saw the look on his face. It was set in a grim mask of concentration, deep lines at the corners of eyes and mouth the only hints of the effort he must be making to push away his pain. Even so, he managed a grim smile in return.

"I can't—" he started to say, then he shuddered.

For a moment his body sagged in the air, but then with a visible effort he regained control and continued levitating. Alarmed, Halisstra fumbled with the reins of the horse with near-frozen hands, trying desperately to slow it.

Ryld groaned aloud, then gasped, "Halisstra . . . I . . ."

He released his grip on her cloak and fell to the ground. In that same instant, the horse turned back into swirling mist, becoming non-corporeal once more, and Halisstra found herself flying through the air. Snow-covered branches whipped at her face as she struck the trees ahead. She landed heavily, knocking the air from her lungs, and lay for a moment, too stunned to do anything but gasp. Then she realized they'd done it—they'd reached the forest.

Scrambling to her feet, she staggered out of the trees. She could no longer feel her feet—they were like lumps of ice, somewhere at the bottom of her legs—but somehow she managed to walk. She was relieved to see Ryld sitting up, apparently unharmed by the fall. She knelt beside him and draped one of his arms across her shoulder.

"Can you walk?" she asked.

He shook his head.

Looking more closely at him, Halisstra was alarmed by the grayish tinge of his skin. She hurriedly dropped his arm.

"Wait, then," she told him. "I'll pray."

"Pray . . . quickly," he gasped, then his eyes closed and he sank back into the snow.

Halisstra gasped in alarm. Was he dead?

No, Ryld's chest still rose and fell. Leaning forward, she placed a hand upon his chest, forcing her frozen fingers into the shape of a crescent moon.

Eilistraee, she prayed silently, unable to speak the words aloud because of the trembling of her lips. *I beg of you. Help me. Send me the magic I need to drive the poison from his body. I could not sing your praises this morning as the sun rose, but I beg of you—let me do that now. Bestow your bounty upon your servant, and give me the blessings I need so that I can save the life of this male who serves . . .* She paused then, and sobbed, then corrected herself. *This man that I love.*

That done, she began humming the morning prayer. Singing the words was impossible—she was shivering violently again, and her lips didn't seem to be working properly.

She paused. Was that the crackle of a breaking twig in the woods?

It didn't matter.

Continue the song, she told herself.

Teeth chattering, she resumed her humming, but it was difficult to concentrate. The fiery tingling had left her hands, leaving a comforting numbness. All she wanted to do was lie down in the snow beside Ryld and sleep. . . .

Was that someone calling her name? No, she must have been hallucinating.

Keep humming, she told herself. Keep praying. Ryld's life depends on it.

But what song had she been humming? Her teeth had at last stopped chattering, but with the shivering gone, Halisstra found herself unable to remember the melody. Instead she sat, staring, at Ryld. Was he even alive?

None of it mattered. Not any more.

Her prayer unfinished, Halisstra sighed, then crumpled to the ground. Strangely the snow was warm, not cold, like a comforting blanket. She lay in it, watching the flakes drift down from the wide gray sky. Funny, she'd never dreamed she'd die with so much space above her. . . .

There. That dark patch. That was the ceiling of a cavern . . . wasn't it? Then why was it moving? Why was it bending down and taking her hand?

As if in a dream, Uluyara's face swam down toward hers. Fragments of a sentence drifted down into her ears, like falling snow.

"We . . . scrying . . . found you."

Halisstra felt hands lifting her and for a moment thought that Uluyara was shifting her body so she could remove the Crescent Blade and songsword from her backpack. Then she heard the melody of a prayer—that was Feliane's voice; she must have been here, too—and she felt a tingle of warmth. Halisstra realized that her pack was being removed so Feliane could hold her, warm her with her body . . . and her magic. At first she was shocked—then she realized she was still thinking like a drow of the Underdark. Knowing that she was saved, she cried in relief, then she realized she was being selfish.

"Ryld. . . ." she whispered.

"Don't worry," Feliane said, her voice growing more intelligible as magic flowed into Halisstra, warming her and driving away the icy hand of death. "He's alive. Uluyara is driving the poison from his body even now."

Sighing, Halisstra allowed herself to relax, to drink in the warmth of Feliane's spell. She'd done it—she'd gotten Ryld to safety. And herself. She'd even managed to recover the Crescent Blade.

Now all she had to do was kill a goddess with it.

T H I R T Y - S I X

Gromph waited in the great chamber of House Baenre's temple, watching through Kyorli's eyes as members of the House guard dragged in prisoners, bound at the ankle and wrist, for execution. A company of soldiers from House Agrach Dyrr had attempted to break out of their compound after House Baenre pulled its troops away to fight the tanarukks, but fortunately soldiers of House Xorlarrin had been able to capture them. House Baenre had claimed its share of the resulting prisoners, who were being "sacrificed" in the temple—for all the good it would do. With the goddess silent, did it really matter?

As yet another captive from House Agrach Dyrr was hustled into the temple—one, unlike the others, not too badly damaged—Gromph stepped into the path of the House guard who was dragging him in and held up a hand. The guard came to an immediate and obedient halt.

"Yes, Archmage?"

Gromph squatted, bringing Kyorli down to the level of the prisoner. Using the rat's eyesight, he stared into the eyes of the captive, who glared defiantly back at him.

Yes. They might just do.

"This captive is not to be exec—*sacrificed*," he told the guard. "Take him to Sorcere, instead, and deliver him to Master Nauzhror. Tell the master that I require the battle-captive . . . for my own purposes."

From deeper in the temple—behind the adamantine doors that led to Lolth's inner temple—came a high, sharp scream, followed by a drow voice pleading. Slaves, meanwhile, carried the body of the last soldier to have been executed past the spot where Gromph stood and flung it outside at the feet of a riding lizard. A moment later Gromph heard a crunching, gulping noise—the sound of the lizard enjoying its victory feast.

The prisoner looked back and forth between the body being consumed by the lizard and Gromph, as if trying to decide which was the lesser evil.

"Thank you, Archmage," the Dyrr cousin said. "I'll serve you well."

Gromph smiled and said, "Perhaps you will. Part of you, anyway." Then, standing, he addressed the guard. "Take him away."

As he waited for the "sacrifices" to end, Gromph craned his head back and squinted up at the temple ceiling. Using Kyorli's eyesight, he could see movement—the quick scurrying of the spiders whose webs filled the great dome above—but no detail. The webs were a white haze, their lines indistinct. Kyorli could see only a limited distance. Rats relied more upon smell and whisker touch than they did on eyesight.

Gromph would have to be careful. Triel had learned from

And-zrel about what had happened to Gromph. But for the time being she had been fooled by Gromph's assurance that the potions had fully restored his vision. Like the other nobles of House Baenre, she took no notice of Kyorli—the familiar often rode on Gromph's shoulder—but if she learned that the Archmage of Menzoberranzan was blind, she could deem him weak. And the weak—in House Baenre, as in all the noble Houses of Menzoberranzan—were swiftly dispensed with.

Keeping that in mind, Gromph turned as he heard footsteps approaching from behind the adamantine doors. Looking through Kyorli's eyes, he picked Triel out from among the priest-esses who fanned out into the great chamber.

"Matron Mother," he said, bowing deeply. "I have news. Good news."

Triel strode over to where he stood. Whiskers tickled Gromph's cheek as Kyorli strained forward, sniffing eagerly. Gromph saw lines of red crisscrossing the matron mother's face and hair, sprays of blood from the flayings she'd recently inflicted. The serpents in her whip swayed gently, tongues dabbing at the bright blood that had stained a weblike pattern across the front of her white tunic.

"You've heard from Quenthel?" Triel asked.

Gromph nodded and said, "I have."

Ever aware of the political web and his place in it, Gromph omitted any mention of Pharaun. Gromph's underling would be spoken of only if specifically asked about.

"Quenthel and the others have discovered the whereabouts of a ship of chaos and plan to sail it to the Abyss," he told Triel. "There they will find out what has become of Lolth. Our troubles will soon be at an end. Assuming, that is, that our sister proves worthy of the task you have set her."

Just as Pharaun hoped she would, Triel smiled at the barb Gromph had tossed.

"Our sister is less brilliant than some, but she is loyal . . . when it suits her," Triel conceded. "Especially in matters concerning Lolth."

Gromph swore silently as Kyorli's attention wandered to one of the spiders that had descended, suddenly, just in front of them. Triel's face was a blur, and he couldn't read it—but causing Kyorli to whip her head around suddenly could reveal his weakness.

The archmage nodded thoughtfully and said, "I see."

"Do you indeed?" Triel asked, and her tone was slightly mocking.

Thankfully, the spider Kyorli was watching swung behind Triel, bringing her into the rat's field of view. Staring out through Kyorli's eyes, Gromph saw Triel's fingers moving.

Then you know that Quenthel has been to the Abyss more than once, she signed.

"Of course I do," Gromph answered smoothly. "You covered up her death quite carefully, but I have my methods of learning our House's darkest secrets. Where else would Quenthel's soul have gone, during those four years that elapsed between her death and eventual resurrection, but to serve her goddess in the Abyss? I can see why you chose her. I only wonder . . ."

"What?" Triel snapped.

"Why the goddess sent her back," Gromph continued. "Quenthel certainly was a loyal servant. Wouldn't Lolth have wanted to keep her close to hand?"

"Perhaps she had other plans for Quenthel," Triel answered. "Assuming the leadership of Arach-Tinilith, for example, which is precisely what happened."

"Or carrying out her current mission," Gromph added. "It's certainly within the powers of the goddess to have seen this crisis coming and have prepared years ago to meet it."

"Indeed," Triel answered. "Who better than someone who

LISA SMEDMAN

knows the terrain to lead an expedition to the Abyss?" She paused. "Is that all you have to report?"

Gromph bowed and said, "For the moment, Matron Mother. I'll let you know as soon as I receive another report."

Dismissing him, Triel strode away.

Sighing his relief, Gromph shook his head. If Triel knew he was still blind, she was letting it pass. If Lolth had been granting her spells, Triel herself and any number of other priestesses could have restored his eyesight in a heartbeat. The fact that none of them could do it was just another reminder of the powers they no longer commanded. Leaving him his pretense of sight would only help Triel maintain her own pretense of power.

As he made his way out of the temple, Gromph wondered what Quenthel would find in the Demonweb Pits and why she had been returned to Menzoberranzan all those years before, only to lead an expedition to her own afterlife. Perhaps his sister had indeed been tapped by the Spider Queen for some higher purpose. If so, upon her return to the City of Spiders the balance of power could shift in her favor—certainly would if she was successful in her quest. He would have to keep an eye on Quenthel.

So to speak.

✵   ✵   ✵

Aliisza crouched on the ledge overlooking the lake and stared down at the ship below. It was of demonic manufacture—that much was clear from the bone and living tissue that had gone into its construction. On the deck stood four drow and a draegloth—Pharaun and his companions.

The wizard and the priestess Quenthel were arguing—just as they had been when Aliisza had first encountered them near Ammarindar. Behind them, the draegloth taunted an uridezu demon that appeared to be bound in place to the deck. The uridezu strained forward, teeth gnashing, as the draegloth held a rat out by the tail—then bit its head off. The other two drow—the mercenary and the pretty little female that irritated Aliisza so—seemed to be keeping out of the argument, waiting patiently for it to end.

Aliisza's eyes lingered on Pharaun who was dressed elegantly, as always, and with that lovely long white hair. She was glad to have found him again, but her timing seemed to have been off. From the snatches of argument that drifted up to Aliisza's perch on the cliff, it seemed the group of drow would soon be departing—though there was apparently some question about how many of them would make the journey. Someone—or something—had to be fed first . . .

Ah. That was it.

"That's a ship of chaos," Aliisza said, proud of herself, then thought, Now *that* is a detail Kaanyr will want to know.

"Where do you plan to sail it to, my dear Pharaun?" Aliisza mused. "The Abyss?" She laughed and tossed her curly black hair. "Surely you'd rather stay here and spend some time with me than visit that nasty goddess of yours. I, at least, am alive . . . and responsive to your prayers."

Chuckling, she decided to delay her report to Kaanyr Vhok—who was all too busy with that dreary siege of his, anyway. Instead she'd stay in the Lake of Shadows and have some fun.

Pleasure, she mused, should come before business.

Always.

R.A. SALVATORE'S
WAR OF THE SPIDER QUEEN

THE EPIC SAGA OF THE DARK ELVES CONTINUES.

EXTINCTION
Book IV
Lisa Smedman

For even a small group of drow, trust is the rarest commodity of all. When the expedition prepares for a return to the Abyss, what little trust there is crumbles under a rival goddess's hand.

ANNIHILATION
Book V
Philip Athans

Old alliances have been broken, and new bonds have been formed. While some finally embark for the Abyss itself, others stay behind to serve a new mistress—a goddess with plans of her own.

RESURRECTION
Book VI

The Spider Queen has been asleep for a long time, leaving the Underdark to suffer war and ruin. But if she finally returns, will things get better... or worse?

April 2005

The New York Times *best-seller now in paperback!*

CONDEMNATION
Book III
Richard Baker

The search for answers to Lolth's silence uncovers only more complex questions, allowing doubt and frustration to test the boundaries of already tenuous relationships. Sensing the holes in the armor of Menzoberranzan, a new, dangerous threat steps in to test the resolve of the Jewel of the Underdark, and finds it lacking.

Now in paperback!
DISSOLUTION, BOOK I
INSURRECTION, BOOK II

CHECK OUT THESE NEW TITLES FROM
THE AUTHORS OF R.A. SALVATORE'S
WAR OF THE SPIDER QUEEN SERIES!

VENOM'S TASTE
House of Serpents, Book I
Lisa Smedman

The New York Times Best-selling author of *Extinction*.
Serpents. Poison. Psionics. And the occasional evil death cult. Business as usual in the Vilhon Reach. Lisa Smedman breathes life into the treacherous yuan-ti race.

THE RAGE
The Year of Rogue Dragons, Book I
Richard Lee Byers

Every once in a while the dragons go mad. Without warning they darken the skies of Faerûn and kill and kill and kill. Richard Lee Byers, the new master of dragons, takes wing.

FORSAKEN HOUSE
The Last Mythal, Book I
Richard Baker

The New York Times Best-selling author of *Condemnation*.
The Retreat is at an end, and the elves of Faerûn find themselves at a turning point. In one direction lies peace and stagnation, in the other: war and destiny. *New York Times* best-selling author Richard Baker shows the elves their future.

THE RUBY GUARDIAN
Scions of Arrabar, Book II
Thomas M. Reid

Life and death both come at a price in the mercenary city-states of the Vilhon Reach. Vambran thought he knew the cost of both, but he still has a lot to learn. Thomas M. Reid makes humans the most dangerous monsters in Faerûn.

THE SAPPHIRE CRESCENT
Scions of Arrabar, Book I
Available Now

ADVENTURES IN THE REALMS!

THE YELLOW SILK
The Rogues
Don Bassingthwaite

More than just the weather is cold and bitter in the wind-swept realm of Altumbel. When a stranger travels from the distant east to reclaim his family's greatest treasure, he finds just how cold and bitter a people can be.

DAWN OF NIGHT
The Erevis Cale Trilogy, Book II
Paul S. Kemp

He's left Sembia far behind. He's made new friends. He's made new enemies. And now Erevis Cale himself is changing into something, and he's not sure exactly what it is.

REALMS OF DRAGONS
The Year of Rogue Dragons
Edited by Philip Athans

All new stories by R.A. Salvatore, Richard Lee Byers, Ed Greenwood, Elaine Cunningham, and a host of **Forgotten Realms®** stars breathe new life into the great wyrms of Faerûn.

FATHER AND DAUGHTER COME FACE-TO-FACE IN THE STREETS OF WATERDEEP.

ELMINSTER'S DAUGHTER
The Elminster Series
Ed Greenwood

Like a silken shadow, the thief Narnra Shalace flits through the dank streets and dark corners of Waterdeep. Little does she know that she's about to come face-to-face with the most dangerous man in all Faerûn: her father. And amidst a vast conspiracy to overthrow all order in the Realms, she'll have to learn to trust again—and to love.

ELIMINSTER: THE MAKING OF A MAGE

ELMINSTER IN MYTH DRANNOR

THE TEMPTATION OF ELMINSTER

ELMINSTER IN HELL

Available Now!

From *New York Times*

Best-Selling Author

R.A. Salvatore

In taverns, around campfires, and in the loftiest council chambers of Faerûn, people whisper the tales of a lone dark elf who stumbled out of the merciless Underdark to the no less unforgiving wilderness of the World Above and carved a life for himself, then lived a legend...

The Legend of Drizzt

For the first time in deluxe hardcover editions, all three volumes of the Dark Elf Trilogy take their rightful place at the beginning of one of the greatest fantasy epics of all time. Each title contains striking new cover art and portions of an all-new author interview, with the questions posed by none other than the readers themselves.

HOMELAND

Being born in Menzoberranzan means a hard life surrounded by evil.

EXILE

But the only thing worse is being driven from the city with hunters on your trail.

SOJOURN

Unless you can find your way out, never to return.